FOR THE SAKE
OF THE GAME

STORIES INSPIRED BY THE SHERLOCK HOLMES CANON

EDITED BY **LAURIE R. KING**
AND **LESLIE S. KLINGER**

PEGASUS CRIME
NEW YORK LONDON

FOR THE SAKE OF THE GAME

Pegasus Books Ltd.
148 West 37th Street, 13th Floor
New York, NY 10018

First Pegasus Books cloth edition December 2018

Interior design by Maria Fernandez

Library of Congress Cataloging-in-Publication Data is available.

ISBN: 978-1-68177-879-2

10 9 8 7 6 5 4 3 2 1

Printed in the United States of America
Distributed by W. W. Norton & Company

To Sir Arthur Conan Doyle: Steel true, blade straight.

CONTENTS

INTRODUCTION

by Laurie R. King and Leslie S. Klinger

In "Adventure of the Bruce-Partington Plans," Sherlock Holmes declares himself without interest in honors or recognition for his work. Instead, he tells his brother Mycroft, "I play the game for the game's own sake." In part, this is his declaration of independence from the normal rewards of a working man, a clear message that he is above such forms of bribery. It is also his way of pointing out that his position is so rarified, he could not expect his performance to be judged and measured in relation to others—or even *by* others. (Although in point of fact, he does accept an emerald tie-pin from a Certain Gracious Lady.)

Considering what is at stake in the story, far beyond the scope of everyday London crime, a reader might well marvel at Holmes's detached attitude. The case Mycroft has brought his brother is not some abstract puzzle or piece of intellectual fancy. Rather, he asks for Sherlock's help in the matter of a man's uncanny death and the theft of government documents—documents so vital that they could change the very nature of war, and cost millions of lives. Yet neither the tragic fate of young Cadogan West, nor the bereavement of his fiancée, nor even the fears of the government itself seem to have any effect on Holmes. Instead, he is drawn in because of the "points of interest" in Mycroft's presentation; he is eager only as a foxhound might be; he even goes so far as to exhibit "hilarity" (Watson's word) as he is closing in on the criminal. The potential use of top-secret submarine plans by a foreign power seems to faze him less than the problem of railway points, and the chief interest in the investigation seems to be the relief it offers from the boredom produced by London's everyday criminals.

The story's rather cold-blooded portrait of Sherlock Holmes is fortunately uncommon in the Conan Doyle canon. In other tales, we can take comfort in his compassion for a victim, or share his anger with a villain, or echo his outrage for the falsely accused. Seeing Sherlock Holmes as essentially human, rather than a Victorian thinking machine, is at the core of the Sherlockian "Game," allowing us to believe that Sherlock Holmes really lived and that Dr. Watson's tales are true. We accept that they were real men, thus making us students of history rather than of clever fictions.

The Grand Game of learned essays treating the Holmes canon as biography, rather than invention (not to be confused with the Great Game, as in Kipling's Asian border struggles) has a long tradition. The first appeared in 1901 (see *The Grand Game: A Celebration of Sherlockian Scholarship,* two volumes edited by Klinger and King). The tradition is alive and well today in the *Baker Street Journal* and countless other venues for the study of Holmes, Watson, Doyle, and the Victorian age. Thankfully, the Grand Game has spilled over into the work of later writers, who extended the Doyle canon with further tales of the Great Detective, the Good Doctor, and the other figures from their lives. Others have imported Holmes into their own worlds, either literally or by showing the influence of his life and work on the lives and adventures of their protagonists. It is axiomatic that no writer of mysteries in the twenty-first century is uninfluenced by the stories of Arthur Conan Doyle; hence, this collection.

For the Sake of the Game—our fourth of its ilk—brings together a brilliant assemblage of writers from many genres and branches of literature. Thriller writers, traditional mystery authors, "cozy" writers, authors of horror and supernatural literature, creators of hard-boiled detectives and mercenaries, and even fantasists have come together here to play The Game. As with Holmes himself, these brilliant writers did not respond to our invitation for reasons of profit or fame—although they might perhaps accept an emerald stick-pin as supplement to their royalties. Rather, we'd like to believe that they are gathered here for the sake of the game.

And now, as we set off into the lands of foggy London and muggy night-time LA, following in the footsteps of rookie police officers, professional assassins, and insect protagonists, the time has come to speak the words:

The game is afoot!

DR. WATSON'S SONG

by Peter S. Beagle

Raised as I was on Arthur Conan Doyle's tales of Sherlock Holmes, which in my turn I read aloud to my children (my daughter Kalisa became so involved in the stories that she began having Sherlock Holmes dreams), my real soft spot has always been for Dr. Watson. Between his incarnations by Robert Duvall, Jude Law and James Mason, the Nigel Bruce cartoon of Watson as a cheerful but utterly useless boob has been pretty well put to rest. Doyle was casual about his details—he couldn't always remember how many wives Watson had had, and he kept moving that *jezail* bullet wound from the Second Afghan War up and down the poor man's body—but he did make it clear that Watson was neither a fool nor unperceptive. Holmes was certainly his hero, but that didn't make Watson an unqualified hero-worshiper. I've always believed that he quite often felt completely exasperated with the great detective—and just as often understood, as no other could have done, the cost of being Sherlock Holmes.

DR. WATSON'S SONG

"I never get your measure, Watson . . ."
"You see, but you do not observe, Watson . . ."
"You know my methods, Watson—apply them . . ."
"The fair sex is your department, Watson . . ."
"The game's afoot, Watson!"
"Elementary, my dear Watson . . ."
"Elementary . . . elementary . . ."

I know he's a ruddy genius,
I know he's a mastermind,
I know it's an honor to be his pawn,
his chronicler, his sidekick,
his comrade, his companion,
whenever he bothers to tell me what on earth is going on.

Keeps playing that ruddy fiddle,
keeps shooting holes in the wall,
knows where I've been and what I've done with whom.
Drives Mrs. Hudson crazy,
broods about Irene Adler,
and goes on about Moriarty till the ruddy crack of doom.

"I never get your measure, Watson . . ."
"You see, but you do not observe, Watson . . ."
"You know my methods, Watson—apply them . . ."
"The fair sex is your department, Watson . . ."
"The game's afoot, Watson!"
"Elementary, my dear Watson . . ."
"Elementary . . . elementary . . ."

Stinks the place up with chemicals,
shoots himself up with cocaine.
turns his bedroom into a ruddy lab.

2

He tells me what I'm thinking,
lectures me about Wagner,
wakes me up in the middle of the night to catch a hansom cab.

> *"I never get your measure, Watson . . ."*
> *"You see, but you do not observe, Watson . . ."*
> *"You know my methods, Watson—apply them . . ."*
> *"The fair sex is your department, Watson . . ."*
> *"The game's afoot, Watson!"*
> *"Elementary, my dear Watson . . ."*

"Elementary . . . elementary . . ."

I know he needs me to show off for,
I know he needs to amaze.
He needs "By Jove, Holmes!"—he needs glory,
he needs me to write the story,
and good lord, does he need praise!
I even think he rather loves me,
though the words will never come—
but sometimes the legend's a bit of a pain
in my weary old British bum.

And for all the gifts and wonders,
sometimes I'm sorry for him.
the best and wisest man I've ever known.
There's no one does what he does,
nobody he can talk to—
He's Sherlock Holmes,
he's the master,
he's Sherlock Holmes,
and he's all alone.

THE ADVENTURE OF THE ABU QIR SAPPHIRE

by F. Paul Wilson

AN UNWELCOME VISITOR

It has been five years since I last put pen to paper for the purpose of recording one of my cases. Apparently, even after nearly a decade in retirement, my reputation persists in London. Since Watson is unavailable, I shall once more assume the task of my own biographer, as I did in regard to the affair of the lion's mane.

For someone who needed cocaine to survive the ennui that dragged him down during the interstices between cases, it still surprises me how much I've grown to love the quiet country life. And as I approach my sixtieth birthday—I find it difficult to believe it's but two years away—I confess to having become somewhat set in my ways. Creeping ossification, one might say. As a result, I tend to loathe anything that interrupts my quotidian routine.

Considering my circumstances, how could it be any other way? I have my villa, enviably positioned on the South Downs of Sussex with its magnificent view of the Channel and the chalk hills that tower over the shore. I have my old housekeeper to tend to my needs as I in turn tend to the needs of my bees.

So you will understand, then, why I was somewhat less than gracious when young Arran Davies arrived unannounced, seeking my assistance.

A sunny Friday in July—the 19th, to be exact. My housekeeper was shopping in Fulworth to replenish our larder and I was in the rear orchard tending my hives, when a car skidded to a halt before my villa. Through the mesh of my netted hat I saw a young man emerge from an open Benz roadster.

"Mister Holmes?" he cried, waving. "Mister Sherlock Holmes?"

He carried an air of desperation that told me he wanted to engage my services. Immediately I began moving towards the back door of the villa.

"Mister Holmes!" he repeated, hurrying around the side. "I need your help!"

I yanked off my bee hat. "I am retired and you are uninvited. Leave immediately."

"I have driven all the way from London to seek the use of your investigative skills."

I was halfway to the door. "There's not that much daylight left and you've got seventy miles to retrace. You should start back immediately."

"I wish to hire you. I'll pay any fee you ask."

Ten feet to go. "Have you not been listening? I am retired."

"My reputation is in ruins. I'm being accused of stealing the Abu Qir Sapphire from the Egypt Exploration Society."

My hand grasped the doorknob. "If you are innocent, you will find the police quite capable of catching the real thief."

"But she appears to know you. She mentioned your name."

Neither knowing nor caring who "she" was, I pulled the door open and stepped through. "For obvious reasons, my name is often mentioned in criminal circles."

"She said she visited your old lodgings on Baker Street in the hope of renewing an acquaintance, but you had moved on."

I thought that odd, but wasn't about to let myself be drawn in. *Retired*. That was my current state of being. Twenty-three years in the consulting detective business had been quite enough.

"Good day, sir," I said and slammed the door in his face.

At the last moment I thought I heard him say, "She calls herself Madame de Medici."

I opened the door.

"What did you say?"

"De Medici. She goes by the name Madame de Medici."

Here was a name I had never expected to hear again.

"Really."

"You know her then?"

"I doubt anyone truly knows that woman. But are we talking about the same Medici?" I found the ease with which I recalled her face a bit disconcerting. "Amber eyes?"

"Yes—yes! Astonishing eyes."

"Then indeed, I did know her, but a long time ago."

He rubbed a hand over his face. "So she's real. I'd begun to think Medici wasn't her real name."

"I'm quite sure it's not. I suspect no one but the Madame knows her real name."

Madame de Medici . . . I hadn't heard that name since—when was it? Before Watson and I joined forces . . . two years at least. That would be 1879. One of the most remarkable women I've ever met, eclipsed only by the redoubtable Irene Adler.

He looked puzzled. "You say you knew her 'a long time ago.' How long?"

"Quite long. Thirty-three years, to be exact."

"Well, then, she cannot be the same. The woman I am speaking of is herself only in her mid-thirties at most."

"Perhaps her daughter, then."

Madame de Medici as a mother? It didn't ring true, but the woman herself would be somewhere in her seventh decade now.

"You seem to have doubts, Mister Holmes."

"The same name, the same amber eyes. With such limited information at hand, I don't see much choice but to conclude she's the daughter."

His gaze unfocused. "Hair black as night, eyes the color of the fresh honey in your hives . . ."

"You seem smitten, sir."

He shook himself. "*Was*. Was smitten, Mister Holmes. I confess that. She worked her feminine wiles on me, but that's over now. I want her brought to justice—punished for theft and for destroying my reputation."

My instincts told me to close the door again, but I was intrigued now. Perhaps hooked was a better word. That name again, after all these years.

"All right, all right. Come in."

His face lit. "You'll help me then?"

Quite unlikely, but I wanted to hear his story

"I make no promises. Tell me your tale and we'll see."

MISDIRECTION AND LEGERDEMAIN

Mister Arran Davies described himself as an Egyptologist with a B.A. and B.Sc., a member of numerous learned societies, and scion of one of England's oldest families—in that order.

Anyone reading Watson's accounts of our outings—sensationalized, to be sure—would know that I have never been impressed by titles, and retirement has not given me cause to revise that attitude.

"Do not waste my time with your lineage and academic achievements. Tell me your story, and do not skip any details."

We were seated in the front room. I'd desired a whisky so I poured us each one from a bottle of Strathisla given to me years ago.

"Well, then, I suppose I should start with the stone."

I pulled out the Persian slipper and started filling the bowl of my pipe. "This Abu Qir Sapphire you mentioned."

"Yes. I came upon it quite by accident—serendipity in its purest form. I had a day off while researching an excavation in Alexandria, so I decided to take short jaunt up the coast to Abu Qir Bay. I wanted a swim, and where better than in the very waters where Nelson defeated Napoleon's convoy and established the Royal Navy as the preeminent naval power in the Mediterranean? Also, I had developed a fondness for the mussels Al Iskandariya dish my housekeeper made when she could find fresh mussels, and I was determined to supply her with the very freshest possible.

"The tide was out and in no time I found a large cluster attached to a shallow rock. As I worked to pull them free I spotted this grimy rectangular stone in the heart of the cluster. I would not have given it a second thought but for its perfectly symmetrical shape. As I worked it free of the mussels' beards, my fingers detected step-cut facets along the upper and lower surfaces. I knew immediately this was more than a random tidal stone.

"I carried it home and, after much careful toil, managed to remove but a fraction of what appeared to be centuries of grime, opening a window onto some sort of blue gemstone. I am naïve in the matter of jewels, so I took it to an Alexandria jeweler who knew just what to do: He immersed it in a series of solutions that dissolved the grime, revealing a vivid blue stone with odd characters engraved along the largest of its facets. He identified it as a sapphire and appraised it as 'perfect'—ninety-seven karats with no inclusions."

"Your lucky day," I said, lighting the pipe and inhaling.

"So it seemed at the time. When I asked him what he would pay for such a gem, he said he wouldn't take it even as a gift. He said he'd seen two other jewels with similar inscriptions over the years and no good would come of owning it. He did not know the language, did not know what the inscription meant, but he kept saying 'Put it back. No good will come from it.'"

"An odd statement, don't you think?"

"I believed the strange characters of the inscription threw him off."

"Obviously you didn't take his advice."

"Of course not, though now I wish I had. But I did my duty and turned it over to the Egypt Exploration Society, of which I am a member."

"Why your duty?" I asked.

"My trip to Egypt was funded by the Society, and so anything of an historical nature I found belonged to them. The Society showed it to the British Museum which professed an interest in displaying it once its provenance could be established."

"You found it in Egypt, did you not? Isn't it therefore Egyptian?"

"But it's quite obviously *not* Egyptian. It's a bundle of contradictions, in fact. As I mentioned, the sapphire was inscribed—etched—with strange characters that reminded one of the Phoenician *abjad* but were not. Experts at the museum thought they were pre-Phoenician and post-Sumerian, but no one had ever seen anything like them. It reeked of antiquity—the pre-Phoenician theory would put it at 2,000 BC or earlier—yet gemstones were not cut like this in antiquity. The lapidary tools and skill necessary to shape this sapphire's facets did not exist in those times. The stone had many possible origins and the Egypt Exploration Society was determined to sort them out. I'd made quite the discovery, you see, and presented the Society with a delicious mystery. I became their fair-haired boy, as it were."

"So some good *did* come of it."

"Yes, well, for a while it seemed nothing *but* good came of it. And then Madame de Medici entered my life."

Finally he had reached the part of his story I wanted most to hear.

"Just how did that happen?"

"Quite by accident—or so it seemed at the time. I was attending a display of the Oxyrhynchus Papyri put on by the Society. She entered the hall draped in a floor-length hooded cloak, almost like a Benedictine monk's robe, although fashioned from the finest midnight-blue cashmere. Her features were hidden deep within the cowl. I forgot all about the papyri. She immediately became the center of my attention. I watched her lithe figure as it glided from display to display. I angled myself so that I could glimpse her face as she perused the display cases, studying the ancient pieces as if reading them. I even saw her smile once or twice as if she found something amusing."

"You believe she was reading them?"

He shrugged. "Or *pretending* to read them."

"If the daughter is anything like her mother, she has a passion for antiquities."

"She most certainly does. I simply had to meet her. So, girding my loins, as it were, I approached as casually as I was able and asked if she were a member of the Society. She looked up at me and I had my first full view of her face. Her flawless skin, those amber eyes and . . . and . . . ." He shrugged.

"You fell under her spell."

A statement rather than a question, for I remembered her mother's mesmeric gaze.

"How could I not? A beautiful, exotic young woman with, as I soon discovered, an encyclopedic knowledge of Egypt. I was completely smitten. We retired to a quiet corner and conversed for hours that flashed by like minutes. An enthralling creature. I didn't want to let her out of my sight, which was why I was devastated to learn that she lived in Cairo and would be sailing back the very next day."

I recognized certain aspects of the classic confidence scheme. Davies had taken the lure, the hook had been set, and now the clock was running. Very smoothly done.

"Nothing could persuade her to stay on?" I offered.

He shook his head. "No. She said she didn't want to leave but had business back in Egypt that she'd left unattended too long. It had all been a wasted trip anyway, according to her."

"Ah. Wasted how?"

"She told me she'd seen a drawing of the Abu Qir Sapphire in a copy of *Al-Ahram* in Cairo. I knew of the drawing. The Society had released it to the *Times* but also to the Egyptian press in the hope that someone would recognize the stone or its inscription. The image had shocked her because 'a very similar stone'—her words—had been in her family for centuries."

"'Centuries'? Most people would say 'generations,' don't you think?"

"I suppose. I remember her exact words were 'a de Medici possession for many, many centuries.'"

I hid my surprise. Decades ago I had heard that exact phrase from her mother regarding another ancient item.

"She told me," Davies continued, "that she'd traveled all the way from Cairo and visited the British Museum to view it, but was very disappointed when she learned it wouldn't be ready for display until more was learned about it. Allowing her to see it was out of the question since it wasn't even in the museum."

"But you could remedy that, could you not," I said, perceiving how this would play out. "You could make her trip worthwhile. You could be her knight errant."

"Exactly," he replied, nodding with a grim expression. "I wanted so desperately to impress her."

"Were you not the least bit suspicious? She latches on to perhaps the one person in all of London who can arrange a viewing of that stone?"

"I will say in my own defense that such a possibility did occur to me. But only briefly. I immediately realized that it was *I* who had latched on to *her*."

My only response was a dour look that Watson knew well.

"I know, I know," he said sheepishly. "A beautiful young female dangling before a young, unattached male . . . I was a moth to her flame. But I still might have refrained from showing her the stone had she not produced her pièce de résistance."

"The exact same jewel."

Davies started as if he'd received an electric shock. "How could you know?"

"As inevitable as the sun rising in the east, I'm afraid."

He sighed. "Well, easy for you to say at this point. But be that as it may, she removed a black velvet jewel box from her purse and opened it for me. There, nestled in white satin, lay a sapphire identical to the one I had found in Abu Qir Bay. As I told you, I'm no gemologist, but what she showed me appeared to be an exact duplicate, right down to the indecipherable engraving."

"Didn't that arouse *any* suspicion?"

"I'm not saying 'very close' or 'almost like,' I'm saying *exact*. The only image of the Abu Qir released was the simple black-and-white line drawing we gave to the press. She could not know the color from the drawing, and hers was a perfect match. One had to have intimate knowledge of the original to make such a copy. I dare say, one might well have had to *own* it at some time in the past to make that copy."

"Well, perhaps her mother did at one time."

He barked a harsh laugh. "Oh, I doubt that very much. That gem was underwater a *long* time. I'm thinking it might even have washed out of Heraecleion itself."

That made no sense. "The capital of Crete?"

"No-no. They sound the same, but I'm speaking of the ancient fabled city supposedly built on an island in Abu Qir Bay. Legend has it that Heracleion sank in the second or third century BC."

"'Supposedly'?"

"Well, there's no trace of it, but it's mentioned as a trading center in ancient texts, so it must have existed."

I had never heard of it, but then I do not clutter my mind with trivialities such as tales of ancient sunken cities and such. They take up room that might be more usefully occupied by facts and theories related to solving crimes. I recall how Watson was shocked when he learned that I could not name the planets, and had no idea that they numbered eight. But really, of what use is such information? None.

"But no matter," Davies went on. "Since the stone seemed impossible to fake, what this woman showed me had to be a genuine companion piece to the Abu Qir."

"And of course, once you revealed yourself as discoverer of the stone in the paper, she wondered if she could see them side by side."

Another sheepish look. "That, I fear, was my suggestion. As finder of the gem, I'd been given access to it for research purposes, and so I took her to the vault, and we laid our respective stones side by side on a velvet cloth. At that point I could see a variance in color between the two, but so slight as to be unnoticeable when they were apart. I asked her what she knew about the stones. She said the inscription was in what she called the Old Tongue from the First Age and was the name of an ancient god of the sea. Sailors of that time believed sapphires guaranteed a safe journey."

"Did any of this make sense to you?"

He shook his head. "Not a bit. She was vague about dating this 'Old Tongue' and 'First Age,' saying it was wiped out by 'the Cataclysm.' And then abruptly she announced that she had packing to tend to and couldn't stay any longer. She thanked me profusely for the opportunity to see the stones together. No cajoling on my part could delay her departure. With the greatest reluctance I handed back her stone and bid her adieu."

"When do you think she made the switch?"

"I assume while she was telling me about the First Age," he said, looking chagrinned. "I kept gazing into those amber eyes, never thinking to watch her hands. When she was ready to depart, I unknowingly handed her the original and packed away the copy. Two days later Doctor Carruthers immediately noticed something amiss when he saw the stone. He has a better eye than I, and a quick examination with his loupe confirmed that the Abu Qir Sapphire had been replaced with a glass copy. Since I was the last one to sign into that particular vault, I am, naturally, a suspect."

"Of course you are. And since you know nothing more than the name the woman gave you, and are the only one who saw her face, you have nothing to fall back on. Anyone who saw you with her that night will assume her to be your accomplice."

"But I did confirm with the police that she boarded a steamer bound for Port Said the very next day. The ship made its first stop in Brest where French authorities were on hand to arrest her when it arrived."

"But she was not aboard."

He looked upset. "True. But how can you know that?"

"Because if she's anything like her mother, she's too smart to allow herself to be apprehended so easily. The boat trip was misdirection, just like her stories of the 'Old Tongue' and the 'First Age.' She's consistently made you look in the wrong direction—misdirection and legerdemain."

"Where *should* I look, then? Where can she be?"

"Mark my words, Mister Davies: Madame de Medici is still in London. And I think I might know where."

MADAME DE MEDICI THEN

We set out for London immediately in Davies's Benz roadster. The evening was warm and I must say I found the rushing air refreshing. Engine and road noise made conversation all but impossible, so I lapsed into a reverie of my encounter with our quest's mother more than three decades before.

The late 1870s were a time of great foment in the Middle East. The fall of the Ottoman Empire at the close of the Russo-Turkish War encouraged nationalist elements in the Egyptian army to revolt. Their overthrow of the government came at a time when years of abnormally low flooding of the Nile resulted in food shortages and starvation in Upper Egypt.

In 1879, leaving the riots and looting behind, Madame de Medici arrived in London. I knew nothing of this. I was engaged in the late summer of that year—August 24, to be precise—by Sir Reginald Serling to locate an Akkadian tablet dating back to 1800 BC that had been stolen from his home. He told me he did not wish the police involved because the tablet was delicate and he would not risk it being damaged by some blundering constable.

Of course, I didn't believe that for a second. Many private collections contained ancient artifacts obtained through highly questionable channels that would not bear even the most cursory scrutiny. Nevertheless, he was offering a generous finder's fee and the circumstances intrigued me.

To wit: Sir Reginald's collection was eclectic, spanning many cultures, from Japan to East Africa. Upon my inspection of the premises I noted a collection of daggers with jeweled handles. The thief had left these untouched. Also untouched was a display of ancient gold coins which easily could have been melted down and sold off as ingots, leaving no link to the crime. Only a clay tablet had been taken.

Upon questioning, Sir Reginald seemed genuinely puzzled at the thief's choice of the tablet. He said it had arrived in a lot he had purchased from a stall in a Cairo street bazaar before leaving Egypt. He'd had the tablet appraised and was told he might get one hundred guineas for it if he found the right buyer. Unless they were engraved with an image, Akkadian tablets were not terribly sought after. This one supposedly listed ingredients for an ointment. Because of the circumstances of its theft, he now suspected that it might be more valuable than he'd been led to believe. He wanted it back.

I began my investigation and, as it progressed, a mysterious lascar of ill repute surfaced and resurfaced. He ran the infamous Bar of Gold opium den in Upper Swandam Lane, a place I would frequent in disguise often in the future. But he lived elsewhere in Limehouse; his home was an anachronism, a relic from the Georgian era, the time before the docklands were built, before the Oriental influx that eventually resulted in Chinatown. I went there expecting to find this mysterious lascar. Instead, I found Madame de Medici.

I was met at the door by a dark-skinned, white-robed servant in slippers that matched the color of his red fez. His angular face traced a maze of fine wrinkles.

"The Madame is waiting for you," he said with a slight lisp.

Hiding my shock, I followed him down a hallway. I had been expecting to meet a man, and had intended my visit to be a surprise.

The servant's slippers made no sound as he led me down a series of well-lit and luxuriously decorated hallways, ending in a thick-carpeted chamber where an exotic woman reclined on a pillowed divan, smoking a mauve cigarette under the cloth-of-gold canopy obscuring the ceiling. She wore a long robe of Kashmiri silk. A low, inlaid table of Chinese design squatted between us. She exhaled a cloud of aromatic smoke as she fixed me with her amber stare.

"Mister Sherlock Holmes," she said in languid tones. "I have heard your name mentioned in certain quarters. You are developing an interesting reputation."

Carmine lips, ivory skin, ebony hair . . . I suppose she might have been considered beautiful by most men. I am not most men. Even then, in my early days of detection, I did not allow the physical attributes of either client or quarry to impinge upon my consciousness. Once you engage the emotions, you hamper clear reasoning. I tried to assess her ethnic origin but could not. Her age was equally obscure. I put her at thirty, thirty-five at most—about five to ten years older than I at the time—but she radiated a calm authority that was ageless. A woman used to having her way.

"You have me at a disadvantage, Madame."

"De Medici," she said.

The name suggested Italian descent, but she possessed no Italian features.

"Honored," I replied. "I am looking for a certain lascar–"

"No, you are looking for that," she said, pointing her cigarette at a velvet-wrapped bundle that sat between a beige envelope and a delicate silver bell on the table. "I do not wish to waste your time. Do not waste mine. Don't be shy. You may look."

I parted the velvet folds and beheld a dun-colored clay tablet engraved with rows of unfamiliar symbols. Most unimpressive.

"Is this Sir Reginald's?" I asked, for I had never seen it.

"No, it is mine—mine for quite a long time. That is until rioters looted it from my Luxor house earlier this year."

She knocked the ashes off her cigarette into a silver bowl at her side. I noticed a gold ring engraved with an image of Bast. A feline human and a feline goddess. It glinted when she spoke.

"Sir Reginald says he bought it from a street vendor."

"That may well be, but that does not grant him ownership of stolen property. It has been a de Medici possession for many, many centuries."

"Still, it comes down to your word against his."

"Precisely. That is one of the reasons I wished to meet you. The first is because you have been quite dogged and rather clever in tracking me down. I thought I had used the lascar to cover my tracks rather well, yet here you are." She smiled and it changed her face in such a way that it might have melted any other man's heart. "The other reason is so that you can deliver a message to Sir Reginald. The envelope is next to the tablet."

Lifting the square beige envelope, I immediately appreciated the silk paper with fine threads running through it. Handmade and of the highest quality, with "Sir Reginald Serling" inscribed on the front in an odd, squared-off hand, obviously written with a quill. On the back, a disk of red wax with a scarab seal.

I held it up. "May I enquire . . . ?"

"Of course. I wish to live an unobtrusive life, to come and go anywhere in the world as I please with no one caring and no one the wiser. Therefore I despise conflict. It attracts attention, so I always settle conflicts. To that end I have invited Sir Reginald to meet with me, just the two of us, so that we might discuss this calmly and rationally. I intend to offer him another antiquity of even greater value in place of the tablet."

"That seems fair," I said. "Quite generous, in fact."

"I have a rather extensive collection spread all over the world. I store quite a few items right here in London, so I am sure we can arrive at an accommodation that will leave us both satisfied."

"Then it appears our business here is done," I said.

That smile again. "You may linger if you wish."

"Duty calls," I said, pocketing the envelope. "I am obliged to deliver this without delay."

"As you wish." She rang the little silver bell and the red-slippered servant re-appeared. "Good day, Mister Holmes. Until we meet again."

I doubted that would ever happen.

I returned to Sir Reginald and told him her offer of a valuable substitute for the tablet. I presented him with the letter which he tore open, read, then tossed to me.

"Outrageous! She has no idea who she's dealing with!"

I glanced at the message, artful in its succinctness:

> Sir Reginald—
> Regret the inconvenience
> Equanimity is my goal
> Madame de Medici

At the bottom she listed a time—eight P.M.—and an address. I thought it rather odd that the address was not the lascar's house but on a neighboring street, one block south.

When I asked Sir Reginald if he was going to inform the police, he angrily responded that the tablet was his and he would settle for nothing less. He didn't need the police. He would take two "stout men" with him to the address Madame de Medici had given and return with the tablet "come hell or high water."

I might have offered to accompany him were he going alone, but since he was not, I informed him that I had discharged my duty in locating the tablet and the rest was not my concern. He grudgingly paid me my finder's fee and I departed.

I learned later that Sir Reginald and two other men left his house that evening and were never seen again. When the police questioned me about his disappearance—his household staff had, of course, reported me as a recent visitor—I told them about Madame de Medici and gave the address she had given Sir Reginald, as well as that of the lascar's house. They found no trace of the Madame in either place. No one in the neighborhood—mostly Han Chinese at the time—would admit that they had ever seen or heard of her. As for myself, I never expected to hear of her again.

MADAME DE MEDICI NOW

The hour was late when Davies and I arrived in London but I didn't think we should wait until morning. I advised him to park his roadster at his home in Belgravia and we'd take an electric hackney into Limehouse.

"I knew this was not a savory neighborhood," Davies said as we made our way towards the docklands, "but I never imagined . . ."

"Not your usual environs, I imagine. Not mine either, I dare say, although I was well familiar with the area before I retired."

Limehouse had deteriorated even further since I'd departed for Sussex. Shipbuilding and shipping remained its major industries, but the population was now almost completely Oriental. Even at this late hour the streets were full of Chinamen, coolies, and Malaysians, some obviously under the influence of the poppy.

When we arrived at the address I had originally known as the lascar's house, which over the decades had passed to a Eurasian named Zani Chada, the upper windows were lit so I assumed someone was home. Instead of stopping, I told the driver to keep moving and take us around the block.

"There!" I said, pointing at a dark narrow entrance to a house on the neighboring street. "Mark that address well, driver. After you drop us at our destination, I want you to wait right here and make yourself available to a young woman should she exit and look for a cab. No matter where she tells you to go, bring her around to us. And if she fails to hire you, follow her."

The fellow gave me an odd look, but said, "As you wish, sir."

The look from Davies mimicked the driver's. "Holmes, I don't understand."

"I'll explain later," I told him.

The dark house matched the address her mother had given Sir Reginald all those many years ago, and I'd noticed that it backed up to what was now Zani Chada's house. I had a suspicion . . .

Soon we stood before the Chada house.

"This is a long shot," I told Davies as I hammered the door's iron knocker against its plate.

"Surely you don't expect her to let us in."

"Of course not, but this is a place to start. Someone must eventually answer. I'll keep knocking until—"

The door swung open. Instead of the tall servant of my previous visit, a squat, turbaned little man met us. He appeared Nepalese.

"The Madame awaits," he said in thickly accented English.

The sense of déjà vu was almost overwhelming. Like mother, like daughter.

Davies grabbed my arm. "Holmes, this smells of a trap. She could be keeping an army of these little savages ready to overwhelm us."

"We are not characters in a penny dreadful," I told him. "And neither is this woman."

I had an advantage of having lived through this before. If she was anything like her mother, the Madame was planning a negotiation. I could see no mutually satisfactory end to this affair, but decided, for the sake of my companion, to let the drama proceed to its predestined finale.

We followed the waddling Nepalese down the same series of hallways I'd traveled before, ending in the same silk-draped chamber. But this time no languid beauty lounged on a divan. Instead, a raven-haired young woman clad in a snug leather jacket, jodhpurs, and leather boots paced before the low inlaid table. Her frown became a bright smile as her amber gaze found me.

"Mister Sherlock Holmes!" she cried. "What took you so long?"

The sight of her rendered me momentarily speechless. Not because of her question, but because . . .

"You're her!" I said, finding my voice.

"Of course I am," she said. "Who else would I be?"

"I thought you were her daughter but you're the same woman—Madame de Medici herself."

"Daughter?" she said with a laugh. "I have no daughter, no children at all."

"But this can't be!" I felt the need to sit but steeled my knees. "You haven't aged a day!"

"A careful diet does wonders for the skin."

She was toying with me. At the very least she had to be in her mid-sixties, yet she had not aged a day since I'd last seen her. And it *was* her. I pride myself on the ability to pick up on nuances of behavior—they are like a fingerprint. My first meeting with Madame de Medici is etched upon my memory. No question: This was the same woman.

"Daughter, mother—irrelevant!" Davies cried. "Whoever you are, you stole—"

"Please, Mister Davies," she said, aiming her amber stare his way, "you are being rude. I am renewing my acquaintance with Mister Holmes." She turned back to me. "Our meeting was so brief last time. But I have avidly followed your exploits, courtesy of your friend, Doctor Watson, and so I feel as if we are old friends. You were only locally known back then. Now you are world famous."

"And you, Madame," I said, managing to keep my composure. "How have you spent the intervening years? Here in London, or in Luxor?"

Her smile widened. "You remembered! No, my Luxor home is but one of many. I divide my time between a dozen locales, all of which provide easy access to remnants of the ancient world."

"To sate your love of antiquities?"

"Quite."

I could see Davies chafing to speak but I needed more answers.

"Sir Reginald disappeared shortly after our meeting. Do you know anything about that?"

She shrugged her slim shoulders. "He burst into Kwee's house armed with a pistol along with two men carrying truncheons."

"Kwee's house—would that be where you told him to meet you?"

"Yes. Sir Reginald came early, before I'd had a chance to tell Kwee to expect him. Mister Kwee is a very private person and does not take kindly to threats."

"I see. And what happened to Sir Reginald and his companions?"

"I have no idea. Mister Kwee told me that they 'went away' and would say no more. But enough about Sir Reginald. What about you? I was devastated to learn you had retired."

"I decided on a graceful exit."

"I gathered that. And I decided to lure you back for a chat."

Davies could contain himself no longer. "Surely you didn't steal the Abu Qir Sapphire just for that!"

Her voice turned cold. "I did *not* steal it. But I made mention of knowing Mister Holmes so that you would run straight to him when you needed help."

Which was exactly what Davies did. A most clever woman.

"You can't possibly deny you stole the sapphire."

"As I recall, Mister Davies, you placed it in my hand yourself."

"Not knowing you had made a switch! Admit you stole it!"

A smile played about her lips. "My dear Mister Davies, how can one steal one's own property?"

He barked a harsh laugh. "You cannot be serious!"

"I am very serious."

"Then you are mad! That sapphire is ancient—so ancient no one can identify the language of the inscription, let alone translate it!"

The smile returned. "I did both for you a few nights ago."

"The 'Old Tongue'!" he scoffed. "The 'First Age'! The name of an ancient god of the sea!"

"Well, that last part is not quite true. Actually the stone is inscribed with *my* name."

"Madness!" he cried.

"Tell me," I said. "What name is inscribed on the stone? Surely not 'de Medici.'"

She smiled. "Surely not."

"What then?"

"You've already seen the transliteration."

Had I? When?

"Never mind names," Davies said. "The sapphire can't be yours. It has been lying on the bottom of Abu Qir Bay for longer than any human has been alive. It most likely washed out of Heracleion after it sank, and that was over two thousand years ago!"

"Yes," she said. "It sank quite quickly, I was told. They built it on a sandy island and all the weight softened the sand, taking everything down. Those who were there at the time escaped with only the possessions they could carry. Residents who were elsewhere in the world lost everything."

"You speak as if—never mind. I demand you return the sapphire immediately!"

Her expression hardened. "I maintain my claim of prior ownership."

Davies turned to me with his hands raised in frustration. "Holmes! What am I to do?"

I did not have an answer for him. I would have called her mad too except for the fact that this woman had not aged a day in nearly three and a half decades. I could not for an instant accept that she had been a resident of Heracleion, but how old *was* she?

"*La belle dame sans merci*," I said. "The Madame appears more concerned with objects than people."

"Because people are transient," she said. "They invariably depart. Things, on the other hand, are more loyal. Things remain. However," she added, "I am not without sympathy for your plight, Mister Davies. I am willing to offer objects of similar antiquity and value to ease your pain."

"I am afraid that is un–" Davies began, but the woman cut him off.

"Do not be too hasty, Mister Davies." Moving with feline grace, she stepped to the rear wall and slid back a panel, revealing a lighted closet lined with shelves. "You may have your choice."

When she stepped inside, I slipped closer, suspecting it might be more than a closet, but she reemerged almost immediately with a handful of bright yellow disks.

"These, for instance," she said, holding them out. "Ptolemaic coins—solid gold."

"I cannot settle for less than the Abu Qir Sapphire. The Society will accept nothing else."

"Very well, then . . ."

She stepped back inside and I was already moving forward when she slid the panel closed behind her. My fingers were mere inches short of the edge when the panel merged flush with the surrounding wall.

OUTFLANKED

"Davies!" I cried. "Help me find the release!"

He seemed frozen in shock for an instant, then shook it off and leaped forward.

"She's mad!" he said. "Locking herself in a closet proves it!"

"Don't talk like a fool! It's the entrance to a tunnel."

"How can you be sure? Where can it go?"

"To the place she calls Kwee's house. Now stop talking and find a way to open this panel. There must be—here!"

My fingernails had found a shallow groove along the edge. I pulled and a tiny lever angled out, releasing the panel. Sliding it aside, I stepped into the empty closet, only to be met with another barrier.

"One of these cabinets must move. Find it!"

We wasted a good half minute pushing and pulling on the shelves until one of them levered downward under Davies's pressure and a section of the wall, shelves and all, swung back. Utter darkness faced us.

In our rush from Sussex, I had neglected to bring a torch, so I eased my foot forward and down until I found a step.

"Careful, Davies. These will lead us down to an underground passage to Kwee's house."

"How can you possibly know that?"

"Follow me but watch your footing." After we had descended ten steps and were inching our way along a narrow passage, I explained. "As soon as I saw the relative locations of the two houses, I knew there had to be a hidden passage. I assume Madame de Medici is the true owner of both. She told me once she likes to come and go as she pleases, 'with no one caring and no one the wiser.' This passage allows her to enter one house and depart from another—with no one the wiser."

The light from the room behind us provided scant illumination, but was better than nothing. I moved carefully, taking long but slow strides until, after perhaps twenty yards, my leading foot caught the lowest step on a new stairway, leading up.

"Stay close," I whispered. "We don't know what awaits."

I led the way up to find our path blocked by a sturdy wooden door. Finding the knob, I gave it a twist. It turned but the door would not budge.

"We must break through, Davies!"

She was getting too far ahead. The manner in which she had been dressed gave me an uneasy feeling, and I had no idea whether our driver would follow her as directed.

"Shouldn't we call the police?" Davies said as he squeezed beside me on the top step.

"No time! Put your shoulder to it. We'll have at it together on my count. One-two-*three*!"

On the first try I heard the door jamb crack. On the second we broke through and stumbled into a pantry. Its door stood open. As we stepped out into a dank hallway, I heard the faint clatter of a horse's hooves from the side of the house.

"She's outplayed us, Davies!" I'd suspected she had a horse ready when I spied her jodhpurs, but by then I'd committed to a course of action that did not allow proper adjustment. "To the front! Perhaps we can still catch her!"

We burst through the front door and reached the sidewalk just as she galloped past our waiting car. I saw her toss something through the rear window on her way by.

"That's her!" I said to the driver as we jumped into the car. "After her!"

"I'm sorry, sir," the driver said as he put the car in gear. "I assumed she'd be on foot."

"So did we. Go!"

It proved a brief pursuit, lasting no more than two blocks, at which point she guided her mount into a narrow, crowded side street. The pedestrians parted for her, then closed behind her, blocking the way. Despite our driver sounding his horn and shouting at the top of his lungs, the throng of Orientals would not let us pass.

"What are we to do, Mister Holmes?" Davies said.

I could only shrug. "Pursuit is hopeless. She has homes all over the world, and perhaps all over London. She will be aboard a ship today or tomorrow or in two weeks, bound for the continent or the Middle East or the Americas."

"We found her today!"

"Only because she allowed it."

He leaned back and closed his eyes. "Then I am ruined!"

"Not so, Mister Davies. We shall return to the Chada house and empty her closet of antiquities, which you shall transport to the Egypt Exploration Society. I'm sure their total value—especially those Ptolemaic gold coins—will equal or even exceed the worth of the sapphire. You will admit you were duped and offer the Madame's horde as recompense."

He straightened, eyes wide. "Yes! Yes, I think that will work. Oh, thank you, Mister Holmes! How can I ever repay you?"

"Never fear, you will receive an invoice for my services."

As the driver returned us to the Chada house, I noticed an envelope made of familiar silk paper on the floor. I retrieved it and immediately recognized scarab seal on the back, and the quill strokes of the squared-off script forming my name. I tore it open.

Sherlock Holmes—
Regret we could not linger longer
Elsewhere calls me as always
Madam de Medici

She'd told me I had already seen the transliteration of her name, and I believed here I was seeing it again. I'd thought knowing her true name might make her less mysterious, but it succeeded only in making Madame de Medici more so.

THE WALK-IN

by Harley Jane Kozak

It's not every day that you walk into your apartment and find that your cat has turned into a dog.

Okay, it was London, so it wasn't an apartment but a flat; and neither the flat nor the cat was mine, they were my brother Robbie's. But the dog was unequivocally a dog.

It was my second day in town, and because my brother's flat was new, and lacking pretty much everything—including my brother—I'd been out buying random moving-in things: toilet paper, dish-drainer, red wine. I was in the hallway juggling these and trying to get his door open when I heard a clickety-clack on the wood floors on the other side of the door. Inside the flat.

Clickety-clack?

I glanced at the gilt number near the keyhole: 2B. Right flat, wrong sound. Touie, Robbie's annoying cat, padded around on silent paws. So who was this? Setting down my packages—parcels, as the Brits would say—I worked to get the door unlocked. At which point I was assaulted by the dog. A twenty-pound bulbous-bellied dog.

He—the gender was glaringly obvious—was corpulent, gunmetal gray and so hair-free he appeared to have been skinned. His legs were stubby but his ears were large, and sticking straight up, rabbit-like. His face was all frowns and folds, a canine Winston Churchill digesting bad news. But he greeted me like a giant dog biscuit: when I bent to rescue my stuff from the floor, he launched himself at my chest, tangled himself in my crossbody bag and slathered me with saliva. For a small dog, he had a lot of saliva.

I pushed the dog back into the flat and got the door closed behind us. "Robbie?" I called out but my voice echoed through the bare rooms. No surprise. Robbie was my twin; I could feel his absence like a tangible thing.

I pushed aside thoughts of *Where's Robbie?* and made a grab for the dog's tag. "So who are you?" I asked him.

His collar looked just like the one Touie, the cat, wore: scarlet leather, the perimeter dotted with faux gems. One of Robbie's extravagances. Strange.

"Sit still, Dog. Let me read this." But when he did and I had, strange turned to bizarre.

The tag said, "Touie" and the number on the tag was Robbie's cell phone.

My first thought was "WTF?" followed by "Where's Touie?" I wasn't her biggest fan, and she was definitely not mine, but I'd just spent five days relocating that cat from New York to London, a feat, on the misery meter, right up there with digging graves in winter. It just wasn't possible that she'd disappeared. I went through the flat, checking under the comforter where I'd last seen her, inside closets, and even the microwave, which Touie was too fat to fit into. There were limited hiding places. The only things Robbie had brought in, before disappearing, were five boxes of books and a bed, its toxic "new mattress" smell wafting through the flat like bad air freshener.

The real Touie, like Robbie, was gone.

"Now what?" I asked, and the dog responded by sniffing around in a distinctive manner, suggesting a bladder situation. I unclipped the shoulder strap from my pink carryon bag, fashioning a leash, and let the dog lead me outside. He had strong opinions about our route, one block to Baker Street and then a left, and another left, until I lost track of where we were.

The October day was murky with fog. And cold. I was wearing Robbie's red rain slicker, but it wasn't enough. How'd I get roped into doing this

favor-turned-into-an-enigma-wrapped-in-a–*Twilight Zone* episode? Robbie had
a lifetime of practice getting me to do stuff he didn't like doing—pet immigration in this case—but I'd had the same lifetime of practice saying no. Yet here I
was, and minus the pet in question. How had it happened? *What* had happened?
And why? And where was my damned brother? Seriously, what was I supposed
to do? Call 911? Was the number even 911 in England? And then what? I wasn't
one to chalk things up to supernatural forces, but it was a stretch to assume a
criminal act. What self-respecting thief would want a plump, elderly cat? And
why leave in her place this wheezing dog, straining at his makeshift leash, pulling
me through London?

I'd been wrong about the dog's bladder: he was on a mission, and hardly paused
to sniff, let alone pee. Oblivious to other pedestrians, he pushed onward like a
horse heading for the barn at the end of a long day. Perhaps he lived around here?
The thought gave me a glimmer of hope.

Oops. The dog came to a sudden squat and was now doing the unmentionable
alongside an iron gate guarding a storefront. As I hadn't thought to bring along a
plastic bag, I looked around guiltily, but no concerned citizens materialized to scold
me. The storefront bore an ornate sign: THE RENOWNED MIRKO: PSYCHIC AND CARD
READER. This was followed by a phone number, and then, in smaller font, WALK-
INS—BOTH SORTS!—WELCOME. I was pondering that when I heard the tinkling of
bells, and looked up to see a man standing in the shop doorway.

We stared at each other. He frowned at me, his lips set in a horizontal line. He
was tall and thin, the kind of thin that makes you think, for just a second, *stage four
cancer*, but there was a kinetic energy about him, something in his gray eyes that
nixed that impression. A high forehead, made higher by a receding hairline, made
him look aristocratic, and strangely attractive, as did a three-piece suit more suited
to a wedding than a psychic reading. I felt very American, and not in a good way.

"Unbelievable," he said.

"I'm sorry, Mr.—" I glanced again at the sign. "Mirko. I didn't bring a plastic
bag—satchel—whatever you call them here—okay, never mind. If you have a
paper towel or something, I'll happily clean this up for you."

"No."

"Okay, 'happily' might be overstating it," I admitted. "But I'm willing to—hey!
Dog! Stop." The dog was greeting the Renowned Mirko like a long-lost lover and
attempting to mate with his dress pants. I tugged on the leash.

"Go. Just go. Take yourself off," Mirko snapped, and then said, to the dog. "Not now."

"Whoa. Hold up," I said. "Do you know this dog?"

"No."

"You do. You know this dog. This dog knows you."

"Nonsense," he said.

"It's not nonsense. He dragged me right to you."

"Leave."

"I'm not leaving," I said. "I'm walking in. A walk-in. Like the sign says. Both sorts!"

He gave me a curious look, but then glanced past me and said, "Bloody hell. Too late. Go in."

"What?" I look over my shoulder.

"In, *in*, go inside, are you deaf? Quickly." The man took my arm and yanked me—he and the dog—through the open door.

The shop was warm, and musty with the odor of antiques and incense, the signature scents of psychics the world over. The decor was Victorian clutter. I got a fast impression of chintz, wallpaper and books, books, books, as Mirko herded me across the room to a kitchenette.

"Sit," Mirko said, and I thought he was talking to the dog, until he pushed me into an armchair and scooped the dog into my lap. He then hauled over a rococo screen and arranged it in front of me, blocking my view of the room. He leaned in so close I could smell the damp wool of his suit. "Do not make a sound," he said. "Do not let the dog make a sound. This is critically important."

Before I could argue the point, the tinkling bell sounded again, signaling someone entering the shop. "If you value your brother's life, stay quiet," Mirko said, and walked away.

That shut me up.

The dog and I listened as Mirko said hello to someone. Actually, he said *zdravstvujtye*. A man responded in kind. In Russian. I knew a few words of Russian, but after the pleasantries, the newcomer told Mirko to wait. A second later came the sound of Barbra Streisand and Neil Diamond singing "You Don't Bring Me Flowers," a ballad Robbie once said made him want to cut off his ears. The music source was a cell phone, was my guess, and I wondered why we were listening to it, until I realized it masked conversation. I could pick out only random words now, during the song's lugubrious pauses, of which there were many. Then came the sound of a zipper zipping. The urge to peek around the screen was strong, but the dog began to struggle, wanting out of my arms and onto a small, narrow refrigerator next to us, on top of which sat a large frozen turkey, thawing, and a large ceramic Blessed Virgin Mary. As I thwarted his efforts to investigate the bird, the twinkling bell sounded again, and Streisand, Diamond, and Russian left the building.

"You may come out," Mirko said.

I came around the screen to find Mirko taking off his jacket and kicking off his shoes. Alongside him was a wheelie suitcase, fully zipped.

"So how do you know my brother?" I asked, and promptly took off my own jacket, the room being hellishly hot.

"I haven't time for this," he said.

"But you know where he is?"

"I do not." Now he had his vest off and was unbuttoning his dress shirt, as adroit as a stage actor doing a quick change. "I suggest you return to your flat, with the dog-who-is-not-your-dog, and sleep off the jet lag that you're trying to ignore. It's four in the morning Los Angeles time, and that red-eye you took did you no favors even with an exit row and a window seat. Nor does sleeping on floors agree with you."

My eyes must've widened. He smiled, before whipping off his shirt and giving me a view of his naked chest. Not a bad chest, if you don't mind skinny, which I don't, but I wasn't about to be distracted. "I don't know how you know the things you know," I said, "but all I care about is Robbie." The dog, perhaps reacting to my tone of voice, produced a sound that was less a bark and more the yowl of a human infant. "You tell him, Churchill," I said.

"Churchill? I'd have said Gladstone." Mirko walked to a bureau covered with Tarot cards, opened a drawer and took out a some clothes and a pair of Converse high tops.

"Whoever that is."

"Victoria's Prime Minister, who more closely resembles a French bulldog." He pulled a T-shirt over his head, followed by a hoodie, a purple Grateful Dead relic from some bygone decade.

I stooped to let Gladstone wiggle out of my arms and over to Mirko, who was pulling on his sneakers, though not bothering to lace them up. "Fine," I said.

"But you're pretty much the only person I know in London, not counting Pet Immigration, and I'm not leaving until—"

"Suit yourself." He stood up, ruffled his hair and put on a pair of black-rimmed glasses. The transformation from aristocrat to geek was not just fast, it was total. From his pants pocket he withdrew a remote, which he aimed at the wall behind me.

A creaking sound like the opening of Dracula's coffin made me turn and see a wall-sized bookcase move.

Slowly, squeakily, so disorientingly I thought, *earthquake*? the bookcase kept advancing into the room, as freaky as the Haunted Mansion at Disneyland. I fixed my eyes at random on one frayed book called *The Coming of the Fairies*, willing it to stay put, but nope. It moved. When I turned my attention back to Mirko, he stepped over his pile of clothes, grabbed the handle of the wheelie suitcase and moved to a now-palpable gap between bookcase and wall.

Behind the gap was a door. Mirko opened the door and went through it.

I grabbed the dog and followed.

⬦

"What do you think you're doing?" he called out.

"Following you!" I called back. "What's it look like?"

It couldn't have looked like anything, because it was pitch black except for the glow of Mirko's cell, bouncing along ahead of me. What it smelled like was a dank cellar, the scent intensifying as I followed Mirko down wooden stairs. When we reached the bottom, a light popped on.

We were in a long and narrow passageway, low-ceilinged, brick-floored and lined with storage shelves. The kind of place that makes you think, *bomb shelter* except that it was stuffed with . . . stuff. Furniture, art, armaments, and god knows what else, bubble-wrapped, crated up or just scattered about. Mirko pushed aside a Roman helmet and heaved his wheelie suitcase onto a high shelf, showing an impressive set of muscles. He gave me a quick look, then took off down the passageway.

"Keep up," he called over his shoulder. "Unless you fancy being locked in."

I jogged after him, clutching the dog, until some three hundred feet later the tunnel ended in a second staircase. The lights went off behind me and in darkness

I followed Mirko up the stairs, bumping into him at the top. "'S'cuse me," I mumbled, unsettled by his proximity, and his aftershave. Bay rum. Which I liked.

"This is where we go our separate ways," he said, working to unlock yet another door. A moment later we were out of the tunnel and in the back room of a supermarket.

It was a Tesco Metro, a British 7-Eleven. I followed Mirko through swinging doors onto the selling floor and the mundane world of Whiskas catfood and Wotsits Cheese Snacks.

Mirko marched through the Tesco with all the confidence of a store manager. I tried to match his gait and attitude, never mind that I was carrying an unattractive dog the size of a watermelon.

Once outside, he picked up the pace, his long legs at full stride, weaving his way through lunch-hour London, jammed with people. I caught up with him on the center island of some major intersection, waiting for the pedestrian signal. Before the light could turn green, Mirko stepped into the street, narrowly avoiding a speeding Volvo, and took off at a run. I said a prayer—a necessity, since the traffic was of course going the wrong way—and took off too, wincing at the horns honking at me. I followed him onto an escalator and down into London's Underground.

It was luck that I had a metro card—no, Oyster card, as they whimsically called it. I raced after him, dog squirming in my arms, through the turnstiles, over to some tube line or other, onto a platform, into a subway car, and out again at Liverpool Street, where we made our way to the train station. He made a beeline for a self-serve ticket machine and I found one too, as close as I could get to his. We bought tickets, me juggling credit card, dog, and purse. He then race-walked to a platform, and I hurried after, boarding a train labeled "Norwich." I walked the length of several cars, ignoring the stares of the presumably dog-averse until I found Mirko, at a table for four. As I approached, the train gave a lurch and I lost my balance for a moment, grabbing Mirko's shoulder to steady myself and ending up with a handful of shirt, at which point Gladstone scrambled out of my arms and into his lap.

Mirko accepted the dog, but raised an eyebrow at me. "Took your time, didn't you?"

I plopped into the seat across from him, still panting. "Okay, where's Robbie? Also, who do you work for and what do you do, and also, what do I call you, because you're obviously not Mirko and while we're at it, how do you know all those things about me, things not even Robbie knew? And don't say you're psychic, because you're as clairvoyant as a bagel."

He held my look. "One, that's what I intend to learn, but lower your voice, please, because I'm following someone and while he is three cars ahead of us, I imagine the entire train can hear you. Two, a small agency within the British government. Three, call me Kingsley. Four, observation. You're an American because of your accent. Someplace hot, because it's winter, yet you have a tan line near your clavicle from a sports bra, and another at your ankle, from your trainers, so not a vacation tan, but a resident's. Your diction has no tinge of the American south, so not Florida, and the freckles on your left forearm suggest an inordinate amount of time spent on motorways with your arm resting on the window side, more likely in the ungodly traffic of California, than in Hawaii, and from the shade of your hair, Los Angeles. The lead on the dog is fashioned from a luggage strap and still bears the knot of elastic from an airline identification tag." He picked up the slack leash and proceeded to unknot the elastic. "Your neck is stiff," he continued, "suggesting someone who slept with her head against the window on the left side of an airplane. Front row, coach, standby, so last to board. With no seat in front of you to stow your bag, and by the time you boarded, there was no overhead space left, so the flight attendant checked your carry-on, which explains the tag." He set the leash down and Gladstone looked up at him. "You dozed—fitfully—on a floor last night, as evidenced by the bits of shag carpet in your hair."

"Is that supposed to impress me?" I asked.

"It does impress you," he said. "Your turn. How did you know which ticket to buy? You couldn't possibly see my touch screen."

"No," I said. "But I had a clear view of your forearm. I calculated the length of that, plus your fingers, factored in the fifty-five-degree angle your elbow was bent at, which told me where your fingers would land on the touch-screen keyboard, given the destination list from the drop-down menu."

That shut him up.

The train conductor approached. "Tickets, please," he said.

In unison, Kingsley pulled his out of his hoodie pocket and I pulled mine out of my jeans. We handed them over.

The conductor punched a hole in mine but frowned at Kingsley's. "Stansted Mountfitchet Station? You're on the wrong train, sir."

Kingsley blinked.

I gave the conductor my most charming smile. "I'm so sorry. My cousin is legally blind, but refuses to ask for help. May I pay the difference for him?"

With a shake of the head, the conductor accepted the twenty-pound note I offered him, made change, and issued Kingsley a new ticket. "An assistance dog, is it?" he asked, directing the question at me.

"Gladstone? Yes," I said. "Years of training."

Once the conductor was out of earshot, Mirko said, "You nicked my ticket. Nicely done."

"I traded tickets," I corrected him. "Which is harder. Robbie and I played 'pickpocket' as children."

"Not so good, though, at buying the proper ticket. You disappoint me."

"Same. Where'd I go wrong?"

"You assumed I used my index finger on the touchscreen. I type with my thumb. A three-inch difference. Classic schoolgirl error," he said, but I could tell he was warming up to me. "When did you last talk to Robbie?"

"Five days ago," I said. "He texted me, asking if would I please fly to New York, pick up his cat, Touie, and get her to London because his sub-tenant was threatening to drown her and he was stuck in England on a job. So I did. It was hell. Whatever lies ahead, let me tell you I survived Live Animal Border Inspection at Heathrow, which can make grown men cry, so your Russian mafia doesn't scare me."

His long fingers, on Gladstone's tall ears, stopped mid-pet. "Russian mafia?"

"The Streisand fan. At the shop. Some low-level operative, right? A smurf?"

"Beg your pardon?"

"Oh, please," I said. "You're obviously laundering money, you've got a tunnel filled with black market goods, a wheelie suitcase full of rubles—"

"What makes you think rubles?"

"Your Russian friend, during a sappy pause in 'You Don't Send Me Flowers,' said 'eight hundred million.' If that was pounds or dollars, you'd need a U-Haul to transport them. Rubles, on the other hand, come in denominations of five thousand, and yeah, you could stuff fifteen thousand of them into a suitcase. Which is around a million pounds, a million three in dollars." I wondered if, behind those gray eyes, he was checking my math. "Anyhow," I said. "My brother was part of this adventure. Whatever it is, it's got 'Robbie' written all over it, him being a Russian interpreter, as you of course know."

He studied me. "Have you told the police he's missing?"

"Yeah, they're gonna care that some random American won't answer his sister's texts. Or that his cat's been kidnapped and a dog has stolen her collar." The thief in question was now dozing, emitting fitful dog snores. "Nope. I'm gonna throw in my lot with you, Kingsley-if-that's-even-your-name."

"Not entirely your call," he said.

"I can be persuasive."

"Persuade me."

"I've got a gun in my purse," I said. "Once you catch up to your Russian friend, the one we're following to Norwich, it could come in handy."

An eyebrow went up. "Nicked that, too, did you? From the tunnel?"

"Yeah. Which wasn't easy, given that I was in the dark, in a hurry, and hauling a dog."

"Is that it, then?"

"I've also got your wallet. You're flat broke."

The other eyebrow went up. "Pinch any bullets?" he asked, and held out his hand.

"You didn't give me much time." I passed him the wallet and our fingers touched. He smiled. "Fair enough. Even a non-loaded weapon is a weapon."

The countryside out the train window raced by, deeply green, with hills so rolling they looked fake, accessorized by contented-looking sheep. To someone used to the parched fields of southern California, it was downright exotic. Kingsley, in the seat opposite, had a view of coming attractions, while I watched what we were leaving behind.

Kingsley and I had steaming cups before us, thanks to the Greater Anglia Railway dining coach. Kingsley was a far cry from "Mirko"—unrecognizable, even—but even so, it took confidence to risk running into the guy he was tailing, just for a cup of tea. Not that I was complaining; he'd brought me back a black coffee. I didn't ask how he knew my beverage preferences. Perhaps I had a speck of ground espresso on my earlobe.

"I'm a consultant," Kingsley said, stirring his milky tea. "I was hired to investigate the clandestine dealings going on at the shop of Mirko Rudenko. Having tapped his phone, I heard Mirko converse with a woman named Sarah Byrne, in a dialect called *Surzhyk*, a hybrid of the Russian and Ukrainian languages in which I am conversant, but not fluent. So when Sarah Byrne made an appointment with Mirko, I rang up your brother to come eavesdrop with me."

I blinked. "Robbie's a spy? You guys are spies?"

"No, a consultant," he repeated. "Robbie, of course, knows eastern European dialects the way a sommelier knows wine. I needed his expertise."

"Okay, whatever. Go on."

"We met outside the shop—'round the back—and listened through the flap of a dog door as Sarah Byrne and the Renowned Mirko had cream tea and a tarot card reading. All nonsense, of course, the tarot business, but then talk turned to gemstones." Kingsley's eyes lit up. "Mirko told Sarah he'd recently acquired a red diamond for a client. 'Come,' he said. 'I'll show you.' But when she stood, she was suddenly unwell. Mirko expressed concern. We heard the sound of creaking wood, people moving about, and then—silence."

"They'd gone into the tunnel."

"They had. If Mirko suspected foul play, he'd certainly avoid the front door. Robbie and I let ourselves in and found no one in the shop but a French bulldog. He was clawing at the bookcase so near the point of entry they may as well have posted a sign saying, PRESS HERE FOR SECRET PASSAGEWAY."

I glanced down at the snoring Gladstone.

"Although it did take me seven minutes to find my way in," he went on. "Embarrassingly slow. I left Robbie in the shop, as a safety measure. I've been locked in cellars once or twice, and wasn't keen to do it again."

"And did you find Mirko and Sarah Byrne?" I asked.

"No, but I could hear them, at the far end. The woman was growing hysterical. I listened for their exit, and then moved fast. Do you recall the tunnel's final meters, where the brick floor ended and the last bit was dirt?"

"No."

"Try to be more observant," Kingsley said crisply. "Fresh footprints, one of them a lady's spiked heel, size four—six to you Americans—told me she was short, plump, vain, and increasingly unsteady on her feet. Mirko half-carried, half-dragged her those last meters and up the stairs, through Tesco's and onto the street. Which is where I found them. I helped them into a taxi, and in the process managed to acquire Mirko's mobile and the remote that opened the tunnel door.

You're not alone in your pickpocketing skills. By this point Mirko was also feeling seriously ill, so I accompanied them to University College Hospital."

"Didn't they think that was odd?" I asked.

"Not once I saw who 'Sarah Byrne' was. She wore an absurd black wig that fell off as we bundled her into the taxi, revealing her to be as blonde as you are. I recognized her at once as Yaroslava Barinova. I had only to profess myself her greatest fan and beg the privilege of helping her. Frankly, they were both too sick to care."

Poison, I thought. "And who is, uh, Yaroslava—?"

Kingsley sighed. "The greatest mezzo-soprano since Frederica von Stade. I saw them to hospital, got them admitted, and texted your brother with an update."

"And?"

He looked at me steadily. "I've heard nothing from Robbie since that day."

I stared at him.

"Breathe," Kingsley said, and I realized I'd stopped. "I found his mobile on Mirko's bookshelf, its battery dead. Not in itself a sign of trouble; your brother's careless about such things. I returned it to his flat, by the way." He frowned at me. "Stop leaping to dire conclusions. We haven't sufficient data, and you'll be no use to me in Norwich if your amygdala hijacks your cerebral cortex."

"That's an oversimplification of cognitive processes," I snapped.

"Don't quibble with me; I wrote a monograph on the subject."

I said, as casually as I could, "So what happened to Mirko and the mezzo-soprano?"

The pause scared me as much as the words that followed. "They were poisoned, of course," Kingsley said at last. "They'll be dead by the weekend."

Norwich, the end of the line, had an actual train station, old and stately. Kingsley and I strolled through it side by side, with Gladstone waddling between us. "Look relaxed," Kingsley said, "but prepare to move quickly. We'll soon need a taxi."

Our quarry was Igor, the Russian who'd come to the shop.

Igor had been the first call on Mirko's cell phone, after it was in Kingsley's pocket and Mirko off to the hospital. Kingsley could tell, from Igor's Russian and his use of the formal pronouns, that the man hadn't met Mirko. This gave

Kingsley the confidence to impersonate the psychic when Igor offered to come round and collect a red diamond, and hand off a suitcase of rubles.

"He had one moment of doubt," Kingsley said, "but I'm extraordinarily convincing as a gemologist."

"Old school money laundering," I said.

"A refreshing change from offshore banking," Kingsley said.

"Delightful," I said. "But what's Igor got to do with my brother?"

"With luck, nothing. But we must eliminate the impossible."

While Gladstone and I had hidden behind the screen, Kingsley, in a feat of deduction involving Igor's footwear and clods of dirt—he'd apparently written a monograph on that, too—had determined that Igor was bound for Norwich, and on either the 11:52 train, or the 12:04. So here we were in a town with the kind of bucolic vibe I'd come to expect from watching *Masterpiece Theatre*. I had no trouble spotting Igor as the train crowd dispersed, outside the station. He was a hulking figure, mostly bald but with a patch of red hair. Wearing a bright green windbreaker, he lumbered through the cobblestone streets with a bearlike gait.

We followed him to the town center, thick with boutiques and cafés. A large after-school crowd, noisy kids in plaid uniforms and their attendant adults mixing in with gen pop, meant that Kingsley and I didn't worry about being spotted. But Igor never looked back. He headed to an open-air marketplace, an Anglo-Saxon sort of *souk* in the shadow of a Gothic cathedral, with row upon row of vendors under striped awnings. We kept our distance now, and when Igor stopped at a kiosk we stopped too, twenty yards back, and Kingsley bought French fries served in newspaper. We then made our way up terraced stone steps overlooking the plaza.

"I assume Igor's getting his red diamond appraised," I said, nodding at a blue awning marked: *POPOV Fine Jewelry, bought and sold. Walk-ins welcome.*

"Chips?" Kingsley pushed the French fries toward me, but as they were covered in vinegar, I passed. Gladstone, however, helped himself. "And what will the appraiser tell him?" Kingsley asked me.

"He'll say, 'Igor, I hope you didn't pay more than thirty bucks for this because it's a third-rate garnet plucked from some dog or cat collar with a Swiss Army knife.'"

"Very good," Kinglsey said. "Not a garnet, though. Swarovski crystal."

I scratched Gladstone's neck, my fingers finding the empty setting where the crystal had been. "Where's the real diamond?"

He shrugged. "The tunnel, I imagine. Some government functionary will be months getting that place sorted."

"Wasn't it a risk, giving him a fake rock?"

"It shouldn't have been. But I fear I've miscalculated," Kingsley admitted. "I expected he'd go straight to his boss, at Finchlingly Manor, six kilometers down the road. Where government agents are waiting to take Igor into custody. That's where I planned to question him."

"But why *wouldn't* he authenticate the diamond?"

"Because Mirko was well-trusted. The Cartier of money-launderers. The De Beers of Marylebone. You don't survive in his trade by ripping off customers."

"Mirko isn't going to survive," I reminded him.

"And Igor has just reached the same conclusion regarding himself." Kingsley stood abruptly. "Off we go."

Igor lumbered along at a good clip now, leading us across a pedestrian overpass into a working class neighborhood.

"Where's he off to then?" Kingsley asked. "If not to his employer, or the train station, or the airport—"

"Church," I said. "To pray for his immortal soul."

"Nonsense. If he were the churchy sort, Norwich Cathedral was right in front of him."

"But that's Anglican, right?" I asked. "He made the sign of the cross as he left the marketplace."

"That wasn't the sign of the cross, it was psoriasis. He's been scratching regularly. And in any case, Anglicans also cross themselves."

"But Anglicans cross left to right for the Holy Ghost part," I said. "Igor went right to left. What do you bet he goes to a Russian Orthodox church?"

"I'm not going to bet with you. Wouldn't be sporting. I've failed only four times in my entire career, and—*now* what's he doing?"

What Igor was doing was staring at his phone as he walked, twice doing a one-eighty, the sign of a man at the mercy of Google maps. Seven minutes later he reached a one-story brick building with all the charm and spaciousness of a vacuum cleaner store. A sign near the door read RUSSIAN ORTHODOX CHURCH. But the door was locked. Igor rattled it twice, then gave up and checked his phone.

"Let's go question him right now," I said.

"Have you never done a proper ambush?" Kingsley asked. "We need privacy. Pity that church is closed."

"Yes, pity that Russian Orthodox church is closed."

"Don't gloat," he said. "It's unattractive."

Minutes later Igor got his bearings and took off, with us following, until Gothic spires came into view, rising out of the drab suburbs.

"Cathedral of John the Baptist," Kingsley said. "Roman Catholic. He must've converted. And unless there's a mass in progress, that's where we'll make our move."

St. John's was what a cathedral should be, all white marble and stained glass resplendent in the dying light of late afternoon. A dramatic *Pietà* dominated the left half of the church, just past the transept, and that's where Igor stopped. He genuflected, crossed himself and knelt.

Kingsley and I found a pew near the back. "It's weird to be in a church with a dog," I whispered. "And a gun. Why ambush him here?"

"We won't ambush," Kingsley answered. "We'll converse. Note his body language: he's dying to confess."

As if he heard us, Igor straightened his spine, turned, spotted us and bolted.

Kingsley was after him in a flash, leaving me to grab Gladstone and follow, down the nave toward the altar, a left at the *Pietà*, around the back and out the side door. Igor was faster than he looked, sprinting across a parking lot and into someone's backyard.

But it wasn't a backyard, it was an entrance to a park. We sped down a walkway, past a sign saying PAY HERE pointing to an "Honesty Box," through a vine-enclosed path and around a bend, into a glorious sunken garden.

The garden was rectangular, ending in a beautiful stone facade. Igor headed that way, then peeled off to the right, scrambling with difficulty up a terraced wall and disappearing into a thick copse.

"Go left," Kingsley called over his shoulder. "The understory! I'll take the right!"

Having no idea what an understory was, I nevertheless scurried up a side stairway, and into a thicket so dense, day became night. I set Gladstone down onto the forest floor and unclipped his leash so he wouldn't strangle himself, and made my way blindly forward, thinking I may as well have been back in the tunnel. I imagined Kingsley doing the same on the opposite side of the garden while our quarry waltzed back out and onto the street.

And then there he was, on the path in front of me.

Igor looked more startled than threatening. He stared at my hand, and I looked down too, to discover I'd drawn the gun from my purse.

Our eyes met. He was pale, and from the ears up, bald. From the ears down he sported a fuzzy glob of red hair, a clown wig cut in half. It gave him a hapless air, Larry of the *Three Stooges*.

I tried to say "Stop" in Russian but what came out was *zdravstvujtye*, which of course meant "good day" which was equally useless. Because Igor had already stopped and neither of us was having a good day.

"Where's my brother?" I blurted out, and then *"Gde moy brat?"* before realizing that this man would have no idea who I was, let alone my brother, in any language.

"You can shoot me," he responded, in very good English. "Please."

Maybe it was the influence of the Honesty Box at the entrance, but I said, "I'm sorry. My gun isn't loaded."

At that point Kingsley came crashing through the thicket behind Igor. He looked at my gun and between gasps of breath, said, "Let's go down to the garden and find a nice bench, shall we?"

Kingsley was right about one thing: Igor was dying to unburden himself. Mopping his sweaty brow with his windbreaker sleeve, he said, "I was hired by—"

"Spartak Volkov," Kingsley said. "We know all that."

"Wait," I said. "*I* don't know all that. Who is Spartak Volkov?"

"Russian émigré," Kingsley said. "Tons of money, ties to both your government and mine. He hired Igor to assassinate—"

"Sarah Byrne," said Igor, nodding. "A simple job."

"For one with your skill set, yes. You're a poisoner by vocation and a baker by avocation. Your passion is pastry." Kingsley said, and then, noting Igor's surprise, "I saw it immediately."

"But how? You are not psychic!" Igor said.

"There are bits of calcified dough on your collar," Kingsley said. "Your fingers are stained from food coloring. Red Dye #3, which you must've brought from Moscow, as it's banned in England. Only an aficionado travels with his own food coloring."

"I use but a drop," Igor said, a tad defensive. "For my icings. Okay, and my jellies. Because Sarah Byrne, she loves to eat the English desserts. This I learn from Spartak Volkov. He makes my job easy. Sarah Byrne has been a long time from England, he tells me, and she visits now and wants her cakes. She will die for her cakes."

"Victoria Sponge: arguable," Kingsley said. "But Spotted Dick?"

"Banoffee!" Igor said. "Figgy Duff!"

"What on earth are you people talking about?" I asked.

"The remains of their cream tea," Kingsley said. "Masterfully done, Igor."

"I paid the chauffeur," Igor explained. "He tells me she goes on Thursday to a psychic. I set up my cart, outside the shop. I wear my apron. My hat. She comes. She buys. Two of everything! She goes into the shop. I hear through the window: Mirko makes tea, they eat her cakes."

Little hairs on the back of my neck sprang to life, but I couldn't yet account for them.

"But when I report to Volkov, he grows mad! The woman, yes, the woman should die, he says. But Mirko? No. Because Mirko the Psychic, he tells me, is also Mirko the—the—" He waved his hands.

"Money launderer?" I offered.

"Fence?" Kingsley suggested. "Procurer? Black Marketeer?"

"Yes! The whole world trades with Mirko! Everybody loves Mirko! Russian, Ukrainian, Bosnian, Herzogovinian—"

"Yes, yes," Kingsley said impatiently. "We get the drift. So you're in trouble. You call the number on the sign in front of the shop. I answer. You're relieved: Mirko is alive, you think. And Mr. Volkov is particularly relieved, as he has given Mirko a very large down payment on a very small rock. And now Mr. Volkov sends *you* with the balance, to collect his diamond. Like a common courier, but what choice do you have? Come, no need to look amazed, Igor. I happen to be a genius. But tell me: something made you suspect I was not Mirko. What was it? My accent?"

Igor shook his head. "It was the sign. 'Walk-ins welcome. Both kinds.' Do you remember? I say to you, 'I myself would like to be a walk-in. How does this work?' But you did not answer. At first I thought, you don't *know* the answer. But then I thought . . . ." he shrugged. "We were there for business. For diamonds, not for spirits. We did not have all day."

"I don't have all day either," I said. "Can we get back on topic? So the two poisonees, Mirko and Sarah Byrne, went into the tunnel, thinking to get away from you, Igor, because they suspected what you'd done." I turned to Kingsley. "And you went into the tunnel after them. And my brother Robbie stayed behind in the shop. Not thinking 'poison,' just thinking 'hungry,' as he always is anytime he goes an hour without food." I turned back to Igor. "It's not just possible he'd be tempted by your sweets, Igor; it's virtually certain. But my brother's a picky eater. So what I need to know is, did you put polonium in every single thing you baked?"

A silence settled on us, so that I could hear the birds in the garden singing their twilight songs.

"How do you know my poison is polonium?" Igor asked quietly.

"Totally obvious," I said.

"*You* are a psychic!" he said, with awe.

"Nobody's a psychic!" I said. "You take pride in your work, and you like a challenge, and polonium takes talent," I said. "And experience. You probably trained in Moscow. Lab X. And also," I went on, "because everyone in this crazy story either *is* Russian or *knows* Russian, so everyone, upon feeling sick, thinks 'poison' and then they think about Alexander Litvinenko and his teapot of polonium and they're off to the E.R., screaming 'radiation poisoning.' Including Robbie. Which is why he disappeared. So while I feel sorry for the psychic and the opera singer, I need to think about my brother now, so you need to tell me, Chef Boyardee, did you bake polonium into *everything*?"

"No, no," he said, shaking his head. "The Flies' Graveyard, yes, and the Garibaldi Biscuit. But not the—wait!" He stared at me. "What opera singer?"

"Sarah Byrne," Kingsley told him, "was the alias used by Yaroslava Barinova whenever she was in London. She liked to go incognito. She also wore wigs."

If Igor had been pale before, he was now the color of toothpaste. The white kind. "Yaroslava Barinova?" he gasped. "I have killed Yaroslava Barinova? The greatest mezzo since Anne Sofie von Otter?" He clutched at his heart, scrunching his windbreaker in his big baker's hands.

I patted him on the back, but he was beyond comfort. "I deserve to die!" He pointed to Kingsley. "I give you rubles, you give me junk. Yes, I am stupid. I kill Mirko, the fence. Yes, I am sloppy. But now, now—" His voice rose to a scream. "Yaroslava—Barinova!—the pride of Perm!" His screams turned to coughing, and he reached into his windbreaker to pull out a tiny aspirin tin, from which he took a pill. He stuck it in his mouth, swallowing with a grimace. Then he began to cry. And cough. And cry.

"Oh, for God's sake," I said, and handed him my bottle of water. He knocked it back, drinking half, and wailed anew.

"Igor!" I yelled. "Toughen up. I'm sorry about your opera singer, but what about my brother?"

But Igor was done talking. A strangled sound emanated from him, an unearthly noise, like someone screaming with a closed mouth, or the braying of a donkey—his head reared back and then he fell forward. Kingsley and I, on either side of him, reached for him, but he dropped from the bench to his knees and into a kind of seizure, his mouth foaming. A dark calm settled over me as I held on to one arm and felt Kingsley holding on to his other, and Gladstone, one paw on the man's knee, howled. The four of us stayed like that for some moments, arms and legs entwined in a group hug there in the Plantation Garden, until the life drained out of one of us, and we were only three.

"Polonium for the customers," I said, "but old school cyanide pill for himself. Poor Igor."

"Before you get all sentimental," Kingsley said, "consider this: Spartak Volkov had Yaroslava Barinova killed because she jilted him. A slow death, so she could think on her sins. That's what our Igor did. His life's work. Just eat your trail mix and try not to romanticize assassins." We were on the train back to London, side by side, now with Gladstone between us like a snoring armrest. Our adrenaline levels were returning to normal and our fingers and toes thawing.

If Igor's death was operatic, its aftermath was not. Kingsley had me help him remove Igor's green windbreaker, from which prints could be lifted.

"Theoretically," I said. "But practically speaking, unlikely."

"Don't argue. Leaving fingerprints scattered about is unprofessional."

It seemed to me that Igor looked lonely, lying there in a brown polo shirt that didn't cover his belly, and when Kingsley made a phone call to his mysterious government agency, I found Igor's iPhone in the grass, clicked on his iTunes and set it on repeat so that "You Don't Bring Me Flowers" would accompany him to the afterlife.

But Kingsley plucked it from the grass on our way out. "Leave it here? Are you mad? A mobile is a font of information."

Once on the train, Kingston kept up a steady stream of conversation, clearly for my benefit. We tacitly avoided the subject of Robbie. "Shall I tell you what became of the cat?" he said suddenly.

"Touie," I replied, "is stuffed into Mirko's freezer. You had to remove a twenty-pound turkey to make room for her. I hope she was dead when you did it."

"She was. I stopped by Robbie's flat this morning to drop off the dog—my landlady, an excellent woman, claims she's grown allergic to him. I must've just missed you. You, on the other hand, did not even see a dead cat on your brother's bed."

"I saw her. It didn't occur to me to check her for signs of life."

"Ah. You see, but you do not observe."

"Why'd you give her collar to Gladstone?" I asked.

He looked at me, surprised. "Dogs need tags. She had no use for it anymore."

"Well, anyway," I said. "It was kind of you to spare me the ordeal of a dead cat."

"It was curiosity, not kindness. I'm interested in cause of death; I plan to test her for butane and benzene, for a monograph on mattress toxicity." He was quiet for a long moment, then said, "What *is* the other definition of a walk-in? Other than a client without an appointment?"

"It's a New Age term," I said. "It's someone who's tired of living, whose soul vacates their body so a more—*evolved* soul can move in. A spiritual celebrity."

"What nonsense."

I shrugged. "Some souls don't want to waste time with birth and childhood. They've been here before, and they've got work to do. But after the trade happens, the new souls generally forget they're walk-ins. Which means you—or I—could be some kind of historical figure and not even realize it. DaVinci. Michelangelo. A dead Beatle."

"Right," he said. "That is the most ridiculous thing I've heard all day. And it's been a long day."

"Whatever," I said. "But next time you impersonate a psychic, you might want to notice the sign outside your shop."

"I saw the sign. All my senses are excellent. *Evolved*, even."

"You saw, but you did not observe," I said.

He raised an eyebrow. "I *observe* that you are picking out the sultanas in that trail mix I bought you. So you dislike sultanas. Does your twin share this aversion?"

I looked down at the small pile of dark, withered rejects, swept aside on the table in front of us. "What's a sultana?"

"A dried grape. Ingredient in sultana cakes, scones, Garibaldi biscuits, and the like."

"Ah—squashed flies?"

"Precisely."

"Oh, yeah. Robbie hates them. Raisins, currants, all dried fruit."

Kingsley blinked. And a slow smile spread across his face.

As the train neared Liverpool station the *ping!* of an incoming text woke me. I'd dozed off, my head against Kingsley's shoulder. I looked at my phone.

SO LONG STORY SHORT, I'M ALLERGIC TO MY NEW BED, THOUGHT IT WAS SOMETHING MORE SERIOUS AND WENT TO THE ER AND SOME IDIOT GAVE ME PENICILLIN, SO THAT NEARLY KILLED ME, BUT ANYWAY, FINALLY HOME, HOPE U WEREN'T WORRIED AND BTW, WHERE ARE U? AND WHERE THE F IS MY CAT? XOX, R.

"What does that mean," Kingsley said, reading over my shoulder, "when you Americans sign 'xox'? I understand 'x' but what's the 'o'?"

I smiled at him. "I think I'll just show you."

THE CASE OF THE MISSING CASE

by Alan Gordon

The police station on Wapping High Street was unique among the twenty or so stations of the London Metropolitan Police in that it housed two separate divisions of the force. The first was the regular police, who walked through Wapping with truncheons and rattles, watching for the footpads and pickpockets who attempted to ply their trade. The other was the Thames Division, whose members rowed along London's aqueous highway in three-man boats for six hours at a stretch, pulling suicides and drunken unfortunates from the currents with their gaff hooks and navigating the maze of docks in search of mudlarks, rat-catchers, light horsemen and the other plunderers of ships, barges and their crews.

There was a friendly rivalry between the two divisions, manifesting itself most frequently in their respective skills in subduing recalcitrant sailors. The Thames lads liked to swing an oar, catching the offender with the flat of the blade. The Wapping boys prided themselves on the precision of their truncheon work, administering taps to the noggin with sufficient force to render instant oblivion without preventing a return to sober employment the following morning.

It was generally a one-night stay in the Wapping Station jail, long enough to recover from the combined effects of watered-down whiskey and the deployment of wood to skull. The Wapping police understood that these were men come in from sea with a month's wages to spend in only a day or two before shipping out again. The local economy depended upon these marinated mariners, and if word got around that the constabulary was overly enthusiastic in their regulation of public order, then the sailors might very well take their business elsewhere, and no one would benefit from that.

This particular October night had been a quiet one in the annals of criminal behavior. There was a crispness to the air, and the lonely sailors were more apt to find warmth inside, whether it was in the arms of the young (and not so young), female (and not so female) companionship available for a fee, or from the nourishment of meals cooked with ingredients that had been living in recent memory rather than dried and packed in salt, awaiting resurrection through lengthy boiling. The evening's nefarious activities were so much in decline that the station house found itself to be the temporary involuntary lodgings of only two prisoners.

The one was a giant man, not only taking up the entirety of the jail cell bench but overhanging it at both ends. He snored prodigiously, in deep waves that gathered softly in the distance before crashing into the shore. Each made the iron bars quiver in sympathy.

The cell's other denizen sat on the filthy floor opposite the Thunderer, his back against the bars. He was younger and leaner than his new roommate, and wore a brown woolen suit with a dark grey waistcoat. The suit bordered on shabbiness, and appearances were not helped by the spattering of mud and blood on the jacket and shirt.

His face was not immediately apparent, due to the bloodied handkerchief he clutched to his nose. He was trying to sleep as well, but every time his eyes began to close, his companion produced another cannonade, jolting him back into semi-consciousness.

This must be what it's like to be married, he thought, casting a doleful look at the snorer.

Outside of the station, a black brougham halted directly in front of the street entrance. A constable hurried out to remonstrate the driver for blocking it. The driver unhurriedly stepped down from the box seat and casually pulled back the lapel of his greatcoat, revealing a badge that produced an immediate effect on the constable. The latter ceased his demurs and stepped partway into the interior.

"He's here, sir!" he called.

A moment later, a sergeant came out, hastily buttoning his uniform coat.

The driver glanced up and down the street, then opened the door of the brougham, his free hand casually remaining near the pocket of his greatcoat.

The gentleman who stepped down from the interior was verging on thirty, but conveyed authority beyond his years. He was tall, running to stout, and dressed in evening formal wear, as if he had just come from the opera.

The sergeant hesitated, then drew himself to attention and saluted. The man looked at him, bemused.

"You don't salute me, Sergeant," he said. "In fact, you never saw me at all. That goes for you as well, Constable."

"Yes, sir," said the sergeant. "Would you like to see him?"

"The purpose of my interrupted evening," said the man. "Where is he?"

"In one of the cells in back."

The man sighed, almost happily.

"Lead on, my good fellow."

The sergeant escorted him inside the precinct and led him to the cells. The man sitting on the floor glanced up past the handkerchief clutched to his nose, then winced.

It wasn't from the pain.

"How is it?" asked Mycroft.

"Unbroken," said Sherlock, pulling the handkerchief away so his brother could get a good look.

"Pity," said Mycroft. "That might have been an improvement. Sergeant, would you let me into the cell, then excuse the two of us? Family business."

"Certainly, sir."

"I see you've come up in the world," commented Sherlock after the sergeant left.

"Why do you say that?"

"Because you came so promptly," said Sherlock. "Remarkable under normal circumstances, but especially now because I never asked for you to be notified. Therefore, they had my name on a list with explicit instructions to contact you if I found myself in these straits. Given the rapidity of your arrival, I conclude that you are now a man of extreme importance in order to have this co-operation from the police. How did you know I would wind up at this particular precinct?"

"I didn't," said Mycroft. "Your name is at all of them."

"Yes, of course," muttered Sherlock. "Why the fancy dress? You're not an opera-goer."

"Heaven forfend," said Mycroft. "It was a special occasion. The opening of a club."

"You went to a club?"

"I am one of the founders," said Mycroft. "The Diogenes Club. It is intended to be a place of silence. A haven for men who desire peace and quiet after the turmoil of the day. Imagine how delighted I was to be interrupted with the news of my little brother's arrest for brawling in the back alleys of Wapping."

"It wasn't a brawl," said Sherlock. "A brawl is between two groups. This was one group versus, well, me."

"How did it turn out, Horatius?"

"Let's call it a draw," said Sherlock.

"Was he part of it?" asked Mycroft, nodding toward the snoring giant.

"He was," said Sherlock. "Once he went down, things became considerably easier. Then the bobbies intervened."

"And this was where?"

"St. Katharine Docks."

"You went into the docks dressed like that?" exclaimed Mycroft.

"This is how I dress," said Sherlock.

"Good God, Sherlock, it's a wonder you weren't killed!"

"I can take care of myself."

"Apparently not."

"My dear brother—"

"Don't you 'dear brother' me!"

"You forget that I am proficient in many of the martial arts."

"Oh, really?" laughed Mycroft. "Please, elaborate on your prowess."

"Well, fencing . . ."

"Did you have a rapier handy?"

"I did not."

"I see. Proceed."

"Single stick."

"Also not handy. Irrelevant."

"I am one of the best boxers for my weight that you'll ever see."

"How about his weight?" asked Mycroft, pointing to the man asleep. "How about the combined weight of many?"

"I survived, didn't I?"

"I don't want you to make that the standard for success," said Mycroft. "And I find myself singularly unimpressed by the argument. I propose a test, young one. If you consider yourself so superb in the pugilistic arts, let's see if you can conquer me."

"Don't be ridiculous."

"You're the one with blood on your face, boy," snarled Mycroft. "I'll wager that you don't land a single blow. Come on, little brother, you've been wanting a chance to do this ever since you were old enough to realize you'd never be more than second best in our family. Take your best shot. You will never have this opportunity again."

Sherlock rose slowly to his feet and stripped off his jacket, the rage gathering in his face. Mycroft looked at him blandly, infuriating him even more. Sherlock began to bounce lightly on the balls of his feet. Mycroft watched with interest.

"Have you been studying ballet?" he asked. "Perhaps you should consider—"

Sherlock lunged toward his brother, a growl erupting from the depths of his being, then abruptly stopped, well short of his target.

Mycroft stood calmly, a revolver in his right hand, aimed at Sherlock's heart.

"Bang," said Mycroft.

Sherlock stood frozen in place, breathing heavily.

"Do I make my point?" asked Mycroft. "If you like, you could run home and fetch your stick. I'll wait."

"Put it away," said Sherlock.

"Of course," said Mycroft, pocketing it.

"You've switched to a Webley," said Sherlock.

"I like the weight."

"It has only five shots."

"I need only one. Shall we go? Put on your jacket. It's nippy out there."

Sherlock picked his jacket up from the ground and donned it, then folded his bloodied handkerchief neatly and tucked it into the pocket.

"What about Bill?" he asked, pointing to his cellmate.

"You know his name."

"Bill Sparrow. When he fell, the earth shook. If I'm not being charged, then he shouldn't be, either."

"Very even-handed of you. Is it wise?"

"We made up after our arrest. He invited me for a round sometime."

"It's good that you have one friend in this cell," said Mycroft. "Very well. I will advise them that you've decided not to press charges."

He rapped on the bars. The sergeant returned, unlocked the cell door, and held it open for the brothers.

"My compliments to your men," said Sherlock. "They were very professional."

"I'll be sure to tell them," said the sergeant. "Good night, gentlemen."

"Good night, Sergeant," said Mycroft. "Thank you for everything."

They emerged from the precinct. Sherlock looked at the driver briefly, then at the horse, then at the brougham itself, letting his fingers trail across the doorframe as he passed through and sat.

"Well?" said Mycroft as the brougham lurched forward.

"Well what?"

"How did you find yourself brawling—"

"Defending myself."

"Brawling in St. Katharine Docks?"

"I was following a lead."

"Ah. A lead. That's good. That means someone finally hired you."

"Not exactly."

"Explain."

"Do you remember the case I told you about involving Victor Trevor's father and his involvement with the disappearance of the *Gloria Scott*?"

"Where you brilliantly decoded a message that any English schoolboy could have solved, and the rascal at fault disappeared before you could bring in the authorities?"

"Well—"

"Which was the sole justification for your decision to come to London and set yourself up as a consulting detective?"

"Fine, belittle me."

"No, no. Go on. What was your lead?"

"The blackmailer was a man named Hudson. I had been searching for him. I saw him last night."

"Where?"

"Heading towards St. Katharine Docks. But before I could locate which ship he had signed onto, I encountered Bill Sparrow and five of his drunken friends. They sought to relieve me of my wallet."

"Of course they did," Mycroft sighed. "So. You lost your lead, who is now no doubt aware of your pursuit. You have no client, no payment for your expenses, and your nose looks horrendous. All you had to do was summon the nearest constable once you saw the man, but that would have been too practical. You have nothing. We should call this misadventure, 'The Case of the Missing Case.'"

"Are you finished?" asked Sherlock.

"I've barely started. You were thrown out of university after only two years . . ."

"I left."

"You were thrown out. You blew up the chemistry building."

"Just one corner of it. And I licensed that formula to a munitions manufacturer and assigned the income to the university. It's already paid for the damages."

"Nevertheless, you didn't finish your education."

"They had nothing left to teach me."

"You arrogance is appalling," said Mycroft. "Our parents allowed you to embark on this mad venture on two conditions, one for you and one for me. Yours is that you not put yourself at risk of your life. Mine is that I not let you put yourself at risk of your life. We have both failed miserably tonight."

"I am an adult."

"You are twenty-two. The milk isn't even dry."

"You are not my minder."

"Oh, but I am, Sherlock, and you need one, clearly. You know much about chemistry, and little about the real world. There are skills necessary to survive in your proposed line of work that you do not possess."

"I can train in more useful street-fighting techniques."

"I would be happier if you never fought at all. Our parents would be happier. Your nose would be happier."

"Are you telling Mother and Father about this?"

"Certainly not," said Mycroft, noting with amusement the look of relief on his brother's face. "But you must now follow my advice. You are on thin ice. I will send you to someone who will teach you how to skate."

"Very well. But let me ask you this—are our parents aware of the danger that you are in?"

"What do you mean?" asked Mycroft.

"This is no ordinary brougham," said Sherlock. "And that's no ordinary brougham driver."

"It is not, and he is not," agreed Mycroft. "How did you know?"

"His bearing is military, and the pockets of his greatcoat both sag under the weight of something I'm guessing has more stopping power than your Webley. I also spotted the butt of a shotgun protruding from under the seat. The brougham itself sits lower than a normal one on its wheels, and your poor horse is sweating mightily even though the air is cold. Even allowing for the exertions of dragging your enormous bulk around—"

"Come now!"

"—this suggests that the weight of the brougham itself is heavier than normal. I also noticed the thickness of the doorframe as I got on. This vehicle is armored. Given that you came from your club, it must have been waiting for you, so it and the bodyguard driving it are available to you on a constant basis. Which can only mean—"

He hesitated.

"Say it," said Mycroft.

"That you are under threat of assassination," concluded Sherlock.

"Your reasoning is sound," said Mycroft.

"How may I be of help?" asked Sherlock.

"By staying out of danger and giving me one less worry," said Mycroft. "Not to mention one less reason to expose myself."

"Then I am sorry that I put you at risk," said Sherlock.

"Oh, it was worth it to see you behind bars," said Mycroft, chuckling. "I would have gladly paid to see that, and there it was, gratis. Here we are. Montague Street. We'll drop you at the corner, if you don't mind."

"One more thing. This club—"

"Yes?"

"Why Diogenes? Wasn't he the fellow with the lamp?"

"Among other things."

"What does searching for an honest man have to do with silence?"

"Because in my experience, the only honest men are the ones who never speak. Good night, little brother."

Sherlock stepped down. The driver closed the door, climbed onto his seat, and flicked his reins. The horse dutifully trotted away. Sherlock noted the click of the lock on the door as it did.

He walked to his tiny office and rooms and spent the rest of the night scrubbing the blood from his clothes.

In the morning, he staggered to his feet and looked in his mirror. His nose was swollen, and a large, dull purple bruise had taken up residence under his left eye. He sighed, then walked into his sitting room. A bit of white poking under the door caught his attention. He reached down to find a plain envelope addressed to him with neither stamp nor seal to indicate its origins.

He brought it over to the window to inspect it more closely, then sniffed at it. Neither sense provided him with any information, so he slit it open.

Inside was a folded note and a small, thin piece of cardboard.

"You need to have a night out. M," read the note.

Below was an address in Wapping and the time of eight o'clock. The cardboard was a printed ticket, reading, "ADMIT ONE BRETT'S VARIETY."

Either a joke, or his brother's whimsical invitation to skating lessons, thought Holmes. Well. It wasn't as if he had other plans.

Despite the Dock Street address, Brett's Variety was as far from the Thames as one could be while still being in Wapping. Access to the venue was gained through a tavern called the Admiral's Rest, the sign mounted on a ship's wheel over the entryway.

In front of it, a boy was passing out handbills.

"Come one, come all, to Brett's Variety Show!" he shouted. "See Captain Ferdinand and his amazing talking parrot, Chu-Chu, who speak seventeen languages between them! Laugh at the knock-about antics of the Condolini Brothers as they put life and limb at risk for your amusement! Wonder at the miracles of that master illusionist of the Orient, Doctor Thaddeus Wang! Let your auditory senses bask in the beauteous voice of Signora Flavia Trattelli, direct from the great opera houses of Italy, and that sensational, scintillating songstress, Mademoiselle Susan Brett, singing her popular comic ditty, 'The Boy Who Rows on the River!' All under the hilarious supervision of Chairman Piggy Watts with the frequent and uproarious interjections of Tyrone Brett, the Man of a Thousand Disguises! Sixpence for the floor, nine for the gallery, where anything can happen! Come one, come all!"

Holmes made his way through the crowd milling about the entrance. A man sat a a table, yelling, "Tickets! Getcher tickets here!"

Holmes held his up and the man waved him through and turned his attention back to the entryway.

The bar was a good thirty feet in length, with two bartenders in a whirl of pouring and serving. Holmes reluctantly parted with enough coin to purchase a pint of porter, then followed the other customers to a door at the rear. A boy in a pale blue uniform looked at his ticket.

"Main hall, table three at the right," he said, handing him a programme.

The hall was perhaps seventy feet across and crammed with small tables. Gaslights on sconces lined both walls underneath galleries that were divided into private boxes. There was a small stage with a red curtain embellished with gold trim, and a cordoned-off area for the musicians. An upright piano faced the stage; to its right was a trap kit containing not only the usual percussion but a variety of wood blocks, tiny cymbals and bells of varying sizes, and a set of black wooden castanets mounted on a tray. Behind the kit was a pair of kettle drums. An eight-foot high bronze gong hung ominously from an elaborately carved red lacquered frame. To the left of the piano was a solitary chair and music stand.

Holmes sat at his table and sipped at his porter, which was watery. A barmaid immediately appeared.

"Take your order, sir?" she said.

"What's on the menu?" he asked warily.

"Cheese, mutton, kippers, meat pies—" she rattled off.

"Cheapest, least likely to kill me," he interrupted her.

"Hard to have both," she said, winking.

"Cheese and bread," he said.

"Another?" she asked, pointing at the porter.

"Might as well," he muttered.

The hall was filling rapidly. It could hold maybe three hundred on the main floor, and another seventy or so in the galleys. The private boxes held four seats that had actual cushions and upholstering, as opposed to the plain wooden bench on which he sat.

Some gaudily dressed women were making their ways through the galleries, appearing in the boxes to whisper to the top-hatted gentlemen sitting in them. Holmes saw one of them nod, then lean forward and draw the curtains, concealing the box from view.

Disgusting, thought Holmes. The shamelessness of them, to operate like that in full sight of all the world.

One of the more brazen women actually had the temerity to ply her wares in the main hall. She was also older and less attractive than the others, but sashayed regally through the crowd in a dark red gown that was cut low over a more than ample bosom. Her neck was concealed by a choker whose many layers of pearls were no more real than her virtue, and her hair was of a red never found in any Nature known to this world. Her features, coarse and unattractive, were heavily rouged and powdered. Her lips gleamed blood-red, and her eyelashes would have been at home in a colony of tropical spiders.

She must have been known to the regulars, for there were many saucy exchanges between her and the less inhibited. She gave better than she got, and her laugh when she was caught by surprise was raucous and hoarse, echoing through the entire theatre. The other patrons turned in their seats to watch her.

Holmes, on the other hand, turned away, avoiding any inadvertent eye contact that might draw her attention.

It had the opposite effect. Before he could say anything, she was upon him, plopping her not inconsiderable heft onto his lap.

"A fresh one at last!" she cried. "You remind me of the first man who ever loved me, whose kisses brought me so much joy, whose caresses sent me into such flights of ecstasy that it was all we could do not to tumble out of the confessional!"

"Madam, I am not interested," he protested.

"Not interested?" she exclaimed in disbelief. "Do you not know who I am? I am the Comtesse Scirroque de la Flamme, the greatest courtesan ever known. Why, Napoleon himself wrote me the highest references. He had to stand on a ladder to make them."

"Napoleon?"

"Well, he told me he was Napoleon," she sighed. "He was not the first who ever gave me that name. A plague upon these short men! Oh, good sir, will you not help me revive the passions of my salad days? Youth must be served, and I am your waitress."

"I am not—"

"Let me at least show you the menu," she growled.

"Please, leave me alone," he muttered.

"Rejected once again," she said, almost sobbing. "Oh, to be an aging beauty in these perilous times. Young sir, you have no idea what it is like to be me. If only you could truly feel what is in my heart. Wait—maybe you can!"

And with that, she took his hand and pressed it against one massive breast. Holmes turned beet red as the crowd, fully absorbed in his predicament, howled.

There was a rapping noise from the stage. A corpulent man in a checkered suit with a purple waistcoat stood by a small desk, a gavel in his hand. He banged it again.

"You, there," he said, pointing at Holmes' unwanted companion. "Cease these disruptions!"

"No one has disrupted yet," she called. "Must have lost me touch."

"My dear lady—"

"I'm not so very dear," she said. "My rates are more than reasonable."

"No matter how low, too much by half," he said. "Now, I must ask you to leave so that the entertainment may commence."

"The entertainment will commence the moment you retire from the stage," she sniffed, and she flounced out to the applause of the crowd and Holmes' great relief.

"I apologize, ladies and gentlemen," said the Chairman, bowing. "You are here for the theatre, not to be the recipients of unwanted overtures. And speaking of unwanted overtures, Maestro Hardwicke, if you please!"

The pianist, who with a trumpet player and a drummer had taken his place during the colloquy with Holmes' tormentor, raised his arms high in the air, then brought them down into a thundering tremolo as the drummer crashed his sticks into every cymbal in sight. Then the trio launched into a rapid series of phrases that chased one another from the trumpet to the right hand of the pianist.

Holmes found much to admire in the musicians, but there was something missing in the arrangement. An imbalance somewhere. They finished before he could put his finger on what bothered him, then played a fanfare.

Captain Ferdinand's parrot Chu-Chu turned out not to be a parrot at all, but a clever puppet whose squawking voice and language proficiency were provided by the captain himself, a skilled ventriloquist. Chu-Chu kept provoking his beleaguered master while throwing jibes at members of the audience.

The Condolini brothers followed, four men dressed as dockworkers against a backdrop showing a dock by the Thames. With an assortment of barrels and a very rickety cart, they performed feats of tumbling and balancing, interspersed with pratfalls and blows from an artfully wielded plank swung with seeming obliviousness by the youngest as he pivoted this way and that, ignoring the shouts of the others. The plank turned into a seesaw after he leaned it against one of the barrels. When he casually stepped on it, two of his brothers leapt onto the other end, flipping him into a double somersault before he landed on the shoulders of the remaining man.

Holmes applauded enthusiastically, wondering if these were the skills he had been sent to acquire. Maybe if—

"Shame!" cried a man coming down the aisle. "Shame upon all of you! Miscreants and sinners, idolators and wastrels!"

Holmes turned to see an elderly, red-cheeked minister storming down the aisle, his prodigious mutton-chops shaking with indignation.

"Reverend Sneerwich, must you continue to plague us?" asked the Chairman wearily.

"If there will be a plague upon this house, it will be one sent by Our Lord Himself!" shouted the reverend as he stormed up the steps to the stage. "Look at you! Why are you not at evening prayers?"

"It is not Sunday," said the Chairman.

"Every day is the Lord's day. And many of you are imbibing, partaking of the Demon's Rum—"

"Demon's beer for most of them," interjected the Chairman.

"That's the Devil's Beer," said the Reverend. "The Demon's Rum, and the Devil's Beer—"

"Who is responsible for the whiskey?"

The Reverend took a deep breath.

"Fine. The Demon's Rum, the Devil's Beer, the Archfiend's Whiskey—"

"And the wine?"

"Look, confound you, I am trying to save their souls!"

"Too late!" shouted someone from the galleries.

"No, it is never too late!" cried the Reverend, pointing to him. "I am not pleading for abstinence, brothers and sisters. Why, I myself—"

The audience chimed in with the "Why, I myself."

"Why, I myself occasionally will have a tiny nip, a wee dram, a flagon, perhaps an entire jeroboam as I did just before the show, to give me the courage, one might even say the Dutch courage, to set forth into this din of inequity . . ."

"That's den of iniquity," said the Chairman.

"Is it indeed?" exclaimed the Reverend, staggering and clearly drunk now. "That makes so much more sense. And you up there, with your loose women—"

Cheers from the ladies in the galleries.

"Yes, you, ladies. Don't think I don't know what, or do think it, because I do know, I know all too well. Why, I—"

"Why, I myself!" shouted the audience.

"Have preached among the fallen women, have seen many a harlot on her knees before me . . ."

There was a guffaw from the men.

"I'm sure I don't understand your reaction," he said, blinking in confusion.

"You will, Reverend," said the Chairman, coming over to take his arm. "Let's get you someplace where you can sleep this off. Again. In the meantime, ladies and gentleman, it gives me the greatest of pleasure to introduce to you that loveliest of ladies with the sunniest of smiles, our very own Mademoiselle Susan Brett!"

The curtains parted and a vision of beauty stood before them, the same Thames backdrop behind her.

She couldn't have been more then sixteen or seventeen, and the blush in her cheeks was her own, although her lips were painted strawberry red to complement her creamy complexion. Her hair cascaded in brunette ringlets down her neck, and she wore a frilled, floral-patterned dress that swirled about her like rose petals in a whirlwind as she stepped to the front of the stage. A flowered bonnet adorned her head, and she twirled a parasol behind her as the music began.

Holmes found himself leaning forward in his seat as she sang:

"Now hark to my melancholy story:
I love a lad who loves a boat.
It's only a wretched little dory.
It's a wonder that it still can float.

Though he gave me his pledges
That he'd give up his dredges,
He still searches the riverbed for gems.
And against all my wishes
He goes out and he fishes,
Even though there's no fish left in the Thames!"

The music shifted to a waltz rhythm, and she began to sway back and forth with it.

"I love the boy who rows on the river.
I thrill when he pulls on his oar.
He glides with the tides, and my heart starts to shiver.
His muscular arms I adore.
And when he's on land, we will walk hand in hand.
His kiss leaves me longing for more.
Yet I'm left on the banks without one word of thanks,
As he rows away from shore.
As he rows away from shore."

Many in the audience joined in the chorus. Holmes was surprised at their familiarity with the song until his neighbor at the table leaned over and indicated on the programme the lyrics, with the heading importuning them to "SING ALONG!"

Mademoiselle Brett, in the meantime, had begun the second verse:

"You'd think that a fellow would prefer maids,
After spending so much time a-sail.
But my little skipper must like mermaids.
It's a pity I can't grow a tail!"

On this, she turned to the side, leaned forward, and planted her parasol point down, then gave her bottom a minute wiggle as the drummer echoed the movement on his cowbell. This microscopic display of eroticism elicited an immense masculine bellow of approval.

Idiotic, thought Holmes with disdain.

> *"There are others who woo me,*
> *But they mean nothing to me,*
> *For the one man I yearn to have is him."*

What is it about mermaids that fascinates so many men? he mused. Sirens, Lorelei, all the dangerously alluring females of the deep.

> *"Yet I can't be ecstatic*
> *With a romance aquatic . . ."*

What could one even do with a mermaid?

> *"For you see, I have never learned to swim.*
> *I love the boy who rows on the river . . ."*

A low, rumbling noise was emanating from his throat, and he realized to his surprise that he was humming along. Oh, well, he thought.

And Sherlock Holmes sang along with the crowd as Mademoiselle Brett skipped along the stage, pirouetting so that her skirts rose, revealing a dainty pair of ankles and the beginnings of white-stockinged calves, bringing forth another paroxysm of approval.

She finished to lusty applause, curtseyed, and scampered off.

The rest of the evening passed in a blur. The gong announced the magician, who sounded more East End than Eastern and relied heavily on bursts of flash powder. Holmes enjoyed figuring out each trick as it happened.

The final act was Master Brett. He proved to be a quick-change artist, passing several times behind a screen to emerge in a completely different costume and persona, all of whom were immensely amusing. Mademoiselle Brett returned to perform a comic sketch with him, reacting with dismay and bewilderment each time a new character appeared. He finished with a swordfight between two equally inebriated pirates, thanks to a cleverly split costume that allowed him to play both through the simple expedient of turning from one profile to the other.

And then it was over. The cast took their bows and the crowd filtered out, the gentlemen who had been in the private boxes looking satisfied and disheveled. Holmes approached the boy who had handed out the programmes.

"I would like to speak with Master Brett," he said.

The boy led him back into the theater, up the steps to the stage, then into the wings.

"Mind your head," he said, ducking through a low door that led to a stairway going down.

Holmes followed him to a narrow hall with a series of doors. The boy rapped respectfully on the last one.

"Come!" said a man, and the boy held the door open.

Master Brett sans costume and wig was a surprisingly thin man with a head shaved clean. He was sitting at a dressing table crowded with jars of powders and creams. A large mirror was mounted on the wall behind it. Brett was in the middle of wiping off his makeup, but turned to look at Holmes, his washcloth hiding the lower part of his face.

"Well? What business do you have?" he demanded.

"The return of my wallet, for a start," said Holmes.

Brett opened a drawer, pulled it out, and tossed it to him.

"It's all there," he said.

"Do you expect me not to count it?" asked Holmes.

"You'd be a damn fool if you didn't," said Brett. "Sit there while you do, Mr. Holmes."

Holmes sat uncomfortably on a low stool and verified the contents of his wallet.

"You know my name because you went through it," he observed.

"I know who you are because if I took your brother and locked him in a cupboard without food for a month, the end result would be you."

"Could you do that?" asked Holmes. "I would enjoy it tremendously."

"Tempting, but no," said Brett, peering into a mirror and scrubbing diligently at the remains of some adhesive on his upper lip. "Is that all?"

"Don't you want to know how I knew you were the woman who sat in my lap?"

"Everyone knows I'm her," said Brett. "It's the act. But tell me what gave it away."

"The bulge of the Adam's apple under your choker," said Holmes. "And the, um, the way your . . ."

He held up his hand and made a squeezing motion.

"The falsies, eh?" chuckled Brett. "So, you do know what a real one feels like. Your brother had his doubts."

"I worked in a mortuary last summer. I am well acquainted with the human body."

"Not the best way to learn," leered Brett. "Why are you really here?"

"Mycroft sent me. I gather he wants me to learn how to disguise myself."

"For what reason? You're too green to be one of his lads."

"I am a consulting detective," said Holmes grandly.

"What the hell is that?"

"I, uh, investigate matters for people."

"They have the police for that."

"The police are not always effective. Or interested."

"True enough," said Brett. "Very well. I can teach you a few things. My rates are—"

"Rates?"

"Did you think you could come into my inner sanctum and learn the secrets of my trade, secrets that I have spent years in acquiring, for nothing?"

"I thought Mycroft—"

"I charge him for educating his people, and I'll charge you for it as well. Two shillings a lesson."

"Two shillings!"

"Not a penny less."

"How many lessons will I need?"

"To master this would take years."

"How many to pass as a denizen of the docks?"

"If you are apt, six or seven lessons. If you would add other professions and areas of London, then more."

"I am a poor man," said Holmes. "What you saw in my wallet are my current holdings."

"Then you should be more careful with it," said Brett. "Good-bye, and good luck with the detecting, Mr. Holmes."

Holmes rose, then hesitated.

"Could I barter for it?" he asked.

"I have no quandaries that need investigating."

"Could I work here? For my lessons?"

"Doing what?" laughed Brett. "I have no need for slave labor, and unless you have an act—do you have an act? Any theatrical talents?"

"I have declaimed a little Shakespeare in my time."

"I don't need any declaimers, thank you. That's it?"

"I play violin. Could you use another instrument for your orchestra?"

"Interesting. Any good?"

"I fancy so."

"Hmm," said Brett, thinking. Then he came to a decision and stood. "Come with me."

Holmes followed him down a flight of steps. Brett unlocked a door and ushered him into a large storage room filled with shelves of props and costumes. He reached up to a top shelf and pulled down a plain wooden box and handed it over.

Holmes opened it to see a violin and bow inside.

"We had a fiddle-player," said Brett. "Mister Scarpelli. Decent musician, terrible drunk. He'd vanish on benders, come back whenever. Last week, he didn't come back, so we've been a man short. Play something."

Holmes lifted it carefully out of the box and ran his thumb over the strings. They were surprisingly in tune.

"He didn't have a regular case for it?" he asked as he tightened the bow.

"Probably pawned it," said Brett.

"Sarabande in D minor," Holmes announced, and he set the bow to the strings.

The sound, melancholy and beautiful, echoed through the room, and Holmes closed his eyes, feeling the old rapture of—

"My God, that's lugubrious," interrupted Brett. "Got anything up-tempo?"

"Allemande, from the Partita, also by—"

"J. S. Bach, yes, I know. Get on with it."

Slightly rattled, Holmes launched into the piece. He observed Brett had a happier expression this time. Encouraged, he let the music soar.

There was a sudden scream from outside, then the door was flung open and a young woman rushed in, her face pale.

"Is he back?" she cried, then she stopped short as she saw Holmes. "Oh. Forgive me. I thought—"

"Mr. Holmes, may I introduce my daughter, Susan?" said Brett.

She looked tiny off-stage, her flowered dress replaced by a plain, woolen dressing gown. She was just as lovely without makeup as she was in the footlights with it. Lovelier, thought Holmes.

Almost without thinking, he bowed.

"A pleasure, Mademoiselle Brett," he said. "You performed admirably, in my opinion."

Admirably, Sherlock? he thought, mentally kicking himself. Is that the best you can do?

"Thank you, sir," she replied. "Nice mouse."

"Mouse?" repeated Holmes.

She pointed to the bruise under his eye.

"Oh, that," said Holmes. "A bit of a contretemps last night. We sorted things out."

"Would you like her to kiss it and make it better?" asked Brett.

"Stop teasing him, Papa," she said. "Please excuse my behavior, Mr. Holmes. Mr. Scarpelli's violin has a very distinct tone. I thought that was him playing it. I have been worried about him."

"Mr. Holmes is going to fill in until he returns," said Brett.

"I passed the audition?" asked Holmes.

"You did," said Brett. "We do two shows a night, four on Saturdays, dark on Sundays. Come in for your lesson at four, then you'll have an hour to look at the music. Do you have your own fiddle?"

"Not in London," said Holmes.

"Then you can use Scarpelli's. But leave it here."

"Tomorrow at four," said Holmes. "Good evening, Mademoiselle and Master Brett."

The following afternoon, he sat next to Brett at his dressing table.

"Look into the mirror," said Brett. "What makes that face recognizable?"

"The narrowness of the visage," said Holmes. "Surmounted by the noble family beak."

"Good," said Brett. "Now, theatrical makeup works well in the theater. We simplify and accentuate our features so they can be read from the last row of the balcony, allowing for the lighting. But you'll be lit how?"

"By sun at day and lamplight at night."

"Precisely. So, you don't want to look like a man wearing makeup, unless you are venturing into establishments where men wear makeup."

"I won't be."

"You never know, do you? But let's take your immediate quest. The docks. You want to pass for a sailor."

"Obviously."

"What do they have that speaks of a life at sea? Think of their faces. Sunburnt. So, you have to change your skin."

He brought out a jar of powder.

"Mix of red and brown," he said. "Apply gently. Don't overdo it, and—no, that's too much!"

Holmes looked in the mirror at an apparent victim of some conflagration.

"I could tell them I was in a boiler-room explosion," he said.

"Needs more soot," said Brett.

"What would you use for the appearance of soot?" asked Holmes.

"Soot, you ninny," said Brett. "Wash it off, try again."

And so the hour passed.

After the lesson, Holmes went down to the storage room. He removed the violin and bow from the box, then stood on a lower shelf to look at the area where the box rested, running his finger along the edge.

He went to the stage, where Maestro Hardwicke was waiting for him.

"You're the new fiddle player?" he asked.

Holmes held up the violin in response.

"My right hand thanks you," said Hardwicke. "It's been doing double-duty playing the violin lines. Hope you're a sight-reader. Two hardest parts are the overture and the knockabout music. Lots of tempo shifts, glissandos, what have you. Watch my nose—when it goes up and stops, you stop. I give you the tempos, you keep up, hear me?"

"Yes," said Holmes.

A second stand and chair had been placed between the trumpet player's and the stage. The chair wobbled as Holmes sat. He got up and inspected the legs.

"Yeah, one of them is short," commented Hardwicke. "Scarps stuck a piece of cardboard under it."

"I see it," said Holmes, squatting to retrieve it from the floor.

He looked at it, then slid it under the chair leg.

"They clean in here much?" he asked.

"They sweep it out twice a week. Why?"

"Just curious."

He sat, opened up his part, and began to practice until the audience began to file in.

He waited off-stage with Hardwicke, who introduced him to Mal, the drummer, and Derek, the trumpet player. The latter leaned over and whispered, "Watch for Heaven."

"What do you mean?" asked Holmes.

"You'll see."

Brett's dissolute courtesan began working his way through the audience, and the musicians took their places. The Chairman came on, and Hardwicke raised his hands. Holmes brought his bow up. Then the overture began.

Holmes kept pace, and Derek patted him on the arm when they came to their first break during the ventriloquist's act. The music for the Condolinis proved to be fiercely difficult, but Holmes' mistakes were unobserved other than the fierce glares cast by Hardwick. Behind him, Mal winked in sympathy.

His part for Mademoiselle Brett was simple, mostly providing the "pah pahs" to Hardwicke's "ooms." He scanned ahead in the part, and noticed a penciled circle over one bar around the word "Heaven." There was an arrow pointing up and to the left.

Holmes duly glanced in that direction when the measure arrived. It turned out to be the moment in her dance when she twirled, revealing her ankles and calves to the audience. Holmes, from his vantage point next to the stage and almost directly under her, saw a great deal more. He immediately fixed his eyes on his music, hoping his blushes went unnoticed.

They finished the first show. Hardwicke looked at Holmes and nodded curtly.

"I won't tolerate any mistakes like that again," he said.

"There won't be any," promised Holmes.

"Come on," said Derek, plucking at his arm. "They put out a cold supper for us between shows."

Apart from those crew members resetting the stage, the entire company crammed into a small room to share the meal.

"Well?" said Derek, nudging Holmes in the side. "Did you get a glimpse of Heaven?"

"Shut up," said Holmes.

"I'm sorry they replaced Scarpelli," continued Derek. "I had the prime view with him gone. Maybe we could switch seats?"

"You depend on your mouth for your livelihood," commented Holmes.

"Yeah, so what?"

"So if I were to punch you very hard in that mouth, you'd have to find other means of employment."

"Here, now!" protested Derek.

"I will treat Mademoiselle Brett with the respect due to a lady," said Holmes. "I recommend that you do likewise."

"Prig," muttered Derek, walking away.

Holmes turned to see Mademoiselle Brett watching from across the room, her eyes shining.

The call came for the second show. This time, Holmes got through the knock-about music flawlessly and received an approving nod from Hardwicke.

The second time through Mademoiselle's music, he found himself distracted by the knowledge of his predecessor's illicit ogling. He also found the musical arrangement boring. Almost without thinking, he threw in an arpeggio for ornamentation at the end of a phrase, receiving an immediate condemnatory look from Hardwicke. Holmes lowered his own gaze in apology, hoping that he had not earned his dismissal.

Yet on the very next phrase, another arpeggio leapt into the performance. Only this one came from Mademoiselle Brett herself, a silvery "ha ha ha HA!"

Holmes looked up at the stage in surprise, and she threw him a smile. Encouraged, he added another arpeggio, and she improvised a response. They continued in this back-and-forth manner within the space available in the arrangement, and she finished with a cadenza into a trill that had Hardwicke scrambling to find an ending.

Under the applause, the most tumultuous of the evening, Hardwicke pointed at Holmes, then drew his finger across his own throat.

They finished without further incident. As the musicians exited backstage, Hardwicke stepped in front of Holmes.

"How dare you!" he thundered. "Where do you come off tampering with our music, you impudent snail? As far as I'm concerned—"

"I thought it was lovely."

They turned to see Mademoiselle Brett standing there.

"You did?" said Hardwicke.

"I did," she said. "We shall keep it in."

"Very well, then," said Hardwicke. "But this fellow—"

"Should come in early tomorrow," she said. "I will need to work out the arrangement. Shall we say three o'clock, Mr. Holmes?"

"I am at your service, Mademoiselle," said Holmes.

"Until then," she said. "Good night."

She walked away. Hardwicke turned back to him.

"You'd best be careful," he said. "I've got my eye on you, boy."

Shortly before three the next day, Holmes arrived at the theater. Mademoiselle Brett was nowhere to be found. He went down the steps to the storage room. As he entered, he was aware of a light flickering in a corner, concealed from view by the shelves.

"Is that you, Mr. Holmes?" called Mademoiselle Brett from that direction.

"It is," he replied.

"Bring your violin, and we shall get to work."

He removed it from its box and went to join her.

She sat before a desk in the corner, sheaves of music piled upon it, along with inkpots and a box of pens and pencils. A small, faded rug extended under everything.

"Cosy," commented Holmes.

"This is where I write," she said, turning to him. "My sanctuary away from the bustle."

"You compose?"

"All of the music for the show."

"I noticed the S. Brett on my score, but I didn't know it meant you."

"It does. Now, what can you tell me about this?"

She pointed to Scarpelli's "Heaven" notation in the score.

"By my predecessor, apparently," said Holmes. "I had no idea what it meant."

"But you did look," she said.

"Forgive me. It shall never happen again."

"Yet you haven't erased it," she said sternly.

He produced a rubber eraser from his pocket. "I was planning to do so today."

"Well, no harm done," she said, taking it from him and removing the notation. "Now, I've written out those ornamentations and sketched out a call-and-response for a cadenza at the end. Shall we give it a go?"

They rehearsed until she was satisfied with the new arrangement. At the end, Holmes bowed to her.

"Impressive work, Mademoiselle," he said. "I am honored to be part of your creative process."

"Truthfully, Mr. Holmes, I am happiest when I am down here, lost in my music," she said. "The performing runs a distant second."

"I would think you'd find this place isolating."

"On the contrary—my mind, unfettered by the distractions of the world, runs free. And there is one thing down here in the depths that stimulates it. Shall I demonstrate?"

"Certainly."

"Then close your eyes—and listen!"

He did. He heard nothing at first, then gradually became aware of the low sound of rushing water.

"We must be—" he began.

Then he stopped as her lips met his. He didn't open his eyes until she had parted from him.

"That was for your gallantry yesterday," she said, her eyes gleaming, "and this—this is because I want to."

She stepped forward and kissed him again, her arms encircling his neck.

"Have you never had a proper kiss from a girl?" she asked when she was done.

"I'm not sure that any of this is proper," he replied.

"No need for propriety," she said. "You're in the theatre, now."

She took her handkerchief and dabbed at his lips, then patted him on the cheek.

"I would have kissed your mouse, but you're too tall," she said. "Time for your lesson with Papa." She gathered up her music and left.

He stood for a long while, then looked down at the floor. Something small and reddish-brown caught his eye. He reached down and plucked a splinter of wood protruding from the base of the shelves. He examined it thoughtfully, then put it in his pocket.

At his lesson with Brett, he once again applied a sunburn.

"I think I did it," he said, examining his work in the mirror.

Brett shook his head. "Go outside," he advised. "Come back and report to me."

Holmes left. He returned shortly thereafter. If a blush could have appeared through the powder, it would have.

"People laughed at me," he said.

"Of course, they did," said Brett. "Whatever works in here will be too much for daylight. Always use about half of what you think you should use. Now, wash it off and try again."

This time, Holmes returned looking sunburnt and happy.

"Success," he said.

"Well done. Now, about that noticeable nose of yours—"

"What would you recommend?" asked Holmes, staring at it in the mirror. "Broaden it with some form of putty?"

"Too obvious, too time-consuming," said Brett. "Put these on."

He handed Holmes a pair of spectacles with thick lenses.

"Describe the man in the mirror," commanded Brett.

"A sunburnt fellow with glasses," said Holmes.

"Did you notice the nose?"

"Not particularly."

"Here endeth the lesson. Wash up and go play your fiddle."

Holmes played flawlessly that night. When he came to the measure where "Heaven" had been, he stared rigidly at the page, only glancing up when he came to the dual cadenza. Mademoiselle Brett's voice soared through the hall like an angel's, and when the applause thundered in response, she winked at Holmes as she curtsied.

The next day was Saturday, and they had four shows to play, starting at two. Holmes rose at the crack of dawn and made his way to Dock Street. He stood outside the tavern and listened. Then he began to walk towards the river.

He stopped periodically, cocking his head, occasionally stooping to touch his fingers to the ground. When he reached Wapping High Street, he spotted a narrow stone stairway going down to the river's edge. It was low tide, and the bottom steps were slippery. He negotiated them with care, then stood, looking up and down as the waters swirled and flowed by him.

To his left, a boat pulled into the dock at the rear of the Wapping Police Station. Three officers stepped out, and three more took their place. Holmes watched as the new shift rowed away, then climbed the steps and walked to the precinct. The sergeant at the desk directed him to the offices of the Thames Division, where another sergeant looked up expectantly as he entered.

"How may I help you, sir?" he inquired.

"Do you have a recent list of bodies pulled from the river?" asked Holmes.

The sergeant pointed to a sheet of paper pinned to a board behind him. Holmes looked at the last several entries.

"Where are they kept?" he asked.

"Think you might know one?" asked the sergeant.

"I might," said Holmes. "A man. It would have been this past week."

The sergeant plucked a ring of keys from the desk.

"Come with me, sir," he said. "I hope you didn't have a large breakfast. This is an unpleasant experience."

"The dead are not strangers to me," said Holmes. "Lead on."

The sergeant took him outside.

"We pull one or two corpses out of the river every day," he said as they walked toward a nearby church. "We take 'em to the dead-house at Saint Saviour's until someone comes to claim 'em."

They went around the back of the church where a small, badly painted building stood at the rear of the graveyard. The sergeant unlocked it, then tied his handkerchief over his mouth and nose. Holmes did the same, and the sergeant opened the door.

There were no coffins or mortuary tables. The dead, in various states of decomposition and bloat, were unceremoniously laid out on stone slabs that might be fashioned into tombstones when no longer used here. The only protection allowed to each corpse was a filthy sheet. The collective stench in the closed quarters was horrendous, much worse than anything Holmes had experienced in his previous summer's employment.

The sergeant consulted his list, then uncovered the body of a man. Holmes squatted down, looked, then shook his head.

The sergeant replaced the sheet, then moved to another.

This time Holmes looked more closely at the deceased, who appeared to have reached the end of his life in his forties. There was a large bruise near his left temple, as well as some older mark on his neck.

"Where was he found?" asked Holmes.

"Washed up at the Isle of Dogs on Wednesday," said the sergeant.

"Any inquest yet?"

"On Monday, one o'clock at Daughtry's Pub."

Holmes looked at the bruise on the temple.

"Any other marks on him?" he asked.

"Back of the head," said the sergeant. "Worse than the front."

"May I see?"

"You may not," said the sergeant. "You may not touch him in any manner or— Here, what do you think you're about?"

Holmes had pulled a pair of calipers from inside his jacket and, to the sergeant's bewilderment, measured the fingers on both of the man's hands.

"What on earth is that for?" asked the sergeant.

Holmes stood, absentmindedly tapping the calipers on the palm of his left hand.

"The fingers on his left hand are longer than those on the right," he said. "Did the surgeon note that?"

"He did not," said the sergeant. "Does it mean something?"

"It means everything," said Holmes. "Was there water in his lungs or not?"

"There was not," said the sergeant. "Which means what, clever boy?"

"That he was dead before his body went into the water," said Holmes impatiently.

"Do you know this man?" asked the sergeant.

"I've never seen him before in my life."

"Right," said the sergeant. "I'll be wanting your name and address now."

"Sherlock Holmes, 17 Montague Street."

"Sherlock Holmes," repeated the sergeant. "I know that name."

"It's on a list at the station house," said Holmes. "But it's only of interest if I'm arrested as I was last Tuesday. Talk to your land-based colleagues, they'll tell you. Thank you, Sergeant. I will see you at the inquest."

He walked quickly out of the dead-house, then ripped the handkerchief from his face and bent over, retching. The sergeant followed him out and observed him with amusement.

"Happens to everyone the first time," he said sympathetically as he locked the door. "You get used to it."

"Wonderful," muttered Holmes as he straightened and wiped his mouth with his handkerchief. "I look forward to that. Good day."

He glanced at his watch. There was no lesson on Saturday due to the extra shows. He stopped at a tea shop to replenish his emptied stomach, then went to the theatre, hoping the stench of his breath had dissipated with his lunch. He arrived some twenty minutes before the first show. He ran down the stairs to retrieve the violin from the storeroom, then ran back up to tune it and warm up.

His thoughts raced, even as the part of his brain responsible for producing music operated by some automatic process. He made no errors, but there was little interaction with his fellow musicians, and none at all with Mademoiselle Brett.

At the supper break, he had no appetite, taking only a mug of porter. Mademoiselle Brett came over to him, her lovely face cast in an expression of concern.

"What is the matter, Mr. Holmes?" she asked. "You've barely acknowledged my existence today. Were my kisses so distasteful to you?"

"Quite the contrary," said Holmes. "In fact, I can think of little else at the moment, but I don't want to lose my place in the music because of the distraction."

"That's more like it," she said.

"Perhaps you could distract me again later?" he asked, smiling.

"Perhaps I could," she said, smiling back. "Now, go play the overture."

He sailed through the last show, then almost fled to the storage room. He placed his candle on her desk, made his arrangements, then tucked the violin under his chin and began to play softly.

She appeared at the other end of the room as if the music itself had summoned her, stepping from the darkness into the pool of light cast by the candle.

"I may not have much time," she whispered. Then she stopped and stared down at Holmes' feet.

He had rolled back the ancient carpet by her desk, revealing a circular grating set flush with the floor.

"What are you doing?" she asked.

He placed the violin and bow gently in their case, which rested on her desk.

"Every occupation takes its toll on the body over time," he said. "Even music leaves its traces."

He pressed his hands together in front of his chest in an attitude of prayer. "Notice anything?" he asked.

"No. What am I supposed to see?"

"I may not be a professional, but I have played for years," he said. "Anyone who plays a string instrument from childhood will end up with longer fingers on the left hand, due to the constant reaching up and down the neck in pursuit of larger and larger intervals. The fingers on the right, whether they bow or strum, will remain the same."

"I never knew that," she said.

"Now, a longtime violinist or violist will end up with a mark on his neck where the instrument meets the skin. There is a man in the Saint Saviour's dead-house with such a mark and with the disparity of length in his fingers. He also bears signs of violence upon the front and back of his head."

"What are you saying, Mr. Holmes?"

"*You loved a man who sank in the river,*" Holmes sang softly. "*It's too bad he's surfaced again.*"

"I never loved him!" she shouted hotly. "Never!"

"He died here," said Holmes. "In this room. On this spot. He was struck with his own violin case on the side of his head, tumbled back, and struck the back of his skull there."

He pointed to a crate, which had one corner sawn off. Traces of sawdust were still clinging to it. Then he tapped the grating with his foot.

"There are many streams that have been buried under the spread of this city," he said. "This grating has been removed and replaced recently. You tumbled his body into it, and he was carried off into the Thames. Then you cleaned this area of any traces of his blood. It's always suggestive to find one section of a storage room to have been cleaned, while the rest is not."

"This is where I work," she said, regaining her composure. "I like it orderly."

"No doubt," said Holmes, reaching into his pocket, "but you missed this."

He pulled out the fragment of wood that he had found.

"Rosewood," he said. "Lovely color, often used for the better violin cases."

"This is ridiculous."

"Is it? Your father led me to believe that Mr. Scarpelli had failed to return last week."

"That's right," she said.

"His chair wobbles," said Holmes. "He used a folded piece of cardboard under one leg to steady it. It was still on the floor by the stage when I came for my first performance. Had it been removed when he failed to turn up last week, that piece of cardboard would have been swept away before I began my tenure in that chair."

"Unless the boy who does the sweeping didn't do a thorough job," said Master Brett, stepping behind her. "Forgive the intrusion, Mr. Holmes. I was in search of my daughter, and couldn't help but overhear your most interesting analysis. So, you believe that you have found Mr. Scarpelli among the dead? A pity—I had advanced him a small sum against his future wages. I fear that I shall not get it back now."

"It doesn't seem likely," agreed Holmes.

"But do you really think that you can prove a killing based on a splinter of wood, a piece of cardboard, and some missing dust?" continued Brett.

"There is this," said Holmes, picking up the violin. "I had my suspicions the moment I picked it up."

"Why?" asked Mademoiselle Brett.

"Because no violinist, no matter how desperate his straits had become, would have left this instrument behind or put it in a plain wooden box without padding. This is a Stradivarius, one of the finest violins ever made."

He put it under his chin and began to play.

"Your kisses were exquisite, Mademoiselle," he said, "but this is what I will miss most of all when I leave here. Most violinists only dream of playing such an instrument. When you heard me play it in my audition, you recognized its unique tone. Hence your scream, your pallor, all the reactions of shock thinking that a man you believed dead had somehow returned."

"You kissed him?" Brett asked his daughter.

"Do shut up, Papa," said Mademoiselle Brett. "Mr. Holmes, let us say for the sake of argument that you are correct: That he stood—there, and that I struck him—there, and that he fell—there. Does that tell you anything about why I might have done so?"

"It does not," conceded Holmes.

"What if I told you that I struck him to prevent him from forcing himself upon me? Would that make a difference?"

"It would be completely consistent with the evidence and what little I know of his character," said Holmes.

"And therefore not murder."

"I never said murder, Mademoiselle. For what it's worth, I believe that is what happened."

"For what it's worth," she said bitterly. "Then it is still your intention to go to the authorities."

"The disposition of the body remains a crime," said Holmes. "That man, any man, should be treated at death with more dignity. His family should have knowledge of his demise, and the chance to make peace with the circumstances."

"Then there is nothing more to be said," she said.

"The inquest is on Monday at one at Daughtry's Pub," said Holmes. "Make your case to the coroner, not to me. Good night."

He placed the Stradivarius gently in the box, rested the bow next to it, then walked past them and out of the theatre.

The next day was Sunday. Had he been a churchgoing man, he might have found something to reassure him that his actions were the correct ones. Surely a woman was justified in defending herself against such an attack. But could he be certain that it wasn't murder, her protestations notwithstanding?

Why hadn't he gone directly to the police?

Because she had kissed him? Was he that credulous?

How could he have faith in a woman's kiss when he had faith in nothing that could not be proved?

He could have let it go. Had he never investigated what no one asked to be investigated, then none would have been the wiser.

And he never again would have been able to look into her eyes without suspicion.

He wanted very much to look into her eyes.

On Monday, he rose and made himself as presentable as he could. By mid-morning, he could no longer stand the sight of his office, so he walked to Wapping.

The theatre was on the way to Daughtry's. On an impulse, he turned onto Dock Street, only to be greeted with a rude shock when he came to the Admiral's Rest.

A crude poster had been slapped over the sign for Brett's Variety. "CLOSED FOR ONE WEEK. WILL REOPEN UNDER NEW MANAGEMENT. ALL NEW ACTS! WATTS' VARIETY!"

Holmes dashed into the tavern, which was nearly empty. One of the bartenders waved him over.

"You left this here," he said, reaching under the bar. "Mr. Brett told me to make sure you got it."

He pulled out a familiar-looking box and placed it before Holmes. Inside was a violin case, a jar of powder, and a pair of envelopes addressed to him. Holmes opened the one from Brett.

"Now I understand what a consulting detective is," read the letter inside. "All we knew of Scarpelli was that he was on the run from the authorities in Italy. We never knew his real name. If you can find his heirs, return the violin. Until then, it might as well be yours. I bought it a better case. It's not rosewood, but it will serve. I am also giving you a jar of sunburn, and recommend you continue your lessons with Mr. Harper, a former apprentice of mine at the Lee Theatre. One last thing, Mr. Holmes: There is a difference between Law and Justice. I hope that you come to appreciate that in time. B."

His hands shaking slightly, Holmes opened the other envelope. It contained a photograph of Mademoiselle Brett. There was nothing written on the back, but she had left an imprint of her lips in the strawberry color that was burned into his memory of her.

"Where is Brett?" asked Holmes, his heart sinking.

"Gone," said the bartender. "He and the girl. Offer of a new venture somewhere, didn't say where. Said you were all paid up otherwise."

"He owes me nothing," said Holmes.

He walked outside and looked around.

They could be anywhere, he thought. They could be anyone.

His shoulders sagging, he walked away in the direction of Daughtry's Pub.

An elderly couple passed going the other way. The woman turned and watched Holmes from under her veil.

"It's too bad, Papa," said Mademoiselle Brett. "I liked him."

"It never would have worked," said Brett. "Now, where shall we go next?"

"Someplace where fools are treated with respect," she said.

"America, it is," he said. He offered his arm. She took it, and they walked away.

ONE MONTH LATER.

Mycroft emerged from the Diogenes Club, refreshed from two hours of reading the evening papers uninterrupted by anything other than the replenishing of his glass of sherry. Thomas was waiting with the brougham, glancing up and down the street. There was no one in the vicinity other than a drunken sailor lurching along the opposite side, bellowing "The Tale of the Rat-Catcher's Daughter," painfully off-key.

"Drink, Thomas, is the great equivocator," observed Mycroft. "It inspires one to sing while destroying one's intonation."

"Yes, sir," said the driver.

"That was meant to be witty, Thomas," said Mycroft.

"Then it was entirely wasted on me, sir," said Thomas, holding the door for him.

Mycroft sighed and stepped in, bolting the door after it was closed. He settled back contentedly in his seat as the brougham lurched forward.

There was a cry, a thud, and the horse neighing in terror. The brougham rolled to a halt, and the door jolted under the repeated blows of a sledge hammer. Mycroft drew his Webley and waited.

Then came a second series of cries and blows, accompanied this time by several sharp cracks. Then there was silence.

"Mycroft, don't shoot," shouted Sherlock from outside. "I have the situation under control. You can come out."

Mycroft cautiously unbolted the door and opened it. The sailor, no longer drunk nor singing, stood over three men who were sprawled on the street. He looked up at Mycroft and held up a wooden baton.

"As you see, I brought my stick this time," said Sherlock. "Don't say that I never listen to you."

"I wasn't expecting them for another three days," said Mycroft.

"They moved up their timetable," said Sherlock. "Long story, I'll tell you later. Your driver needs medical assistance. I take it you can hold these three while I get help?"

"I should be able to do so."

"Good," said Sherlock. "Is there a reward for their capture? I'm a bit out of pocket on this one."

"I'll see what I can do," said Mycroft.

"Right. I'll be back shortly."

And he ran down the street, blowing a whistle as he disappeared around the corner. Mycroft watched and shook his head.

"Very well," he said. "You can stay."

SHERLOCKED

by Rhys Bowen

The room was becoming hotter and more unpleasant by the minute. It had been unusually warm for May in the Thames Valley and the meeting room that had been selected at the local posh hotel was really too small for the number of people who had shown up for the demonstration. And not all of them had been over-generous with deodorant, Clare Patterson thought as she moved as far back from the offending odor as possible. There was an expectant buzz of conversation and Clare heard a voice behind her wondering how soon they could go to the pub. She had positioned herself in a far corner, as befitted a lowly detective constable, and examined the crowd. There were Thames Valley police top brass, looking uncomfortable if smart in their uniforms; the plainclothes branch distinguishable from the forensics lot and the press, because they were wearing ties and had neat haircuts. The forensics boys sported longer hair and a few untucked shirts, while the pressmen were identifiably most shaggy and casual of all. The female reporters, on the other hand, wore impressively high heels and smart, short skirts.

"Such an interesting mix," Clare thought and studied faces. She was determined to make a success of her new career and had been told by an old sergeant that you could learn more from a face than any amount of forensic evidence. "You'll pick up right away if someone's uneasy, or cocky. If you watch carefully, the cocky ones will allow themselves a little grin because they think they've pulled one over on you. A dead giveaway."

She had observed about half the room when the door opened. A hush fell as Chief Superintendent Barclay walked in.

"Welcome," he said, looking around the crowd. "Good of you all to come on this momentous occasion. First of all, a warm welcome to our fellow officers from around the British Isles. And to our various forensics teams, our technical geeks—or should I say geniuses—without whom this would not have been possible. And last but not least, to our friends in the media. I feel I'm safe in saying that what we are going to show you today will blow you away."

He paused. He had the sort of face that always looked smug but at this moment he looked positively self-satisfied. "And," he went on, "if everything progresses according to plan, we may all find ourselves out of a job soon."

A nervous titter ran around the room.

"I wish he'd get on with it," a voice said behind Clare. "Always did like the sound of his own voice."

"Some of you have caught whispers of what we've been doing, here in the Thames Valley," the Chief Superintendent went on. "And finally I'm happy to unveil something that will revolutionize policing around the world. Ladies and gentlemen." Another long and dramatic pause. "May I present to you Sherlock."

He looked toward the open door. All eyes followed his gaze, and in through the door came what looked like a rather superior vacuum cleaner. Again there was an uneasy titter from parts of the crowd. The robot moved easily over the carpet and came to a halt in the middle of the room. It could not have been called handsome or even impressive. It was about three feet high with a round base, a long neck ending in a glass ball, upon which someone had placed a small deerstalker cap. The ball rotated from side to side, giving the impression that while the crowd took in the robot, it was equally examining them.

"Doesn't look like much, does it?" CS Barclay went on. "We discussed making it more human looking, or even more like what we've come to expect a robot will look like. C-3PO? Is that what it was called in *Star Wars*? But we've kept the design pared down so that it's easily transportable in any police vehicle—and frankly, it can do the job."

"And what is that job, exactly?" one of the braver press boys asked.

"Sherlock is the ultimate crime scene investigator," Barclay said. "When we send out a CSI team to a crime scene there's always a chance of contamination, of destruction of minute evidence, of things that will be overlooked. That will never happen with Sherlock. He will move across the crime scene, disturbing it as little as possible, and examining every inch of the floor as he goes. He can pick up the smallest trace of evidence—say, a soil particle carried in on a shoe—and tell us where that soil came from. Likewise plant fibers, clothing fibers, even dandruff. He can examine footprints and tell us when they were made and what kind of footwear made them."

Someone must have pressed a remote because the robot started to move silently across the floor.

"What about evidence that isn't on the floor?" one of the female reporters asked. "Not all murder victims fall to the ground. Some might be killed sitting in a chair."

"Good point." CS Barclay nodded appreciation. "Sherlock is equipped with two arms, just like us. And the end of each arm has a powerful sensor on it."

Two metal crane-like arms extended. Sherlock went over to the reporter in question and one of the mechanical hands skimmed over the female reporter's skirt. This got a chuckle from some of the younger men.

"Sherlock will be able to tell you where you have been recently," CS Barclay said. "What you might have brushed against. Where you sat. And when it comes to analyzing a murder victim, he'll tell us the time of death and be able to make a fairly reliable assessment as to what killed the person. His all-seeing eye will examine the walls for blood spatters and tell us how far away the gun was fired, what type of weapon . . . He'll examine fingerprints and send data to be matched. Things that would normally take ballistic and SCI experts hours or days can now be accomplished almost instantly."

There was a pause as the audience took all this in.

"Any questions at this stage?" Barclay asked.

"What about psychological profiling?" an older officer from another police jurisdiction asked. "What about the human element? What about experience?" It was his turn to look smug.

"We're working on that," Barclay said. "I'm told by the technical team that Sherlock will have a companion up and running within a year. Naturally we're calling him Watson. He will be able to examine facial expressions, detect a rise in pulse or temperature from suspects, in short do what the most accomplished and experienced of police investigators can now do."

Another pause. Sounds of shifting feet as if people were now uncomfortable or impatient to leave.

"Have you actually tried this thing out on a real case?" a young reporter asked.

"We have run simulated crime scenes but no, we have not used Sherlock on a real crime scene yet. We don't get many juicy murders in the Thames Valley, you know." And he gave his self-satisfied chuckle. "As soon as we've tried him out, you can be sure we'll let you know!"

They were dismissed. Some of the reporters surrounded Sherlock and Barclay with more questions. Photographs were taken. The top brass hung around conferring with one another.

"Well, that's me out of a job. I suppose I'd better go and sign up at the labor exchange and it will be behind the counter at Starbucks." Charlie Tanner, a young CSI agent, fell into step with Clare as they left the room. He gave her a friendly grin.

"Me too," she agreed. "They won't need as many people on the force, will they?"

"Only one or two to look important like Barclay or to oil little whats-his-name."

"You mean Sherlock?"

"Sherlock." He grimaced. "How pretentious. I bet the thing doesn't even work."

"We'll have to see, won't we?"

Clare's governor, DI Hammond, was equally skeptical when she returned to police HQ. He was a comfortable, middle-aged man with three daughters and he treated Clare like a fourth.

"What will they think of next?" he said. "What a load of old codswallop! I bet someone's modified a vacuum cleaner and got a large grant to do this."

"It might be a useful tool if it actually works, sir," she said hesitantly.

"Then I think it's up to you and me to prove that it doesn't," he replied.

"You're not suggesting sabotage?"

He chuckled. "No. I'm suggesting we show that you can't beat good old human intelligence and intuition, Clare. I'm hoping that test case will be on our patch and that we'll be assigned to it. Then we'll see: man versus machine and may the better man win!"

As it happened they were in luck. Two weeks later Clare was summoned to the incident room as soon as she reported on duty.

"This is it, Patterson," he said, grinning at her. "The game is afoot."

"Pardon, sir?" Clare looked blank.

Hammond gave a sigh. "Don't tell me you haven't read Sherlock Holmes."

"I tried him once, sir. I'm afraid he annoyed me with his supercilious, know-it-all attitude. I mean, 'I deduce this spent match was struck by a left-handed librarian!' Give me a break!"

DI Hammond chuckled. "You do have a point there, but now you may have to change your attitude. You're about to see Sherlock in action."

"You mean the robot?" Clare's eyes lit up. In spite of herself she was excited. "There's been a murder?"

"There has. At one of the Oxford colleges. St. Clement's." He picked up his phone from the desk. "Come on. Grab your notebook and get in the car. I'll fill you in on the details as we go."

Soon they were heading through the outskirts of Oxford, the drab suburban streets giving no indication of the glorious buildings that lay ahead.

"So who is dead?" Clare asked.

"A professor of English called Orville. Theodor Orville. He lives in faculty rooms at the college, as do several other unmarried dons, one gathers. His body was found this morning when the college servant couldn't get into his sitting room. It was apparently locked from the inside. She alerted the college porter, who has a master key, and they found him lying on the floor."

"So he was alone in a room locked from the inside?" Clare asked. "Then how did his killer escape? Out of a window?"

"Apparently not," DI Hammond said. "The building dates back to the fifteenth century. The windows have small leaded panes."

"Then how . . . ?" Clare started.

Hammond interrupted her. "No doubt Sherlock will have it all sorted out by the time we get there."

St. Clement's was situated between Magdalen and St. Edmund Hall facing the High Street, with meadows leading down to the Cherwell behind it. It was built in mellow cream-colored stone, aged with centuries of coal fires and passing cars to a dark gray. Like all of the ancient Oxford colleges, it was constructed around a quad, with the only open entry through the central gateway, manned by a porter. As they arrived a group of undergrads were coming out, their gowns flapping out in the stiff morning breeze. The porter met them, saying that a Chief Superintendent was already at the scene and implying that since such a senior man was there they needn't have bothered. He grudgingly led them along the cloister on one side of the quad. A groundsman was mowing the lawn in perfect lines. At the end of the cloiser they were led up an ancient stone staircase, its tread worn down by centuries of feet.

"So this is faculty housing?" DI Hammond asked him.

"This is where the dons reside, yes, sir," the porter replied stiffly.

"And how many dons would there be in residence at the moment?"

"Well, there's the master and the dean—they have the ground floor to themselves. One floor up was poor Professor Orville, and Dr. Tanner of the classics department, and Professor Treadwell of modern languages. Up on the second floor there would be Dr. Heathcliff and Dr. Ransom. Both lady dons, you understand."

"Which is why they've been relegated to the top floor?" Clare asked, then realized she should have kept silent. The junior officer does not ask questions unless told to.

The porter gave her a hard stare. "It's only recently that St. Clement's has had women on the faculty," he said. "It was felt they would be happier away from the pipe-smoking males."

"Quite," DI Hammond intervened, giving Clare a warning glance.

They followed the porter along a dark hallway, their feet echoing on the tiled floor.

"The dons each have two rooms?" Clare asked, noting names on doors.

"Sitting room and bedroom, next door to each other," the porter replied. "They share a bathroom at the end of the hall."

At the far end of the corridor they could hear voices. A door was half open, but most of the light from the doorway was blocked by the chief superintendent's impressive bulk. He turned at the sound of their footsteps.

"Ah, Hammond. Glad you could make it."

"Well, it is a death on my patch, sir," Hammond said easily. Then he added, "Wouldn't miss it for the world."

Chief Superintendent Barclay stepped out into the hallway and let them get a glimpse of the room. One young man stood inside the door and Sherlock was moving slowly across the floor, looking more than ever like a rogue vacuum cleaner, skirting around a body that lay sprawled on the carpet.

"As you can see," Barclay said, "he's already hard at work. And what's more he doesn't want to stop for coffee breaks." He chuckled at his own joke.

Clare stood back from her DI, trying to take in as much as possible. From where she was standing she couldn't see a clear cause of death. But she noticed a window was open and the breeze ruffled papers lying on a table. It was an old-fashioned room. On the far wall was a big marble fireplace. Above it hung a hunting print. Apart from the table under the window there were a leather arm chair and a couple of upright chairs. The Spartan room of an unmarried academic, she thought. No photographs, no bright cushions. And no smell of pipe smoke either. But it was also a messy room. Papers and books were piled on every surface. A cup and plate set on the floor beside the chair. A bottle and glass rested on a side table. Professor Orville would have expected the college servant to clear up for him, Clare thought.

"So what do we know so far, sir?" DI Hammond asked. "Before Sherlock tells us whodunit?" He intended it as a joke, but Barclay's face was serious when he replied.

"Initial examination tells us he was dead for less than an hour when found. Blow to the back of the head. Door locked from the inside. Key still in the lock."

"Interesting." Hammond glanced at Clare. He went to take a step into the room but Barclay put out a hand to stop him.

"Well, we'll leave Sherlock to finish his task, shall we?" he said. "Why don't you interview the other residents of the building and the cleaning lady?"

Clare could see DI Hammond glowering as they walked away. "Keeping us happy and out of the way. What a farce. I bet that overgrown vacuum cleaner turns up nothing useful."

They were taken down the hall to a small kitchen where Ada, the college servant, was sitting, being consoled by a young policewoman. She glanced up and smiled as DI Hammond entered. "Oh, hello sir. This is Ada Johnson. She was the one who found the body."

"Hello, Ada," DI Hammond said kindly. "Bit of a shock, eh?"

"Oh yes sir," Ada turned a mournful face to him. She had been crying. "He was a lovely gentleman. Ever so kind. Of course, he wasn't the tidiest of gentlemen. Especially not when he was working on something. Your typical absentminded professor, so to speak." She smiled wistfully. "Always spilling things on the rug. But at least he didn't smoke so he didn't burn any holes, like some of them."

"So tell us exactly what happened this morning," DI Hammond said.

"I went to clean his room as usual about nine o'clock," Ada said. "I always start with him, seeing he's got the end rooms. I made his bed as usual, and then I tried his sitting room and it was locked. That surprised me because I know he teaches a nine o'clock class on Tuesdays. He always leaves the key in the lock so I can go in and clean for him. I wondered if he'd been working late and fallen asleep in his chair." She looked up at them. "He's done it before, you know. And he likes his whiskey on occasion."

"So what did you do?"

"I knocked, sir. I banged on the door. Professor Treadwell came out to see what the commotion was about. I told him and he went to get the porter with the pass key. We opened the door and there was the poor professor lying there, dead as a doornail, sir. It quite took me funny. And the professor went and phoned for the police."

"When did you last see the professor alive?"

"Well, sir, I didn't see him yesterday when I went to clean his room, but I heard him."

"Heard him?" DI Hammond asked.

"Yes, sir. He wasn't in his rooms when I came. I made his bed and then I went through to his sitting room and I was sweeping the floor when I heard a right old barney going on upstairs. Dr. Heathcliff's rooms are directly upstairs from his and the sound echoed down the chimney. They were going at each other. She called him a pedantic old bore who was past it and should step down, and he called her a meddling and ambitious harpy who wasn't above stealing someone else's research." Ada paused and looked up at them. "I left them at it, sir, and went on with my cleaning. These scholarly folks, they do get quite het up about their work sometimes."

"Has Professor Orville argued with any other colleagues lately?" DI Hammond asked.

"Not that I've overheard, sir. He gets on well with everybody most of the time. He's especially thick with Professor Treadwell and with the master."

"And what about outside visitors?"

"I believe his sister comes to visit him sometimes, and of course students come up to his rooms on a regular basis. Any outsider would have to go past the porter's desk and sign in."

DI Hammond turned to Clare. "Any questions you'd like to ask, Constable?"

"Yes," Clare said. "Did he often keep his door locked?"

"Not usually in the mornings, because he knew I'd want to get in to clean for him, but I imagine he did lock himself in when he wanted some privacy. They don't just want undergrads barging in on them, do they?"

"And who might have access to the pass key besides the porter?" DI Hammond asked.

"Oh nobody, sir. The porter guards that key with his life."

"Besides," Clare pointed out, "if the door was locked from the inside then the key would have been in the lock, wouldn't it? When the porter pushed his pass key in, the inside key would have fallen to the floor."

"Quite right," DI Hammond nodded approvingly. "Thank you, Ada. You've been very helpful. Now if we might have a word with Dr. Heathcliff, if she's available?"

"She should be in her rooms still," Ada said. "She doesn't teach until a tutorial at noon. Up the stairs to the rooms at the far end."

Clare fell into step beside DI Hammond. "What do you think, sir?"

"Since we haven't been able to view the body, I have no idea," he replied. "The door locked from the inside? Someone's been quite clever."

They went up a second stone staircase and tapped on the end door of an upstairs hallway, if anything more gloomy than the first.

"Enter," boomed an authoritative voice. They entered a very different room. This one was clearly a woman's room. The walls were lined with bookcases and there were neat stacks of papers on a desk against the far wall. But the window seat was piled high with pillows and there were embroidered pillows on a chintz-covered sofa. On the coffee table there was a dish containing Murano glass beads and a half-finished necklace beside it. And plants—lots of plants everywhere. Clare detected the faint smell of smoke in the room and wondered if the plants were an attempt to cover up the woman's smoking. There was a slight movement and Clare noticed a large white cat asleep amongst the pillows.

"Miss Heathcliff?" DI Hammond asked pleasantly.

"It's Doctor Heathcliff," she said curtly. The woman came toward them. She was large but not fat—a draught horse, not a thoroughbred. If she had been wearing a suit she would have come across as a formidable presence, but she was wearing a loose, flowing dress and an intricate beaded necklace. Clare wondered if this was a deliberate attempt to soften a dominant personality. She was interestingly complex—the orderly shelves of books and papers and the hand-embroidered pillows and folksy attire showed two very different sides of the same woman.

"I beg your pardon, Doctor," the DI said. "I'm DI Hammond and this is Constable Patterson. I wonder if we might have a few words."

"About Professor Orville, I presume?"

"You've heard?"

"Of course. And I'm very sorry. We didn't always see eye to eye but he was a good man. An intelligent man. Was it a burglary? I wouldn't have thought he had much worth stealing."

"We haven't had a chance to view the crime scene yet," DI Hammond said. "But we wanted speak to potential witnesses first."

"I'm afraid I can't help you. I haven't seen him since yesterday morning," she said.

"When you apparently had an argument," DI Hammond said evenly.

"We did."

"Would you mind telling me what it was about?"

"Bacon," she said.

"One of you is a vegetarian?"

She gave a rather patronizing laugh. "I'm talking of Francis Bacon. I am writing a paper on new evidence proving he wrote some of Shakespeare's plays. Orville disagreed strongly. He urged me to drop it." She looked up sharply. "You can't possibly think I had anything to do with his death. You don't kill somebody because you disagree academically."

"Of course not," the DI responded. "But would you like to tell us what your movements were this morning?"

"This morning? Is that when he was killed?" She shook her head in disbelief. "I heard nothing."

"You were in your room all the time?"

"No. I always go for my walk at eight o'clock. The same every morning. I cross the meadows to the Cherwell, go along the river and back through Magdalen. If you want to check on my movements I always pass the same people: a couple with a small white poodle; Professor Tweedie from Brasenose; and I generally exchange pleasantries with the porter at Magdalen. I return home between eight forty-five and nine. I have been in my room since then preparing for a tutorial."

"Can you think of anyone who would want to harm Professor Orville?" DI Hammond asked.

"He could be infuriating at times," she said. "Completely disorganized. That room of his. . . . Hopeless. I gave him one of my plants, but I suspect he's let it die by now. But hating him enough to kill him? One of the students went off his rocker, I suppose. They do, sometimes. It's the pressure of exams."

"I wouldn't like to get on the wrong side of her," DI Hammond muttered as they left Dr. Heathcliff's room.

They proceeded to interview those members of the faculty who were still in their rooms. None had seen Professor Orville that morning nor heard any sign of a fight. They returned to Barclay.

"Well?" Barclay asked. "Anything suspicious?"

"Only that the female don upstairs had an argument with Orville yesterday. But she is out on her walk between eight and nine and you suggest the time of death was around eight thirty?"

Barclay nodded.

"And besides," Hammond went on. "She's a rather large lady. She wouldn't fit through Orville's windows and I doubt she could climb down the wall."

"Sherlock's done with the floor and now he's collecting fingerprints," Barclay said. "In an hour or so we should know something. I suggest you keep yourself busy by getting fingerprints from the occupants of this building."

"Good idea. Why don't you do that, Constable Patterson?" DI Hammond said.

Clare nodded and went to collect a fingerprint kit.

"You again," Dr. Heathcliff said, frowning, as Clare returned. "Fingerprints? Of course they'll find our fingerprints all over his room. We met for sherry every Friday evening. Is there anyone competent handling this investigation?"

"A robot," Clare answered.

"There is no need to be facetious with me," Dr. Heathcliff snapped. "Now, if you will excuse me, I have a tutorial."

Clare handed in her fingerprints and then she went with DI Hammond to break the news to Orville's sister, who lived in a terrace house on the other side of Folly Bridge over the Isis. She was a tiny sparrow of a woman and she looked up at them fearfully as DI Hammond broke the news.

"I was worried when he didn't telephone me this morning," she said. "He always did, at eight o'clock on the dot. Was it his heart?"

"We're not sure yet," DI Hammond said. "May we come in?"

She offered them tea and seated them in a tiny sitting room. A calico cat rubbed up against their legs.

"So tell me about your brother," DI Hammond said.

"I did my best to look after him," Miss Hammond said. "He was hopeless. He'd never have changed his clothes or washed his shirts if I hadn't made him. Head up in the clouds. Always, even as a boy."

"When did you last see him?"

"He came to me for Sunday lunch regularly. And sometimes he'd come over and we'd play Scrabble. But Sunday, that was the last time." She put a hand to her mouth as if she'd just realized what she had said. "The last time," she repeated.

"Was your brother worried about anything? Did he have any enemies?"

"Enemies?" She shook her head. "He was the most gentle of creatures. Easygoing. Mild-mannered. Content with life."

They left soon after and returned expectantly to St Clement's. As they entered they heard a booming voice coming from the upstairs hallway. "Don't be so ridiculous! Keep your hands off me!"

Barclay appeared. "All sewn up while you were away, Inspector. It was the woman upstairs. The one he was arguing with. She couldn't stand him."

"Dr. Heathcliff? How could you tell?"

"It was Sherlock who told," Barclay said with his self-satisfied smile. "The carpet had been cleaned yesterday morning so anything found on it was fresh. And what was found were the following: damp soil. A blade of grass . . . and we know that woman crossed the meadow on her walk—which she clearly took earlier than usual today. A white cat hair and we know she has a white cat. And a spent match . . . she smokes, he doesn't. And the phone was hanging down from its cord. He went for the phone and she struck him from behind. Maybe on impulse. Maybe she didn't mean to kill him."

"But the locked door?" Clare asked.

"Clever." Barclay nodded. "The woman is into craft work. She does beading and has a pair of long-nosed pliers wrapped in silk cord to prevent her from damaging expensive beads. She put them through the keyhole and turned the key from the other side, leaving no marks on the key. Brilliant."

"And do we know how he was killed?"

Barclay was still smiling. "That fireplace surround. Those marble balls come off the fender. She hit him with it and then replaced it, wiping off her fingerprints. But there are still traces of blood and hair."

He went to walk away.

"Do you mind if we take a look now Sherlock is finished?" DI Hammond asked.

Barclay shrugged. "Please yourselves. They are coming for the body soon."

He went out, closing the door behind him.

"Well that's nice and neat, isn't it?" Hammond turned to Clare. "Do you think she did it?"

"I suppose it does all make sense," Clare said. "You said she was a woman you wouldn't want to cross."

DI Hammond knelt to examine the body. There was an ugly wound on the side of the head. Clare looked around the room. The marble ball on the fireplace fender still had clear traces of blood and hair on it. Why not wipe it clean if you had wiped off fingerprints? And on the windowsill was the plant Dr. Heathcliff had given him. Indeed in a sorry state, but it had been watered recently. He must have been trying to revive it. She glanced into the fireplace. The weather had been warm so there was no fire, but there were a few ashes.

"I think he burned something recently," she said. "That would account for the match on the floor."

DI Hammond stood up.

A breeze came in through the window and ruffled the papers on the sill. Clare stood there, frowning. If that breeze had been stronger it would have knocked over the plant, and soil would have spilled onto the floor. And the lawn in the quad was being mown. A blade of grass could have easily blown in through the window. And the white cat hair? He had visited his sister with the calico cat and he never brushed his clothing. . . .

Then she looked down at the body and a big smile spread across her face. "I don't think it was a murder at all, sir," she said. "It was an accident."

"How do you make that out?"

"Look, sir. We were told he was absentminded and didn't take care of himself. One of his shoelaces was untied. He tripped over, fell and hit his head on the fireplace. He tried to crawl across to the telephone, reached for it, but passed out and expired."

DI Hammond nodded with satisfaction. "I think you may be right. Come on. Let's rescue that poor woman before Barclay has her locked in a cell."

Clare was lying in bed that night, thinking with satisfaction about the outcome of the day. She had been praised for her powers of observation and deduction, and yet something was worrying her. Suddenly she remembered what the old sergeant had told her—that real coppers watch faces and learn to read expressions . . . and that cocky criminals give themselves away. Dr. Heathcliff's face when Clare had taken her fingerprints. As Clare had put away the kit and Dr. Heathcliff had thought Clare wasn't looking she had grinned. A momentary, fleeting grin.

What if Sherlock had been right after all?

A STUDY IN ABSENCE

by *Reed Farrel Coleman*

Holmes was in one of his peculiar phases or, more accurately, one of his particularly peculiar phases. Most souls, I suspect, would judge his usual state of being, as it were, bordering somewhere between certifiable madness on the one hand and quaint eccentricity on the other. I, of course, knew him to be both of these and neither. He was, simply, Holmes. What I suppose I'm saying is that between cases, Holmes could turn his considerable intellect and powers of observation and deduction outward like a weapon to fairly torture those of us who chose to remain in close proximity to him—or turn them inward on himself. Although I must confess a distinct preference for the latter, as it removed the proverbial bull's-eye from the rear of my dressing gown, the former was still a cause of great consternation. For one never knew with Holmes if he would reemerge from these introversions.

So it was with little fuss that I passed Holmes gazing into the hallway mirror at Baker Street on my way to the breakfast of toast, eggs, and tea provided by Mrs. Hudson. Ninety minutes later, after having dispatched my breakfast and a second pot of tea, I spotted Holmes still gazing into the mirror. I was concerned. If I did not know that it was anatomically impossible, I would have sworn that the man hadn't blinked or moved in all that time.

"Holmes," I said to him, "what are you up to?"

"Am I here, Watson?"

"Holmes!"

"Answer the question."

"Are you here? Of course you are."

"But how can you be certain of that?"

I placed my hand around his right biceps. "Because I can feel you, see you, hear you, and, frankly, I can smell you. Do freshen up. Just how long have you been at this . . . whatever this is?"

"Yes, John, you can detect a physical presence, but can you be certain that it is *mine*?"

"Holmes, you are in one of your moods. Go play the violin or do something to occupy your mind until you have another case. Anything to deal with your boredom—except your cocaine."

That's when Holmes smiled, or what passed for a smile from Holmes.

"Do I seem bored to you, John? On the contrary, I do have a case and the client should be arriving at ten. If you had been paying careful attention, you would have noticed I've been at work on the case all morning."

"By staring into the looking glass?"

He made that face of his, the one that let you know he knew he was the smartest fellow in the room. It was most annoying when I was the only other person present.

"The very point of my questions, John. You judge the physical presence before you by observing the exterior, but what can you know of the internal processes or of the essence of the being?"

"Holmes, you are the keenest of observers and have often drawn wild extrapolations about such things from twitches and idiosyncrasies, some so slight as to be nearly imperceptible."

"We are not talking about me." His smile vanished. "But please do answer my query. How can you be certain the person before you is me?"

"I am well acquainted with your physical appearance, your voice, your quirks and tics."

"For argument's sake, I will grant you that the physical presence before you seems to meet all of those aspects and expectations you have for the person you know as Sherlock Holmes, but how can you know that within this physical vessel the being you know as Holmes resides?"

"For heaven's sake, Holmes, I am a medical doctor. I will leave the metaphysics and discussions of essence and souls to philosophers and the clergy."

"So then you do admit this is not an issue of body, but of spirit?"

"I said no such thing."

"Of course you did, John. I've no time for idle chatter now. I must, as you suggest, freshen up." And with that, Holmes was gone.

The doorbell sounded promptly at ten. Less than a minute later, Mrs. Hudson appeared at the top of the stairs with a handsome and smartly dressed woman of indeterminate age who clutched a neatly brown-papered-and-tied bundle to her chest. The woman's porcelain skin and white smile suggested youth. The traces of faint lines at the corners of her eyes and mouth spoke of age. The sparkle in her flecked blue eyes hinted at sagacity and experience. All that, however, was overwhelmed by the crushed flowers and citrus scent of her perfume that, like fine wine, became more complex with exposure to it. After the initial burst of flora and citrus, I noticed the earthier harmonic notes of sandalwood and patchouli. I, too, possessed the power of observation. An indispensable asset for a medical man.

"Miss Rosetta Sebastian for Mr. Holmes," Mrs. Hudson said before withdrawing.

Miss Sebastian eyed me with suspicion. Understandable, as I was not whom she had come to see.

I stood, gently taking her hand in mine. "Dr. John Watson, an associate of Mr. Holmes."

"Of course, Dr. Watson." Relief displaced the suspicion in her eyes. "How thick of me not to recognize you. I have read your accounts of Mr. Holmes's exploits . . . and yours."

For reasons known only to Holmes, it seemed he was determined to make an entrance. Ten minutes on, both of us straining the limits of polite chatter,

Holmes had failed to appear. Miss Sebastian removed a small pocket watch on a fob hidden in a tiny slit pocket on her dress and checked it.

"Mr. Holmes is aware of our appointment?" Her voice was strained with concern and the seeds of anger.

I stood. "I do apologize, Miss Sebastian. Holmes can be . . . unpredictable. Let me—"

"No call for you to make apologies on my part, John," Holmes said, stepping out from behind the thick draperies of the drawing room.

"Holmes. Were you standing there this whole time?"

"I was." He strode directly to where Miss Sebastian was seated. "Forgive me, but surely you see the point I was attempting to make."

She shook her head. "Frankly, Mr. Holmes, it escapes me."

"Very well," he said, barely able to mask his impatience and disappointment in her intellect. "I was showing you, by example, that it is possible to hide oneself in very close proximity to those who might wish to find you. It is often simply a matter of will."

That youthful white smile broke across her face. "I see, Mr. Holmes."

I had had enough of Holmes's cryptic questions and queer behavior. "Well, I don't, and I would very much appreciate someone giving me a notion of what is going on."

Miss Sebastian turned to me. "Forgive me, Dr. Watson, I wrongly assumed that Mr. Holmes had discussed the details of my problem with you."

"No need for apologies. Holmes sometimes delights in keeping me in the dark."

"You do such a fine job of that yourself, John. It is only on rare occasions that you require my assistance in that endeavor."

I ignored Holmes. "Please do continue, Miss Sebastian."

"I am an editor at Partridge House and—"

I interrupted. "An editor! Isn't that an unusual position for a woman to hold?"

"Nevertheless, Dr. Watson, it is my title, and one, I assure you, that was hard-earned."

Holmes laughed. "John can be rather provincial, Miss Sebastian. Please excuse him. Do go on."

"Several months ago I received a manuscript for a crime drama, but not at all the usual fare. It is a most dark tale of a former mercenary soldier who, through acts of selflessness, seeks a redemption that remains beyond his grasp. Dr. Watson, this is something of superior quality, featuring the finest, most well-drawn characters that have ever lived on the page."

"Finer than Dickens's characters?"

Miss Sebastian blushed. "I must confess to you, Doctor, I am not a great enthusiast for Dickens. While his talent is undeniable, I find his characters too often to be just one thing, and representing some moral virtue or deficit. I also find the dreadfully unlikely coincidences on which his tales often turn beyond the limits of credulity. I am afraid I enjoy more realistic works, for I have encountered no person to be one thing or representative of anything but him or herself."

Holmes, growing impatient with our literary banter, cleared his throat. Miss Sebastian heeded his prompt.

"As I was saying, I received a manuscript for a novel entitled *The Absent Man*, a copy of which is on the table, there. You may read it at your leisure. The work is by a gentleman named Isaac Masters Knott."

I happened to look at Holmes at that precise moment and saw him rolling his eyes. Sometimes, as earlier during his mirror gazing, he was unreadable. At other times, as with the clearing of his throat, he was exasperatingly obvious.

I pushed ahead. "And the reason you have come to see Mr. Holmes this day is . . . ?"

Holmes could no longer contain himself. "*The Absent Man* by I. M. Knott . . . John, really. Clearly, Miss Sebastian cannot get in touch with the author because Isaac Masters Knott is a nom de plume, and a rather ham-fisted one at that."

"Don't be too distressed, Doctor," Miss Sebastian said, blushing again. "It was not until I failed in all of my efforts to contact the author that I came to the realization about the title and his name. Of course, when I put it together, I felt so much the fool. But Mr. Holmes is quite right.

"Partridge House is most excited to enter into negotiations with the writer of the manuscript, whoever he may be, in order that we might publish it this coming autumn. To this point, all of our efforts to locate the author have led to naught. We have tried ourselves and have gone so far as to hire an expatriate American, a former Pinkerton detective. He, too, has made no progress."

Holmes got that familiar glint in his eye. For Sherlock Holmes, this was ideal. Not only was he taking on a new case, but in competition. Whether it was a vestige of his childhood relationship with Mycroft or simply an integral part of his nature, Holmes derived a particular delight in competition.

"Very well, Miss Sebastian," Holmes said, sounding as if he had a hundred better things to do, "I'll locate this absent man for you. Have you the name and address of this American?"

She reached into her small bag and handed Holmes a slip of paper and a calling card. Miss Sebastian stood. "Thank you, Mr. Holmes. I cannot express how pleased I am to know you and Dr. Watson are on the case."

Holmes and I escorted her to the stairs.

"Thank you, Dr. Watson, for making me feel so at ease. When this affair is over with, I would very much enjoy a continuation of our discussion on Dickens, and other writers on whom we might share more commonality of opinion."

"I would enjoy that very much."

I can't say what it was that drove me to do it, but I took the opportunity to kiss her hand in the continental manner. In spite of her attractiveness, it wasn't a matter of carnal desire or flirtation. That much I can say.

"Mr. Holmes, I'm afraid I misspoke when I said that the detective we hired had made *no* progress. Please do consult with him."

"I shall, of course. I am, after all, a consulting detective."

I was stunned at Holmes's attempt at low humor. It seemed Miss Sebastian's presence had affected the both of us.

When she had gone, I turned to Holmes. "There is something about that woman."

"She is indeed very lovely and her perfume is made for her and her alone."

"But it isn't that. There is an air about her that I cannot adequately describe."

"Tragedy."

I wasn't having it. "Don't be ridiculous, Holmes."

"I am never ridiculous."

Now it was my turn to roll my eyes. "We shan't argue the point, but I was not thinking of tragedy when discussing her *je ne sais quoi*."

"Yet it is there, John, like the richer and more elusive aspects of her perfume, lingering in the air just beneath the obvious and perceptible."

"But on what basis can you proffer such a judgment? She is distressed by the circumstance of the manuscript and its author, certainly. Still, I heard no words from her that indicated a tragic situation. There was nothing in her tone that hinted at it. Nothing in her actions."

"It was not in her actions that I became sure of my judgment."

"Blast, Holmes, make some sense."

"It was not in her actions, but in our reactions to her as males of the species. Not even I am immune to the allure of a woman and tragedy. Our urge to rescue is primal."

I considered asking him to explain further, but whether I understood how he had arrived at his conclusion or not, I knew he was correct.

The American's garret was above a Hebrew's tailor shop and family flat, down a grubby little street in Deptford, only several hundred yards from the spot on which Christopher Marlowe was mortally wounded. I nodded at the Hebrew as we passed the window of his establishment. He nodded in return, lowering his spectacles to the tip of his nose, following our progress.

After hearing our unsuccessful attempts at getting the American to come to the door, the tailor stopped pumping the foot pedal of his machine and came out of his shop to inquire as to our purpose.

"May I be of assistance?"

I answered, "We would very much like to speak to the gentleman who rents the upper-level flat."

The Hebrew laughed a joyless laugh. "This American is no gentleman. He is a *shiker* like you shouldn't know from it," said the bent man, nodding upward, holding his skullcap against the wind. "I wouldn't be surprised if he was dead up there."

I was confused. "*Shiker?*"

"A sot," Holmes said.

"Yes, yes, a drinker. Still, he pays his rent and makes no trouble. There is a great sadness in him, this fellow. He is scarred. Do you mind me asking who you gentlemen are and why you are wishing to see him?"

"My name is Dr. John Watson and this is Sherlock Holmes. We have business with him."

The Hebrew's eyes widened and he extended his right hand. "Such an honour to make your acquaintance, gentlemen. I am Chaim Rosenbaum and I have read about your—"

Holmes interrupted. "You say there is a great sadness in him and he bears scars. Has he ever discussed these subjects with you?"

"Mr. Holmes, my people know from sadness and scars. Our history is more sadness and scars than almost anything else. Some of this man's scars are plain to see. Some, not so much. He is not a Jew, but he is a fellow traveler. Of this, you can be certain."

The tailor then reached into his pocket, removed a small keyring, found the correct key, and unlatched the door. When that was done, he retreated to his shop.

Although Rosenbaum's remark about the American being dead was, I suppose, meant to be facetious, it was, unfortunately, correct. We found the American supine in bed, barely clothed, his unseeing eyes open. The skin of his neck was still warm to the touch. A cloying, bitter odor in the air cut through the stench of fresh death and the ambient tang of raw alcohol. Holmes and I immediately and simultaneously recognized the scent of laudanum.

"The tailor may not have had this man's addictions diagnosed perfectly well. He was, however, spot on about his scars." I stepped back from the bed, pointing at the corpse. "Prominent scarring on both legs. Observe the type and placement of the scar tissue on his upper right arm. I would venture to say the wound there was caused by a large diameter bullet. Those suture scars on the far left side of his abdomen are from the repair of puncture wounds. This chap's body tells a sad history."

"Curious."

"How so, Holmes?"

"How old would you estimate him to have been?"

"Forty at most."

"I concur. At first blush one might be tempted to attribute all of his scarring to his having participated in the American Civil War."

"That would be wrong."

"Precisely, John. Some of the scarring, like that from the wounds, is aged and faded and is indicative of hasty, slipshod battlefield surgery. The bullet wound, while not recent, is fresher. The suture scarring of puncture wounds even more so."

"He must have been in constant pain, hence that tincture of opium. A curse in itself that killed him in the end."

"I'm not at all certain of that." Holmes approached the body, knelt down beside the bed, and removed a small magnifying glass from the pocket of his waistcoat. "As I suspected. An opiate may well be the cause of his demise, but not from the laudanum. See for yourself."

He handed me the glass and pressed his index finger to a spot on the inside of the dead man's forearm.

"Yes, Holmes, I see it, a tiny puncture wound. But what's to say this wasn't self-inflicted?"

Holmes laughed. "Did you stumble upon a syringe?"

"Point taken."

"A theme emerges, John."

"A theme?"

"Another absent man. Another man who is not."

"Is it safe to assume the author is this man's killer?"

"Nothing is safe. What we need to understand is our part in this."

"How so?"

"Were Miss Sebastian's intentions pure? Did she seek out my help simply as a last resort or was the entire point to involve me?"

"Holmes, I am never quite sure which of your foibles is the stronger: your paranoia or your narcissism. Can you really imagine this man's murder as nothing more than a means to pull you more deeply into the case?"

He waved a dismissive hand. "Of course. I think an unplanned visit to Miss Sebastian is in order, but first, some research."

Partridge House was located on the Strand, very near a slight bend in the Thames. We were greeted by a junior clerk, a lad whose red neck was chafed by his too-tight collar.

"Who is it you wish to see, gentlemen?"

"Miss Rosetta Sebastian."

The lad's face went utterly blank. "Excuse me, gentlemen, can you please repeat the name?"

I did so, putting the clerk's ignorance down to his apparent newness in the position.

"Whom shall I say is calling?" he asked, stalling for time, thumbing furiously through the registry.

"Dr. John Watson and Mr. Sherlock Holmes."

"Pardon me, sir. Did you say you were Dr. John Wat—"

"—son, yes, and Mr. Sher—"

"—lock Holmes?" The clerk's face turned as red as his chafed neck. "I am terribly sorry, gentlemen, but there is no person by that name listed in our firm's registry."

Holmes removed Miss Sebastian's calling card from his pocket and handed it to the lad. The young man had a queer reaction. He could not contain a laugh.

"Very good, Mr. Holmes," he said. "I've read about tricks like this in the penny dreadfuls. Inks that are invisible to the naked eyes that must be treated with chemicals to be seen. I like it, sir. I like it very much."

I'd had quite enough. "What are you going on about, boy?"

He handed to me the card Holmes had handed to him. It was blank.

"Holmes, what is going—"

Anticipating Holmes's next move, the clerk handed him the registry. "You can see for yourselves, sir, there is no one by the name of Sebastian employed here."

"Would it be possible for us to see the publisher, do you think?" Holmes asked.

"I have no doubt that he will want to meet you gentlemen."

While we waited for the clerk to have a note brought upstairs to the publisher, Holmes deflected any of my attempts to question him as to what he believed was going on. He was deep in thought and considered my questions to be like the whining of mosquito wings in the dark.

Ten minutes later, we were seated across an ornate, warship-sized walnut desk from Helton Partridge. Partridge was a corpulent man in his late sixties, his face hidden behind enormous grey muttonchops and overgrown mustache. A ring of untamed steel-colored hair formed an untidy U around his bald pate. His distracted eyes were a faded blue and not even a meeting with the great detective seemed to focus him.

"Yes, gentlemen, what's this nonsense all about? Some woman claiming to work here as an editor? Ridiculous. Ridiculous."

I explained the situation while Holmes observed. Partridge shook his head the entire time as if physically denying every word that sprang from my lips.

"As I say, ridiculous."

"Yes," Holmes commented, "as you say."

"A manuscript . . . *The Absent Man* . . . Never heard of it. Isaac Masters Knott, never heard the name. Rosetta Sebastian. An American murdered in Deptford . . . Ridiculous. Ridiculous, all of it. Well, if this manuscript does exist, send it my way. Now, if you'll excuse me . . ." He didn't bother finishing the sentence.

When we exited onto the street, Holmes was quite breathless and hailed a cab.

"What is it, Holmes?"

There was both a twinge of dread and a sparkle of delight in his eyes as he answered, "The manuscript."

"What of it?"

"Is there an *it*, if *it* never was?"

"Not that bent again."

The cab pulled to a stop in front of us before I could ask Holmes to explain.

"221 Baker Street, double quick," Holmes told the driver. "There's an extra shilling in it for you if you can get your horse to cooperate."

"Don't you fret none about that, sir," said the sooty-faced cabman, touching the bill of his tall hat. "Old Padraig will have us there in jig time."

When we pulled up in front of 221, Inspector Lestrade was pacing a rut into the street in front of the flat.

"Pay the fare, old man, while I attend to Lestrade. And, John, do remember to give him that promised shilling."

Holmes was out of the cab before I could respond. Sometimes it was difficult for me not to suspect Holmes of wanting to bankrupt me one cab fare at a time. Even as I handed the coins up to the driver, I could hear the anger in Lestrade's voice.

"I've had just about enough of your games, Mr. Sherlock Holmes. I really have. I realize there is usually a point to your methods, but what do you mean by wasting Scotland Yard's time and me own on false reports? A murdered American, indeed."

But if I expected Holmes to act surprised or shocked by Lestrade's assertion, I was to be severely disappointed. He seemed almost reassured.

"Would I be correct in my assumption that when you and your men arrived at the address in Deptford that you found no body, and that when you went to interview the tailor at his shop the shop was closed, and no Mr. Rosenbaum was to be found?"

"You would, Holmes. Now would you care to explain all this to me?"

"I assure you, Lestrade, I would be glad to at some time in the future when I come to understand it myself. What I can say without question is that someone has gone to great lengths to impart a lesson."

"A lesson?"

"A lesson. Now, if you'll excuse me, Lestrade, it has been a long and taxing day."

"I know better than to expect an apology from the likes of you, Mr. Sherlock Holmes, so I'll be on my way. And you can keep your explanations to yourself, thank you very much. All the explaining in the world won't give me or my men our time back."

Inspector Lestrade strode over to me as our cab drove away. "I'll confide in you that at times, Dr. Watson, I envy you, but on days like this one I want no part of your friend Mr. Holmes. Good day."

I watched Lestrade head off in the opposite direction from our cab.

"Watson, come up here."

"What is it, for heaven's sake?" I said even as I walked into the house behind him.

Just before he reached the kitchen, Holmes came to a sudden stop and turned. The aroma of herb-roasted chicken was powerful. One didn't require the deductive skills of Sherlock Holmes to know that Mrs. Hudson was gathering china and silverware to set the table. All one needed was ears.

"Listen to me carefully, Watson," Holmes whispered. "If I'm right, some of Mrs. Hudson's responses to my questions will . . . surprise you. I urge you not to challenge her, for it will serve only to upset and confuse her. Do I have your word?"

"Holmes, what is this—"

"Your word?"

"Of course, Holmes. You have my word."

I followed Holmes into the kitchen and Mrs. Hudson's face brightened at the sight of us and then she feigned anger. "And what are the two of you doing in my kitchen?"

"Please forgive us," I said.

"Yes, I beg your indulgence, Mrs. Hudson," Holmes seconded, mustering all the charm he could. "But I was wondering if you could help settle a small dispute between Dr. Watson and myself?"

"If I can."

"Very well. John claims that a woman came calling on us this morning at ten and that you showed her up to our flat and I say he's mistaken."

"I'm afraid Mr. Holmes is right, Dr. Watson. There was no one who came calling today."

I opened my mouth to argue, then remembered my word to Holmes and the bizarre nature of the entire day, beginning with Holmes's mirror gazing.

"Thank you, Mrs. Hudson," I said and raced up the stairs.

She called after me, saying something about cleaning up for dinner, but all I could think of was the neatly bundled manuscript we had left on the table in the parlor. It was gone. Of course it was. Holmes came up behind me, a smug smile on his face.

"Did you actually think it would be there, John?"

"I hoped more than expected."

"What is this all about, Holmes? A desperate woman who doesn't exist, a dead man gone, a calling card with disappearing print, a manuscript vanished. I overheard you saying something about a lesson to Lestrade."

"A lesson is most assuredly being taught."

"What lesson is that?"

"I believe we are each meant to draw our own conclusions from the evidence with which we have been presented today."

"And who, pray tell, was the teacher in this scenario?" I wondered.

"A most devilishly shrewd and clever instructor."

"Moriarty?"

Holmes gave me that dismissive laugh. "No, no, John. Someone even more sly and cunning than the Professor."

"Mycroft?"

"Really, John, you do credit my brother beyond his talents."

"Then who is it, man?"

Holmes smiled and said, "I believe dinner is served. Best clean up or face the wrath of Mrs. Hudson."

I thought it only good form to let it go until dinner was over with, afters had been finished, and the dishes had been cleaned away.

"Holmes," I said at last, "can you please answer me this one question. Am I going mad or was there a lovely woman here today bearing a manuscript and a story?"

"I cannot say with any certainty, Watson. I surely cannot prove it beyond what would be your corroboration. Can you prove it beyond mine? Goodnight, Watson."

Hours after Holmes had retired and I had turned the day's events over in my mind so many times that I had even begun to doubt my own part in it all, I caught a faint trace in the air of sandalwood and patchouli. Suddenly it came to me. I understood the lesson and realized my tutor had long ago gone to bed. As I shut my eyes, I carried the scent of perfume with me into sleep, a question ringing in my ears: "Am I here, Watson?"

THE ADVENTURE OF THE SIX SHERLOCKS

by Toni L. P. Kelner

Tilda Harper had just picked up her Baker Street Con name badge and swag bag when the argument broke out.

"I can't believe you're taking Noah Anderson's side," said Sherlock Holmes. Well, said *a* Sherlock Holmes. From where she stood, Tilda could see nearly a dozen incarnations of the famous fictional sleuth scattered around the hotel lobby: most were wearing the classic deerstalker cap and Inverness cape, some had dressed as modern TV and movie versions, and a sprinkling had chosen interpretations like Space Sherlock and 1960s Sherlock. There were also quite a few Dr. Watsons and a couple of Irene Adlers, *the* Woman whom Holmes admired from afar.

The disbelieving Sherlock, who wore traditional Holmes garb, went on. "Anderson screwed up. He shouldn't have been cooking with peanuts. The whole point of his portion of the show was—"

A Sherlock dressed like the Jonny Lee Miller Holmes in *Elementary* said, "What do you mean 'his portion of the show'? *Sherlock's Home* was his show! He wrote it, he produced it, he was the host. Lee just acted out snippets from the stories—Anderson was the expert."

"Then why was Anderson serving peanuts? Peanuts aren't Canonical."

"Technically, no, but they were eaten in Victorian England," *Elementary* Sherlock said. "And it wasn't peanuts—it was peanut oil. Nobody would have known the difference if Lee hadn't been allergic."

"Michael Lee almost died, which is why you never cook with peanut products without asking about allergies."

"Most kinds of peanut oil are perfectly safe, even for people with allergies. And if Lee was that allergic, why didn't he ask before eating? Why wasn't he wearing a medic alert bracelet?"

Traditional Sherlock threw up his hands in disgust. "He was in costume! Of course he wouldn't have worn something so far out of period."

A gender-swapped Watson wearing a tweed skirt, matching jacket, high heels, and a trilby hat joined in. "If either of you knew anything about television, you'd know Anderson didn't do the cooking. That's what production assistants are for."

"So what?" Traditional Sherlock said. "Anderson must have provided the recipe."

"As if nobody ever substituted an ingredient in a recipe," Gender-swap Watson retorted.

"I still say it's the responsibility of the person with dietary limitations to check on the ingredients," *Elementary* Sherlock insisted.

"You're all assuming that Lee is actually allergic," said a woman in a tailored Inverness cape and a classier-than-usual deerstalker. "I heard he was just faking the allergy to get out of his contract."

"If you believe that, you ought to be working with Lestrade," said a Sherlock in a coat and scarf à la Benedict Cumberbatch. "It wasn't a fake allergy and it definitely wasn't an accident. Anderson was insanely jealous of Lee's popularity when it was supposed to be his show! He used peanuts on purpose, and he didn't care if Lee died or just quit."

Gender-swap Watson scoffed. "Seriously? The show barely lasted a month with Lee's replacement—those episodes were so bad they didn't even put them on the DVD. You really think Anderson torpedoed his own show on purpose?"

Cumberbatch Sherlock rolled his eyes. "Of course he didn't expect that. He thought that with a less charismatic actor playing Holmes, everybody would love him instead, so he recruited a production assistant or something. He was delusional."

"*Somebody* is delusional," Gender-swap Watson muttered.

Tilda thought all of them were delusional if they expected to change anybody else's mind. What had come to be known as the Food Feud had been raging for two years, ever since the basic cable show *Sherlock's Home* was canceled.

As it turned out, the feud would be definitively settled later that weekend, but nobody knew it then.

Tilda moved along, dodging people taking selfies in front of cardboard backdrops of Holmesian locations like 221b Baker Street, Scotland Yard, and a hansom cab. It was only Baker Street Con's second year, but it had drawn a good crowd of Sherlock Holmes fans, enough so that they could afford to comp Tilda's hotel room and meals in return for her moderating a few panels. The idea that she would write an article or three reflecting well on the con was unspoken, but hinted at, and in return, Tilda had hinted that she would appreciate private interviews with con guests of honor Noah Anderson and Michael Lee, the former stars of *Sherlock's Home*.

"Tilda! Tilda!"

She looked toward the hotel bar and spotted a familiar face. Vincent Peters was hanging over the low railing that separated the bar from the lobby, waving wildly. "Come have a drink!"

She checked her watch, saw that she had over an hour until her first panel, and headed over.

"The only way to start a con is at the bar," Vincent said, pulling out a chair for her. "Which is also the perfect place to end a con. And honestly, when it's in a open area like this one, it's the best place to spend the majority of the con."

"It is a good view," Tilda admitted, "but how's the service?" She was haunted by the memories of overwhelmed hotel bars.

"Not a problem." Vincent waved at the waiter on duty, and miraculously, he came directly over, ignoring two other tables on the way. "Ed, this is Tilda Harper. Tilda is one of our pro guests."

"You're an actress?" he said.

"No, a freelance reporter."

"Tilda writes for *Entertain Me!* magazine. She found Mercy Ashford, broke the *Leviathan* story, and interviewed all the Cartwright Brides."

Ed looked blank.

"I specialize in classic and cult TV shows and movies," Tilda explained. *Classic* and *cult* sounded better than *totally obscure* or *formerly famous*.

"Sounds interesting," he said, though Tilda could tell he didn't mean it. "What can I get you?"

"A Coke, please."

"And an order of nachos," Vincent added. "With—"

"With extra cheese. Got it," Ed said and left.

Tilda was impressed. "At the risk of sounding like a cliché, do you come here often?"

"Listen and learn. There are three things to do to get great service at an understaffed, overcrowded convention bar."

"All convention bars are understaffed and overcrowded. It's tradition."

"True. So Step 1: Come early, the night before, if you can swing it. Then you'll have time to get a drink or a snack at the bar before things go crazy, so you can move on to the next step."

"Which is?"

"Step 2: Make friends with the wait staff. Use their names, ask where they're from, find out about their families. Ed, for instance, is the single father of a college student named Penny."

"You learned all of that since you got here?"

"Well, no. I met Ed and Penny here last year, and I take notes, which is how I knew that Penny is studying theater at Emerson. That's why he asked if you're an actress."

"Because a pro actress might be able to help her in the business?"

"Exactly. You can also ask if they're interested in the convention, but if they think we're weirdos, agree with them."

Tilda eyed a Steampunk Sherlock, complete with egregious gears and a pair of goggles, and a dude in a costume that mingled elements of Cumberbatch's outfit in the *Sherlock* series with the one from *Dr. Strange*. "Con attendees can be pretty odd."

"Of course we are—that's why we come to cons," Vincent said. "Step 3: Tip well. Not outrageously—then they figure you're trying to impress people or maybe you're drunk and they'll have to cut you off. Just a little higher than the norm. Follow those three steps and they'll treat you better than they do their own family."

Vincent's methods seemed to work. Ed arrived a moment later with her soda and promised that the nachos would be following soon.

"Truly, you are wise in the way of cons," Tilda said, though she couldn't help thinking that as a freelance writer, she usually couldn't afford extra nights at a hotel or hotel-priced drinks. When she wasn't being comped, she could barely tip adequately, let alone generously. At least she was good with names, and might be able to fake the friendly part. "I wasn't expecting to see you here this weekend—I didn't realize you were such a Sherlock Holmes fan."

"Are you kidding? I'm a Sherlockian, a Cumberbunny, an Elementapeep, and a Sherlock's Homeboy. Which are you?"

"Just somebody who likes Sherlock Holmes." She'd read the Doyle books and seen enough theatrical productions that she'd had to do very little prep for the weekend, but she didn't think she was devout enough to deserve a title.

Vincent, on the other hand, never liked anything without becoming an ardent fan. Though he was an entirely average-looking man in height, build, and features, even in the world of fandom he stood out because of his pure, unbridled enthusiasm. Since many of his favorites were on the obscure, formerly famous side, he was a great source of information.

"I am really looking forward to your first panel," Vincent said. "I volunteered as room monitor to make sure I get a good seat."

"You think it's going to be crowded?"

"Are you kidding? It'll be standing room only. This is the first time Noah Anderson and Michael Lee have appeared together since Lee walked off the set of *Sherlock's Home*! Everybody wants to hear about what happened."

"Then they'll be disappointed. I'm not supposed to mention the Food Feud or entertain questions about it from the audience. It will be referred to if, and only if, Anderson or Lee bring it up, and since they're the ones who made the rules, that's not likely. I think the reason I was asked to moderate the panel is because I haven't taken sides."

"Of course. In your position, you can't say anything publicly." He lowered his voice. "But privately? What do you think? Did Anderson do it on purpose, or did Lee fake it all?"

"Not saying a word." She resisted his entreaties to give her opinion. Even the bribe of half the plate of nachos didn't sway her, especially since she knew Vincent would let her share anyway. When he finally gave up, they traded movie gossip while noshing on nachos until it was time for Tilda to go.

She said, "I'm heading on to the panel room. Somebody is supposed to meet me there and introduce me to Lee and Anderson."

"I'll come with to make sure the room's ready. You know, room monitor stuff."

"And if you get a chance to meet Lee and/or Anderson, that would just be a lucky happenstance."

"Of course." Vincent left cash to cover their tab, plus a tip that matched his criteria. Then he surveyed the lobby, which had grown considerably more crowded as additional Sherlocks, Watsons, and even non-costumed fans arrived for the weekend. "Fortunately, I know a shortcut to the big ballroom."

"Because of course you scoped out the layout ahead of time."

"When it comes to cons, I'm Sherlock Holmes. You can be my Watson."

If it got her where she was going, she would accept that.

The door Vincent led her through was marked EMPLOYEES ONLY, but as they made their circuitous way through utility corridors, she spotted at least one person in a deerstalker and Inverness cape, so perhaps others were following the teachings of Vincent. They emerged from a door in the back of the bland hotel ballroom.

"Hey, Regina," Vincent said to a sturdy-looking woman with a long dark brown braid and a blood-red t-shirt with IRREGULAR printed on it. "Tilda, this is Regina—she's in charge of con security. They're calling them the Irregulars because—"

"Dude, I know who the Baker Street Irregulars are," Tilda said.

"Regina, this is Tilda—she's moderating the panel."

Tilda said, "I'm supposed to meet Lee and Anderson ahead of time."

"Right. I'll be escorting them from the green room shortly. And just so you know, when I met Lee last year, he was kind of a jerk. Thinks he's hot stuff."

"I've seen the type before."

"Anderson is okay, I guess, but he won't talk to Lee, and Lee won't talk to him."

"That sounds lovely," Tilda said dryly. In her experience, the best panels included plenty of back-and-forth between panelists. Apparently this was not going to be one of those panels.

The walkie-talkie at Regina's belt buzzed. "That's probably them now. Excuse me."

After Regina left, Tilda said, "Vincent, is meeting con staff part of your convention prep?"

"The trick is to volunteer to help with setup. I spent hours last night stuffing con swag bags—we bonded over that." He went to chat with other Irregulars at the front of the room. If he didn't know them already, he would soon.

Tilda saw that the setup for the panel was the usual convention design: a low platform, a long table with a white tablecloth that faced the audience, chairs with a modicum of padding, microphones, and cardboard name tents to identify the panelists.

As a nice touch, reusable water bottles had been left for each of them. Two had labels with names on them in script letters. *Noah* and *Michael*. The third had *Moderator*—written in marker. Tilda accepted it philosophically. Once the celebrities she was interviewing got engraved glass mugs while she got a red Solo cup.

She was checking her notes when the back door opened.

Noah Anderson entered first. He was a distinguished man, and Tilda saw he was wearing the same style of academic chic he'd adopted while hosting *Sherlock's Home*: a tweed jacket with suede elbow patches. Behind him came Michael Lee. Lee was more handsome than the traditional Sherlock Holmes, but he had the requisite long, aquiline nose and dark brows. Tilda had wondered if he'd dress in an Inverness cape, but he was wearing tight-fitting jeans and a button-down shirt, with a black leather backpack slung over one shoulder at a determinedly casual angle.

Regina, looking annoyed, followed them inside. "Mr. Lee, Mr. Anderson, this is Tilda Harper, who will be moderating your event today."

Anderson cordially shook her hand and said, "Call me Noah, please." Lee just nodded.

As Regina had warned, the two men did not speak to each other. In fact, they were working hard to not even look at each other.

Bowing to the inevitable, Tilda stood equidistant from the two men to explain her plans for the panel.

This time Anderson nodded, while Lee said, "And no mention of the incident, right?"

"Absolutely not. If anybody in the audience brings it up during Q&A, don't answer—I'll shut them down."

"Good." Lee almost turned his head in Anderson's direction, but stopped himself just in time.

Vincent pretended to ignore them as he attended to his room monitor duties: checking to make sure the microphones were working properly, removing detritus that had been left on the panelists' table, and putting a RESERVED FOR MONITOR sign on a chair in the front row. Once everything was arranged to his satisfaction, he glanced hopefully in Tilda's direction.

Figuring she owed him for the nachos and the shortcut, she said, "Hey, Vincent, can you come over here a minute?"

He didn't quite sprint.

"Gentlemen, this is Vincent Peters. He's our room monitor and will help keep us on schedule. If there's anything you need during the panel, just flash him the high sign."

"Anything at all!" Vincent put in.

Lee went back to perusing his Twitter feed, but Anderson offered Vincent a handshake and said, "Nice to meet you, Vincent. Looks as if we're in good hands."

Vincent beamed.

Tilda checked her watch. "We should sit down. They're going to let the crowd in soon."

Regina opened the doors while Tilda and her charges settled, and every seat in the room was quickly filled. Vincent kept busy greeting friends, but not so busy that he didn't let Tilda know when it was time to start. She cleared her throat and began.

There were grumbles when she announced that the Food Feud was off limits, but otherwise, the panel went well. Lee and Anderson kept the audience thoroughly entertained, and though they didn't interact, neither did they interrupt or run over one another. In fact, they were so well-behaved that Tilda started to wonder if they were really as antagonistic as she'd been led to believe. Could they have been playing up the Food Feud? Controversy kept fan interest high, and arguments between fans—like the one she'd seen in the lobby earlier—drove DVD sales and YouTube views.

As Anderson finished a funny story about researching Victorian era toilet paper, Vincent held up the fifteen minute warning sign, so Tilda went to her standard final question. "I'm going to open it to the audience in a moment, but I want to give Noah and Michael a chance to plug upcoming projects."

The two men looked at each other directly for the first time all evening, then grinned, as if they'd been waiting for somebody to ask that question. The audience could tell something was up, and phones came out, camera apps ready.

Anderson said, "There is an announcement I wasn't intending to make tonight, but we just can't keep it quiet anymore. *Sherlock's Home* is returning to television next year—with both Michael and myself on board." The two men stood as if they'd practiced—and they probably had—and shook hands, both going for a two-handed clasp that evolved into a manly hug. The standing ovation was deafening.

After that, there was no way they were ending the panel on time. It was ten minutes before people even calmed down enough to take their seats, and then Lee and Anderson took turns explaining that the feud had been blown completely out of proportion, and how they couldn't wait to work together again. Tilda thought Lee came off a little more genuine, but of course, he was an actor. At least Anderson was convincing enough that more trusting fans would report that the announcement was spontaneous instead of the publicity stunt Tilda suspected it to be. From the number of people tapping on their phones, the story was already trending on social media.

After fifteen more minutes of mutual admiration, Tilda saw Vincent emphatically waving the STOP sign. So she said, "I hate to do this, but we've got to clear this room for the next event. I want to thank both of you for letting us all be the first to know—"

Before she could finish her "thanks-and-get-out" spiel, somebody in the audience yelled, "A toast!" Others echoed the call, and Lee and Anderson were willing to oblige. They picked up their metal water bottles, clinked them—pausing just long enough for people to take more pictures—and took big swallows as the audience applauded once more.

Tilda was starting to gather her notes when she saw the expression on Lee's face change from a smile to a grimace. He opened his mouth as if to say something, but no words came out, and after a couple of labored breaths, he toppled over onto the platform.

That's when Anderson saw what was happening. "Michael! MICHAEL!"

"Vincent, call 911!" Tilda yelled. "Regina, get hotel security!" She thought she smelled peanuts when she knelt down beside Lee, and knew what that had to mean. He was wheezing so hard it hurt to hear, and there was a blue tinge around his mouth. She'd never realized how horrible anaphylactic shock was.

Anderson was crouched on the other side of Lee. "He needs his EpiPen."

Tilda patted the actor down the best she could, but there was nothing like that in his pockets. "Does he have a bag?"

Vincent joined them on the platform. "Here!" He pulled out Lee's backpack from under his chair and started rummaging around in it.

"Just dump it out!" Tilda said.

He did so, and a variety of stuff tumbled onto the platform. Tilda had never seen an EpiPen, but there was only one item that looked like a good possibility: a tube about the size and shape of a fat marker with an orange cap on one end and a blue one on the other. Vincent tried to hand it to her.

"I don't know how to use that," she objected.

"Me, neither."

They looked at Anderson, who shook his head.

"There are directions on the side," Vincent said, still trying to give it to Tilda. Then a guy dressed as Dr. Watson, with a ridiculous mustache that covered half his face, hopped onto the platform. "I'm a nurse—I know what to do."

Evidently he wasn't a trauma nurse, because he wasted valuable seconds by dropping the EpiPen back into the pile of Lee's belongings and having to fish it out again. Then he popped off the blue cap and jammed the EpiPen onto Lee's thigh so hard Tilda winced. He held it there for several seconds while they watched for a reaction.

There was no change.

"He must have gotten a big dose," Nurse Watson said. "Is there another EpiPen?"

Vincent scrambled around but found nothing in the backpack, so Tilda grabbed the microphone to yell, "Does anybody have an EpiPen? We need an EpiPen NOW!"

A Mrs. Hudson ran up. "Take it!"

Nurse Watson held out his hand for the EpiPen—which he promptly dropped just as he had the first one. Tilda wanted to push him out of the way and take over, but restrained herself until he found the thing and then used it on Lee's other leg.

Tilda could tell the second injection wasn't helping, either. If anything, Lee seemed worse.

"Why isn't it working?" Anderson said. He took Lee's hand. "Stay with me, Michael. Stay with me!"

A phalanx of panicked con and hotel staff members burst into the ballroom, but could do nothing but stand around watching Lee try to take a breath. An eternity later, hotel security led in two EMTs with a gurney, and Tilda backed out of their way, pulling Vincent with her.

They watched the EMTs work, but after a few minutes, they lifted Lee onto the gurney and wheeled him away, with Anderson following along. Tilda remembered Lee's scattered belongings, and scooped them all up to shove into his backpack, then trotted after them. She caught up with them in the lobby, and thrust the bag at Anderson. He murmured his thanks as they headed out the front door.

By the time Tilda got back to the ballroom, it had cleared out except for hotel staff prepping the room for the next event, but Vincent was waiting for her.

"He's going to be okay, right?" he asked.

"I don't know." She picked up her notes, got her satchel, and after a quick look to make sure she hadn't missed any of Lee's stuff, said, "Do you think your private waiter is on duty? I could use a drink."

The bar was full of people who'd seen Lee's collapse, but Ed squeezed them into a corner and brought beers promptly. Tilda craved something stronger, maybe several somethings, but as much as she hated the thought, she was going to have to write up both Anderson's announcement and what had happened to Lee.

"He's going to be okay, right?" Vincent asked again.

Tilda shrugged, and they quietly sipped their beers. Half an hour later, they got their answer. A cluster of people in the lobby started talking loudly, sounding upset. Vincent rushed off to find out what had happened, but Tilda was sure she knew even before he returned.

Michael Lee had died.

He'd never even made it to the hospital.

Though she wasn't normally a hugger, this once she allowed Vincent to tearfully embrace her as he told her the news. Truth be told, she kind of needed it. She'd seen death before, but not like this. She could still hear Lee struggling to breathe.

She and Vincent spent the rest of the evening at the bar. Neither had any interest in the other scheduled convention events and they shared an unwillingness to be alone. Instead Tilda reluctantly pulled out her laptop to write up the story.

Though she was normally as enthusiastic about breaking a story as any reporter, this time she took no pleasure in it.

At least she didn't have to go far for background material. The convention program provided plenty of detail about Lee's life, enough people came by their table to mine quotes for a dozen articles, and Vincent had several good photos of Lee and Anderson before Lee fell ill. Some of Vincent's friends offered shots of Lee afterward, including while the EMTs were working on him, but Tilda declined those with extreme prejudice.

The capstone to her piece would have been a quote from Anderson about his lost friend, but if he'd returned to the hotel, he'd done so discreetly. Conflicting accounts from Vincent's friends said he was suicidal, strangely unmoved, distraught but only for the sake of his TV deal, and under arrest for murdering Lee. Though Tilda and Vincent consulted their best sources, both at the con and online, Tilda was unable to find out which of the first three was the true story. She didn't give credence to the latter tale. Given that Lee and Anderson were poised to work together again, she couldn't imagine what Anderson's motive could have been.

Finally Tilda finished up several versions of her article for different markets and sent them off, feeling like a ghoul. While she indulged in another beer to reward and/or console herself, she listened to Vincent and acquaintances try to guess whether or not the convention would be canceled. Nobody knew for sure until nearly eleven, when Regina came to their table.

"I thought you'd want to know that the convention will continue as planned," she said. "Well, mostly as planned. We're canceling the Victorian dance Saturday night—it didn't seem appropriate. And we've moved two panels Sunday morning to make room for a memorial service. Mr. Anderson says it's what Mr. Lee would have wanted."

"And the police are okay with that?" Tilda asked. "Aren't they investigating?"

"Oh, they've come and gone. Anderson told the cops that somebody was eating peanuts on the flight from Vancouver—Lee texted him all about it. He had a mild reaction to them but took an antihistamine, and thought he was okay. It wasn't until the panel that he had what they call a delayed reaction. They're rare, but can affect people hours later."

"Why didn't the EpiPen work? He had two injections."

"Was it because it took me so long to find the EpiPen?" Vincent asked. "Or because I was afraid to use it?"

"It wasn't you, Vincent. EpiPens don't always work, even when they're administered immediately. You did everything right—Lee's death was just a tragic accident." She left to continue spreading the word about schedule changes.

Tilda took a final swallow of beer. "I should get up to my room. I'm moderating another panel in the morning." She didn't remember what the topic was, but she'd wing it if necessary.

"You're just going to leave it like this?" Vincent said.

"Leave what like what?"

"Of course, you're a reporter, not a detective, but you have done this kind of thing before."

"What kind of thing?"

"Solving murders." Before she could answer, he went on. "Tilda, I know the way I overprepare for a con amuses you, but cons are important to me. Especially these days, when the country is in such a mess. All the fighting."

"Like the Food Feud?"

"That's a safe argument. We all know— Well, most of us know it's just a distraction from real life. Family members would never quit talking to me because of the Food Feud, not like they do over politics."

"Oh."

"Yeah. So I need this oasis, and I need it to be safe, without a murderer running loose."

"Regina said the police are satisfied it was an accident."

"They didn't even question us."

"Which means they didn't need to."

"Or that somebody covered his or her tracks." He lowered his voice. "Lee got sick immediately after the toast, which was the first time he'd drunk from his bottle. I videoed the whole panel, so you can watch if you don't believe me."

"I believe you, but—"

"And I smelled peanuts when I was on the platform."

"I thought I did, too, but it should be easy enough to test. Except—" She stopped.

"What?"

"Right before we left the ballroom, I looked to see if anything from Lee's bag had been shoved under the table. There was nothing."

"So?"

"So where were the water bottles?"

"Did the EMTs grab them? For testing?"

"Maybe. I don't suppose you filmed them working on Lee."

"God, no!" He looked resigned. "But I know other people did."

"Then our first step is for you to track down those people and look at their footage. Find out what happened to the water bottles."

"Does that mean you're taking the case?"

She knew she should have said *absolutely not*, but Michael Lee had been poisoned in front of a whole roomful of people who'd been doing just what Vincent said, taking a respite from the world's ugliness. She wasn't a big con goer herself, but she recognized their importance—the appeal wasn't that different from that of her work. "Let's just say I'm following the story."

"Excellent! We'll be like Holmes and Watson!"

"Vincent, you know I don't play well with others." That was why she was happier as a freelancer, rather working an actual job, and why she was once again between roommates. "Yes, I've done this kind of thing before, but I've always worked alone."

"But—" He took a breath, turned toward the lobby, and started pointing people out. "See that guy over there? He writes some of the best *Elementary* fanfic on the web. That woman? She's a college prof, and teaches the canon in her classroom. Those two teenagers don't even like Sherlock Holmes, but they come every year to spend time with their grandfather."

"And this matters why?"

"It matters because I'm a Sherlockian, which you said you're not. I know these people and I know the fandom. You need me."

He had a point. Look at how he knew all about Ed. Tilda had been eating at the same restaurant at least once a week for years, and only remembered the serving staff's names if they were wearing nametags. Maybe she didn't need Vincent, but having him on board would make things a lot easier. "Okay, we'll work together. Just remember, I'm Holmes."

"Yes!" He started to pump his fist in the air, but Tilda stopped him in mid-pump.

"Vincent, this is not a game. You have to be careful."

"Absolutely." But he couldn't keep from grinning.

Tilda was expecting to help Vincent track down video and photos, but he said he could handle it better on his own. So after getting his promise not to go down shadowy corridors with suspicious characters, she went up to her room. As she got ready for bed, she admitted there might be something to the idea of having a Watson after all.

As soon as she woke up the next morning, she checked her phone and found a series of texts from Vincent:

11:45 P.M.: Found proof. The only thing the EMTs took were the used EpiPens for disposal. Didn't touch water bottles.

12:45 A.M.: Can't find photos of anyone taking water bottles.

1:05 A.M.: Have a lead re: water bottles.

2:15 A.M.: Giving up for the night.

There'd been no additional reports, probably because Vincent was still sleeping. So she went to her morning panel, an interview with a YouTuber who'd adopted the persona of Schlock Holmes and dressed in a cheap Inverness cape and deerstalker to film humorous reviews of bad B-movies. Since he'd never made the mistake of mocking a Sherlock Holmes movie, the panel was controversy-free. Just in case, she'd brought sealed bottled water from the gift shop for herself and Schlock.

After the panel, which was reasonably entertaining considering that Schlock was hungover, she received another text from Vincent.

10:30 A.M.: May have a witness. Meet me in bar.

She found him with sodas and nachos already on the table, looking like a kid waiting for Santa Claus, and suspected that despite her warning, he was enjoying their "case" more than he should. "You found a witness?"

"And it wasn't easy. First I hunted for pictures and video, and verified that the EMTs did not take the water bottles."

"So you said in your text. But you found a witness?"

"Unfortunately, nobody filmed anything showing where the water bottles went."

"So you said in your text," she repeated. "Did you find a witness?"

"One picture did show hotel staff members starting to straighten up the room. That would have been while you were returning Lee's backpack." He looked embarrassed. "I was talking to people, so I didn't notice them."

"One, you were upset. Two, you're not Sherlock Holmes so you don't remember everything you see. Three, neither am I, because I didn't notice them either. And four: witness or no witness?"

"Witness. I found footage of one of the people assigned to ballroom cleanup, and I recognized her. She's coming by with the whole crew. That took some doing." He started to explain a process that Tilda imagined would include three or four levels of networking, but fortunately they were interrupted by a trio in burgundy hotel uniform shirts: a trim black man, an older Asian woman, and a girl with streaks of purple in her pixie cut hair.

"Vincent?" the girl said hesitantly.

"Penny? Your hair looks fabulous! Tilda, this is Ed's daughter, Penny. I met her at last year's con. Penny, this is Tilda. Penny, I don't know your friends."

"This is Samuel and Mrs. Dao."

"Please, have a seat." He arranged chairs so they could all sit.

Tilda was used to thinking of Vincent as kind of a goof, but he was good with people. Maybe they were more like Holmes and Watson than she'd realized.

"Did Regina speak to you?" he said.

"Yeah, she said something was left in the ballroom after—" Penny faltered. "After what happened."

"I'm sorry," Vincent said. "I remember from last year that you were a big fan of Michael Lee's. This must be really upsetting."

She looked away. "No, not a fan. I mean I'm sorry about what happened to him, but—"

"We found nothing in the ballroom," Mrs. Dao said firmly. "If anything was taken, it was not by us."

"That's right," Samuel agreed.

Vincent said, "Of course not! We're not accusing you guys!"

He was so upset about upsetting them that Tilda took over. "Did you guys set up the room, too?"

"Yes," Penny said nervously.

"Okay, I was on that panel with Anderson and Lee, and when I got to the ballroom, there were three water bottles on the table. Can you tell us who put them there?"

"Metal bottles?" Samuel said.

Tilda nodded.

"I saw those when I came to check that the mics were hooked up."

"They didn't come from us," Penny said. "I brought in a pitcher of water and glasses for the head table like usual, but since the bottles were already there, I just made sure they were filled and took the other stuff away."

"So none of you know who put the bottles there?"

All three of them shook their heads.

"What about afterward?"

"We came back just before they took that poor guy away," Samuel said. "Once he was gone, we started straightening the room."

"Did you see what happened to the water bottles then?"

Penny and Samuel shook their heads again, but Mrs. Dao said, "Yes, a man took them."

"Who?"

"One of your people. He came in through the door behind the platform—it's supposed to be employees only, but I keep seeing guests in there." She gave Vincent and Tilda a significant look. "He picked up all three bottles, put them in one of the bags they've been giving away, and went out the same way he came in."

"Did you recognize him?" Tilda asked.

Mrs. Dao raised an eyebrow. "Sure. It was Sherlock Holmes."

Tilda and Vincent stared at each other. At least Vincent was staring—Tilda was pretty sure she was glaring.

She finally said, "Vincent, how many people are at this con?"

"I think registration got up to six hundred."

"How many of them would you say are dressed as Sherlock Holmes?"

They looked around the lobby. There were plenty of people who weren't in costume or were in other Sherlockian costumes ranging from Inspector Lestrade to a Solitary Cyclist, but there were still an awful lot of Sherlocks.

"Maybe a tenth?"

"So sixty Sherlocks."

"If we lined them up and walked them past Mrs. Dao—"

"I only saw him for a minute," Mrs. Dao objected. "I couldn't pick him out."

Of course not, Tilda thought. No, they'd have to investigate all sixty Sherlocks. With a month and a lot of luck, it would be no problem. Unfortunately, they had just over twenty-four hours until the convention ended.

More Sherlocks came out of the elevator and lined up for the photo backdrops. At least she could cross one off the list—some guy had an impressively realistic skeleton costume under his Inverness cape and deerstalker, and a nametag that said SHERLOCK BONES. Mrs. Dao would have noticed a skeleton. All she had to do was use the process of elimination on the other fifty-nine Sherlocks.

She considered that thought, taking long enough that the trio of hotel employees was getting restless when she finally spoke.

"Vincent, remember when I said that murder isn't a game? I was wrong. Solving this murder *is* going to be a game." Tilda knew she was going to hate herself for saying what came next, but she couldn't resist. "And the game is afoot!"

Two hours later, she, Vincent, Mrs. Dao, Regina, and as many Irregulars as could be spared were in Security HQ, which is what Regina called the spare function room cluttered with equipment, a mix of full and empty soda bottles, and a lot of pizza boxes.

"Ms. Dao, these guys have photos of most, if not all, of the people at the con dressed as Sherlock Holmes." Tilda, Vincent, and the Irregulars had gone through their own files and social media accounts galore. It helped that most of the people who'd used the backdrops in the lobby had used the Baker Street Con hashtag.

Mrs. Dao looked skeptical, but said "I'll try, but like I said, I didn't get a close look at the guy." The only reason she'd come was the tip Vincent had offered. For once he'd broken his rule and gone for extravagant. "I could flip through pictures all day and still not be sure."

"You're not going to look at the pictures—we are."

"Huh?"

"I used to have a board game called Guess Who?, kind of a kids' version of Twenty Questions. Players had pictures of suspects, and would use questions to find a criminal through process of elimination. 'Was it a man?' If *yes*, you'd eliminate the women. 'Does he have facial hair?' If *no*, you'd check off the men with beards and mustaches. Eventually you got down to the answer. So I'm going to ask questions, and these guys will go through their pictures and see if we can eliminate some of the Sherlocks."

"Okay." She sounded marginally less skeptical.

"First question. Was the Sherlock you saw a man or a woman?"

"Man."

"You're sure?" Tilda had seen several gender-swapped Sherlocks.

"Either a man or a really unendowed woman, and he moved like a man. Like my daughter says, the person presented as a man."

"People, take the obvious women off of your lists."

She waited for the Irregulars to go through their files, then went on.

"You said he was dressed as Sherlock Holmes. So he was wearing a deerstalker and Inverness cape, right?"

"What's that?"

"A double-billed cap, and a half-cape, half-coat thing. The stereotypical Sherlock Holmes costume."

"Of course. I told you it was Sherlock Holmes."

"Good. That eliminates the *Elementary* and *Sherlock* cosplayers."

"The flashback episode of *Sherlock* had Holmes and Watson wearing Victorian dress," a pedantic Irregular said.

"Fine. Then it eliminates all the *Elementary* Sherlocks and most of the *Sherlock* Sherlocks," Tilda conceded. They also eliminated three steampunk Sherlocks, an anime Sherlock, and various cross-cosplays including a bedazzled Liberace-Sherlock getup.

Once they'd finished weeding through their files, Tilda asked, "Was he Caucasian?"

"He could have been Hispanic, but on the lighter side."

"People, eliminate some more."

"What about the guy who was dressed as Data from *Star Trek: TNG* dressed as Sherlock Holmes?" the pedantic Irregular wanted to know.

"Did he have unnaturally white skin or yellow eyes?" Tilda asked Mrs. Dao.

"I didn't see his eyes, but the skin looked normal."

"Cross off the android."

There were a few more questions about lighter colored variants including a pale-pelted furry Sherlock, Vampire Sherlock, and a Sherlock with a white beard from *Sherlock Gnomes*.

Next Tilda was able to pare down the list by body size and shape. Unfortunately, Mrs. Dao couldn't answer any questions about hair, eyes, or other distinguishing marks, so they let her go about her business.

The Irregulars emailed their remaining candidates to Tilda, and she and Vincent eliminated the duplications—people who'd had pictures taken by more than one Irregular. Once all that was done, there were half a dozen choices left.

"What next?" Vincent asked.

"Now we track down the six Sherlocks."

Even with only six, it wasn't going to be easy. None of the people in the photos were identified and nobody recognized them. So the Irregulars were tasked with keeping an eye out for them, and Vincent went to find a central vantage point from which to watch. In other words, the bar. Meanwhile, Tilda had a final panel to moderate on a subject she barely remembered two minutes later because she was so busy scanning the audience, looking for any of the targets. She was unsuccessful, but a text from Vincent proved that hanging at the bar had more benefits than excellent service.

She rushed over, but wasn't expecting to find the suspect sharing nachos with Vincent, nor was she expecting him to be wearing a black frock coat, wide-brimmed hat, and wire-rimmed glasses.

"Tilda!" Vincent said. "Meet Oscar. I was telling him how much I admired his costume."

"It's certainly different." Then she remembered seeing something like that getup before. "'A Scandal in Bohemia'?"

"Good catch," Oscar said. "It's Sherlock's Nonconformist clergyman disguise."

"Oscar has ten different costumes for this weekend," Vincent said.

"Ten?"

"That's right," Oscar said proudly. "Yesterday, I started out with the classic, but there were so many Inverness capes wandering around that after I got some pictures, I switched to the Jeremy Brett version. Today I'm running through Sherlock's disguises. I started with the doddering opium smoker, then the French laborer. Next up, I've got the book collector, the Italian priest, and I'll wrap it up with the drunken groom. Tomorrow—"

"Wow. You are devoted." Trying for subtlety, Tilda said, "I think I saw you at the panel with Lee and Anderson."

"Yeah, I was in the back so my top hat wouldn't block anybody's view. Then when . . . you know . . . happened, I was glad to be so far away that I couldn't see much. It must have been awful for you."

"Yes." Tilda didn't elaborate.

Vincent tactfully switched the conversation to the nuts and bolts of packing so many costumes and the accompanying accessories. Tilda was only moderately interested, but took a few notes. It might make for a salable story, given the popularity of cosplay. Fortunately for her attention span, Oscar was on a tight schedule and soon took off to change.

"What do you think?" Vincent said.

"He could have lied about what he was wearing," Tilda said. "Do we have photos of the back of the ballroom?"

Vincent did, and they quickly spotted Oscar and his hat.

"That's one Sherlock down," Tilda said.

Over the course of the evening, the Irregulars brought over three more suspect Sherlocks, all of whom they eliminated.

One hadn't arrived at the con until long after the panel ended, which they verified with the hotel valet who'd parked his car.

Another said he was at a different panel, and when Vincent talked to the monitor for that panel, she remembered the guy asking long-winded questions and buttonholing a panelist afterward to argue with him. Tilda neither asked nor cared what they argued about.

A third Sherlock had been in the right panel, in the right costume, but he was mostly confined to his wheelchair. He was only able to stand long enough for photos, and couldn't walk unassisted.

After that, they stalled. One was a partial view of a Sherlock in bad light, but should have stood out because he had red hair and freckles, unusual for a Sherlock, and his deerstalker was too big. The other was both more and less promising. On the good side, he was slipping through the same EMPLOYEES ONLY door Vincent had taken Tilda through to get to the ballroom, which seemed suspicious, and he had a more muscular build than most Sherlocks. On the bad side, the actual subject of the photo was a pair of Moriarty cosplayers, leaving Sherlock out of focus. Maybe it was staring at them so long, but both pictures looked almost familiar—Tilda just couldn't figure out why.

They stayed at their station well into the evening, eating dinner off the bar menu, but even though the lobby was thick with Sherlocks, they couldn't spot either of the ones they wanted. When Vincent wandered off to consult with cronies, Tilda decided it was time for a beer, and looked around for Ed. He saw her wave and started over.

That's when Tilda realized why Out-of-Focus Sherlock looked familiar.

Ed asked, "What can I get for you, Tilda?"

"How about an answer?" Tilda said. "What were you doing in the hall behind the ballroom right before Michael Lee's last panel?"

The waiter wouldn't meet her eyes. "Who says I was there?"

Tilda hoped his daughter Penny's acting skills were better than his. Rather than answer, she waited him out.

After a pause, he folded. "Okay, I was back there. So what?"

"In disguise?"

"What disguise? I dressed up to join in on the fun."

"You're not in costume now."

"My manager said it was against policy."

"Right. And you were behind the ballroom because . . . ?"

"I had to get something, and the main halls were crowded, so—"

"Not buying it, Ed. You were looking for Lee, weren't you?"

He sat down at the table. "Okay, I wanted to talk to him. Maybe do more than talk."

"Like planting a water bottle dosed with a peanut product?"

"No! I mean I wanted to punch him for what he did to my daughter!"

"What did he do?" Tilda said gently, with Harvey Weinstein–like crimes in mind.

"A fat lot of nothing!"

She blinked. "You've lost me."

"You know the con was here last year, right? Penny was a big fan of Lee, so she makes sure to work that weekend. When he comes in here for a drink, I get her to come by and introduce them. Like I told Vincent, she wants to be in movies, and I thought he might have some pointers. Networking, you know. They must have talked an hour. He even pulls out a script and they read lines together. Here where I could see them, of course. I wouldn't have let her go up to his room."

Obviously Tilda wasn't the only one thinking about Weinstein and his ilk.

"He says she has real talent, and that he knows the perfect project for her, so he's going to talk to his agent and call her next week. Penny's over the moon! She tells her friends at school how she might have to drop out and move to Hollywood.

"Only he doesn't call. Another week. He doesn't call. Another week. No call. Penny isn't doing her homework, she isn't eating, she isn't sleeping. She thinks he's lost her number. So I get his phone number from when he registered at the hotel, and I give it to her.

"She calls him and leaves a message, then waits for him to call back. Nothing. A couple of days later, she calls again, leaves another message. Nothing. The kids in her classes are laughing behind her back, saying she made the whole thing up, and trashing her online. But she still believes it's just a misunderstanding. Until the day she calls and the bastard has blocked her number." Tilda jumped as he slammed his fist against the table. "He didn't even have the guts to tell her it was all talk, that he isn't going to do anything for her."

"Honestly, he probably didn't have the juice to help her," Tilda said. "One cult TV show does not a power player make, and he'd done nothing but minor guest shots since *Sherlock's Home*."

"Then he shouldn't have broken my girl's heart! If I'd seen Lee on fire, I wouldn't have bothered to spit on him to put it out."

"I don't blame you, but why go after him in the ballroom?"

"I didn't want him in my bar—if I lose my temper here, I lose my job. I thought if I got to him somewhere more private, it would be my word against his. But he wasn't there, and other people were, so I decided to try again later. I came back to work. And the next time I saw him was when they were wheeling him out."

She kept at him a while longer, but she was sure Ed wasn't their guy. Maybe he could have left the water bottles, but if he'd been on duty at the end of the panel, he couldn't have retrieved them. He left just as Vincent came back.

"Wow. Poor Penny," Vincent said when she told him what had happened.

"Tell me you got something."

"Nothing to help, just a rumor that Anderson is moving ahead with the plan to bring *Sherlock's Home* back. Here's hoping he finds a better actor than Lee's last replacement."

"Pardon me if I don't care a lot right now."

"Hey, we're down to the last Sherlock," he said. "That's good, right?"

"Only if we find him." She sighed. "I'm ready to call it a night." Not only was she tired, but she suspected that Ed wasn't going to come back to their table anytime soon. Their golden hours of VIP service were over.

Tilda was not feeling optimistic the next morning. The convention was coming to an end, and with it, their chance of solving Lee's murder. When Vincent texted to ask her to join him for breakfast, she almost turned him down, but figured she had to eat, so she met him at the hotel restaurant. She could tell he was discouraged, too—he hadn't bothered to chat up the waitress.

Still, once they'd filled their plates from the breakfast buffet, he said, "So what next?"

"I've got nothing."

"What about the last Sherlock?"

"What about him?"

"He's got to be the one, Tilda."

"It doesn't matter if we can't find him. He's probably already left anyway." She'd love to skip out early, too, but had a market that wanted a write-up of the memorial service, no matter how tediously maudlin it was.

"We could post his picture online. I'm in a lot of Sherlockian fan groups. Someone must know him."

"Then what? Once the con's over, how could we find any proof that he's a killer? No, if he's gone already, we're out of luck."

"Then maybe it wasn't the sixth Sherlock after all. Let's look at the other five again."

"Which one? The Sherlock who changes costumes at the drop of a hat? The one who wasn't even at the hotel at the time? I know, maybe they were in it together!"

"Hey, be nice!"

She took a deep breath. "I'm sorry, I don't know why you've been putting up with me."

"Because you're my best shot at saving this con, for me anyway. If we can't solve it, I won't come back."

"I'm sorry."

"There are other cons," he said, "but I do like this one. Why did he have to kill somebody here?"

A thought struck her. "Why *did* he have to kill somebody here? Why commit murder in the middle of a convention, of all places?"

"I don't know. What are you thinking?"

"Access to Lee is the obvious answer. Like Ed waiting for his chance to slug him. And Lee was kind of a jerk, so somebody else could have had a grudge, but did he really have enough time to give somebody a reason to kill him?"

"The con kept him pretty busy."

"So if it wasn't access, maybe the point was camouflage."

"Meaning what?"

"If you killed somebody at your office, the police would look at all the people who worked there. If you killed somebody here, they'd look at you, but they'd also have a lot of other people to look at."

"Lee didn't have an office, and hadn't had a regular job since *Sherlock's Home*. Do you think Anderson did it?"

Instead of answering, she pulled out her laptop and started tapping away. It didn't take long to find the pictures she was looking for. "Finish up your breakfast—we need to find Regina."

Just before noon, subdued fans filed into the ballroom. Regina had stationed Irregulars around the room armed with photos of the man Tilda thought was the killer, and they would have no trouble spotting him if he was in the audience.

In the meantime, she, Vincent, and Regina were waiting for Anderson in the green room, which was no more plush than Security HQ, but at least it was free of pizza boxes. The plan was to explain the situation to Anderson before the service to enlist his help, but under the circumstances, his aid wasn't needed. The killer walked in with him. Though he was dressed in a somber dark suit, Tilda recognized him immediately as the last Sherlock.

"Tilda," Anderson said. "I've been meaning to thank you for what you tried to do for Michael. You, too, Vincent."

"I just wish we'd been able to do more." She spoke to the man with him. "I'm sorry, have we met?"

"I don't believe so," he lied.

"Tilda, this is Jeremiah Bourreau. You may remember him from the later days of *Sherlock's Home*."

"Of course!" she said. "You replaced Michael Lee in the Sherlock re-creations. Didn't I see somewhere that you started out as a production assistant on the show, and got promoted when Lee left?"

"That's right."

Anderson said, "In fact, we'll be making an announcement about Jeremiah stepping in for Michael again. Not today, of course. I don't think that would be appropriate."

"Wow, that's big news. Mr. Bourreau, will you be playing Sherlock or Watson?"

He looked puzzled. "Sherlock, of course."

"Really? You did so well as Watson Friday night. That mustache you were wearing was a bit over the top, but otherwise, a solid performance. Though you might want to brush up on your medical skills if you're going to play a doctor. Or a nurse."

"I don't know what you're talking about," he said. "Noah, shouldn't we be going in for the service?"

"There's still time," Tilda said, noting that Regina was blocking the door. "You know, you really confused us, showing up as both Holmes and Watson that night. But it was an easy switch, wasn't it? Put on the Inverness cape and the deerstalker, and you were just one Sherlock among many so it was easy to leave the poisoned water bottle for Lee. But you were worried some of the fans would recognize you, so you added a wig and drew on some freckles. You'd have been perfect for the red-headed league."

Tilda was disappointed he didn't seem to recognize the reference.

She went on. "Even the wig and freckles might not have fooled Lee or Anderson—especially Anderson, because he was used to seeing you dressed as Sherlock. Plus you needed to get up close for the next part of the plan. So you dumped the cape and wig, put on a different hat, and used the ridiculous mustache to cover the freckles and most of your face. Then you could be Nurse Watson. What did you do with Lee's EpiPen anyway? I didn't see it, but you must have made a switch when you pretended to drop Lee's, and then did the same thing with the one the woman from the audience gave you. I imagine you got the EpiPens you used in Canada—you can get them without a prescription there. Did you just empty them or dose them with more peanut?"

Bourreau said, "Noah, I don't know—"

"Never mind. Mere details." Tilda was hoping the police would be able to locate the discarded EpiPens at the hospital or wherever they'd been disposed of to verify her suspicion. "Once the EMTs came, you ducked out and switched back to Holmes so you could take the tainted bottles away. You really lucked out when it turned out Lee had been exposed to peanuts earlier, making it look as if he'd had a delayed reaction. But even without that, you were in the clear because nobody knew you were here."

"I wasn't here!" Bourreau protested. "I only came in yesterday to support Lee."

"That'll be easy enough for the police to check on, especially if they can find the hotel you stayed at Friday night. Besides, people love to take pictures at a con. We've already got plenty of you pretending to help Lee, and one of you as Sherlock." It struck her that hiding a Sherlock among the Sherlocks owed more to Poe and his purloined letter than it did to Doyle's work, but Tilda didn't think Bourreau would appreciate the literary irony.

"Jeremiah, is this true?" Anderson asked.

"Of course it's not true! It's nuts! This woman is a crazy fan! You know what they're like!"

"Noah, I do have one question for you," Tilda said. "That meal that started the Food Feud, the one where peanut oil was used? Did you cook it yourself?"

"No, Jeremiah—" He looked at Bourreau with his eyes wide, then stepped away from him. "God, Jeremiah. You didn't!"

Regina took over after that, bringing in hotel security and police to take custody of Bourreau. The memorial service ended up starting an hour late, but it did go on, and pictures of Anderson breaking down in tears went viral immediately.

Unfortunately, Tilda wasn't there to cover it, because the police wanted to talk to her, but Vincent took enough pictures and notes on her behalf for several articles.

As she told Vincent later, there's that something Bourreau hadn't realized, but all Sherlockians know: a Sherlock is only as good as his Watson.

THE CASE OF
THE NAKED BUTTERFLY

by William Kotzwinkle and Joe Servello

THE CASE OF THE NAKED BUTTERFLY

AN INSPECTOR MANTIS MYSTERY

BY WILLIAM KOTZWINKLE ART BY JOE SERVELLO

Doctor Hopper insisted Inspector Mantis give his great brain a rest.

THE ANNALS OF CRIME HAVE DRAINED YOU, MANTIS. YOU NEED THE MUSICAL STAGE TO REVIVE YOU.

THE MEDICINE OF MUSIC, DOCTOR? PERHAPS YOU'RE RIGHT.

Mantis had been on the trail of Malcom Malworm, untouchable now, having gone to cocoon, from which Malworm would emerge with a new identity. He'd given Mantis the slip, and was immune to prosecution, his transformation from worm to moth a clean slate, legally speaking. He would fly to the light, one moth among many, his crimes forgotten.

Later, as they walked toward the Bugland Follies...

YOU NEED THE FULL EXPERIENCE OF FORTUNA FIREFLY SINGING *LULLABY OF BUGLAND.*

HOPPER, LOOK!

GREAT GRASSHOPPERS!

A butterfly was fluttering over them, her wings completely naked, her scales gone. She was as transparent as glass.

HAVE YOU SEEN SUCH A THING BEFORE?

NEVER.

IS THERE SOME MEDICAL REASON FOR HER TO HAVE LOST HER SCALES, EVERY LAST ONE OF THEM?

NO REASON THAT I KNOW OF. IT SMACKS OF VIOLATION.

They hurried after the butterfly but she was moving quickly through the night, dipping and darting through the shadows until she was beyond reach.

Inside the theater another shock awaits them...

Fortuna Firefly, star of the Follies, is wearing a gown made of butterfly scales!

YOUR BUTTERFLY IS WELL-NAMED. THE UNUSUAL IRIDESCENCE OF ITS WINGS COMES FROM MIRRORING IN THE TWIN LAMINA OF THE SCALE.

I HAVE SEEN THIS SAME PATTERN ON A GEMSTONE.

THERE IS NO SUCH PATTERN HERE, MANTIS. THE GEM YOU SAW MUST BE EXTREMELY RARE.

I FEAR YOU'RE RIGHT. MUCH TOO RARE.

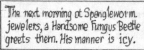

The next morning at Spangleworm jewelers, a Handsome Fungus Beetle greets them. His manner is icy.

IS THERE SOMETHING I CAN HELP YOU WITH? SOME LITTLE ITEM THAT CATCHES YOUR FANCY?

THAT ONE, WHERE IS IT FROM?

SCOUTS BRING US TREASURES FROM EXOTIC LANDS. I DOUBT IF YOU WOULD HAVE HEARD OF SUCH PLACES.

AND SPANGLEWORM, WHERE IS HE?

MR. SPANGLEWORM IS A DEEPLY PRIVATE BUG. I'M NOT AT LIBERTY TO DISCUSS HIS WHEREABOUTS.

I NOTICE YOU'RE WEARING SCENT.

WE COMPOUND OUR OWN VERY FINE COLOGNE. IT ADDS A PERSUASIVE TONE TO INTIMATE MOMENTS.

AS DO YOU, HANDSOME FUNGUS BEETLE. GOOD DAY.

outside the shop...

PASSION FLOWERS AGAIN, MANTIS.

WE NEED TO KNOW MORE ABOUT THEM, HOPPER. AND ABOUT THE MYSTERIOUS MR. SPANGLEWORM.

A police vehicle pulls up, and Captain Flatfootfly hails them.

I NEED YOUR HELP, MANTIS.

SURELY NOT, FLATFOOTFLY.

YOU'VE MADE SOME SLIGHT CONTRIBUTIONS TO MY INVESTIGATIONS IN THE PAST, MANTIS, AND I'M NOT TOO PROUD TO CONSULT YOU AGAIN.

THEN I'M AT YOUR SERVICE. WHAT IS THE PROBLEM?

THE WHOLESALE DISAPPEARANCE OF AN ENTIRE BUGLAND FAMILY. JOLLY LITTLE BUGS. NEVER HARMED ANYONE. NAME OF LAC.

I CAME BACK TO THE HOUSE AND EVERYONE WAS GONE. THE DOOR WAS SMASHED IN, THE PLACE WAS A WRECK.

MR. LAC, YOUR FULL NAME, I THINK, IS GUM-LAC.

WE SHORTENED IT.

IT COMES FROM THE PERSIAN, MEANING A RESINOUS RED GUM, WHICH AS WE CAN SEE COVERS YOUR BODY.

MANTIS, WHAT THIS LITTLE CHAP IS COVERED WITH ISN'T THE PROBLEM.

MR. LAC, I'M SURE YOU'RE FAMILIAR WITH THE WORD SHELLAC.

NEVER UTTER THAT WORD!

BECAUSE YOU LIVE IN FEAR OF BEING TURNED INTO SHELLAC.

Mantis drew the butterfly scale from his pocket and held it up to the light. A burst of color appeared in it. Then he looked at Lac, his gaze moving thoughtfully over the little insect's body...

5

WE MUST GET TO POLLEN LANE, FLATFOOTFLY. QUICK AS YOU CAN.

WHAT'S IN POLLEN LANE?

A NUMBER OF SOLITARY BEES.

STILL NOT WITH YOU, MANTIS.

YOU'VE READ MY MONOGRAPH MAKING SENSE OF SCENT?

I MISSED THAT ONE.

...OFF TO POLLEN LANE.

147

MIDNIGHT...

The windowless walls of the vineyard warehouse gave off a sinister air...

A nasty substance hits Hopper's hat.

CANTHARADIN! THEY'RE USING BLISTER BEETLES AS SECURITY GUARDS!

THEY *WERE* USING BLISTER BEETLES.

A shout from Flatfootfly took them to the other side of the building.

GET BACK, FLATFOOTFLY. ONE BITE FROM THOSE FANGS AND YOU'RE A DEAD BUG!

Mantis struck out with his great arm.

The spider was bound by his own silk.

I WAS ONLY DOING MY JOB.

THE KEYS.

I'M BASICALLY A DECENT BUG.

YOU'RE AN UNWHOLESOME, MURDEROUS WRETCH.

I FELL INTO BAD COMPANY.

They ignore this pathetic appeal.

They enter the warehouse. The sight that meets their eyes is grotesque. Hanging in chains are dozens of Shining Mirror butterflies, waiting to have their wings stripped. But more horrible...

DEAD, EXECUTED TO KEEP THEM FROM TELLING ABOUT THIS PLACE.

Lac flies were held in a cage beside a boiling vat. "They're going to boil us alive!" cried the unfortunate flies. More unfortunate were the flies who had preceded them into the vat. All that was left of them was a layer of resin floating on the surface.

Deathwatch beetles, employed to carry out this filthy business were hurrying to escape. Flatfootfly flattened them with his nightstick.

Mantis reveals the tragic combination of butterfly scales and shellac ...

THEY FADE WITH TIME. BUT PRESERVED IN SHELLAC FROM THE LACS THEY WILL KEEP THEIR COLOR FOREVER.

AND THERE IS THE MISCREANT WHO ENGINEERED THE PROCESS!

PRIVATE

IT'S OVER, SPANGLEWORM.

A FORTUNE IN GEMS. HIDDEN, OF COURSE, I ALONE KNOW WHERE. LET ME GO AND THEY'RE YOURS.

THEY ARE NOT TRUE GEMS, SPANGLEWORM. THEY ARE VILE PRODUCTS OF YOUR DEMONIC ART.

SAY WHAT YOU LIKE, BUT ONLY I AM WORTHY TO DRESS THE EMPRESS. THIS IS TO BE HERS. IT BELONGS IN THE ROYAL WARDROBE.

IT BELONGS IN THE BUGLAND MUSEUM OF CRIME.

SEE THAT IT'S WELL-LIT.

8

The butterflies, now released from their chains attack Spangleworm.

MONSTER!

FIEND!

PLEASE, LADIES, THE LAW WILL TAKE CARE OF THIS GOOD-FOR-NOTHING.

CONTACT THE EMPRESS! ONCE SHE SEES MY GOWN, SHE'LL DECLARE ME A NATIONAL TREASURE.

Mantis stepped away in disgust. If he hadn't seen the greed and vanity in Spangleworm's eyes, he would have thought him insane. But Spangleworm was of sound mind all right, and terribly clever. He simply had no moral compass. A bug who would turn other bugs into shellac lacked any trace of conscience.

WELL, MANTIS, WHAT NOW? THE WRETCH SAID A FORTUNE IN GEMS IS HIDDEN SOMEWHERE.

I HAVE NO INTEREST IN FINDING IT. LET IT REMAIN IN THE DARK.

WHERE IT BELONGS....

And so the marvelous creations are to languish forever in their secret hiding place, Shining Mirrors of Evil...

MANTIS WAS RIGHT. BETTER LEFT UNSEEN. TO LOOK UPON THEM WOULD BE CORROSIVE TO A BUG'S SOUL.

After much searching...

Mantis and Hopper found the naked butterfly hiding in a camp of gypsy moths.

Her escape from Spangleworm's warehouse was written up in every newspaper and her heroism became the stuff of legend.

BRAVE BUTTERFLY ESCAPES FROM FIEND!

Max Mayfly recognized a star in the making and gave her a part in the New Bugland Follies.

In the proper lighting, her transparent wings produced a touching effect, especially when she sang *My Fluttering Heart*.

The dandyflies loved her. They tossed her necklaces and bracelets – cheap stuff Spangleworm would have despised, were he there to see it but he was languishing in prison.

Doctor Hopper tossed her a bouquet of passion flowers.

MOST APPROPRIATE.

THEY EXPRESS MY FEELINGS ENTIRELY.

Now fireflies filed onto the stage, forming a chorus line behind the butterfly. The effect was startling, as if she were some new form of butterfly, never seen before.

Then the fireflies shut off their lights and the curtain closed.

A CHARMING CREATURE. I HOPE SHE FINDS LOVE.

YOU SEEM A STRONG CONTENDER.

I ALLOW MYSELF TO HOPE. AND YOU?

MY COURTSHIP IS WITH CRIME.

THE END

BOTTOM LINE

by D. P. Lyle

"It don't make no sense," Billy Whitehead said.

He was standing across the cold, metal table from Wilbert Scoggins, owner of Scoggins' Funeral Home and the county coroner for more years than Billy could remember. The man he'd worked for going on five years now.

"What don't make sense?" Wilbert asked.

"Why would Carl kill hisself?"

The body on the table was one Carl Draper. He looked nothing like he had two days ago, the last time Billy had seen him, standing behind the counter in his store, that friendly lopsided smile on his face. Now he was pale, waxy, face mottled with blue-gray splotches, head lolled to the left, a blood-crusted hole just above and behind his right ear clearly evident beneath the harsh overhead bulb light.

"Don't know for sure," Wilbert said. "I hear tell his business wasn't doing all that good and he was worried about the future—how was he going to keep things going? That kind of thing."

"That don't make sense neither. Back when I worked for him we was always busy. Ever time I go in there now, he and Cora are hopping like one-armed paper hangers. Far as I could see anyway."

Wilbert sighed. "That's the tricky part of owning a business. Things can get out of sorts pretty quick." He waved a hand. "I'd be lying if I said I was doing as well now as I was five years ago, the last time you worked for Carl over at the hardware."

"You're doing okay."

"Yeah, mostly. But we've had fewer customers lately. Comes with the shrinking population around here. Ever since the shoe factory closed. That, and all my expenses have crept up. Little things like caskets and embalming fluid. Cost nearly half again as much as they did a few years ago. It adds up. And I suspect Carl was going through the same thing. Ain't cheap to keep a hardware store stocked. And the drop-off in home building around the county sure don't help much."

"I suppose."

"Well, all I know is both Carl and Cora have been stressed lately. Money getting tighter."

"We going to do an autopsy?" Billy asked.

"Don't see much need for that. Pretty obvious what happened."

"That's a fact."

"The sooner I get my report done the quicker Cora can plan the funeral."

"She'll appreciate that."

"Let's cut his clothes off and then we can make a better examination."

Took five minutes to scissor away Carl's pants and bloody shirt, the leakage from his head wound having soaked down onto the shoulder and back of his white shirt. Looked rusty brown now. Wilbert gave Carl a good look-see, head to foot, then they rolled him over.

"Only got the entry wound," Wilbert said. "Bullet's still in there somewhere."

"Shouldn't we take it out?"

Wilbert shook his head. "No. If we open him up, his head anyway, it'll make the embalming messier. And I'm sure Cora don't want his head all bandaged at the visitation. She'd rather it be an open viewing. Closed caskets make folks uncomfortable."

Billy nodded.

"What is it?" Wilbert asked.

"You sure he did it to hisself?"

"Sure am. He was lying on floor, the gun was right there beside him."

"Someone could've put it there."

"Now, who on God's green earth would want to shoot Carl?"

"Don't know." Billy walked around the table. He pointed to the wound. "But don't you think that's a funny place to shoot yourself?"

"In the head? Happens all the time if someone wants to make sure."

"Seems like it's pretty far back."

"Not if he turned his head to the left before he fired."

"I guess."

"You been reading again, haven't you?"

"Never stopped."

Wilbert smiled. "Too many of those mystery novels'll make you think all sorts of things. Maybe you should put Agatha Christie and Sherlock Holmes aside."

"Agatha's pretty clever and Sherlock is about as smart as smart gets."

"You know those stories are made up. Right? And Sherlock Holmes weren't even a real person."

"He was based on one."

"That right?" Wilbert asked.

"Dr. John Bell. Arthur Conan Doyle knew him—was one a his students. Bell had a knack for looking at crimes and seeing what others skimmed over."

"Like Sherlock?"

"Exactly."

"They're still stories, Billy. Not real life."

"You can learn a lot from stories."

"How so?"

"Lot's of stuff," Billy said. "Like the Bible. It's mostly a bunch of stories."

Wilbert chuckled. "Better not let your mama hear you say that."

"Ain't that the truth. She'd box my ears in for sure."

"That she would," Wilbert said.

"But I read other stuff, too. Real stuff."

"Like what?"

"Edmond Locard and Hans Gross. A guy named Goddard."

"Who're they?"

"Crime experts. Locard was French and Gross was from Austria. They more or less changed everything when it came to murder investigations."

"Murder? We ain't got no murder here. Carl was simply down in the dumps and made a poor choice."

"Maybe."

"Okay, Sherlock, tell me why you're talking about this?"

"Two things. First, like I said, that's not exactly a comfortable position to shoot yourself from."

"Is there a comfortable one?"

Billy smiled. "You know what I mean. To do this, Carl's hand would've had to be all twisted around." Billy made a hand pistol pointing his index finger barrel behind his own ear, cranking his elbow way back to create the right angle. "See? Not easy to do."

"Again, unless he turned his head." Wilbert rotated his own neck as if working out a kink. "That's what it looks like to me."

"Plus that, Carl was left-handed."

"So what?"

"I think most folks shoot with their best hand. Carl would've used his left."

Wilbert eyed him. "You're a smart boy. Always was. But I suspect someone committing suicide ain't overly concerned with what hand they use."

"That's what I'm saying. He'd of done what was natural. Use the left one."

Wilbert gave him a fatherly smile.

"And there ain't no powder burns on his head or neck," Billy said.

"So?"

"If the muzzle was near his head there'd be powder burns on the skin. And his hair."

"That so?"

"That's what the books say."

"Maybe he held it back a few inches?"

"Couldn't do that." Again, Billy aimed his hand pistol at his own head. "Arm ain't that long."

Wilbert rubbed his chin. "Look, as sad as it is, Carl took his own life. That's a fact. And I damn sure ain't going to stir up a mess of hornets by suggesting otherwise."

Billy nodded. "You're probably right."

"I been at this for a while. And I do know what I'm doing. Your books aside."

⬥

Billy sat at the dinner table with his mama. He ate one pork chop, not his usual two, and only a spoonful of pintos and greens. Not a single yam.

"You okay?" she asked.

He took a bite of cornbread and looked up. "Sure."

"Don't look like it to me. You hardly ate nothing."

"Not hungry."

"That's what I mean. Your father, God rest his soul, was the same way. Whenever something lay heavy on him he didn't eat." She smiled. "I could always tell."

"It ain't nothing."

"That's what he'd say. Weren't the truth though." She eyed him. "It's Carl Draper, ain't it?"

Billy nodded.

"It's a pure tragedy. I'm here to tell you. I can't imagine what Cora's going through. I mean, losing your father was bad. And he died of the cancer. But Carl taking his own life? That's got to be hard for her."

"If he did," Billy said.

She dropped her fork on her plate. A sharp clank. "What's that supposed to mean?"

"Nothing."

"You telling me someone killed Carl? Who? Why?"

"Don't know."

"That's crazy talk." She stood, collecting her plate, then Billy's, ferrying them to the sink. Over her shoulder she said, "I know you, Billy Whitehead. Don't you go making no waves. Talking nonsense. You hear me?" She turned and looked at him.

"I won't."

In his upstairs bedroom, Billy pulled his books off the shelf. He opened the collection of Sherlock Holmes stories, flipping through the pages until he found the one he wanted. He adjusted the lampshade so the light fell over the bed, stretched out, and began reading.

⊰◈⊱

Carl Draper's visitation was held the next day in the large room for such events at Scoggins' Funeral Home. Must've been 150 folks. The mood was mostly somber, visitors knotted into small groups, some smiling, even laughing softly, probably sharing some remembered story about Carl. The brushed-bronze casket rested on a white pedestal along the far wall and Billy made his way in that direction. Carl lay nestled in the cream-colored satin lining. He wore a blue suit, white shirt, lighter blue tie. His Bible lay near his left hand. Wilbert had done his usual good job.

"He looks good, doesn't he?"

Billy turned to see Cora next to him.

"He does." Billy studied her for a few seconds. "How're you doing?"

"Not well." She reached down and clasped her husband's hand. "I just don't understand why he did it."

"It sure shocked me. Last time I saw him, just a couple of days ago, he seemed more or less like his ownself."

She stared at her husband's face, unmoving for nearly a full minute before finally letting go of his hand, as if reluctant to do so. "Don't know what I'm going to do now."

"Anything I can help with?"

She shook her head. "Not sure anyone can help with this."

"Maybe I can pitch in at the store," Billy said.

She turned and gave him a weak smile. "You're a good man, Billy Whitehead. But you have your own life, your own job, to tend to."

"I got the time."

Tears collected in her eyes.

"Tell you what," Billy said, "I'll drop by Monday morning and we can talk about it."

She sighed. "If I can just get through the funeral tomorrow."

"You'll do fine, Cora. You're tough."

"Don't feel that way right now."

Billy pushed through the front door of Draper's Hardware just after ten on Monday morning. Sunday had been a beautiful day, clear and bright. The funeral, attended by well over 300 people, had been a mournful event, but Cora held up well, clutching her Bible to her chest, eyes watery behind the black veil. During the night, weather had blown in and today, rain whipped down in sheets and thunder rumbled above the hills to the west. Billy stamped water off his shoes and shook more from the canvas satchel he carried over his shoulder.

Raymond Eldridge looked up from behind the counter. "Billy. You look like a drowned cat."

"It's coming down pretty good," Billy said.

Raymond, late forties, thin, long neck, big Adam's apple, graying hair, had worked for Carl and Cora for more than a dozen years. Mostly stocking the shelves and making sales. He had also taken over the bookkeeping when Billy left.

"What can I do for you?" Raymond asked.

"Is Cora here?"

Raymond shook his head. "No. I told her to stay home. She ain't in no shape to work today."

Billy nodded. "I wanted to see if I could help out."

"I appreciate it but not much to do. I already shelved the stuff that came in Saturday and I suspect there won't be too many folks traipsing in with all this weather."

Billy nodded.

"I stopped by and talked to Cora this morning," Raymond said. "She's thinking of selling the place."

"To Olsen?"

Robert Olsen owned a couple of businesses in town—the drugstore and a nursery—and had repeatedly offered to buy out Carl and Cora. Pestered them as far as Billy could see. But, nothing ever came of it.

"Yep." Raymond leaned his elbows on the counter, hunched over. "I think Cora's heart ain't in it anymore. I suggested she wait a few weeks. Get her head right. Then decide."

"Makes sense."

"Don't know if she'll change her mind though."

"What will you do? If she sells?"

Raymond straightened. Shrugged. "Don't rightly know. Maybe try to stay on with Olsen. If he's the one what buys it. Maybe I'll mosey on up to Morgan City. Work for my brother. He could use the help, for darn sure."

Billy scratched an ear. "You got any idea why Carl would've done it?"

"He's been down lately. Things haven't been going too well." Raymond's gaze roamed around the store, toward the stocked shelves, the stand of brooms near the front door, finally back to Billy. "Costs have climbed up there but prices sure ain't. We been on a razor's edge here for a couple of years."

"I don't understand how," Billy said. "This is a good business."

"It ain't like it was when you worked here. Cash flow has been pretty slow."

Billy nodded. "Well, let me know if I can help out."

Billy braved the rain for the two blocks to the courthouse, where Sheriff Blake's office nestled in one corner of the first floor. He debated the wisdom of talking with Blake all the way over. Was he making too much of this? Was he seeing it all wrong?

Blake, sorting through a stack of papers on his desk, looked up when Billy rapped a knuckle on the door frame.

"Got a minute?" Billy asked.

"Sure. Come on in. Take a load off."

Billy sat in the chair that faced Blake. "I got a question for you."

"Okay."

"Did you see Carl's body?"

"Sure did. Why?"

"Anything seem off to you?"

Blake leaned back, folded his hands over his ample belly. "Like what?"

Billy explained his concerns. The angle, the gun in the right hand, the lack of powder burns.

Blake's brow furrowed. "What exactly are you getting at?"

"Maybe Carl didn't do it."

"Come on, Billy. You believe that?"

Billy reached inside his satchel and removed the Holmes book, opening it to the page he had marked with a torn piece of paper. "Let me show you something. It's from a Sherlock Holmes story. 'The Reigate Squires.'" He slid the book across the desk toward Blake. "A man named William Kirwan, a coachman on the Acton estate, got hisself shot, apparently wrestlin' with a burglar. That according to a guy named Alec Cunningham who saw the fight. The Actons and the Cunninghams were in some property dispute. Anyway, Holmes said that the lack of powder burns on the victim meant the shot couldn't've been fired at close range like it would've been in a situation like Alec described. Sort of like what we have here."

"So this concern of yours is based on a made-up story?"

Billy reached over and turned a couple of pages. "Read this part here." He tapped a finger to indicate the passage.

Blake read. Billy waited.

Finally, Blake looked up. "You do realize this is a fictional tale."

"I do. But Sherlock always seemed to find just the right clue. And here it looks like what happened to Carl."

"The gun was Carl's. You know that? Right?"

"I didn't but I knowed he had one."

"Kept it right there in his desk," Blake said.

"I knowed that, too."

Blake shook his head. "So someone came in the store, at night, while Carl was working, took his gun out of the drawer, shot him, and left the gun lying there so it'd look like Carl shot himself?"

Hearing it that way did make Billy think a minute. But still. "That's surely possible."

"But does it seem likely?"

Billy had no answer.

"It sure don't to me," Blake said. "So, let me ask you, who would do that?"

"I don't know. Maybe you can snoop around and see."

"Billy, Carl ain't even cold yet. Cora's a mess. And I damn sure ain't going to dig into something that don't need digging into." He closed the book and handed it back to Billy. "Not based on some story."

Billy lay awake, staring at the ceiling above his bed. It was spidered with cracks in the paint, every line familiar. How many times had he lay right here, thinking on stuff? Like now. But, right now, his mind seemed to twist in the wind and rain that battered the window.

Who would've killed Carl? Why would they? His mind sorted through all the stories and books he had read. Why'd people kill? Rage? Jealousy? Money? Was the killer a robber? If so, how'd he get Carl's gun from the drawer and use it on him? Wouldn't Carl have put up a fight? There weren't no overturned furniture or stuff knocked all to hell like a struggle had broke out. And from what he'd heard, the cash register hadn't been messed with. Nothing was missing.

Why would the killer leave the gun behind? Make it look like Carl did hisself in? Why not just run?

No, someone wanted Carl dead. And didn't want no one thinking Carl didn't do it. Who would gain from such a thing?

He sat up on the edge of his bed, elbows on his knees. Rain pecked at the glass panes, thrummed the roof. He stood and walked to the window. Wind buffeted the crab apple tree just beyond, its branches scratching against the side of the house.

The only thing that made sense was Carl knew something. Something that could bring trouble down on another person—the one that killed him. But what could Carl've known? Who could he have had friction with? Carl had no enemies. He was a good man. Never said an unkind word. Never harmed anyone.

"Let it go, Billy," he said out loud. "You'll only make trouble for yourself."

Lightning pulsed, backlighting the tree. Billy mentally counted. Four seconds before the thunder grumbled.

What would Sherlock think? How would he figure this out? If it indeed needed figuring out. One thing Billy knew for sure, Sherlock would try to connect the evidence in some logical fashion.

What exactly did Billy know? That Carl was shot in the head. That Carl might've done it, but the angle and lack of powder burns surely looked like someone else must've. That Carl had been depressed by his money troubles. Which, to Billy, made no sense at all. Carl and Cora ran a good business.

So, how did all this fit together? Did Carl's money woes figure into this? If so, how?

Billy knew he shouldn't stir anything up, but ignoring his gut feelings wasn't something he could abide. Truth be told, every time he did, he later regretted it.

So, again he braved the rain and walked the six blocks to the hardware store. He couldn't shake the feeling that the answer lay somewhere inside.

It was nine at night and the town, as usual for this hour, slept. Not a soul on the street. He still had his key and came in through the rear door. He didn't turn on any lights as he looked around, using the meager glow from the streetlamps outside the front windows to navigate. Everything seemed normal. Nothing out of place. The cash register stared at him. He popped open the drawer. About eighty bucks and some change inside.

He walked into Carl's office, pulling the door closed behind him. The room had no windows so he turned on the desk lamp, brass with a dark green shade. He sat in the chair where Carl's body had been found, facing the entry door across the desk. If someone came in and shot Carl it was someone he knew. No way to sneak up behind him.

The desktop was neat. Lamp, phone, "In" and "Out" trays, letter opener, a pen, two pencils, and a smudged rubber eraser. Billy slid open the middle drawer. More pens and pencils, a role of tape, a ball of rubber bands, a couple of note-books. The left drawer held neat files of receipts. Each vendor block printed on the file's edge. Billy's printing.

In the right drawer rested the current year's ledger book. Thick and heavy. Like the nine others that stood like soldiers along the top shelf of the bookcase to his left. Each labeled by the year. Also, Billy's work.

Carl had been great with people, and a good businessman, but he hadn't been much for keeping records. Stuffed receipts and other papers into paper bags and shoved them here and there. Most of his transactions were in cash—both the customers paying him and he in turn paying his suppliers. He rarely wrote checks.

When Billy began working for Carl, during his junior year in high school, he'd organized the receipts and set up the ledgers. Took the better part of two months but in the end he'd created a workable file system and annual ledger books that kept track of expenses and income. He smiled. He never could get Carl to use checks though. Never could shake his comfort with cash business. Old dogs didn't like new tricks.

Billy lifted the ledger from the drawer and flipped it open. Columns of expenses and income. He remembered sitting in this same room and showing Raymond how to add entries, total columns, do all the things needed to keep everything in line. Looks like Raymond had continued the same system after Billy left.

Billy leafed though the pages. It took twenty minutes before he realized the income columns read as they had five years earlier but the expenses had risen. He didn't remember ten penny nails going for that much.

Over the next two hours he went through four years of ledgers. The cost of supplies began to increase about two and half years ago. And, when he dug through the receipt files, he found the ledger entries and the actual invoices didn't match. The cost of five pounds of ten penny nails hadn't budged but the entries in the books showed they had. Same for screws, shovels, rakes, rawhide strips, hammers, everything.

Around midnight, the truth settled over him like a rain-soaked blanket. The invoices and the ledger entries simply didn't match. And by his loose calculation, ten of thousands of dollars couldn't be accounted for.

Raymond. No one else could have done this. And it had been easy. He controlled the books and the money. Carl only saw his business losing ground.

Then another truth dropped.

Raymond killed Carl. That thought sounded ridiculous inside his head, but as soon as it sparked to life, he knew it to be true.

He tugged Carl's address book from the middle drawer and quickly found Sheriff Blake's home number. He spun the rotary dial. Blake answered after two rings, his voice heavy with sleep.

"Sheriff, it's Billy Whitehead."

"Billy, what the hell time is it?"

"You need to see something."

"Right now?"

"Yes, sir. I'm over at Draper's Hardware."

He heard shuffling as if Blake was rolling out of bed. "What are you jawing about?"

A sound. The dream of footsteps. Beyond the closed door.

"Someone's here," Billy whispered.

"I can't hear you. What was that?"

The door swung open. Raymond, a hammer in his right hand.

"I saw the light beneath the door," he said. "Thought someone was robbing the place. What're you doing?"

"Maybe I should ask why you're here this time of night?" Billy said.

Raymond's gaze danced left, then right, no doubt searching for a reasonable answer. He finally found one, of sorts. "I was just checking on things."

"No, you were going to destroy the proof."

"Proof? Of what? You're not making much sense."

"It was you," Billy said.

Raymond's gaze now landed on the open ledgers and stacks of invoices on the desk. His face hardened, eyes narrowing. He raised the hammer a notch. "Put the phone down."

Billy did, but not in its cradle. He laid the handset on its side, facing Raymond.

"You've been stealing from Carl," Billy said.

"The hell I have. Are you crazy?"

"For nearly three years."

"I never . . ."

"It's too late, Raymond. The evidence is right here." Billy waved a hand over the desk. "And you killed Carl when he found out."

Raymond's entire body tensed. He stood frozen for a few seconds, and then charged toward Billy, the hammer high.

Billy snatched up the closest thing to a weapon that he could see, a fancy letter opener that lay beside the phone.

It had all happened so quickly and when it was over nausea swept over Billy. Cold sweat erupted on his face. He had managed to hold it together while he hung up with Blake and called Wilbert Scoggins. He then walked to the employee washroom. Just as he finished washing Raymond's blood from his hands, watching it swirl down the drain, his stomach knotted. He dropped to his knees before the toilet and retched. Only hot, acidic liquid came up. When his stomach finally unwound, he struggled to his feet, grasping the sink for support. The cold water he splashed on his face settled things somewhat.

Ten minutes later, Billy stood next to Sheriff Blake over Raymond's body. Blake looked disheveled, shirt wrinkled, eyes sleep swollen, hair flipped up on one side from the pillow he had just vacated. Raymond looked worse. Pale, waxy, mouth slack, a dribble of blood at one corner. The letter opener protruded from his chest, a blossom of red around it.

"Looks like you hit his heart," Blake said. "Got a lung, too, I'd surmise."

"I wasn't trying to kill him," Billy said. "But he didn't give me much choice."

"So I heard." Blake glanced at him. "Clever leaving the phone line open."

"I figured if it was me lying there, you'd know who did it and why."

"What the hell?"

Billy turned to see Wilbert Scoggins in the doorway behind him.

"Raymond messed up," Blake said. "Badly."

Billy explained what he had discovered, and that Raymond had attacked him. He walked to the desk. "Raymond's been fixing the books. Making it look like everything cost more than it really did. Stealing from Carl and Cora."

"I can't believe it," Wilbert said.

"It's a fact," Billy said. "Been doing it for years."

Wilbert shook his head. "No wonder Carl's business has been bad."

Billy nodded. "Hard to keep a good bottom line when someone's emptying the pot as fast as you can fill it."

Wilbert looked at Billy, then gave a brief nod toward the papers on the desk. "How'd you even know to look at all this?"

Billy glanced at Blake, and managed a smile. "Sherlock Holmes."

BUY A BULLET

AN ORPHAN X STORY

by Gregg Hurwitz

She takes the pain, takes it so well. This is evident the moment she enters the upscale coffee shop in downtown Palo Alto. She is on the arm of a trim man with artfully tousled hair, two-day growth, and Bono sunglasses. Or rather, he is on *her* arm, his fist wrapped around her slender biceps, steering her, conveying ownership. She winces against the pressure of his grip, allowing a slight crimp of the right eye, but her grin doesn't so much as flicker. Experience has taught her.

Bringing up the rear is a head-taller, broad-chested specimen of a bodyguard, ex-military judging by hair and posture. His deferential bearing suggests that when tasked, he also performs the services of a personal assistant, as do most employees in the orbit of the very rich. He is youthful. His body fat is single digit; muscles sheathe him like armor.

In the corner of the shop, a man notes this little retinue over a lifted cup of espresso. He is around thirty years old, not too handsome, unobtrusive. Just an average guy. At his feet sits a bag bulky with night-vision gear handed to him hours ago through the rear door of a Sand Hill office in exchange for a banded stack of bills. He is not a regular in the Bay Area; having collected what he came for, he has pit-stopped for a quick cup before the five-hour haul back to Los Angeles. But now his interest is piqued by this woman and the man clamped to her.

The coffee shop on University Avenue gets all kinds—or rather, all Silicon Valley kinds. A trio of Scandinavian engineers in their Dockers and rumpled short-sleeve button-ups. Entrepreneurs-to-be hunched over slender silver laptops, plugged into headsets. Twentysomethings wearing Havianas and slurping free-trade coffee, key-chain carabiners dangling off their belt loops. The wood-paneled confines smell of Guatemalan roast and ambition, and hum with caffeine and a variety of pleasingly accented voices.

At the couple's entrance, activity ceases for a moment but it is not, surprisingly, at the woman's considerable Midwestern beauty. The ensuing stir appears to be due to the man in the yellow-tinted shades. From the whispers making the rounds, a name emerges—Steve Radack.

The watcher at the corner table lowers his demitasse to the tiny saucer. The name rolls around in his mind for a moment before slotting into place. Radack is a dot-com success story, which makes him, in these parts, royalty. A member of the three comma club, he is unaware of the attention or, more likely, inured to it. His knees jiggle beneath tailored pants. An unlit cigarette bobs from his lips. Sweat sparkles at his hairline. He is amped on something and the condition seems not unfamiliar to him.

Radack orders the bodyguard to bring him a Dead Eye—three shots of espresso added to drip coffee—and leads the woman to a table, his fingers still indenting her smooth pale skin. Patrons clear a path. At the table, the woman says, "Would you mind getting it to go?" and he slides his hand to her wrist and deals it a cruel twist. Her full lips part but she makes no sound. She lowers her head and sits, her emerald eyes slightly dulled. One side of her neck is streaked with faded bruises. Finger-width. Her nose is sloped just right with a scattering of freckles across the bridge, and her front teeth are Brigitte Bardot–pronounced, just shy of buck. She is stunning, and yet there is a blankness behind her features, the blankness of compounded trauma.

The watcher at the corner table knows this expression. He knows it well.

He has spent a lifetime in the vicinity of trauma, usually inflicting it. He is known by some as Evan Smoak. To a few, he is known as Orphan X. But generally he is not known at all.

He decides to extend his visit.

Steve Radack's background and proclivities prove to be amply detailed on the World Wide Web. He is the visionary behind *Thumbprint*, a software that allows one to press a finger to a smartphone and pay for a variety of items in a variety of ways. To the watcher, this doesn't seem like a concept worth a seven-hundred-and-fifty-million-dollar buyout, but he is not an arbiter of the whims of the Silicon Valley gods. Sitting on a muted floral duvet in a Los Altos hotel room, sipping a Grey Goose over ice, he scrolls and clicks.

Radack is the self-described bad-boy of the software world, and though this seems a comically low bar, his accomplishments in self-debasement are impressive. Shortly after *Thumbprint*'s acquisition five years ago, he was ousted from the company's board after the replacement CEO filed battery charges. Radack went on to total a Tesla Model S Signature and an Audi R8 Spyder in a three-day period. After the latter wreck, despite blowing nearly six times the legal blood-alcohol limit, he got his DUI overturned on a technicality by a team of attorneys. A run of thrill-seeking adventures followed, from big-wave surfing in Peru to BASE jumping from Dubai skyscrapers, the party culminating in a protracted cocaine bender that stopped his heart for a full seven minutes. A gaggle of concierge doctors at the Stanford University Medical Center and a pacemaker got him up and running again, and according to various accounts, he hadn't lost a step. In a recent *Wired* interview, when asked to give his religion, Radack names Social Darwinism. Expounding upon the rights and obligations of the powerful, he quotes everything from *The Art of War* to the Leopold and Loeb trial.

But he is not the watcher's focus. The focus is Radack's girlfriend, the lovely Leanne Lattimore, who hails from Kansas City. The daughter of an insurance salesman and a schoolteacher, she came west to attend San Jose State, where she studied computer science. An internship at *Thumbprint* six summers ago brought her into contact with Radack and she'd been attached to him ever since. Or him to her. The watcher finds footage including her backstage at one of Radack's TED talks. A well-timed pause captures her in close-up.

When he finally looks up from the screen, the windows are dark with night. He finishes his vodka, rises, and sets the glass neatly on the tray above the wet bar, nudging it until it is perfectly centered on the paper doily. An urge turns his head. He looks across at the bed and the open laptop on which Leanne's image is frozen. The situation she is in appears to be unmanageable. It's a complex problem, one that will require a solution worthy of Sherlock Holmes.

He stands motionless with his fingertips tented on the brim of the empty glass, regarding Leanne's image, feeling the pull of instinct and muscle memory, his thoughts reshaping themselves until they form something dark and unyielding and true.

Perhaps she will be his first.

In the trunk of his Honda Accord is a black sweatshirt, a pair of Night Owl tactical binoculars, and a Wi-Fi antenna with good gain. A few exits up Interstate 280 in Atherton, he finds Radack's oft-referenced estate with little trouble. The fifteen-acre compound features multiple safe rooms, a fully stocked fish pond, and self-sustaining gardens and crops in the event of a nuclear winter or zombie attack. The watcher takes a single pass around, noting a sheltered dog run just east of the guest house. He parks on the back side of the compound in a blind spot between cameras mounted on the spike-topped fence. The binoculars' night vision provides decent vantage through to the main house. He wonders which window Leanne is behind. Then he shakes his head: *I never guess, Watson.*

He opens his laptop and, with the help of the antenna and a thirty-dollar long-range Wi-Fi modem, finds the network—TECHWARRIOR. It is password-protected. While he is hardly a tech warrior himself, he knows which tools to apply. Using the Kismet and Aircrack suite of programs, he recons the hidden wireless network and finds the encrypted credentials. These he e-mails off to a double-blind account at Hashkiller, and sets its 131-billion-password cracking engine to work.

Two Dobermans appear at the fence near his car, vibrating the windows with resonant barks. He checks the time—it took them three minutes and twelve seconds to notice his presence. They are overfed, boxy around the middle, further evidence of their owner's lack of discipline. It is time to go; even fat dogs can raise an alarm.

Sliding his laptop onto the passenger seat, he drives off. Ten minutes away in Woodside, he finds an upscale restaurant, The Village Pub. The bar has the usual selection of vodkas. He settles on a Cîroc, up, with a twist, and tells the bartender to bruise it. It pours properly, with a film of ice crystals, and it drinks even better.

He sips it halfway down, tips the bartender handsomely, returns to his car, and checks the laptop. Hashkiller has already delivered the network authorization passwords. Holmes would have figured them out himself, but that was then.

He drives back to Radack's estate, this time parking two blocks away, and inputs the new-found passwords. Access granted. His laptop is now a member of Radack's internal Wi-Fi network. Once inside the system, he finds the security cameras with ease. The links to the hundred-plus webcam and security feeds are neatly aggregated on a single webpage. The configuration of the web server tells him the location of the router as well as the VPN gateway. Hashkiller makes short work of those credentials as well, and the watcher is set up to access the estate's security camera feeds over the Internet from any location.

Heading back to the hotel, he rolls down the window. The maples, spotting the vast lawns, have gone to orange and yellow, and the heavy air tastes of autumn.

In his room, he scrolls through the feeds. Library, kitchen, bowling alley, screening room, all empty. He finds Radack in the cigar parlor drinking mezcal and playing darts with a pair of bodyguards—the one from the coffee shop and a second man, Hispanic, even more sturdy. The latter strains a T-shirt at the seams and has a circular tattoo covering one biceps. The watcher waits for the right angle to identify the tattoo, but the lighting is tough. Finally, he picks up what looks like a black spear inside the circle. He places it as the emblem from the United States Marine Corps Special Operations Command. Both men look to be in their late twenties, far too young to be out of MARSOC for any good reason, which points to disciplinary discharge or drug-testing. He picks up names from the banter—Kane and Padilla. Padilla sports a hip-holstered Glock, while Kane wears a single-action revolver in an upside-down shoulder holster. Radack throws back another shot and spreads his hand on the dart board, daring his lackeys to a steel-tipped game of chicken. The watcher leaves them to it.

He clicks through various cameras, finding Leanne trying to sleep in the master bedroom down the hall from the parlor. She is curled around a pillow, covering her exposed ear. Every time a burst of laughter reaches her, she starts.

He observes her for a time.

She needs him. She really does.

When he clicks back to the parlor, Radack and his henchmen have disappeared. All that remains are two empty bottles of mezcal on the bar, next to a few residual lines of cocaine. There is blood on the dartboard.

He finds the trio in the bowling alley. Radack is firing a submachine gun at a target painted in blood above the middle lane. He is tearing up the wall, Sheetrock dust clouding. The shots climb off the target, the gun running him rather than the other way around.

Despite the bravado, Radack is afraid of the gun. This is good to know.

Crimson drips from Padilla's left hand; he appears to be the dartboard casualty and the fingerpainter behind the target. After Radack empies the magazine, Padilla applauds dutifully, radiating droplets of blood. From his front right pocket, Kane removes a baggie and a military folding knife and offers Radack cocaine off the blued tip. As Radack leans over to snort, the submachine gun comes into clear view. It is an H&K 94, illegal in California even without its clandestine conversion to full auto. Radack likes his toys and dislikes protocol.

The watcher captures the image of Radack's nose nearing the blade and enlarges it. The knife is an Emerson, popular with former military. This, too, is good to know.

Back in the bedroom, Leanne sits with her shoulder blades pressed to the corner, hugging her knees, rocking herself. Her lips move but the sub-par audio picks up nothing.

In the bowling alley, Radack jams home another magazine and, to cheers and encouragement from his paid admirers, resumes shredding the wall above the target. Two hours and three bottles of mezcal later, the men stumble outside, leaning on one another, barely keeping their feet. Radack throws a grenade in the stocked fish pond. The pop is muffled. Water sprays the laughing men and dozens of white spots bob to the surface. They drink more and pass out on the lawn. The Dobermans tentatively approach, pull dead fish from the pond, and feast.

Inside, Leanne stays in the corner, trembling. She does not sleep.

The watcher does not either.

In the morning, he calls the Stanford University Medical Center, Radack's hospital of choice, and identifies himself as a consulting physician for Ms. Leanne Lattimore. Would they be so kind as to send the medical files from her emergency room visits? They would, provided Ms. Lattimore signs a release. This of course will not happen, but he has confirmed his hunch that Ms. Lattimore is a frequent flier at the Stanford ER.

A medical supply shop on El Camino Real sells standard teal scrubs. He changes into them in his car, drives to the hospital, and steps into the bracing air-conditioning of the main lobby. Rather than heading for the bustling ER, he detours to the medical floor, lingering by a water fountain until he sees a pretty Indian physician leave her office. He waits for a break in foot traffic and slips inside. The doctor has left her computer logged on to the Epic medical records system. The watcher types in *Leanne Lattimore* and brings up her files.

Her injuries and admitting complaints are telling. A gashed lip and broken cheekbone she claimed to have incurred in a fender bender. When presenting with suture-worthy tears at the introitus and vaginal mucosa, she confessed to being into rough sex. Clavicle and distal radius fractures she chalked up to a snowboarding fall. Deep scrapes to her upper arm required antibiotic ointment and dressings; she explained that she'd been clawed by a dog. Photographs had been taken at the nurse's insistence for legal reasons, should Leanne want to press charges against the dog's owner. The watcher studies them. He has been clawed by many a dog and her wounds feature none of the trademark gouges. They do however look familiar. He has seen this nasty little trick twice before, once in Zagreb, once in Bangkok. The lacerations are caused by a potato peeler.

He is now ninety-nine percent sure, but with what he's considering, there can be no shadow of a doubt, not an eyelash of uncertainty. This is the First Commandment: *Assume Nothing.*

Before he acted, he would be well acquainted with every last detail, as intimate with each particular as Sherlock was with the number of steps leading from the ground floor to the door of his flat at 221B Baker Street.

He slips out of the hospital unobserved, stops for a quick lunch, and returns to his hotel. The woman behind the reception desk is attractive and her eye contact direct, but he pretends not to notice.

As he passes, she asks, "In town for business?" and he gives a benign nod.

In his room, he again accesses the security cameras from the estate, splitting the screen to watch multiple feeds at once. Radack's goons are only now stirring. Radack is in the pool house, showering. A squat, middle-aged housekeeper finishes cleaning up the bowling alley with a dustpan and broom. In the screening room, Leanne sits on a padded bench, tapping at an iPad. She wears large round retro eyeglasses that accent her round face and somehow make it prettier still.

When Radack emerges from the shower, he admires himself in the mirror. A scar runs zipper-like from above his navel to the base of his throat where they cracked his chest to resuscitate him. Another scar to the side indicates where the pacemaker was inserted. He dresses and enters the main house, crossing paths with Padilla in the foyer.

"Erase the footage from last night," he says. "Bowling alley and front yard. The pond. Get that shit gone."

Padilla nods and shuffles off to the adjoining study. Deleting evidence seems to be a habit of Radack's, a habit that will prove useful.

As Padilla sits at the computer, the watcher brings up another screen. From inside the system, he sees the previous night's footage vanish from the net video recorder application. The watcher notes the precise time of Padilla's meddling—15:31. The archives already look like Swiss cheese, showing an extensive history of holes where Radack has ordered illicit activity excised from the record.

Back to the live feeds. Radack is walking down a long hall. He enters the screening room. Leanne jolts upright and turns off her iPad. Radack crosses his arms.

"You e-mailed your mom to get you a plane ticket," he says.

The air leaks from Leanne; she seems literally to deflate on the bench. Her fingers twist together in her lap, tugging.

"I'm a software visionary, you dumb cooze. Do you really think you can do *anything* without me noticing?"

Her words are almost too quiet to be picked up by the speakers. "Why don't you let me go?"

Radack leans back on his heels, appeals to the upholstered ceiling. "I don't want to break *up* with you," he says. "I want to ruin you so no one else will ever want you." He wipes at his nose with finger and thumb. "What do you have to say to that?"

She has nothing to say to that.

He points through the wall. "Kane and Padilla, they are my blood brothers. My guard dogs. Wherever you go, they will hunt you down. And bring you back to me."

She says, "Go to hell, Steve."

He moves like a flash, two quick strides and a backhand, and she is sent sprawling off the couch. On all fours, she gropes for her broken glasses.

He stands over her, wide-postured, legs spread. "Hell ain't a *place*. It's a state of mind."

He walks out. She waits frozen for a few moments and then clamps a palm over her mouth and sobs into it. Finally she rises, weak on her legs, clutching her shattered eyeglasses. She pokes her head through the doorway, then moves quietly down the hall and turns left. The watcher loses her, not knowing which feed to pick up. He finds her in the maid's quarters, where the housekeeper looks stunned to see her. Leanne asks her to read the Bible with her, and the woman nods. They kneel together at the side of the bed before the worn book. Leanne holds up one intact lens to read through. She laces her free hand in the housekeeper's.

In the living room, Radack gathers his H&K 94 and his bodyguards. They head to the screening room first and find Leanne missing. They begin a march through the house, prowling, opening doors.

Leanne reads faster. Her body tenses. Her eyes squeeze shut. The housekeeper looks terrified.

The hunting party nears. The door to the maid's quarters opens.

Radack says, "Go home, Marisol."

Marisol rises. She has to pull her hand free of Leanne's. Marisol nods respectfully to Radack and slides out through the men. Rushing down the hall to the foyer, she begins to weep soundlessly.

In the room, Leanne has still not looked up. Her eyes remain closed; her lips are moving soundlessly. Radack steps forward and places the muzzle of the submachine gun to her forehead.

The watcher knows now. She is the one.

She is the catalyst for his reinvention.

Leanne's lips stop moving but even now she does not open her eyes.

"The killings in Rwanda," Radack says. "Know what the Hutu tribesmen did? They made their victims buy the bullets they'd be killed with if they didn't want to get hacked to death."

Behind him, Kane laughs at the thought of this.

"So," Radack says. "What do you say, Leanne? Wanna buy a bullet?"

Leanne remains very still for a long time, maybe a full minute. Finally she shakes her head. He clocks her with the barrel of the carbine, knocking her over. Then he tugs down his pants and advances. The bodyguards look on. He finishes and rises. There are smiles and high fives.

As Radack exits, he says, "Have a go."

The men are willing. They step forward, already unbuckling, and set upon her like dogs. The watcher does not flinch. He does not look away.

When it is over, he turns to the window. It is night.

Night is good.

He packs up, walks downstairs, and checks out. The receptionist says, "How was everything?" and he smiles and says, "Fine, thank you."

He drives over to Radack's estate, abiding the speed limit, and parks on the quiet street behind the compound. A check of the laptop shows Radack shirtless, playing a first-person-shooter video game in the living room, the real submachine gun resting on the cushion beside him. He has seemingly ordered Leanne to the facing couch, for she lies there fetally, shuddering. Padilla mixes margaritas on the kitchen island behind them, and Kane patrols the halls. Both bodyguards wear satiated grins. There are white lines on the coffee table before Radack and white lines on the granite slab of the island and the three men's motions have more zip than seems standard.

The watcher applies Superglue to his fingertips, covering the prints, and then pops the hood and trunk. He climbs out, removing the floor mat and hanging it over his open door. He takes the battery from the engine and jumper cables from the back and throws them over the fence. He pays the security cameras no mind; he will make sure later that no footage from tonight exists. In the archives, it will appear as though Padilla shut down the security cameras altogether during his visit to the study at 15:31.

The watcher slings the floor mat up to cover the spikes and scrambles over the fence.

The wet wind is blowing out, buying him time before his scent travels. He slices through the maze of the gardens, darting between pea planting beds. Emerging from a row of corn stalks, he sprints for the fish pond.

At the bank, he kneels. He has just attached a jumper cable to the positive terminal on the battery when he hears the dogs' snarling approach. He slings the other cable into the pond and trawls it, a few paralyzed fish rolling up to the surface.

The Dobermans explode into view. He drags the cable clear of the water to preserve the battery for his ride to Los Angeles, and puts the pond and its offerings between him and the dogs. Sure enough, they catch sight of the fish and their interest is diverted. They wade heavily into the pond, dip their snouts, and come up with dinner. He walks boldly between them, signaling his fearlessness. They pause from gnawing, their eyes rolling to track him.

"Sit," he says in a low, hard voice.

They sit.

He walks to the house. The front door opens, Kane ambling out onto the porch, already shouting: "Thor! Zeus! C'mon, b—"

Kane stops, on his heels.

The watcher is ten feet away.

Now five.

Kane's hand flies to his shoulder holster and the revolver is out, swinging toward the watcher's head. Hopping the step onto the porch directly into the path of the muzzle, the watcher grabs the gun around the wheel, clenching so the cylinder cannot rotate and the weapon cannot fire. For a split-second, he is staring straight down the bore. Kane is still tugging the trigger, confused, when the watcher torques Kane's gun hand, forcing him to spin to keep the elbow intact. The watcher slides neatly behind him. His free hand moves to Kane's front right pocket and he rakes the Emerson knife free, knowing that the shark-fin hook riding the blade top will snare the pocket edge and snap the knife open. Kane is arched backwards, his vitals bared, and the blade work is direct and efficient. The scents of tequila and deodorant are joined by a fresh, coppery tang.

Better than Baritsu, the watcher thinks.

He eases the collapsing form to the concrete and pivots to the door, his momentum barely slowed.

He is inside.

The house smells of teak and lavender—it smells of *money*. He strides through the foyer but Padilla is already stepping into view from the living room on the far side, surprising him. It is clear now just how large Padilla is.

The men halt and consider each other across the six-foot span.

"What the hell?" Radack calls out from behind. "Where'd Kane *go*?"

The watcher lunges before Padilla can go for his hip holster. Padilla leads with a jab and the watcher sidesteps and flicks the Emerson. But the big man is well trained, parrying the swipe and countering with a cross that whistles overhead. The watcher lunges with the blade and Padilla catches his arm midflight, one giant hand crushing his wrist. His arm and the knife are going nowhere; the men are locked up. Padilla draws back his fist, but before he can swing, the watcher does the unexpected; he opens the hand clenched around the knife handle. The blade tumbles past their eyes, their chins, their chests, Padilla seeming to realize what is coming an instant before it does.

The watcher's free hand darts forward, grabbing the tumbling knife as it falls between them and driving it into Padilla's gut. He punches it two more times up Padilla's left ribs—*smack smack*—and the man falls away in slow motion.

The watcher is already gliding down the steps into the sunken living room, angling for the kitchen. As the watcher hoped, Radack has the H&K 94 in hand. He swings the submachine gun blindly as the watcher hip-slides across the sleek granite slab and drops behind the island.

Radack dumps all thirty-two rounds in a single wild burst. Wine bottles shatter. Bullets ping off the Sub-Zero. The Viking stove crumples inward and emits a puff of gray smoke. Lighting fixtures spark overhead. Chunks of the ceiling dump down. Somewhere on the floor beside the couch, Leanne screams.

The island remains, predictably, untouched. The watcher could have stood in plain view and every last bullet would have sailed overhead.

He rises now and crosses to Radack, who struggles to drop the magazine from the useless gun, his panic tangible. Drops of sweat cling to the tips of his disheveled hair. As the watcher nears, Radack gives up on the mag and clubs at him with the barrel. The watcher knocks the weapon wide and, with the butt of his palm, delivers a single stun blow to the heart.

Radack makes a noise like a bark and veins pop in his throat. He takes a step back, his clawed hand hovering an inch off his chest. The skin has gone to scarlet, the sutures scars standing out in defiant white. He lean-sits against the couch back and his eyes widen and widen some more and then his head lolls forward and he is dead.

The room is thick with smoke and dust billowing from the torn-open ceiling.

Leanne resolves through the debris-filled air. She lies on her stomach, half twisted over one hip like the crippled girl from that Wyeth painting.

The watcher says, "You're safe now."

He takes the knife and balls it into Radack's hand for the prints, then lets it fall to the carpet by the man's bare feet.

"Radack went crazy," he tells her. "Hopped-up on coke. They beat and raped you. Then he went paranoid. Killed his own guards and shot up the place. The security cameras will be wiped."

She pulls herself up to sit against the base of the couch, holding one hand to the side of her head. Bruises are coming up around her left eye and there are small cuts where Radack shattered the eyeglasses against her temple earlier. Tears stream, though she makes no noise.

He crouches, keeping a distance, not wanting to crowd her. In the air is the familiar hot-metal taste of a gunfight's aftermath. "You're free."

Her face is tilted to the ceiling and her lips move in a quiet murmur. It seems she is speaking more to herself than to him. He thinks he makes out her hoarse whisper.

—thank God thank God thank—

"I have to go now. I have one thing to ask of you. Only one thing. So please listen carefully."

She tries to speak but coughs dryly instead. Then she squints at him through the swirling dust. "Who *are* you?"

He hesitates. He hasn't used the name, not in several years and never in this context.

"The Nowhere Man," he says.

THE GIRL IN THE KEY OF C

by Weston Ochse

Los Angeles was the sort of town that, if you aren't watching television, you might not even know it was Christmas. What's Christmas to a movie star who has a three-picture deal and graces every red carpet at the Kodak Theater? What's Christmas to a homeless guy who just wants his next meal? What's Christmas to a surfer other than a bullshit story about a red and white fat man whose entire gig was to be a mythical creature who gives children toys they don't need? No, Christmas might be important to some, but to the denizens of Los Angeles, especially those of us working the docks down in L.A. Harbor, Christmas meant only two things: you weren't with your family and you were getting time and a half.

And of course, the occasional hooker in red spandex and a white fleece collar was the added bonus.

She was a relatively new addition to our dock-side mart, and looked as out of place as a sleigh and reindeer—although I admired her skin-tight red pants tucked into her loosely laced army boots as she bent into the window of the beat-up Cadillac Seville. I couldn't hear her but imagined a sweet voice as she tried to talk her way into the driver's wallet. He could be a lovelorn husband sick and tired of the holidays, or a middle-aged divorcée with no one to share hot chocolate, or a cop—a serial killer, even—but she didn't care. She was on the job and ready to let strangers tour her architecture for a few twenties and a possible smile.

She backed out of the window and turned to gaze back at me, as if my attention had all the power of the moon and she was unable to resist its tidal effects. In a surprising moment of audacity, I held her gaze. We stared at each other and I felt my stomach begin to flutter. Then she ended it, opened the car door, and got in. The pair were silhouetted in the dark front seat by the lights of the cranes for a brief second, then the driver put the Caddie in gear, and took her away.

I sighed as I turned back to my hotdog cart. I checked the temperature of the water, peered at the condiments to make sure no flies had settled in, and slouched against the cool metal. Night shift in L.A. Harbor. Who ate hotdogs at night? I'd wondered when I'd taken the job. The longshoremen who came on shift at 8 P.M., that's who. The commercial fishermen coming in from several days fishing the western shoals of Catalina Island for yellowtail, that's who. The cops and Homeland Security officers who patrolled the place for possible terrorist incursions, that's who. And more often than not those who came needed more than hot dogs.

I glanced over at the coffee truck that also sold meth if you knew the signal. Next to it was the chowder truck, offering seven different kinds of clam and fish chowder, served either in a plastic bowl or one made with sourdough, which was primarily reserved for the odd tourist who had absolutely made a wrong turn.

We were an unhappy lot. We lived in a world with no sun. The smell of diesel engines and the constant metal-on-metal noises from the longshoremen unloading and loading containers on the ships was our constant tympanic soundtrack. That this was Christmas made us doubly unhappy. The longshoremen got overtime, and all we got was the same bullshit like it was any other night.

Frank, the guy who sold coffee and other stimulants—I didn't know his last name and had never thought to ask—had been in the military until an IED took the lower third of his right arm. He lived hand-to-mouth in a one-room shack in Wilmington. The meth belonged to the Eighth Street Angels, and he was lucky to get a one percent cut.

Edna Carruthers ran the chowder truck. Her husband had started it five years ago, sinking their entire savings into it and mortgaging their small home in Gardena. Then the bastard had died while getting a blow job from a prossie in Koreatown, leaving her chained to the chowder, even though she'd never wanted anything to do with clams or chowder or sourdough-fucking-bread bowls. Now she was the owner, manager, cook and server, and she had no other life than to serve the tourists over at Ports of Call during the day, and at night the longshoremen and denizens who called the docks home. I'd often see her snoring gently, her head on her arm as she waited for the odd customer to creep out of the shadows. She'd at least tried to celebrate the season with a scraggly old length of lights around the serving window. Red, green, blue winks like they were laughing at us.

And then there was me.

I'd been going to Harbor College, working toward a degree in law enforcement, for so many years now it seemed ridiculous to still call myself a college student. I lived on the couch of a one-bedroom five-hundred-square-foot apartment in Lomita. I paid half the rent, which came to six hundred a month. My bills and college loans came to another six hundred. In a good month, I might clear fourteen hundred dollars running the hot dog cart, leaving me with two hundred dollars mad money, which normally went to bus fare so I could get back and forth to work. When I had more, I'd take a class if I could find the books cheap enough. If it wasn't for the hot dogs on the cart, I'd have nothing to eat. But then again a good hot dog consisted of all the food groups, especially if you understood that ketchup was a fruit. In between sales—and there was a lot of in-between time—I read mysteries. I'd gotten hooked on Sherlock Holmes when I was a kid; now I entertained myself by making deductions about my customers, telling myself I was practicing skills for the future.

An hour later my Christmas Elf was back.

I checked my watch. We were fifty-five minutes into Christmas morning.

Edna snored.

Frank rattled his fingers in a meth-fueled rat-a-tat-tat on the metal serving ledge of his truck. He was going to be in the shit if the Angels found out he was using their product.

We were five minutes away from the longshoremens' union-mandated break.

"Gimme one with everything," came a voice I'd been aching to hear.

And there she was. All the times I'd seen her, all the times I'd watched her, she'd never come to me, instead getting pastries from Frank or chowder from Edna instead.

"Everything? Even peppers?" I managed to say.

She had fairy features. Small nose. Small chin. Slightly slanted eyes, revealing something Asian in her genetics. My gaze was drawn to the space between her brown eyes, wider than that of most women, forcing my own eyes to dash back and forth to take in the whole of her elfin beauty. I couldn't tell anything else about her, not from just looking. I wasn't very good at being Holmes.

"Oh, 'specially peppers," she said, drawing out the words.

I tried to look cool while I made her hot dog. I'd always been nervous around beautiful women. This one seemed to be more beautiful than most, if not completely intriguing.

"I see you watching me. Watching me talk to the customers. Thinking about me, like you're Sherlock Holmes or something."

I felt my heart skip as I spooned onions over the ketchup and mustard. I suddenly wondered if she kissed her johns. With the onions, one would think she didn't. I felt her watching me, knowing she wanted a response. "I didn't mean to stare," I managed to say.

"Of course you did, Mister Hot Dog Man," the last coming out as if it were part of a song. *Mister Hot Dog Man.*

I relished the words and forced myself to gaze at her.

"I know how I look," she said as straight as any businesswoman. "I work at it."

I smiled weakly. The last time I'd had a date, it was a divorcée in my building. She was ten years older, burdened by her three kids, and just wanted a good fuck. Two glasses of chardonnay and a piece of pizza and she had me doing her like a dog in the middle of my living room floor amid a battle array of Power Rangers and a talking teddy bear that she kept bumping, which made it sing. Even thinking of it made me feel dirty in front of this prostitute.

I added a swirl of mayo on top of the finished product, then wrapped it in paper and handed it to her.

She held out a ten.

I shook my head. "I got this."

She frowned. "Don't do that."

"No, really. Merry Christmas."

"I said don't do that, Sherlock."

"Don't do what?"

"This isn't a date. It's business."

"But it's Christmas."

She thrust out a hip. "Do I look like a kid waiting for Santa Claus?"

"But what if I *want* to give it to you?"

"Never give away what you can't afford to give."

"How do you know I can't afford to give it away?"

She laughed throatily, a bite of hot dog rolling in her mouth. "You out here slinging sausage tells me you can barely afford to breathe, sugar. The only people worse off than you is Frank, who's about to get shanked for using product, and Edna, who's thinking about walking away from everything and living on the street just so she can get a day off."

I thought about what she said as I watched her eating the hot dog. Finally, I asked, "And you? Can you afford to give it away?"

She lowered her head and smiled, a speck of ketchup caught in the corner of her mouth. "Sherlock, this girl doesn't give nothing away."

As we laughed together, the horn blew, signaling the longshoremen's break.

She finished her hot dog and wiped her mouth. "Time for both of us to get to work, right?" She pointed her chin to the dozens of men heading our way. "I know several are going to want a Christmas special."

I nodded, realizing too late that I'd forgotten to ask her her name. I was soon swamped as the hungry men descended on the three food venues and the lone whore.

By one-thirty we were alone again. A pickup pulled up, and out she hopped. She glanced once in my direction, but remained standing where she was. I wanted to go see her, but I wasn't supposed to leave the cart. Looking around, there was no one except Frank, Edna, her, and me.

Fuck it. What could happen to the cart?

I cinched up my bravery and strode over to her, adjusting my cap, smoothing my apron.

"Hey," I said.

She turned to me. She'd been crying.

Anger blossomed inside me. "What'd he do to you?"

"It's not that. I'm okay."

"But you're hurt."

She shook her head and wiped a tear away. "I'm not. It's okay." She turned to me. "I'm fine."

"Then why are you crying?" I glared at where the pickup had disappeared. "Did he do something to you?"

She sighed and bit her lip. "I know what's best for me."

I felt the need to be a hero. I persisted. "How can you know—"

"I know. I just do. Get it?" She turned away. "Just go!"

I rejoined my cart. I noticed that Edna had watched the whole episode and rolled her eyes. What was I getting myself into? I turned away from her and stared up into the lighted cranes. I knew that they were merely machines, but they'd always seemed a little eerie to me, as if they were monsters, waiting to be called to life.

"Hey," came her soft voice from behind me.

I turned. She was no longer crying. She stared up at me, worry in her eyes. She was so beautiful.

"Sorry," she said.

I shrugged. "That's all right. I can be pushy."

She smiled weakly. "All men are pushy. It's in your DNA." She put her hand on the cart, giving her manicured nails something to tap against. "Listen, I know things. If I tell you to leave, then you need to get far away from here, okay?"

What did she mean? "How can you know?"

Now it was her turn to shrug. "I just do. It's like I was born knowing."

"Knowing what?"

She sighed. "Everything. Nothing. It doesn't matter. It's silly."

I let the silence surround us for a moment, but it became too heavy too quickly. "It's not silly," I said. "I think you are something awesome," then died inside as each word fell lamer and lamer.

"No. Don't say that. I'm just a regular girl."

Still, I persisted. "There's nothing regular about you."

"You just don't know. I'm simple. Basic. I'm—I'm a girl in the key of C."

Just then an old but beautiful Chevy lowrider rumbled slowly by. Carlos Santana blasted from big trunk speakers. Two heavily-tattooed *cholos* slouched in the front seat of the car, which was the metallic green color of a June bug. Hats cocked, eyes lasered in on Frank's food truck, they were oblivious to us. I watched the man in the passenger seat, distinctly aware that I couldn't see his hands. I followed his gaze to the coffee truck. The light was on but Frank wasn't there. The bangers didn't stop, but kept going.

Edna and I locked gazes, as the music receded.

Where was Frank?

"Be careful," said the girl, then she slipped into the night.

A ship's horn blew.

Then silence.

One hundred and twenty minutes into Christmas, I fed two port police officers. Fifteen minutes after that, a foreman from a nearby loading crew came over and bitched and moaned about the quality of workers he had that night. He had nothing but management working to get overtime, and wanted real workers because this crew was way too slow. Longshoremen made between twenty and fifty bucks an hour. I'd give anything to get one of those jobs, and told him so. He mumbled something about the union and having to know someone, then paid up and went back to yell at his men. I didn't have a chance to ask how one gets to know someone.

The Girl materialized once more twenty minutes later, looking more and more like a Christmas elf.

I wonder if she'd grant me a wish. Then I shook my head to dislodge the idea. She'd never go for me. I was just Mister Hot Dog Man. Still, I went over to her, hands in pockets, confidence balanced on the tip of a smile.

"Hey," I said like a conversational genius.

"Hey," she said back. She glanced worriedly at Frank's truck, then back at me.

"My name's not Sherlock. It's Danny." I stuck out my hand.

She took it like it was someone else's used Kleenex and gave it a brief squeeze.

"What's that mean, that you're a girl in the key of C?"

She paused a moment, then pulled out a nail file from her tiny white handbag. She began working on her right hand as she asked, "Are you familiar with music?"

"I listen to it."

"But you don't play it."

I remember when my mother wanted me to play the trombone. I'd thought it a totally stupid instrument at the time, but now I wished I'd had, if only to have something to talk about with the Girl. So instead of conversation, I let a "No" escape from my lips.

"Never evs?" she asked, grinning.

I couldn't help but reciprocate her cuteness. "Never evs."

"So, a key is a kind of guide on how to play the other notes. A song will sound different depending on the key it's played in. C, or C major, is one of the simplest keys, 'cause it doesn't have any sharps or flats. Get it?"

I nodded. "C is the most . . . common?"

She nodded. "It's the first key beginning students learn."

"So what does that have to do with you? It's not like you're a musical instrument. It's not like you're common at all."

"Don't be so sure." She cracked a smile. "'A Girl in the Key of C' means I'm the normal. I'm the simple that people look for. When their lives get so hard . . . so sharp . . . so flat . . . they want nothing more than to find the center. The C of it."

"C as in Christmas," I said.

She looked at me oddly. "Why do you say that?"

I tried to come up with a reason, but I'd only said it because it had come to me. Now I cursed inwardly for even saying anything and disrupting her flow. "Cause it's Christmas day?"

"Christmas isn't the center. Christmas is the sharpest of sharps and the flattest of flats," she said. "I'm anything *but* Christmas."

You're my Christmas every day, I said to no one ever, but wanted to now. What I actually did say, I tried to make serious, but it came out almost reverent. "You're anything but normal."

There was an awkward moment. Then, "If you say that, it means you're so far away from normal that you can't even recognize it."

I thought about that as she strode away. So I was one of her sharps. I was one of her flats. It bothered me to hear her say it. What was normal? Was it normal for a thirty-year-old man to be living on a couch, still going to college with teenagers, living hand to mouth, his only method of transportation the city bus, and whose entire diet was hot dogs? It could be argued that it was normal for L.A. I knew plenty of people like me—but no, I didn't really know anyone. To use her musical metaphors, if my life was an old vinyl record, I lived in the scratchy grooves at the end of the album. My music had played and I was caught between the music I'd already heard and the music that had yet to start.

So how could I get my life to the new music?

Frank returned on a bike ten minutes later. He stopped by my cart. His whole body trembled like it was in the middle of a methquake.

"Anyone come looking for me?" His normally combed hair was mussed. His gaze moved frantically from object to object.

"Two bangers in a lowrider," I said.

"Shit. Shit." He swiveled in his seat to look at the road behind him. "Did they say they'd be back?"

"Didn't say nothing at all." I watched his eyes dart back and forth. "And I didn't bother to ask," I added.

He put foot to pedal and without any further words, went to his truck. He disappeared inside for five minutes, then appeared at the counter, his elbows resting on it as he listened to KROQ playing softly on a portable radio as if everything was normal.

I suddenly remembered a science teacher I had in ninth grade—Mr. Southard. He had this gravitational experiment he liked to show us. He had an immense metal bowl with a clear plastic top. He'd put a marble into it and shake the bowl so that the marble would travel all the way up to the rim, then circle, and circle, until it eventually found the center.

"Everything wants to go to the center. It seeks it. It wants it."

Then he'd remove the cover and do the experiment once again. At first, it had the same result, but then he'd shake the bowl harder and harder until the marble finally flew free.

"Sometimes it can escape the center," he'd said. "But once it does, there's no going back. That marble escaped gravity. It's out there looking for a new center. Maybe it will find it, maybe not."

Strange how that memory had sprung forth. I hadn't thought of Mr. Southard in years. I'd always wondered what the hell he'd been talking about, but I suddenly understood. The center in science was the large object that everything else rotated around. In life it was normalcy. As I thought the word, I broke it down once more—and laughed: *normal-c*—The Girl in the Key of C. It was too perfect to be coincidence.

Once again, I realized that I didn't even know her name.

One hundred and eighty minutes into Christmas saw another shift break. We were all busy. I noticed that when the longshoremen came across the walk, the Girl was nowhere in sight. She must have gotten good work. Edna, Frank, and I did brisk business for half an hour, then it was a ghost town once more.

The Girl appeared ten minutes after that and went straight to Frank's truck. They appeared to argue for a few minutes, then she stomped away. She stood in the middle of us, staring at the ground, her eyes furious, but concentrating. Then she slowly raised her head, her gaze first falling on Edna, then eventually falling on me with so much weight, I could hardly breathe.

She glanced once at Frank, then strode toward me, now with the ferocity of a dark rider from *Lord of the Rings*. "Listen," she began, her words low but forceful. "You're going to go to the police and report what you're about to see. Ask to speak with the FBI. Ask them for protective custody. They're going to change your life. They're going to make it normal again. This is your chance. This is your redo."

Was this is my flipped album? Was I going to escape the groove? But how? She was talking nonsense and I said as much to her.

"Remember when I was crying earlier and you thought someone hurt me?"

I nodded.

"The man I was with then . . . he's going to die later on this morning in a car crash, heading to his ex-wife's house to give his son Christmas presents. I tried to see a way out of it, but if it's not him, then it's a four-year-old girl, or a mother of three, or a young man who's destined to create a new vaccine. I can see it all if I concentrate, and it's . . . it's just too much."

I stared at her, aware that my mouth was open. I closed it. "I thought you said you were normal."

"Are you listening to me? Did you *hear* me? Go to the FBI. Ask for protective custody."

"FBI," I repeated. "Protective custody. Got it." Then I shook my head. "I don't get it."

She sighed in exasperation, then glanced over at Edna. "Watch her. She's going to touch her ear when the next customer comes over, then she's going to laugh and then she's going to hand over a cup of chowder, but then watch as she lets it go, spilling it on the man."

I watched, and everything the Girl said came true, every last thing down to the spill of steaming hot chowder.

"How did you—did she do it on purpose?"

"I never know the whys; I just know the whats . . . as in *what's going to happen*."

I blinked at her several times. Was she for real? If so, why wasn't she famous, studies done on her, TV programs . . . Then it hit me. "It's why you're out here with us in the dark. Anywhere else and there are too many people. Too many variables. Here you can control it. Am I right?"

She nodded. "You're pretty smart, Mister Hot Dog Man. Maybe you are Sherlock Holmes after all." A hint of a smile slipped across her otherwise serious face. "I can't stand the knowing. My mother had it, and she took her own life. So did her mother before her."

"Can you see your own future?"

"No. And it's both wonderful and frustrating."

He remembered the look on her face when she'd gotten into the Caddie earlier and the pickup truck later. He'd thought of it as excitement, or sexual energy, but maybe it was a carefully held sense of wonder. "It's the only thing that gives you excitement . . . the not knowing."

She nodded again. "The not knowing is such a blessing."

"Then you see the rest of us." I shook my head. "You're amazing, you know that?"

"Not me. I'm just a Girl in the Key of C." Her eyes went wide. She pointed to the large trash bin a dozen feet behind my cart. "Over there. Hide! And whatever you do, don't come out!"

I stared at her, dumbfounded.

"Now!" she screamed, slapping me across the face.

I ran and dove behind the bin just as three cars came screeching around the corner. One was the same lowrider which had come by earlier. Behind it was an immense boat of a gold Caddie with white rim tires and behind that was a candy-apple-red 1972 Cutlass Supreme. Bangers poured out of the cars and surrounded Frank's trailer. Two of them separated and went to my hot dog cart. One of the bangers peered into the darkness after me, while the other got distracted by my cart and started to make himself a hot dog. I ducked my head and pulled my legs further into the shadows.

I heard a man scream, followed by the sickening sound of flesh on flesh.

Then I heard another scream, this one from a man in agony.

I spared a glance in time to see an immense *cholo* in a wifebeater and khakis climb out of the back-seat of the Caddie. He wore Doc Martins on his feet and enough gold chains around his neck to strangle a basketball team. He turned to the guy with the hot dog and told him to "Put it the fuck down," giving me a perfect view of his face . . . the mole, the gold tooth, the scar . . . all good enough for me to identify in a lineup and testify in a court of law.

I shifted my position and peered around the other side of the bin.

I could see Edna kneeling behind the counter in her cart, shaking, her eyes closed, one hand holding her rosary to her lips, the other on a .38 Special.

I could also see the Girl . . . my girl . . . the Girl in the Key of C. They had her kneeling on the ground next to Frank. Both of them had their hands on their heads.

I wanted to rush out.

I wanted to save her.

Then her gaze found mine, and we locked eyes. She shook her head slightly as if she knew what I was thinking . . . of course she knew.

Fuck it, though. I couldn't let her go out this way. Not her. God dammit, I didn't even know her name.

I started to get to my feet, when the huge guy stepped up to the kneeling man. The gang leader was so big, he blocked out Frank in an eclipse of wife-beater white. I saw his arm raise high into the air, revealing a bat. Then I saw it come down.

Once.

Twice.

Thrice.

Each time it came down the sound was like a melon breaking.

Each time it came down, the Girl in the Key of C's eyes became wider, the sense of wonder stoked by the fires of violence, a hint of a smile growing at the corners of her perfect elfin mouth.

When the gang leader backed away, Frank's dead eyes stared into nothing.

And then the man brought out a pistol and shot my Girl in the Key of C through the head. She fell lifeless to the ground, eyes closed, smile slipping away.

Then I watched another man walk into Edna's cart and take her pistol away from her. I was still shocked at what had happened to the girl, but struggled to rise. He must have heard me because he spun and saw me.

"Hey!" he yelled, pointing the pistol at me.

I ducked around the back of the bin with nowhere else to go. I wedged myself into molding cardboard remembering that bit of conversation. *"You're anything but normal,"* I'd said. And she'd said, *"If you say that, it means you're so far away from normal that you can't even recognize it."* I sobbed into the cardboard as I imagined the pistol to the back of my skull. Whatever happened, I didn't want to see it coming.

I heard a series of shots.

I heard men running.

And then I heard sirens.

There was shouting, curses—and the sounds of engines revving, tires burning rubber, the cars taking off.

Los Angeles was the sort of town that if you aren't watching television, you might not even know it was Christmas. What's Christmas to a movie star who has a three-picture deal and graces every red carpet at the Kodak Theater, or to a homeless guy who just wants his next meal? What's Christmas to a thirty-year-old midnight hot dog vendor whose life was going nowhere until a Girl in the Key of C came into it? She *was* the center. She was the normal we all sought. Then when I finally connected with her, I became that marble that soared free from this reality into a new one . . . a reality where everyone knew what Christmas was.

Of course, she knew that.

She knew what was going to happen. She'd played it all out in her head until she'd figured out how to save me.

Part of me thought that maybe I'd just been in the right place at the right time, an accidental beneficiary to her wanting an end to the constant knowing. But the part of me that figured out patterns, and the part that still wanted to touch her, kiss her, be with her, both thought that maybe it was something about *me* that made her do it. Some reason she chose me over Edna.

Because who'd have guessed, other than her, that I'd end up in the witness protection program, enrolled in a law enforcement program in No Name, USA? Who'd have guessed that her one and only Christmas present, this girl whose name I never knew, would push me at the FBI and open the door to a future? A future I can't see, but that might give me the chance to save others. My Girl in the Key of C finally gave me *normal—c.*

Elementary, once you see the pattern.

THE GHOST OF THE LAKE

by Jamie Freveletti

Hester Regine tore herself away from an article on telomere strings and DNA strands to pull the screaming tea kettle off the flame. The weak October sun rose on a cold, Chicago day. She lived in a renovated three-story house with an expansive yard in a beautiful but deeply troubled Chicago neighborhood. Trouble didn't scare Hester. She loved the neighborhood's wide boulevards and stately brick and stone homes, many standing empty and built when the area was one of the finest in Chicago. She'd bought hers four years ago, restored it to its former glory, and spent her free time assisting in community service to help turn things around. A fence surrounded her property, hedge lined the fence's perimeter, and a camera mounted at the home's eaves scanned the yard for unauthorized move-ment. Just three hours before, an intruder had triggered her burglar alarm, and she was still tired from the broken sleep.

This latest would-be thief managed to climb the fence, fight through the hedge, and make his way halfway across the yard before he triggered the second line of defense. A spotlight high above bathed the yard with glare, the burglar alarm shrieking to life. The masked intruder froze to stare upward as a Gatling gun positioned on the roof rose noiselessly from behind a three-foot high stone parapet. The red LED tracking beam on the gun scythed through the dark sky above and then the lighted yard below as the internal eye sought the source of the vibration on the lawn. It began tracing a line along the ground toward where the man stood.

The gun roared into life, pounding rubber bullets into the dirt and creating divots in an ever advancing line of fire toward the intruder. The staccato sound of rapid gunfire, coupled with a cloud of billowing smoke from the rattling weapon and the shriek of the burglar alarm, usually sent the average thief screaming toward the hedge. Not so this one. He feinted at a tight, ninety-degree angle and then moved closer to the house, a clever tactic that allowed him to duck underneath the beam as it began a second sweep for the source of movement. The tall, thin figure jogged to the side hedge, shoved a boot into it at the place where the branches formed a perfect foothold, and vaulted up and over the fence. He landed on the other side, his knees bent and in a crouch to absorb the impact, then rose and ran away, his form and pace worthy of a trained sprinter.

Hester, woken from a sound sleep, had watched the entire performance on a house monitor. When it was over, she used an app to stop the rooftop gun, turn off the smoke machine that mimicked gunpowder, and silence the alarm. A second click reset the system.

The police knew not to bother to respond to an alarm at Hester's address. Neighborhood thieves were well aware that the yard was booby-trapped in an endless number of ways and most gave the house a wide berth. This one was of a different sort, and she contemplated that fact as she fell back into bed.

She was still contemplating it now.

She took a chair at the kitchen bay window, allowing herself a moment to gaze at the beauty of a new day, and then flipped open her computer and accessed the latest news. SCORES VISIT SITE OF VIRGIN MARY PHENOMENON; POLICE STILL SEARCH FOR BOMB SUSPECTS. The headlines repeated on every news site. Two weeks ago, a city worker noticed that a water stain on the concrete wall of a Chicago underpass appeared to be an image of the Virgin Mary. He snapped a photo, uploaded it onto social media, and it went viral. In a city where the citizens still referred to their neighborhoods by their parish, the fascination with the image rose to a fever pitch within days.

Then the bombings began. Two in as many weeks, with rumors that Satan was creating the bombs, and the image was the Virgin Mary's attempts to warn the city. People ran to their houses of worship and prayed. The city hummed with a low level of panic.

Hester rarely panicked. As a consultant for some of the most top-secret governmental agencies in the world, her days were spent almost entirely online or in the field, addressing some of the darker aspects of mankind's inability to live in peace. Panic was a luxury she could not afford.

She dumped two heaping scoops of fragrant, dark coffee into the French press, added another of decaf, and stirred it together with a wooden spoon. As she pressed the timer that she'd affixed to the handle, her laptop played the beginning strains of Carl Orff's "Carmina Burana, O Fortuna." She walked over to the table and tapped open the app.

Beatrix Walker's face filled the screen. The banked intensity in her eyes relayed the seriousness behind her phone call—but then, Walker's calls were always serious. As the head of the National Cyber Terrorist Security Agency, she intervened in some of the most heinous crimes perpetrated worldwide.

"Good morning. You look grim," Hester said.

"And you look surprisingly chipper for a woman woken up at three o'clock in the morning."

"NCTA watching my burglar alarm feed?"

"We do have a vested interest in keeping you alive. You're our top analyst, after all. I'm told that last night's intruder was a cut above the average. Outsmarted the tracking beam for an instant and calmly escaped. Not usual."

Hester nodded. "I've been ruminating on it this morning. Deciding what to do."

"I don't envy him, whoever it is. If you need any assistance, let us know."

"I will. But you didn't call to discuss Chicago's criminal population. What can I do for you?"

"I have a rather . . . unusual assignment."

Hester shifted the computer so it would follow her as she stood and moved back into the kitchen. "Go ahead."

"It's a local matter. We've been asked to consult along with the FBI. It seems as though the nephew of the mayor of your fine city has gone missing."

Hester took a coffee cup from the cabinet. "Sounds like a job for the Chicago police, not a federal agency."

"Not when the nephew in question is an expert in particle physics and works on various secret federal projects."

Hester turned to look at the computer. "George McPatrick has gone missing?"

"You know him?"

"He works at the University of Chicago. I've bumped into him at various scientific conferences." The timer started beeping and she pressed the plunger down.

Walker tilted her head. "You time your coffee?"

"Absolutely. Four minutes, no more. Some prefer to steep six, but I find that to be overkill." Hester poured the coffee into her mug and added some heavy cream. "How long has he been gone?"

"No one is quite sure. I guess he lives alone and spends most days and some nights in the lab. He has no wife, no kids, and the two colleagues that work in the same lab say he stays to himself. They described him as odd."

Hester walked back to the table and sat down. "He's weird as hell. Claims that one day he'll prove parallel universes exist. What's he working on for the feds?"

"That's classified, even for someone with your clearance. But suffice to say it involves new ways to program and deploy missiles."

Hester stopped with the cup halfway to her lips. "The very idea of McPatrick in control of anything involving the discharge of missiles is terrifying."

"And yet, it's true." Hester's email pinged with an incoming note. "That's from me. I've attached a dossier prepared by the local FBI agent there, a . . . Karl Drake. You have an appointment with him this morning at ten."

"That's an hour from now."

Walker raised an eyebrow. "Is that a problem?"

"I haven't showered, you watched me make my first cup of the day, I usually drink two before even considering positive motion, and the federal building is thirty minutes from here by subway."

Walker waved a hand. "For a woman of your talents, that's nothing. Good luck."

The screen went dark. Hester picked up her cup and took it to the master bedroom. Thirty minutes later she grabbed a jean jacket from a front hallway closet, filled her thermos with the rest of the coffee, and headed to the subway.

⊰◇⊱

Hester stood in front of a seriously tall, late-thirty-something black man in a dark blue suit with the barest hint of a pinstripe and a muted blue tie with tiny red diamonds. His trimmed hair and clean-shaven face gave him the air of ex-military. His demeanor read current FBI agent. He took in her jean jacket, black pants, also jeans, and black combat boots.

"Dr. Regine? I'm Karl Drake. Pleased to meet you. Come on back to my office and we can talk." Drake passed by the receptionist, a forbidding looking older woman in a wheelchair, and led Hester through a door and down a hall. Near the corridor's end he waved her into a small office with a standard issue reddish wood desk and a bookshelf behind it. A framed certificate hung on the wall that recognized Drake for meritorious service. He waved her into a chair opposite the desk.

"I've been told that you're on loan to the FBI, but only for a short while and undercover. I'm to introduce you by whatever name you give me, and pretend you're an agent from another jurisdiction."

"If that's so then my cover's already been blown, because your receptionist heard you refer to me by my real name."

Drake took his own chair behind the desk and tilted back a bit.

"Marta is a trusted member of the team. Former Israeli military. And she keeps a nine millimeter in her right drawer at the ready, so not someone to mess with. You want to tell me the name I should use?"

"Agent Percy is fine."

"All right, I'll get some documentation for you." He typed an email, then returned his attention to her.

"I read the dossier," Hester said, "but it merely contained the statements of colleagues confirming that McPatrick was missing. Can you fill me in?"

Drake leaned back further and the chair creaked.

"They trashed his house. Stole equipment from his home office, and his PC is gone. Oddly enough, no one's used his bank cards and his accounts remain untouched. We checked for strange withdrawals or payments in the weeks before and there are none."

"So he isn't running from debt collectors or blackmailers," Hester said.

"Or the IRS," Drake added.

"How common is that?"

A hint of humor crept into Drake's eyes. "More common than you'd imagine. All sorts of people disappear. Or attempt to."

"How successful are they?"

Drake shrugged. "I would think your organization knows as much as mine."

"Perhaps, but I don't work in that area. I'm have a Phd in chemical engineering and handle biochemical weapons and experimental chemistry. So if you get pricked by an umbrella and fall dead, or drink tea and die of a slow poison, then I'm your woman. If your credit card is hacked, not so much."

"Got it. Well, fifteen years ago a civilian could manage it fairly easily. With current technology that's no longer true. It takes real dedication."

"Best places to go?"

"Foreign, not Europe, but also not a place where your skin is a different color or facial features unusual for the area."

"Why not Europe?"

"Too many cameras. And you'd be surprised how many people can remain in the United States and still avoid scrutiny despite our technology. But the suburbs are better than a rural area. Small towns are just that, and everyone knows everybody else. A stranger sticks out."

"McPatrick would stick out in a suburban area too."

"You know him?"

"Only in a professional capacity. He believes in parallel universes and lectures extensively about them. He's also a vocal member of a skeptic society."

Drake's phone rang once, then silenced. He made no move to answer it, which Hester liked. He could focus.

"You sound like you don't believe in this theory."

"I don't."

"How about ghosts? Believe in them?"

"Ghosts? No."

"And McPatrick did?"

"I have no idea. Why?"

Drake placed a file at the end of his desk, facing her. The word CONFIDENTIAL stamped across its cover in bright red made her pause. Drake waved at her.

"That's for you. Go ahead. It's not going to be confidential in exactly ten minutes when the local papers report."

"Okay," Hester said.

She opened to the first page: a grainy black-and-white photo of Lake Michigan at night, taken by someone on shore. The moon cast a line of light along the water and the camera's lens registered an eerie white glow. Within the glow and hovering above the water was a man. Shadows covered his face, and though his eyes were shrouded one got the sense that he was staring at the camera in fear, or hate. He held his arms out to the photographer, as if beseeching the viewer to come forward. The man's body was transparent. Hester could see right through him. If she didn't know better, she would have thought she was staring at a ghost. She glanced up at Drake.

"Double exposure? Misfiring camera?"

"Both possibilities ruled out by our labs."

"Photoshop?"

"That was our first thought. But look at the others."

Hester moved aside the page to find another nighttime photo. This one faced south and depicted the curving lakefront along Oak Street beach with a view all the way to Navy Pier. Hester could see the bright lights of the Ferris wheel in the distance. In the foreground, though, over the water, hovered the same man. This time his mouth was open in a scream, hideously contorting his features. The image sent a chill through Hester, and she could feel the hairs on her arms rise. She leafed through three more photos, all from different locations along Chicago's lakefront, all at night, and all featuring the same figure. In the last one his arms were spread wide and he stared malevolently at the camera. To Hester it seemed that she was gazing upon the face of evil. She turned the photo over so as not to have to see it, surprised at how rattled she was by the images.

"Any idea who the deranged man is?"

Drake shook his head. "Face recognition software came up empty."

"How many photos in total?"

"Nine. Taken by nine different people."

"Are they connected in any way? Family members? Coworkers?"

"Not that we can find. One was a fisherman headed to his usual spot to cast a line, another was a man who jogs nightly along Oak Street beach, and a third was a father of three playing some evening soccer with his kids up at the Lawrence Avenue soccer fields. It goes on like that. No real connections."

"Did you find any projection equipment at the site?"

"None. And no holographic equipment either. But we do know that aerial 3-D technology exists in its experimental phase that would enable an image to project without a screen. The ghost photos began right around time of McPatrick's disappearance. You know if he had any equipment like that?"

"Not sure, but I wouldn't be surprised if he did. You think these came from some of the equipment stolen from his house?"

She picked up a random image and peered more closely at it.

"Why are they all in black and white?"

"Aerial 3-D images are hard to create in color. You would need several lasers and I would think one of the witnesses would have seen the equipment. Also, all of the witnesses claimed to hear a scream right before the image disappeared."

"A scream," Hester said.

Drake waved at the file. "Read the quote in the statement about picture number six. The deranged one with the Ferris wheel in the background and his evilness in the foreground."

Hester turned over the photo. "You don't like this one either."

Drake exhaled. "That's the one I can't get out of my head at night. I'm not sure why."

Hester found the statement. "He screamed. A hideous, high-pitched sound of rage. I've never heard something like that before and I never want to hear it again." She held up the document. "Which one was this?"

"The fisherman."

"So how does any of this relate to McPatrick?"

Drake waved at the file again. "In the separate envelope. That photo was from two nights ago."

Hester fished out a small manila mailing envelope and slid out yet another picture, facedown. She took a deep breath to brace herself. If this one outdid the others she wasn't sure she wanted to let it reside in her brain. She flipped the picture over. Once again a black-and-white photo with a ghostly image hovering. But this time the ghost was someone new—and this one's face twisted not in rage, but in fear.

George McPatrick stared back at her.

⋯◇⋯

Hester held the photo up. "Who took this one?"

"A social worker who trolls the lakefront at night, searching down the homeless to try to get them into a shelter. That's Fullerton Avenue, and he's floating against the wall of the theater there."

"Did McPatrick scream like the other guy?"

An emotion passed over Drake's face that might have been sadness, Hester wasn't sure.

"He said, 'I believe' and then disappeared."

"Hmm," Hester said.

"I have some additional bad news for you. Two of these images were taken at the exact spots that the two recent bombs detonated."

"Coincidence?"

"Could be. But we're cordoning off every photo location to sweep it. The bomb squad's been working night and day. They've cleared five of the nine sites." Drake rubbed his face. "In light of the Virgin Mary image and the Satan rumors, we've been trying hard to keep the ghost photos contained so as not to create any more panic. We lost that battle this morning when a member of the press located one of the photographers."

"Where'd the reporter find him?"

"At church. Praying. He's the one that snapped the evil picture."

"Taking that one might have driven me to church as well," Hester said.

"I hear you," Drake said. His phone buzzed and this time he picked it up. He listened a moment and then set it down.

"That was the Chicago police. They're having a problem at the latest site. Let's go."

Hester followed Drake back down the hallway, and as she passed Marta, the woman turned from the phone banks.

"Ms. Regine, here's your temporary FBI card identifying you as Agent Percy." She placed a slim wallet on the desk.

Drake put his hands on his hips and smiled down at his shoes as Hester picked up the ID.

Twenty minutes later Drake drove into the area bordering the theater, but was blocked from getting close by an assortment of news vans, their roofs cluttered with satellite equipment. He wedged the car in between two and waved her out.

"Looks like the news hit," he said. "Let's go." Hester followed him as he wound his way toward the wooden theater building. A large group of people with press credentials on lanyards around their necks and some holding microphones grappled for position in front of a line of yellow barricades.

Farther away and toward the water an even larger crowd gathered and a man stood six feet above them, on the stone abutment that blocked the waves from splashing over the sea wall. He held a megaphone and waved a Bible in the air.

"You have seen it for yourselves. The famous skeptic felled by his lack of faith. Repent your sins now and tithe so that your prayers will be heard!" He waved at an open box at his feet that was rapidly filling with cash.

"This is a real circus," Drake said.

Hester followed Drake as he pushed his way through the crowd, flashed his badge and was allowed past it into the protected area. They headed toward two uniformed officers who looked perplexed as they stared at the theater. As Hester neared the scene, she saw the source of the officers' consternation.

A tall, slender man dressed in black pants, dark ankle boots, and a black trench coat crept along the perimeter of the old theater. His body curled downward as he bent to examine the walls. The wind blew his dark hair about his head and his hawkish nose was red at the tip. He'd been out in the wind a while. Drake strode up to the first officer.

"Is the bomb squad here?"

The officer shook his head. "Not yet."

"Then we need to increase this perimeter to get all of these people farther away." Drake pointed at the man prowling by the theater. "And you can start with that one. Who is that, and what's he doing so close to an unsecured site?"

"Guy named Holmes. We told him to back off, but he said he's working with the FBI and licensed in bomb detection and not to worry. Is he?"

"Is that the famed Sherlock Holmes?" Hester asked.

"I guess so," Drake said. "I got a call from the international crime unit saying he'd been brought in on our side. You know him?"

Hester shook her head. "By reputation, sure, but I've never met him. I thought he was a myth. He's discussed at just about every security conference I've ever attended, but I've never met anyone who admitted to a personal encounter."

"The guys said he was a recluse. Only accepts the weirdest cases and demands payment in crypto currency."

"Bitcoin?"

"Yes. You probably know this, but Bitcoin is the favored currency for drug and arms sales worldwide. Wonder what he's got to hide. Then again, at least *he's* been introducing himself by his real name." Drake shot her a look.

"But I accept cash, so there's that."

Drake snorted.

"And Bitcoin is gaining mainstream acceptance. My travel site now takes them to book flights."

"Wonder what *they* have to hide."

"You are a suspicious man, Mr. Drake."

Drake nodded. "That I am. Let's go meet the famous Sherlock Holmes, but not too close, because I'm not risking getting blown up even for him." Drake headed toward the theater, striding with authority. Holmes straightened up from his building inspection to watch him approach. His gaze shot to Hester and she thought she saw speculation in the other man's eyes, quickly masked. Drake stopped well away from the theater and waved Holmes to approach.

"Mr. Holmes? I'm Agent Drake and this is Agent Percy from our New York office." Holmes stepped up, shook Drake's hand, and turned to Hester.

"It's a pleasure to meet you, Dr. Regine. I read your treatise on the ethics of biochemical warfare," Holmes said. Hester kept her face impassive, thinking, *Show-off.*

"This undercover thing is going well, don't you think?" Drake said to Hester.

She shot him a quelling glance as she reached out to grasp Holmes' hand.

His long fingers wrapped around hers and she felt a tiny callus on one of his fingertips.

"I'm surprised you know of it. It wasn't disseminated widely."

Holmes raised an eyebrow. "Just to the entire upper echelons of the intelligence community." He looked at Drake.

"I came straight here to view where McPatrick appeared."

"I understand, but you shouldn't disturb a crime scene," Drake said.

"I in no way sullied the scene, you can be sure," Holmes said, and Hester thought she detected a hint of pique in his voice.

The man with the megaphone yelled, "Nonbelievers, repent. You see what happened to the scientist! Disappeared!"

"That man's been bellowing doomsday prophecies for the last thirty minutes. One wishes *he* would disappear," Holmes said.

"What did you find?" Drake asked.

"No footprints that indicated he stood against the wall, or any other marks indicating projection equipment placed in the area. And your officer mentioned that you were concerned about a possible bomb, but I saw no evidence of that either."

"I'm going to have to ask you next time to wait until after the bomb squad clears the area," Drake said. Holmes nodded and headed past the officers to the water's edge. Hester followed.

"Nice vault over my fence, Mr. Holmes. Perhaps you can explain why you tried to burglarize my house last night?"

Holmes turned away from the lake to look at her.

"I don't know what you're talking about."

She waved at his shoe. "My hedge seems to have scoured the side of your boot."

He turned back to face the water with a slight smile on his face.

"It's against the law to protect your home by lethal methods. At least it is in London. I'm not so sure about Chicago, what with its gun violence."

"Chicago is the same. The gun doesn't have real bullets and is programmed to avoid hitting anyone. It's security theater. Designed to frighten, not injure. You know that as well as I do," Hester said.

"And how would I know that?"

"Because you weren't frightened at all. So tell me why you were there."

Holmes stopped smiling, and though she'd only just met him, she had enough insight into the man to realize that what he would say next would be disturbing.

"Dr. Mary Carleton, an engineer involved in a secret project involving the manufacture of a new type of missile, disappeared from her London town house a week ago. She worked on a highly confidential joint project with the United States. The same project that McPatrick was assigned to here in Chicago. When British intelligence learned that McPatrick, too, had gone missing, they became alarmed and immediately contacted your FBI and sent me here to investigate. They believe that whoever kidnapped Carleton has also kidnapped McPatrick. They think it's a splinter group from a terrorist organization working in Europe. Two of whom entered the United States last week, and promptly disappeared."

"Were there ghostly sightings in London?"

Holmes shook his head. "Not at all. And I am not convinced that the two are connected."

"You still haven't explained why you tried to breach my security last night."

"I wanted to assure myself of your safety."

Hester didn't bother to hide her surprise. "My safety? Why?"

"The name of their joint project is 'Attila.'"

"Oh no," Hester said.

Holmes held her gaze. "You see the problem. You're the final participant in the project. I'm told you're working on a biochemical angle."

"I am, but we're not privy to the others. Complete confidentiality is an NCTA rule. Mostly for our own security."

Holmes nodded. "And so you must understand that the next logical one to be taken is you."

Nothing like an honest man to ruin your day, Hester thought.

Hester turned and walked along the water, trying to collect her thoughts. Holmes fell into step with her.

"Does Beatrix Walker know about this?" she asked him.

"She does. We asked to have you placed under protective security, but she said you'd never agree, and that confidentiality rules required they not tell you about the fact that two other Atilla participants have gone missing. Apparently she found a way to add you to the investigation. I'm not bound by those rules and thought you should know."

"She's right, I wouldn't have agreed. And you're right, I should know. Thank you."

"We need to solve this, and quickly. For your sake as well as the others. With each passing hour, the chances of finding either alive diminishes."

Drake jogged up to them.

"Another bomb just detonated on the south side. Let's go," he said.

They climbed into Drake's official vehicle and he placed a siren on the hood as he spun the car around to follow the police SUV. As they hurtled down Lake Shore Drive, Hester filled Holmes in on the possible links between the ghost sightings and the recent bombs.

"Was this one near a sighting?" Holmes asked.

"Yes," Drake said. "At Northerly Island. A venue for concerts, things like that. It's from the third sighting."

"And the other two? What numbers were they, and in what order?" Holmes asked.

"The first bomb coincided with the fifth sighting, the second with the sixth, and this is from the third."

"No real sequence," Hester said.

Holmes merely nodded. She could almost see him turning the facts around in his head.

"Do you have a map showing the locations of all nine?" Hester asked. Drake waved at the back of the car.

"In the file. Last sheet."

They reached the bomb site, tumbled out of the car, and were stopped immediately by a cordon of Chicago police. Drake showed his badge.

"They're with me," he said. "Keys are in the car if you need to move it." The cop nodded and waved them past. Holmes marched forward, his long coat flapping in the wind. Hester had to admire his ramrod straight posture and air of command. While not as tall as Drake, the two of them together made a formidable sight. Hester kept back a bit to get an overview. She found that distance was often needed for perspective. After a few minutes she headed back to the car to consult the map showing the ghost photo locations.

They spanned the entire lakefront, none far away from the lake, and none in the suburbs. She looked for similarities beyond their lakefront locations. After a few moments the car's back door opened and Holmes slid in next to her.

"Nothing worthwhile to learn. The bomb obliterated most of the evidence."

Hester held up the open map.

"I've been trying to see if there is any logic to the ghost sites. They hug the coastline, and some are at Chicago landmarks," Hester said. "But they're at interesting distances and different locations. I don't see a logical sequence."

"What type of landmarks?" Holmes asked.

Hester pointed to a spot near the curve of LaSalle drive as it headed to the lake. "This is a bizarre thing. The public park is built on a former cemetery. There remains a small mausoleum with the name Couch on it. No one's really sure why it's still there."

Holmes pointed to a second dot. "And this one? What's there?"

Hester turned the map a bit to see the street name.

"Oh, that's the location of the famous St. Valentines's Day Massacre."

Holmes frowned. "You have a museum for such a thing?"

"No. It's a pizza restaurant now. But there's a small plaque and tour companies take visitors around to the various sites involving Al Capone."

Holmes rolled his eyes. Hester smiled. "It's actually an interesting tour."

Holmes leaned near enough that she could smell the scent of aftershave and pipe smoke.

"One finds it hard to believe that a simple plaque at the scene of a thug's murderous crime spree could be interesting, but I'll take your word for it."

Their faces were only inches apart and from this distance she could see a small scratch where he'd cut himself shaving. While not conventionally handsome, the intensity and intelligence that blazed from him was powerful and appealing. Hester forced her gaze back to the map.

"And this"—she pointed at another dot—"is nearby. It's currently a cocktail bar, said to be haunted. When the owners went into the basement they found a pentagram on the floor and Egyptian markings on the ceiling. Many think it was the site for meetings of the American chapter of the Hermetic Order of the Golden Dawn. Not the recent neo-nazi group, but the original spiritualist group from the 1800s."

Holmes nodded. "I'm familiar with it. They started in Great Britain and many famous people were members. Did anyone die there?"

"An elderly woman claims to have witnessed a murder during a Golden Dawn meeting back in the 1930s." Hester's phone vibrated with an incoming text. She pulled it out.

"Another bomb just detonated further south." She pointed to an existing dot on the map. "Drake says to take the car. He's staying here, but called ahead so that we can view the site."

"What ghost photo number matches this new location?" Holmes asked.

"Four," Hester said. "It's definitely a pattern."

She got out of the back and slid into the sedan's driver's side. Holmes joined her up front, but as she pulled away, he shook his head.

"Forget the bomb site, we won't find anything of use there. They're using it as a distraction. Tying up Chicago's resources." Hester thought Holmes was probably right. The entire exercise felt like a wild goose chase. "Take me to the Virgin Mary image," Holmes said. "Is it far?"

"Not at all. But why?"

"It's another strange thing occurring in Chicago right now. Likely a coincidence, but we should at least check it out." Hester wasn't sure that the side trip was worth the time, but a small part of her wanted to see what all the fuss was about.

They pulled up to a corner west of the viaduct and two blocks away. A long line of people waited patiently in the weak October sun. Policemen lined the sidewalk all the way to the viaduct and Hester showed her identification each time they tried to wave her to the back of the line. Half a block from the image, on the opposite side of the street, a bearded man in a tattered black suit stood on an overturned crate, a microphone in his hand.

"Isn't that the same guy from the lakefront?" Hester pointed at the preacher. "They're taking full advantage of the situation, aren't they?"

"Someone needs to confiscate that megaphone," Holmes said.

"Repent your sins! Behold the power of light and turn away from darkness. Place your alms here to show your commitment to the light. I'm Ezekiel the Prophet!" Spittle formed on the man's unkempt beard and he waved the Bible in the air. At his feet was an upturned hat, filled to the brim with dollar bills that those in line added as they passed. Around him stood ten others, all carrying various signs with what appeared to be warnings of the coming apocalypse.

As they neared, the preacher seemed to laser in on Holmes.

"You, in your slick topcoat and with your ill-gotten gains, and you, with your belief in science above the Light, turn away!"

Holmes stopped walking and stared at the man while the others around him raised their signs and began chanting "Turn away! Turn away!"

"You think he knows who you are?" Hester asked in a low voice.

"Not likely. But he appears to know that you're a scientist and probably saw us together at the McPatrick site." Holmes held up his camera, snapped a photo, and took a step closer to the preacher, who hastened to step off the crate.

"The Great One will protect me from harm!" he said as he backed away. Holmes stayed put, staring at the man. The chanting followers surged around their leader as if to shield him.

"Go away! Go away!" they chanted.

"I do believe our pastor is frightened of you," Hester said.

Holmes nodded. "I take a dim view of those who would attempt to profit from another's religious experience."

Soon they stood inside another cordoned-off area with three more policemen. Hester walked up to the first.

"Agent Percy, FBI. Quite a crush here. That the image?"

The police officer nodded.

The water stain did, indeed, appear to be the picture of a woman's bowed head, her veil flowing down over her shoulders. Above it was the faint circle of a possible halo. When Hester stepped to the side, though, it changed into an average line of dripping condensation from the metal struts above. Every few seconds the police waved the next in line forward and they snapped a photo, made the sign of the cross, and were hustled away.

"Who's the preacher?" Holmes asked.

The cop shrugged. "Some guy from out of state. We're told to leave him alone as long as he stops at sunset and doesn't incite violence."

"What happened to the tent city that used to be here?" Hester asked.

"They moved on to the next viaduct. Didn't like all the commotion."

Back in the car, Hester paused.

"Do you mind if I make a stop? Nothing to do with all this, it's just that there's someone from the old tent city that I want to check on."

"Of course. I, too, have eyes and ears all over London and from every walk of life."

"Well, this isn't an informant. Just a man I met though my charitable work. His name is Bruce. He's homeless and an ex-vet."

Hester drove two miles to the next viaduct over the highway entrance, where the roadway shielded pup tents, camp chairs, and laden grocery carts. She climbed out of the car and headed to the cluster. As she did, one man rose from a chair. He wore jeans with holes in them, a dark army coat, and a heavy sweater. He swigged from a beer bottle as he ambled toward them.

"Hey girl, who's your friend?" he said. Hester introduced Holmes, who muttered a greeting. "Nice accent. Smart guy, huh?" Holmes' mouth just quirked.

"I was just checking up on you. I saw that everyone left the other viaduct."

Bruce nodded. "We don't like no trouble, and that preacher man is trouble, I can tell you that."

"Why do you say so?" Holmes asked.

"They came two days before the image thing. I swear they created it just to make some cash. And they were real secretive-like. When they found out some of us were ex-military they started harassing us. Calling us 'war mongers' and said that if we didn't move they'd take care of us, just like the others. You see that preacher man's eyes? Dead pools." Bruce took a swig of his beer and offered it to Hester, who waved it off. Bruce got a sheepish look on his face. "Sorry. Ain't got no coffee." Hester just smiled and patted him on the arm.

"Thanks anyway."

"Did they tell you what others they 'took care of'?" Holmes asked.

Bruce shook his head. "No. But we heard rumors that they take the guys and try to 'convert' them to their way of thinking. Half those people carrying signs were converted. It's a cult, if you ask me."

"I have a photo of him and will arrange to have someone run a background check," Holmes said.

"I'll keep a close eye on them." Bruce drank again from his bottle.

"Be careful. You have any trouble, you call me, okay?' Hester said. Bruce patted his pocket.

"I got that phone you bought me. Don't you worry about me."

Back in Drake's car, Hester started toward her neighborhood.

"Let's go to my house. I haven't eaten all day, and we can analyze the file."

Holmes gave a quick nod. As she drove, he seemed to be lost in thought.

"What are you thinking?" she asked.

"I don't like that the bombs are moving south. Toward . . ." He didn't complete his sentence.

She did. "My house."

"Yes."

Hester didn't like it either. "If you're worried about being there, I understand. We can go back to the FBI offices to work."

"I'm not worried," Holmes said.

"Do you think—"

"Stop!" Holmes spoke so suddenly that Hester startled and jerked the wheel. "Pull over."

Hester did, pulling in front of a white building with a side yard. Holmes bounded out and stood in front of it. Hester joined him on the sidewalk . Holmes pointed at the building.

"Is this building on the map?"

"No."

Holmes breathed a sigh of relief. "Do you know what this is?"

Hester was confused. "Sure. That's the famous Chess Studios. Some of the greatest blues players in the world recorded here. Muddy Waters, Chuck Berry, Howlin' Wolf, Etta James, and Willie Dixon. The Rolling Stones made regular pilgrimages. Unlike the St. Valentine's Day massacre site, this *is* a museum."

"As well it should be." Holmes said. His excitement was palpable and unlike his usual dour exterior.

"You're a music fan?"

Holmes nodded. "Classical. But the blues is an art form that holds its own with the masters. I'm truly glad it's not on the map." Hester smiled at him and he seemed slightly embarrassed. He swung back into the car and a bemused Hester retook her place behind the wheel.

Back at Hester's house, she cooked an early dinner of spaghetti Bolognese and they pored over the file, tossing ideas out and discarding them. Drake called to say that another bomb had been found, this one within a mile of her home, and successfully disposed of by the bomb squad. Holmes asked if there was any news of the missing terrorists.

"None," Drake said, "except that they're known for their improvised explosive devices back in their home country, so the bomb squad believes they're behind this string of explosions." He rang off, promising an update if anything occurred.

"Sounds like your distraction idea is the right one. These guys keep the city busy while they hunt me," Hester said to Holmes. She sounded calm, but inwardly she was anything but. She took a sip of her wine while she contemplated how close the latest blast was to the house. Holmes frowned into his own wineglass, and once again she imagined that she saw the gears of his mind turning.

"What we need to do is to discern where the next ghost sighting will be and catch them in the act," Holmes said. "Then we can find out how they created the McPatrick photo and whether they have him hostage."

Hester headed to the freezer and removed a carton of chocolate ice cream and held it up in a silent question. Holmes shook his head and poured more wine into his glass, and, after a slight pause, refilled hers. Wine and ice cream seemed like an unlikely mix, but Hester thought Holmes had it right and the circumstances called for both.

The map was spread on the table as well as the photos, with the exception of the evil one, which Hester had turned on its face. Now she stared at the dots.

"Each sighting is by a landmark that involves a famous event in Chicago."

"And all involve death in some form or another," Holmes said. "Let's catalog which ones are left." Hester shoved her plate aside and pulled the map closer.

"Here is where Richard Speck killed some nurses in 1966, and here's Rosehill Cemetery, where they buried Bobby Frank, the young victim of Leopold and Loeb. Somewhere in this area was the infamous murder house of the serial killer H. H. Holmes, during the 1893 World's Fair." She looked at Holmes. "No relation, I presume?"

"None, I assure you," he said. "But that site is very close."

"Yes. The house is long gone now." She sighed. "It's a devil's list for sure, but I imagine any large city would have as many, if not more."

Holmes patted through his pockets and came out with a pipe.

"I see you have an outdoor deck." He held the pipe up. "May I?"

"Be my guest." Holmes grabbed the wine bottle and both their glasses and headed outside.

Hester made an after-dinner espresso while Holmes sat on the deck and smoked. It was full dark now, and a luminous moon rose above the trees. She poured her espresso into a tiny cup, pulled an oversized cable sweater over her head, and joined him on the deck. He appeared to be brooding once again.

After a time, he spoke. "You must go to the H. H. Holmes site and keep watch. I will stay here. Do you have a gun?"

Hester sipped her coffee. "Sure. On the roof."

"A handgun."

Hester nodded. "In a safe in the master bedroom. Why?"

"I should like to have it. In case I need it."

"What, here?"

"I expect them to come here tonight. Whoever they are."

"Can you even shoot a gun? Other than using it to tattoo your boarding house walls, of course."

Holmes slanted a look at her. "That story is making the rounds, is it?"

"Yep." She set down her espresso. "Let me get this straight. You want to banish me from my own house in order to ambush and possibly kill an intruder with my gun."

"It's for your own safety," Holmes protested. "If we call Drake and they openly position police around this house you can be sure no one will risk it, which will defeat the purpose entirely."

"What if they toss a bomb over the hedge? Then a gun will be of no use to you."

Holmes shook his head. "That's not efficient. They want you alive to give up the missile secrets. Throwing a bomb is too risky."

"More wine, please," Hester said and Holmes reached over and filled her glass.

"You treat your colleague, Dr. Watson, like this?"

"At times."

"Well not me. We go to the Holmes site together. If they trigger my alarm, my phone will light up—I can even watch the proceedings from it. I'll give Drake the code so he'll see it as well and send in the troops. There's no reason for anyone to place their lives in jeopardy to protect my empty house."

"But they may get away and you will remain a target."

Hester finished the wine and stood, putting a hand out to him. "Come on. Let's go catch a ghost."

Two hours later Hester was hunkered down near a large bush with Holmes at her side while they watched the space that was once a serial killer's house, now a post office building. The moon above their heads cast a glow, and whatever the moon didn't accomplish, the street lights did. They'd been crouched for a long while and absolutely nothing of interest was happening.

"This is a bust," Hester whispered.

Her phone buzzed in her pocket and she pulled it out. Holmes moved closer to view the screen. Immediately her burglar alarm app lit up, and when she tapped it her yard came into view. Two ski-masked men were crab-walking toward her back deck. She watched a split screen as the gun rose from the turret and began spitting fire and belching smoke. It rained rubber bullets down on the men, hammering into their heads and shoulders.

"I thought you'd programmed it to avoid hitting anyone?"

"I may have tweaked the program."

Holmes smiled. "Excellent."

The entire yard filled with uniformed Chicago police and the two men froze with their hands in the air. Drake strode into view of the camera and Hester could see him giving orders. Her relief was profound.

"Well, that's over. Let's hustle back to the house. We can interrogate them and see if they know where McPatrick is." Her phone buzzed again and she looked down. "It's Drake. Said he found a note in one guy's pocket with my address on it and McPatrick's underneath. He texted a photo." She showed Holmes.

Holmes frowned, but said nothing. He waved her toward the car.

"You're right. There won't be a ghost sighting here." Another buzz sounded—this time, Holmes' phone. He read the screen and if anything his frown deepened. "The British agents found Dr. Carleton. She's unharmed."

"That's wonderful news! Why are you still frowning?"

"That note Drake sent you. It showed your address first, not second. People don't write 'to do' lists in reverse order. These two hadn't yet gotten around to McPatrick. They started with you."

"Maybe they were aware of my house's superior security, so they went after the easier target first?"

Holmes shook his head. "Then they would have taken you on the street, not attempted this tonight. Why risk triggering your alarm when they could simply follow you and abduct you off the street? I was right. These two and those who kidnapped McPatrick are unrelated."

Hester beeped open the car. If Holmes' analysis of the situation seemed right, the implications for her future safety were once again dire. She wanted the whole thing to be over. She heard a text come in, and paused before starting the car in order to read it.

"It's Bruce. He said to come to the tent city right away. Something's happened."

The tent city residents milled around, some drinking and others wringing their hands. Hester bounced the car up onto the sidewalk and jogged to Bruce's tent.

"You looking for Bruce?" a wizened-looking woman holding a cigarette asked.

"Yes, is he okay?"

"No. He came running around the corner claiming he'd seen a ghost. Said he was going to text a friend and then took off. Ghost! Not sure what he's been drinking."

"Did you see where he ran? It's important."

The woman shook her head. "He was hallucinating, I tell you."

Holmes stood still, watching the tent city. Hester did her best to tamp down her worry over Bruce. He was former military, after all, and had navigated Chicago street life safely for the past three years.

"Give me a landmark close to here," Holmes said. "And by that I mean within a two-block radius."

Hester shook her head. "I don't know of any." She took out her phone to search. "Google shows no murders."

"Expand the search beyond homicides to strange happenings, and the area to several miles. If I'm right, the people who took McPatrick just took your friend Bruce."

"Well, there's the Biograph Theater, east of here, where Dillinger was shot down by the FBI. South, there's the site of the old Iroquois Theater, with an alley said to be haunted by victims of the fire that burned it to the ground. Then there's the Museum of Science and Industry—the ghost of Clarence Darrow sometimes appears on the bridge where his ashes were scattered into the lagoon."

Holmes snapped his fingers. "That's it."

"Why that one?"

But Holmes was running to the car and Hester took off after him. She hit the street again and fumed as they were caught at a red light.

"Tell me," she said.

"Darrow. Famous lawyer of both Leopold and Loeb *and* defender of evolution in the Scopes trial. Who do you think would hate him the most?"

The light turned and Hester hit the gas. Holmes placed a hand on the dashboard to brace himself. Hester placed her phone on speaker.

"Call Drake," she said. The phone system dialed and Drake answered immediately. "Get someone to the Museum of Science and Industry. We think another ghost sighting occurred there and we're heading to intercept them." Drake agreed and hung up.

"Enter from the west, if you can," Holmes said, studying his cell phone. "They'll be heading back to the Virgin Mary viaduct by now with their projection equipment. There." Holmes pointed to a battered van, its windows blacked out and REPENT drawn on its side. "Follow them. And call Drake back. Tell him to join us."

Within minutes, Drake's car pulled up in the next lane, followed rapidly by three Chicago police cars. They cut off the van, flashing their lights to order it to pull over. Hester parked twenty feet behind and watched as the uniformed officers approached the vehicle with caution. After a moment the van's front doors opened. Ezekiel and two of his followers stepped out, hands raised.

An officer approached the van's cargo doors, gun drawn. Two covered the first as he opened them. They shined their flashlights into the cargo bay and Hester saw McPatrick and Bruce, both tied up with gags in their mouths. Two other followers rode with their hostages, and equipment filled the rest of the cargo hold. Hester sighed in relief.

"I should have known," Hester said. "They targeted McPatrick and whipped up superstition with the ghost sightings. And Clarence Darrow must be their worst nightmare."

Someone tapped on her window, which sent her heart racing, but it was only Drake. She rolled down the glass. "You scared me to death!"

"Excellent work, 'Agent Percy.'"

Hester laughed. "Thank Holmes. He figured it out."

"Mr. Holmes, we appreciate it. Either of you know the second victim there?"

"His name is Bruce. He's former military and living in the tent city under the viaduct near the Virgin Mary images."

Drake pointed at one of the followers, who was rocking back and forth in agitation and chattering to one of the officers.

"That one is already trying to talk his way out. Says it was Ezekial who came up with the scheme to abduct a famous skeptic and force him to recant on camera. When they realized that we were holding back the ghost photos, they came up with the bombs."

"Were they connected to the two terrorists?"

Drake shook his head. "I doubt it. Seems that was a completely unrelated scheme.

"Looks like we solved two crimes in one night," Hester said.

"None of these guys look like the ghost that everyone's been photographing. I wonder if we'll find him among Ezekiel's other followers?"

But with that, Holmes reached across Hester to show them both his phone. On its screen was a grainy photo of the evil man, his hands outstretched and the hate pouring from him.

"I asked Watson to research Ezekial, and he sent me this. It's Ezekiel's grandfather. Turns out he was an old tent preacher from the thirties who warned of the apocalypse. He handled snakes and died when one bit him during a session."

"If I were you I'd delete that link from my phone," Drake said.

Holmes smiled. "Superstitious?"

"In this case? You bet. Keep the car. I'll get it tomorrow." He tapped on the hood and Hester rolled the window back up. She thought for a moment, and then turned to Holmes.

"You up for a celebratory drink? I know a great late-night club."

He raised an eyebrow. "Yes. Where?"

"I'll show you."

Hester and Holmes sat at a table at a blues joint in Chicago and listened as a quartet tore the house down. Holmes stretched out his long legs and cradled his glass against his chest, eyes closed and a smile on his face. When the band took a break he sat up and turned to Hester.

"Thank you," he said.

She nodded and clinked her glass against his. "I should be thanking you. Where's your next case?"

"London. Watson notified me that there's a missing tanker filled with a chemical that, if it falls into the wrong hands, could pollute the city's drinking water beyond repair."

"Sounds like a job for an expert in biochemical weaponry."

"Do you know any who might be free to join me in a flight to London?"

"Paid for in Bitcoin?"

"Naturally," Holmes said as he leaned in close.

She smiled back at him and the next band began to play.

TOUGH GUY BALLET

by Duane Swierczynski

I was hungover the day my partner was killed. Yeah, that sounds lousy, but in my defense I had no idea Chuck would be going after the Multiple Maniac all by himself. We'd been partnered up for six years and the vast majority of the cases we solved were thanks to shit Chuck discovered on his own. Truth be told, he'd carried my ass since the beginning. Sure, he'd bring me in for the rough stuff—a shoot-out in Hollywood, a dockside brawl down in Long Beach. He'd look at me with that cock-eyed grin and give me his catchphrase, *You want to get into some trouble?* But none of it was stuff Chuck couldn't handle on his own, I was sure of that. I don't know, maybe he kept me around so he could lob his tennis balls of brilliance against my stupid wall head. And now Chadwick "Chuck" Ostrander, the smartest homicide detective who'd ever worn an LAPD badge, was no more. What hope do I have now? What hope do any of us have?

But I'm getting ahead of myself. What I really want to talk about are the strange circumstances surrounding Chuck's death . . .

He'd left me a message on my answering machine, which he left God-knows-when but I only discovered around 4 A.M. on the way to the bathroom to vomit or take a piss or maybe both. I should have gone to the movies the night before. When I go to the movies I don't drink. I sit back and sip diet soda and stuff salted popcorn into my mouth and let the images wash over me. Instead I got into a fight with my ex and engaged in some serious self-harm with my longtime nemesis, Mr. Jack Daniel's.

The light blinked red. It would not stop blinking red. Even if I were to blow my brains out right now, I'd be sent to an afterlife of nothing but that red light, blinking. So I pressed the button.

"Howie, if you're up, meet me downtown at the Promenade."

That was Chuck for you. Sure, Chuck, everybody's up at 4 A.M.

I took care of all three bodily functions, not in the best possible order, then brewed some weapons-grade coffee. I brought the whole carafe with me in the car. By the time I reached downtown I'd finished the whole thing and it hadn't helped one bit, except now I was jittery and painfully aware how drunk I was. I also had no idea where this Promenade was. He'd said downtown, right?

Well no, it turned out he meant this new apartment complex in beautiful downtown *Burbank*.

By the time I figured it out and headed back up the 101, sunlight was crawling over the Verdugo Mountains and my brain was ready to explode. I pulled into the strelitzia-lined driveway that led to the interior of the complex. There was a a small roundabout. The name of the place was lit up next to a marble fountain that sprayed water with all of the gusto of an elderly man taking a leak. The apartment complex was only a year or two old and already out of style. Somebody built a series of wrapped wedding presents, stacked them haphazardly on top of each other, and called it "architecture."

Here's the difference between me and Chuck: if Chuck had shown up here, he'd have pinpointed my location within a minute. He had a brain that worked like that. (Or maybe I was just predictable.) I, on the other hand, had no earthly idea where my partner was. Chuck could be in any of the five buildings that surrounded the pool. Underneath one of the buildings in the ground-level parking areas, maybe. On the roof. Lounging in the pool, doing calculus problems in his head.

"Chuck!" I shouted, even though it wasn't even 7 A.M. yet, and most of the good residents of the Promenade were probably sleeping in this fine Saturday morning. "CHUCK!"

"Shut the fuck up, asshole!" someone yelled back from a window somewhere.

"Yeah, yeah," I said. "CHUCK!"

"Are you looking for Detective Ostrander?" a quiet voice said behind me.

I turned around to see a girl, maybe fifteen, in a halter top and boots that went up to her knobby knees. She looked like she was dressed up as a whore for Halloween, only she'd missed the big day by a month and change.

"Who are you supposed to be?" I asked.

"You must be Detective Burton. We don't have much time. Follow me."

I blinked. "Follow you? I don't even know you."

"I'm Nikki. He'll only come to you, so let's get moving."

Nikki the fifteen-year-old pretend whore (she had too sweet a face to be in the life for real) walked toward a metal gate near building 2. I had no choice but to follow her. This was vintage Chuck, too—enlisting random weirdos in our investigations. He called it "pooling brains." See, Chuck had a theory that everyone was useful in an investigation, even if they didn't realize it. He especially loved working with whores and wayward kids and bums, all of whom spent more time on the streets than anybody.

"Nikki, honey, why don't you just tell me where he is and I'll take it from here."

"Because I don't know where he is."

"You just said he'd only come to me. So you must have talked to him."

A microsecond after the word "him" came out of my mouth Nikki was up and over the nine-foot gate like a gazelle. I'd never seen anyone move so fast, especially in whore boots. She stared back at me through the bars.

"You coming?"

"If I try to make it over this gate, whatever's left in my stomach will take two very different exit routes, probably at the same time."

Nikki frowned, then turned the handle and popped open the door for me. "You're disgusting."

Which struck me as funny, considering her career aspirations, but before I had time to craft a dazzling retort she was already moving into the complex. Which was a maze with open-air hallways and a nonsensical layout. I could barely keep up. After a few confusing turns, she stopped so abruptly I almost knocked her down.

"Call out to him."

I sighed. "Chuck!"

"No, not like that, you idiot!" Nikki hissed. "With your mind. He'll sense you, and I'll sense him."

Now, as an adult member of law enforcement, I should have bristled at being called an *idiot*. But something else she'd said tripped me up.

"I'm sorry . . . did you say with my *mind*?"

"*Think* about him!"

And then she was off again. None of this made sense. Then again, nothing about the past few months made any sense.

We were after a serial killer Chuck had dubbed "MM," as in Multiple Maniac. MM struck all over L.A. using such wildly different methods people thought it was the work of at least a dozen different killers. Chuck was the one who figured out it was all the same guy. The way Chuck put it, there was a pattern to MM's non-pattern, whatever the fuck that meant. And night after night, Chuck tried to figure out the next step in this non-pattern.

There was serious pressure to catch this sick ticket. Single-handedly MM had already boosted the county homicide rate about 7 percentage points. And there was no sign he was slowing down. The Maniac killed every night, in neighborhoods rich and poor. L.A. was terrified. So was I. Because one of these days, I knew Chuck would call me up and say, *You want to get into some trouble?* And we'd have to face off against this nutjob.

I turned a corner and almost bumped into Nikki again. She was standing in front of a door, ear to the wood.

"What are you doing?"

Nikki turned to put a finger to her lips and give me the bug-eyed death stare.

"Enough of this shit, Nikki. Is he in there? CHUCK?"

The door flew open and a guy came out waving a utility blade.

Now I'm not the quickest thinker in the world—that was more Chuck's department. But I had two thoughts straight away:

Poor Nikki will probably never look the same

and

I need to blow this fucker away

But I'm telling you, Nikki was a hundred times quicker. Before my left hand reached the butt of my gun, she had done a half-dozen extremely clever things.

Best I can recall, and with God as my witness: she snapped her head back like she was doing the limbo. *The blade missed.* And when he came back hard on the return swing, she used her wrist to block his. Nikki booted the guy in the chest, bouncing him off the door frame. He slashed again and she captured his forearm with her hands, twisted, then jerked him forward so that her bony knee landed up in his rib cage. He fell to his knees, but slashed up at her again. She recaptured the arm and drove her knee up into his face this time. I heard a crunch like a celery stalk snapping in half. Then again. And again. And again. The utility blade fell out of his hand. The guy dropped.

By which point I had my revolver in my hands and I was yelling, "Freeze!"

Nikki just looked at me. *Now* you step in?

My cheeks burned, so I focused on the guy. Khakis, untucked button-down shirt, barefoot, clean-cut yuppie prick. Was this supposed to be MM? If so, where was Chuck?

"Chuck!" I shouted into the apartment.

"He's not going to hear you."

"Why's that? CHUCK."

"Detective Burton."

"CHUCK! What?"

"Your partner is dead."

◇◈◇

Now it was my turn to move like a jackrabbit. I clumsily launched myself into the apartment, clearing corners and feigning sobriety like a champ.

How did she know Chuck was dead? Nikki must have looked into the apartment, saw Chuck's corpse, and knew it was too late. And you know, the strange thing is that I could just feel it, too—like the wattage powering the whole city had dimmed a little. *Chuck was dead.* My friend, my partner, my mentor, my lifeline. Chuck. Dead.

And with every second that passed, I expected to find the most tragic crime scene I'd ever see. But there was no one inside. It was just an ordinary apartment. What the hell?

Back out in the hallway, I pointed my revolver at the yuppie's head. "Where is he?!"

MM played possum. I kicked him in the ribs. He moaned.

"WHERE IS HE!?"

"Detective Burton," Nikki said, "stop it."

I gave him another rib-splitter. He started shrieking and sobbing. Some tough killer he was.

"Detective Burton!"

But I'd had it. For all I knew, Chuck was bleeding out somewhere, in dire need of an ER. This sick bastard needed to talk.

I pointed my weapon a few inches to the side of his head and squeezed the trigger.

Or *tried to*, anyway; my entire hand was immobilized. I looked down to find Nikki's petite hand around my wrist, her fingers curled like she was making a G-chord on a fretboard.

"Stop it," she said, slowly and quietly. "This host body is innocent. The malevolent soul inside has already fled. Probably gone back to join the collective."

I tried to pull the trigger and swear to Christ I couldn't. "What are you doing to my hand?"

"You can't shoot him. It would be murder."

"I wasn't going to kill him. The bullet would have gone into the ground."

"Not at this angle it wouldn't."

"You know what? Fuck you, Nikki."

"Check the angle."

"Who the hell are you anyway?"

"Check it."

So I checked my sights. And at this angle, the bullet would have . . . traveled straight into his left eye.

Which was blinking at us.

"Who-the-fuck-are-you-people!?" he stammered. Even I, the big dummy, could tell this wasn't MM.

Nikki tucked the guy back inside his apartment, told him this was all a dream, and when he woke up everything would be the way it was. I watched this girl, this teenage kid, calm him down like she'd been on the job for a couple of decades. She was totally chill with this scumbag who just a few minutes before had tried to slice up her face like a slab of lunchmeat. I was impressed.

But I also thought about what she'd said before she played my wrist like a guitar. *The malevolent soul . . . back to join the collective.* What the fuck was that about? Did she mean this guy had been possessed?

After Nikki closed the door, she took me by the hand and led me down the hallway, made a few turns, then backed me up against a white stucco wall. There was a surprising amount of muscle in her spindly limbs. Then again, maybe I was still drunk.

"Think about your partner," she said. "Everything is riding on this."

"How about you take a moment and explain to me what the fuck is going on."

"No."

"No!? What do you mean, no."

"No, as in there is no time. Do you want to save your partner or not?"

"You said he was dead."

"Dead but not gone."

"What in the motherloving hell does that mean?"

Nikki sighed. "I want you to think about Detective Ostrander. The sound of his voice. The look in his eyes. The way he moved his body. What he liked to eat or drink. All of this will help us locate his soul, which is clinging to his corpse somewhere in this complex."

"If he's dead like you say," I said, "wouldn't his soul be gone along with him?"

"When someone dies, it takes a while for the soul to understand. Imagine you're in a car wreck. Do you immediately run away from the vehicle? No, you stick around to see what happens next. You wait for the police to show up. You wait for order to be restored. Only then do you abandon your vehicle. It's the same for a human soul."

"So if we find him, we can put his soul back in his body?"

"No," Nikki said. "Would you climb back into a totaled car?"

"So what does it fucking matter?"

"One," Nikki said, "you shouldn't curse so much, it makes you sound like a cliché. Two, it will make all of the difference in the world. Especially if you want to catch the killer you call MM. Detective Ostrander cracked his pattern, and I need to know what he knows."

The weird little chick was throwing so much at me I needed a moment to breathe. Mind you, I was still drunk. Yet, for the first time that morning, I realized I very much needed a drink.

"Trust your partner," Nikki continued. "He's calling out for you. If you think about him, you can lead us right to him."

When you're faced with the absurd, sometimes all you can do is go along with the absurd. So I leaned back against that white stucco wall and thought about my partner. Chadwick "Chuck" Ostrander. The "Chuck" was my idea. No L.A. cop would take a dude named "Chadwick" seriously. How about Chad, he suggested? Get the fuck out, I said. Chad was even worse. Hi, I'm a bad-ass detective named . . . Chad? It just wouldn't work. So Chadwick, to his credit, became accustomed to being called "Chuck," which—like most nicknames—started out as a joke. But, eventually, it became something warm. Something real.

"That's good," Nikki said. "Keep going. Imagine him standing in front of you."

Okay, so Chuck is standing in front of me, looking at me through his horn-rimmed glasses. Another thing that made him a target in the Detective Bureau. But he didn't care. Even when they fogged up at the most inopportune times.

"What was that?" Nikki asked.

"What was what?"

"What were you just thinking about—specifically?"

"His glasses."

"That's it! He left us a clue."

"What?"

"Come on," she said, tugging at my arm and leading me down another hallway.

We ran through this apartment complex that was clearly designed by a schizophrenic. *Look for his glasses*, Nikki said. *That will tell us where his body is.* It would be just like Chuck to leave us a bread crumb like this. But I was sad to think of Chuck, in a horribly desperate moment, pulling down his horn-rims, his vision blurring instantly, and—knowing he'd never see clearly again—tossing them somewhere for me to find later.

As we moved through the buildings, dogs barked at us and people told us to quiet the hell down. Some threatened to call the police. I told them I was the police, and they told me I was a fascist. Good morning to you, too, sweetheart.

We were on the second floor when something caught my eye. "Wait," I said, then peered over a balcony down into this little patch of ground one floor below. A hangover vertigo washed over me, and then something else. A cold reckoning.

"What is it?"

I could barely form the words: "Chuck's glasses."

Only then did I truly believe my partner was dead. Whenever we'd find ourselves in one of those shoot-outs or brawls or fights to the death, Chuck would carefully remove his eyewear and tuck them in the pocket of his blazer. *But you won't be able to see*, I'd say every time. And then he'd give me one of those cockeyed smiles and say, "They cost $179.99 a pair. I can squint."

But here was the weird thing: there were no apartment doors anywhere near Chuck's glasses.

We were looking down into this weird little square of non-used space, enclosed by four walls, visible only from above. Which is what happens when you draw up the architectural plans for an apartment complex while you're in a straitjacket.

"There's no door," I said. "How'd did they get down there?"

Nikki looked up. "The roof."

We went up a series of stairs that left me both winded and on the verge of another epic round of vomiting. I was chilled to my marrow and sweating at the same time. Surely this was my body telling me that it was just giving up. Go ahead and drink yourself to death if you want. I'm done trying to talk to you.

My vision was blurry when we reached the top, which was above the third-floor level. Nikki tried a metal door that opened out on the roof. Locked.

"Step back," she said, balancing herself like a crane—arms extended out, leg up—before smashing open the door with the heel of one of her prostitute boots.

"How did you do that?" I asked, stunned. "You're what, all of 90 pounds?"

"It's not about weight, it's about physics. Now come help me look for your partner."

Chuck and I called it "tough guy ballet"—fancy cop moves. Chuck wasn't the type to leap over a hood and draw his weapon, taking down three bad guys with one bullet, and neither was I. We laughed whenever we saw that shit in a movie. But here was this kid, doing it in real life.

We scrambled across the rooftops. The morning light was soft pink through the pollution of the L.A. basin, which made Chuck's corpse seem to glow like it was radioactive.

Yeah, my partner was up there, and he was definitely dead. MM had done a number on him. I was by no means a forensic expert, but even I could tell Chuck had put up the fight of his life. He'd very much wanted to go on living. I should have been with him. Chances are, it'd be my corpse lying right there next to Chuck's, too. But it would have been one glorious brawl.

A quiet voice snapped me out of the numbness that had washed over me.

"When I collect him," Nikki said, "I'm going to fall unconscious. I need you to take me somewhere quiet and safe and give me time to recover."

"'Collect?'"

"Like I told you, he needs order to be restored. I need to give him a refuge."

"You're going to take in Chuck's soul," I finally said.

"That's a crude way of putting it, but essentially yes."

"So Chuck's going to wake up in the body of a fifteen-year-old girl dressed up like a hooker."

Nikki was offended. "This body is nineteen years old. Do you think they'd do this to a minor?"

"No, course not."

She kneeled on the spongy surface of the roof and closed her eyes, as if in prayer. I walked over to look down at Chuck. I probably looked like I was praying, too, but I wasn't. I took a deep breath, and turned around just in time to see Nikki shudder and keel over.

I threw up.

⬥

So that's how I ended up carrying the unconscious body of a fifteen-year—sorry, nineteen-year-old—girl dressed up like a hooker back down to the round-about . . . right into a six-man team of Burbank PD, all of whom were pointing their service weapons at me.

"Hey," I said. "Let me explain."

Which started a long day of explaining. All I did for hours was explain—our case, my drinking, the girl dressed up like a hooker, the assault on the yuppie, the glasses, how I found the body. I left out the metaphysical stuff, for obvious reasons. I said that my partner had left me a message, and this girl had led me to his body. Along the way, some yuppie attacked us. He was probably high on PCP, I don't know. Does it matter? My partner was dead. I said "my partner is dead" a lot. I told my story so much even I began to believe it. And why wouldn't I? That's what happened, right? Any other version would be too bizarre.

I also said, "the girl is a hero," and that I wanted to talk to her immediately. And eventually, they let me.

They had her in interrogation room D with a Styrofoam cup of coffee and a napkin stacked with a couple of sugar cookies. They were untouched.

"Hey, Nikki—how're you feeling?" I closed the door behind me.

"Hi, Howie," she said. "Glad to see you made it in the end."

"How do you know my name?"

"Howie, I've been your partner for six years."

"Nikki, listen . . ."

"It's *me*, Howie. Your old pal Chuck."

"Nikki, honey, enough with the—"

"Go ahead. Ask me anything."

"I'm not asking you anything because you're crazy. You understand that, honey, don't you?"

But then Nikki began to tell me a series of things only Chuck would know. The things that are shared between partners and partners alone, secrets that *die* with those partners. She—*he*—reminded me of things I did for him, times I pulled his bacon out of the fire. The bullet that caught my hand instead of his face. The sinking boat I pulled him off, lugging him to shore with only one good arm and one sort-of-okay leg. Tackling him at L.A. Coliseum while automatic gunfire sprayed over our heads. The things you tend to forget or downplay when you're hanging around a goddamned genius all the time. But funny enough, those were the very things that Chuck remembered the most.

"Jesus, Chuck. Are you, what—in there alongside Nikki?" I felt like I ought to peer into the girl's eyes to see.

"Yeah, we all sort of share . . . like, a brain hotel, for lack of a better term. We each have our own rooms. And we take turns controlling the body."

"The body of a *teenager*, Chuck. Do you even realize you're in the body of a teenager?"

"This isn't the first body they've occupied," Nikki/Chuck said. "Some bodies just give out, some are killed. But the brain hotel can move to different hosts. There's got to be a dozen people in here with me. It's impressive company. Some of these detectives are legends."

"You're inside this 'brain hotel' with a bunch of dead cops."

"Not all cops. There's this big fat guy who's obsessed with orchids, and some alcoholic lady named Nora, and this British guy who plays the violin and seems to know everything about everyone, and—oh, and Nikki, too. She says hello."

"Hi," I said, which came out like a whisper-choke.

"But that's not even the craziest thing. You know the guy we've been chasing? This MM? Well, he's been running around the country collecting souls, too. He's got over a hundred psychopaths knocking around his skull. Can you believe that? This is why there was no real pattern. He lets a different soul take the wheel every time he kills."

I put my face in my hands. "Please, please . . . stop it."

"What's wrong?"

I looked up.

"*What's wrong!?* Chuck . . . if this is you . . . what the hell, man? What do you want me to do? What am I supposed to *do* with all of this?"

Nikki's face twisted up into one of those Chuck Ostrander–style cock-eyed grins.

"You want to get into some trouble?"

HOUNDED

by Zoë Sharp

"Excuse me, gentlemen, is anyone sitting here?"

The men looked up from their table with the resigned irritation of travellers who thought they'd managed to get three seats together in a first class compartment without having to endure the company of a stranger.

One of them—youngish and tall, with a nose he could have used to spear pickles out of a jar—peered rather pointedly over his gold-framed spectacles at the adjacent table across the aisle. It had only a middle-aged, middle-class couple in occupation, although they'd sprawled their iPads and iPhones and papers across the surface to stake their claim.

I followed his gaze and produced a rueful smile.

"I don't go by train very often," I confided as I slid into the remaining seat. "But when I do I'm afraid I really can't face backwards. Gives me motion sickness."

"Ah," said the man. "Have you thought of taking hyoscine hydrobromide of some kind? It's available at any pharmacy without a prescription."

233

Before I could answer that, one of the others—an older man with a bushy moustache and the upright spine of the ex-soldier—cut in with, "Or antihistamines? A little less effective, perhaps, but fewer side-effects. Hyoscine may make you drowsy, my dear."

Instinctively, I glanced at the third man. He was small and sturdy, his hands and face tanned as much by wind as by sun. He grinned at me from under thick black eyebrows.

"Hey, no use looking to me for advice. These two guys are the physicians. The ginger tea my mom used to make whenever *I* got sick, that's about all I could suggest."

My first thought was *American*, but the slightly Scottish inflection on the word "about" tipped him farther north.

"Is that a Canadian accent I hear?"

The bushy eyebrows wriggled like two hairy caterpillars on his forehead, and his grin, if anything, widened.

"Good call," he said. "Most folks over here mistake me for a Yank."

"Ah, well, I shouldn't let it worry you." I returned his smile. "*Some* folk over here mistake *me* for a lady."

He laughed out loud at that, and after a moment the two doctors allowed themselves a small twist of the lips that might have passed for amusement. The Canadian, meanwhile, leaned across the table with a weathered hand outstretched. "Henry Baskerville."

I took his hand, not without caution, and received a robust shake that threatened to bounce my shoulder out of its socket. Still, at least there were two professionals nearby who could have put it back for me.

"Charlie Fox," I said. "Nice to meet you, Henry."

The beaky-nosed doctor cleared his throat, murmured, "It's *Sir* Henry, actually."

"Really? Should I curtsey?"

"Oh, not on my account, I assure you. A few months ago I was farming in Alberta province. Then my uncle, Sir Charles Baskerville, died suddenly, and now I find myself a baronet with a country estate in Devonshire."

"I thought your last name rang a bell. There was something unusual about your uncle's death, wasn't there? Enough to make the national news, anyway."

"Ah, you're referring to the pet story of my family—the hell hound." Sir Henry smiled again at his own pun. "I've heard of it ever since I was in the nursery, but I never thought of taking it seriously until now."

The doctors' eyes flicked toward each other. Only a tiny movement, but I caught it nonetheless.

"Sir Charles died of dyspnoea—difficulty breathing—and cardiac failure," the beaky-nosed doctor said. "The post-mortem examination showed long-standing organic heart disease. Indeed, as his medical practitioner I had urged him to seek specialist advice about his health. But . . ." He gave a shrug.

"I'm sure you did everything you could for your patient," I offered. "Urging him is one thing, but I don't suppose you could exactly truss him up like a Sunday roast and deliver him to Harley Street, could you?"

He unbent enough then to introduce himself as Dr. James Mortimer. That left the older of the men, who quickly followed suit, even though recognising him was the reason I'd begged the spare seat at their table in the first place.

"Dr. John Watson."

I manufactured a reasonable facsimile of surprise. "Of course," I said. "I follow your blog. The exploits of Sherlock Holmes, consulting detective. If even half of it is true, it makes fascinating reading."

"If anything, I tend to play *down* some of the more sensational aspects of Holmes's cases," Watson said, looking almost sheepish.

A firm nudge against my leg beneath the table had me looking down, to find a curly-haired spaniel eyeing me dolefully. I stroked the dog's ears, and said, "Do I take it there might be a hint of the sensational going on in Devon?"

"Indeed not," Watson denied quickly. "Or Sherlock Holmes himself would be travelling with us."

"Which, plainly, he is not," Mortimer added, trying for an air of nonchalance that he failed to pull off.

"Even so, to bring along not one but *two* doctors, Sir Henry, you must be wary of something serious happening to you?"

"I guess it might look that way," said the baronet. "And there have been a couple of interesting occurrences since I got to England. I don't mind admitting I feel safer in company."

Aware of a certain relief, I opened my mouth to ask more about that, but Watson jumped into the gap with a question about my own reason for heading down to Dartmoor.

My turn to shrug. "Oh, I've booked a week away in one of those little holiday cottages on the moor," I said, still fussing the spaniel under the table as an excuse not to make eye contact. "It's almost more a yurt than a cottage, from the pictures I've seen. A bit basic, but the season's just about over, so I'm told I'll have the whole development to myself."

"I know the ones. They *are* rather remote," Mortimer said. "Are you sure you'll be all right out there on your own?"

"I needed a get-away-from-it-all break." The story tripped convincingly from my tongue. "Having no Internet and no cellphone coverage sounded like a blessing rather than a curse."

I didn't think it necessary to mention the military-grade GPS unit tucked into my rucksack. Nor the 9mm SIG Sauer lying snug in a concealed-carry rig at the small of my back.

If they weren't here to interfere in my business, at this stage of the operation I had no intention of interfering in theirs.

The station was tiny, little more than a roadside halt, bordered by a white fence from which hung flower boxes overflowing with late blooms. Sir Henry, the two doctors, and I were the only passengers to climb down when the train made its brief stop.

Two vehicles waited outside the gate, but neither of them was for me—or at least I hoped not because as well as a Land Rover Discovery there was also a liveried police BMW with two officers in tactical black standing by. They eyed us with suspicion as we passed.

The Discovery driver hopped out and opened the rear doors to take his party and their bags. Mortimer lifted the wriggling spaniel into the rear luggage compartment.

I hovered, looking up and down the deserted road and frowning, until Sir Henry, who'd taken the front passenger seat, called to me through the open window.

"Hey, Miss Fox, you need a ride?"

"Well, it looks like mine hasn't turned up, for some reason. That's very kind. Are you sure I won't be taking you out of your way?"

"Dr. Mortimer tells me we'll pass the cottages on our way to Baskerville Hall," he said.

"In that case, I'd be very grateful to accept. I know I was hoping to do some walking while I'm here, but there *are* limits."

As the smallest, I squeezed into the middle of the rear seat, between the two doctors. The driver placed my rucksack in with the luggage and the spaniel. The dog huffed down the back of my neck through the grille that separated us.

As we set off, I asked, "Why the police presence?" with as much innocence as I could muster.

The driver spoke over his shoulder. "There's a prisoner escaped from HMP Dartmoor. He's been out three days now and they watch every road and station, but they've had no sight of him yet. The farmers here about don't like it, miss, and that's a fact."

"After three days in the outdoors without anything by way of food or shelter," I said, "he's unlikely to be much of a threat to anyone."

"Ah," the man said, "but it isn't like any ordinary convict. This is a man that would stick at nothing."

"Oh?" said Mortimer. "Who is he, Perkins?"

"It is Selden, the Notting Hill murderer."

I'd spent a lot of time over the last few years living and working outside the UK, but the man's crimes had been vicious enough to attract international coverage.

"And it will be dark by the time you reach your cottage tonight," Mortimer put in with a dubious glance. "Perhaps you should delay until daylight tomorrow?"

I made a show of indecision. "Well, if I might borrow a phone so I can call the woman who was supposed to meet me with the keys, I should be fine."

Perkins unhooked his elderly cellphone from its holder on the dashboard and passed it to me without hesitation. I dug the booking confirmation out of my pocket and dialled the number. A minute or so later I handed the phone back.

"It seems she mistook the time of my train and is shopping over in Exeter," I said. "She'll be on her way home shortly. If you'd drop me off by the cottage, I'm happy to wait there."

"Out of doors, with a man like Selden on the loose?" Sir Henry said. "I won't hear of it. Besides, the light will soon be gone, and the last thing Mr. Holmes said to me when we left London was to quote one of the phrases from that queer old family legend: 'Avoid the moor in those hours of darkness when the powers of evil are exalted.' Come dine with us at the Hall and have this woman meet you there. I couldn't live with myself if you fell victim either to this psychopath or the infamous hound!"

We saw the twin crenellated towers of Baskerville Hall long before we reached the intricate wrought-iron gates. The original gate lodge was derelict, but a new construction had been started on the other side of the drive. Sir Charles Baskerville, I recalled, had made a fortune in South Africa. Clearly, he'd been spending lavishly on his property at the point of his demise.

An avenue of trees lined the driveway, darker in the falling light. The Discovery's headlights threw elongated shadows into the tunnel of thick foliage, creating an even more eerie effect.

"Was it here?" Sir Henry asked in a low voice. "That my uncle . . . ?"

"No, no," Mortimer said. "In the Yew Alley, on the other side."

The avenue opened out onto a lawn area with the house centre stage. The central section was swathed in creepers, cut away from the odd window or coat of arms. The towers we'd seen protruded from the top, and a porch jutted out at the front. The wings at either side had to be later additions, in dark granite with mullioned windows. A few dingy lights showed through the glass, but overall it looked like someone had gone mad with low-energy bulbs and really needed to swap them out for much brighter LEDs.

We were met by the Barrymores, husband and wife, who had apparently looked after the Baskervilles for years. They didn't bat an eye at my unexpected inclusion for dinner. Still, they didn't have extra to cater for. Dr. Mortimer made his excuses and disappeared with Perkins in the Discovery. Once I got inside, I discovered why he'd been keen to get home.

The interior of the Hall was as gloomy as it had appeared from the exterior. The walls were hung with murky portraits of Baskervilles through the ages, painted by artists who'd evidently got bulk discount on tubes of Burnt Umber and Lamp Black.

The dining room, which opened out of the hallway, was even more depressing. It didn't help that both Sir Henry and Watson had worn dark suits for the journey. I had on a navy blue fleece and felt positively gaudy by comparison.

After we'd eaten—a subdued meal with little conversation—we moved through to another dimly lit room, this time containing glass-fronted bookcases and a full-size billiard table. The wind had begun to pick up across the moor, rattling the windows as if seeking an unguarded place to enter.

"My word, it isn't a very cheerful place," Sir Henry said. "I don't wonder that my uncle got a little jumpy if he lived all alone in a house such as this."

The sweep of headlights across the front of the house and the crunch of tyres on the gravel heralded the arrival of the caretaker of the holiday cottages. She was a large lady who bustled in with great energy in a long skirt and unbelted raincoat, so she took on the appearance of a galleon under sail.

I said my thanks to the household before being whisked away to bump across a moorland track in her elderly Daihatsu 4x4. She was full of apologies and explanations, and never seemed to stop talking long enough to draw breath.

The cottage was one of a group that had once been peasants' huts, huddled in a hollow on the moor to escape the worst of the winter gales. The sparse nearby trees all grew at extreme angles to show the direction of the prevailing wind. I reckoned that if I lived out here I'd soon develop a permanent lean from the force of it.

"I confess I half expected you to cancel, lovey, what with this madman loose on the moor. Shocking, isn't it? In fact, I'm in two minds about whether you *should* stay out here all alone, I really am."

The last thing I wanted was for her to try to stop me from staying. The cottage was isolated and unobserved—the perfect vantage point from which to study the habits of my target, and to finalise my plans.

"If they've had no sign of him in three days, he's probably long gone by now," I said quickly. "I'm sure I'll be fine."

Although the accommodation was tiny it was enough for my needs. Heating and cooking were via the wood-burning stove in one corner, but the building had been well insulated, and I'd been fed already, so I didn't feel the need to light the stove tonight.

Instead, I switched out the lamp and sat below the window, looking up at the clouds rushing past the stars in the light from a pale half moon, while I stripped, cleaned, and reassembled the 9mm pistol by touch alone.

◇

The following morning I woke early, splashed cold water onto my face, and shrugged into my clothes knowing I had a lot of ground to cover and limited time in which to cover it.

The wind of last night had died down. As I stepped outside I was immediately aware of a faint odour of wood smoke. I stilled in the watery sunshine and heard a shrill, burbling whistle that sounded very like an old-fashioned kettle coming to the boil.

Reaching behind me, I eased the semiautomatic pistol in its rig to make sure it wouldn't foul on my clothing, and moved softly towards the source of the sound.

Unless I was mistaken, it had come from the end cottage of the little group. As I approached, I saw the door was slightly ajar, leaving a strip of internal frame visible along the leading edge.

I paused a second just outside, mind flashing through my options. Not the entry—that I could do in my sleep—but the excuse I'd need for it if the occupant turned out to be a legitimate guest.

"Don't stand on ceremony," called a man's voice from within. "I've taken the liberty of preparing breakfast for both of us."

He sounded friendly enough, but I've come across too many smiling killers not to draw the SIG first. Holding it down by my leg, I shoved the door open and slid rapidly to the side of the aperture as I went through.

A spare man with a thin face and high forehead sat with a chair pulled up close to the wood-burning stove, on the top of which he was nudging with a spatula at bacon, eggs, and tomatoes frying in a small pan. He barely glanced at me as I came in, but I got the impression there was little he didn't see.

"Ah, a woman of caution as well as action," he said. "Good. That makes things so much less worrisome."

It was not the opening gambit I'd expected, causing me to ask blankly, "How so?"

"Because clearly I need not concern myself with your safety while this man Selden is still at large, and therefore you will not distract me from the task at hand," he said as if it were obvious. He lifted the pan off the heat. "Now, there's bread on the table, if you wouldn't mind cutting a couple of slices? The kettle, as you no doubt heard, has just boiled. I can offer you Earl Grey or coffee—both black. No milk, I'm afraid."

"Excuse *me*, but my mother always warned me never to put anything offered by a stranger into my mouth."

He gave a bark of laughter, swapped the frying pan to his left hand and stuck out his right. "Your mother is evidently a woman of good sense and sound judgement," he said. "Sherlock Holmes, at your service."

I put away the SIG and shook his hand, murmuring a cautious, "I'm Charlie" as I did so.

"Well, Charlie, my thanks to you. It's due entirely to your arrival last night that I can indulge in a hot meal this morning."

"Ah, you mean if anyone saw the smoke"—I nodded to the wood-burner, "they would assume it was mine."

"Absolutely. So it's only right that I should offer to share my good fortune."

I hesitated a moment longer, then shrugged and moved across to the table. By the time I'd sliced two chunks from the crusty loaf, he'd served the contents of the pan and laid out cutlery. Automatically, I took the chair opposite the window and we both dug in. It felt somewhat bizarre to sit down to a campfire breakfast with such a man, only seconds after we'd met.

He ate with the same single-minded focus I imagined he did everything. Only when he'd finished the last bite, wiped his plate clean with bread and sat back with his mug of tea, did he turn his scrutiny in my direction.

"Tell me, Charlie, how long is it since you were in the military?"

I allowed myself a raised eyebrow. "Not everyone who knows how to handle a firearm is necessarily an ex-squaddie."

"True. But in this country, where guns are far more uncommon than in America, it's certainly indicative. As is the way you lace your boots."

"Damn." I glanced down at my hiking boots, frowning. "Old habits, I suppose."

"Indeed."

"I take it that Dr. Watson and Sir Henry are not aware of your presence?"

"Just so," Holmes agreed. "And I would be grateful if I could prevail upon you to keep them in ignorance of the fact. Our opponents in this case are formidable, and I thought it prudent to remain an unknown factor in the business, ready to throw in all of my weight at a critical moment."

"They won't hear anything from me," I said. "But I don't suppose you'd care to tell me what the *business* you're concerned with might be?"

He shook his head, smiling. "No more, I suspect, than you yourself would be willing to tell me what brings *you* to the wilds of Dartmoor."

I took a sip of my coffee, which was thick, dark, and sweet, like treacle. "I *might* be here on a straightforward walking holiday . . ."

"But then again, you *might* not . . ."

"Care to hazard a guess?"

He looked offended. "I never guess. It is a shocking habit—destructive to the logical faculty."

"My apologies. To *deduce*, then?"

He put down his mug and leaned both elbows on the tabletop, steepling his fingers as he regarded me. I sat without fidgeting and stared right back.

"Hmm. Whatever you did in the army, it was a role that was out of the ordinary," he said at last. "And your experiences either during your period of service or since have had a profound effect on you."

That was closer to the mark than I was expecting, even from a man with Holmes's reputation. I resisted the urge to shift in my seat and said only a non-committal "Oh?"

"You are too intelligent, articulate, and far too aware of your surroundings to have been merely a *squaddie*, as you put it," he said. "By choosing a seat with your back to the wall, facing both doorway and window, you take great pains not to put yourself at a tactical disadvantage, despite the fact this puts me between you and any means of egress."

"From what I've read about you in Dr. Watson's blog, you're pretty handy at Bartitsu. If anyone comes through that door they'll have to deal with you first."

He ignored my flip remark, gesturing instead to the mug I was clutching. "You are clearly right-handed, and yet—even after you have ascertained that I am not a threat—you are careful to drink only with your left, leaving your strong hand unencumbered."

"Perhaps it isn't *you* I'm worried about."

"Thus confirming that you have come to the moors with a purpose. One that is not without considerable dangers attached."

Still, I hedged. "Aren't you forgetting this prisoner on the run, Selden? My precautions could be all because of him."

"If you were so concerned about an escaped lunatic, you would not have come at all," Holmes said. "And he's still hereabouts, by the way, so do watch yourself."

"Thanks for the warning—and for breakfast," I said, rising. "I'll leave you to whatever it is you're working on." I stepped past him, pausing at the doorway. "Unless, of course, there's anything *else* about me you'd care to add?"

"You present quite the conundrum, Charlie. You have the appearance of someone who is only too willing to resort to violence, and yet is equally determined to avoid doing so, from which I might conclude that your own reasons for being here contain that combination." Holmes regarded me steadily, his smile no longer in evidence. "Be aware that I am dealing with an ugly, dangerous business, and if by any chance our undertakings should coincide, you will need all your skills about you."

I walked over rutted stone tracks into the nearest village of Grimpen. It was a low-lying place of cottages huddled down against the elements with few people in sight. The only large buildings turned out to be the local pub and the house of Dr. Mortimer. As I passed, I was amused to notice an old phrenology bust in the window of his surgery.

There was an open-all-hours village store, combining Post Office and greengrocer as well as a couple of café tables. They had Wi-Fi, though, and I was able to pick up my emails, including an attached folder of jpeg images that provided me with added motivation, if that were needed, to complete my task. I sent a brief response saying I was in position and had begun to recce for my opportunity to act.

I bought a few supplies, stowed them in my rucksack, and set off walking back. The day was clear and the sun had solidified the turning colours of the moorland into shades of russet and gold. All-in-all, a lot cheerier looking than it had appeared last night.

According to my GPS unit it was about a 5.4-km hike, and although the rough ground meant I had to take care where I put my feet, it was easy enough to give me thinking time. I would guess I was about halfway back to the cottage when someone shouted my name.

I turned quickly, to see two men approaching. One of them I knew already—Dr. John Watson. The other I recognised, although we had not yet met, and for a moment I wished heartily that I had been either quicker or slower along the track.

"This is Jack Stapleton," Watson said when they'd caught up to me. "He lives at Merripit House. You may have seen it—or at least the smoke from the chimney—if you've had a chance to do any walking yet."

"Only into the village," I said, shaking Stapleton's hand. He had an expensive-looking Nikon camera on a strap over his shoulder. I tried not to let the possible range of the telephoto lens bother me. "That's a serious bit of kit."

"I'm a naturalist," the man said. He was a little shorter than the doctor, clean-shaven, with fair hair showing beneath a battered straw hat. He lifted a shoulder to indicate the Nikon. "We don't catch butterflies in a net and pin them to a board anymore."

"I'm glad to hear it," I said, but photos of a different kind were printed large in my mind's eye. Photos of bruised and swollen flesh, and of long-term misery. I couldn't quite prevent myself adding in an entirely neutral tone, "The moor must be an ideal place for you to indulge in your passion."

He stilled, cocked an eyebrow. "Oh?"

"All this undisturbed flora and fauna for you to study." I gave him a bland smile. "Does your family enjoy living out in the wilds, also?"

"Of course."

I caught the flash of a frown pass across Watson's features, then it was gone.

"Yes," Stapleton went on. "I've been here long enough to know these moors like the back of my hand. But I would not advise *you* to wander too far from the marked trails, if you value your health."

I tried not to bristle. "Meaning?"

Watson turned to point. "My dear, do you see the patches of bright green scattered across this great plain? Stapleton was just telling me that's the Grimpen Mire." He suppressed a shudder. "I've just seen for myself what happens to even large animals that find themselves stuck in it."

"Certain death." Stapleton's pale eyes were fixed on mine for a second. Then they shifted to a point over my shoulder and he darted to the side, unslinging the camera as he went. "Excuse me an instant," he called over his shoulder. "It is another Cyclopides."

Watson and I stood and watched him pursue the butterfly, leaping from tuft to tuft with camera poised.

Not knowing how long he would be occupied, I turned to Watson and said bluntly, "Something about meeting Stapleton's family that worried you, Doctor?"

He looked surprised, then shook his head, and frowned again. "A misunderstanding, I think, between myself and his sister," he said. "She lives at Merripit House with Stapleton. At first, she mistook me for Sir Henry and was most insistent that I—or, rather, *he*—should leave the moor and never return."

His sister? Ah . . .

"Did she say why?"

"No. But afterwards she definitely did not want her brother to know she had said such a thing . . . It was most strange. Perhaps she, too, is worried about strangers becoming engulfed in the Mire."

"Or it could be that living here was more his choice than hers," I ventured. "And she's giving every newcomer the benefit of her unfortunate experience."

"Indeed. She claimed to be happy, but her voice didn't quite match her words."

And there's a damn good reason for that . . .

Stapleton was returning, eyes fixed on the view screen on the back of the Nikon as he checked his shots.

"I think I have him that time," he told us, gaze flicking from one to the other. "Ah, yes." He turned the camera around and showed us a sharp close-up of a fairly ordinary-looking brown-and-yellow butterfly. "Really quite beautiful, isn't he?"

The gentleness in his voice almost made me shiver. I left it to Watson to make the right noises.

"I must be getting on, if you'll excuse me, gentlemen?"

"Of course," Watson said. "Oh, just one last thing before you go, Miss Fox. A few minutes before we met, you didn't happen to hear a loud, well, *howling* sound, did you?"

"A howling?" I repeated. "As in a wolf, or a dog?"

"Yes." Watson seemed almost embarrassed to ask. "It was the weirdest, strangest thing I've ever heard in my life."

I shook my head.

"I told you, Dr. Watson, I should not be surprised to learn that what we heard was the cry of a bittern," Stapleton said. "At one time they were practically extinct in England, but the population has boomed in recent years."

I had never knowingly heard the sound made by a bittern, but I was not convinced. And if the look on his face was anything to go by, neither was Dr. Watson.

Stapleton invited me to join the pair of them for lunch at Merripit, but I declined—much, I suspect, to his relief. Instead, I continued on the track leading me towards the holiday cottages, not breaking stride until I was out of their sight.

Then I ducked off the trail and left the rucksack marked by a small pile of stones, turning back without it. I employed every stealth technique I'd ever been taught to cover the ground between me and the Stapletons' without being seen. That telephoto lens of his was a hazard I could have done without. I had no choice but to work around it.

I managed to creep into position nearby, and lay waiting while Watson no doubt enjoyed a pleasant lunch with Jack Stapleton. I'd been told he could be charming company when he set his mind to it.

And downright bloody nasty when he was thwarted.

Watson left Merripit House sooner than I expected and started out in the direction of Baskerville Hall. I debated going after him, hesitating long enough over the decision for it to be taken out of my hands.

A slim, dark-haired woman slipped out of a doorway at the side of the house and hurried across the moor on an intercept course with the doctor. Knowing I wouldn't reach her beforehand—not without risk of exposing us both—I stayed put.

It wasn't long before I saw her returning, and this time was able to slip out of my hiding place and stop her before she got back to the house. Her stride faltered when she saw me waiting for her by the path, glancing sideways at Merripit as if to satisfy herself that we were not going to be seen.

"Beryl Stapleton?"

I hardly needed her tentative nod of reply. She wore a pair of jeans with a polo-necked sweater, and hugged thin arms around her body, though it was hardly cold.

"When?" she asked.

"As soon as you're ready," I said. "Pack a bag and I'll have you out of here this afternoon."

A cloud passed across her face, stricken with indecision. She glanced behind her again, over towards the house. Or it might have been cast further, in the direction Watson had taken.

"I–I need another day," she said, her voice broken but still with the lilting South American accent of her birthplace. "Two at the most. I—"

She broke off as I stepped forwards, took her wrist and pushed back her sleeve. The bruises on her forearm were livid, and fresh.

"Why, when he does this to you?"

She wrenched her arm loose with more force than it needed. "I cannot explain. I know only that he plans a great wrong, and I must stop him—"

"If you tell me, I'll stop him for you," I said. I thought of Holmes hiding on the moor, and of Watson staying close by. "Help may be closer to hand than you realise."

"It would be my word against his, and what's the use in that?" she cried. "He has doctors lined up to swear I am incapable of knowing my own mind, that I am delusional. All you will succeed in doing is making him more devious and more cruel than he is already."

I sighed, pulling together a patience I didn't feel. "Beryl, you asked for help to get away from this man. That's why I'm here. Why risk your safety any more than you have to—any more than you have already?"

She hunched down into herself, wouldn't meet my eyes. "Because this is partly my fault," she whispered. "And because it is not only *my* safety that is at stake."

And with that she whirled away and ran back towards the house, her dark hair streaming out behind her like a pennant.

"Come in, Mr. Holmes," I said, answering a quiet knock on the cottage door. "My turn to cook for you, I think."

I'd spent another soggy day keeping obs on the comings and goings of Merripit House, returning to the cottage tired, wet, cold, and irritable. A hot shower and a change of clothes, though, had improved my mood no end, as did getting the wood-burning stove lit and a stew bubbling away on top in a cast-iron pot.

Sherlock Holmes made himself at home in one of the dining chairs while I dished up the stew into bowls. We ate in companionable silence. It wasn't until he'd set aside his cutlery that the intensity of his gaze turned on me in full.

"Well, Charlie, it would seem that our purposes do indeed intersect."

"Oh?"

"You have been keeping an eye on Sir Henry, I believe."

"Not as such," I said. "I'm keeping an eye on the Stapletons. It just so happens that Sir Henry is spending more and more time there."

"Ah. I allow the distinction." He lifted his coffee mug in salute. "He seems much enamoured of Miss Stapleton, from what I can gather."

"Yes, he does rather, doesn't he? You may want to nip that in the bud."

He made no comment other than to raise one eyebrow. "Is there some reason a wealthy baronet would not make the lady a most suitable husband?"

"None at all . . . if she weren't already married," I said. "Jack and Beryl Stapleton are not brother and sister—they're husband and wife."

Holmes absorbed this news in silence for a moment. "You have proof?"

"Check the records. He used to run a school somewhere up north. The pair were pictured in the news reports when it closed."

He nodded slowly, spoke almost to himself. "Ah, yes, of course. And no doubt he foresaw that she would be very much more useful to him in the character of a free woman." His gaze turned sharp. "But she has tried to warn off Sir Henry several times—first the note, and then mistaking Watson for Sir Henry here."

"Note?"

"In London, before Sir Henry came down here."

I nodded. "I don't know about that, but I believe Stapleton coerced her into falling in with his plans. He certainly physically and psychologically abuses her."

"And what is your role in this, if you *are* now prepared to tell me?"

"I'm here to get her out."

"So, why haven't you?"

I sighed. "Not for want of trying. I don't do kidnapping. She asked for help and she has to *want* to leave. The arrangements were all in place before I came down here, but since Sir Henry's arrival she's turned . . . reluctant, shall we say. She believes he's in danger."

"From Stapleton? Indeed, he is," Holmes said, his gaunt face grave in the fire-light. "Stapleton is a Baskerville. He knows if he can rid himself of Sir Henry, he's next in line for both title and fortune. I very much doubt he will let the lady—be she wife or sister—stand in his way."

I woke in the night and found myself grabbing instinctively for the SIG Sauer, which I'd left covered by a shirt on the chair next to the bed. Heart pounding, I sat upright with senses straining against the darkness for whatever had startled me from sleep.

A second later it came again, the thud of a heavy shoulder to the door of the cottage, followed by muttered curses as the sturdy oak held fast.

I reached toward the lamp, mind flipping through scenarios. Someone was clearly trying to break in. Were they doing so because they knew I was in here? Or because they thought the place was empty?

Could be Jack Stapleton, come to put a stop to his wife's escape plan . . .

Putting on a light would either warn the intruder I was awake and prepared, or warn him I was here at all. Neither option was bad.

I flicked on the light.

The thudding ceased, then a fist began to bang against the wooden planks more desperately than before. I heard a man's voice, high with alarm, his words incoherent.

Throwing back the duvet, I slid my feet into the boots I'd left by the bedside and scooped up a flashlight and the pistol. I was still otherwise fully dressed, so it was only a moment before I was by the door, watching the latch jump and rattle with the force of the assault from the outside.

"Back up!" I shouted. "Move away from the door."

"Let me in!" roared the man's voice. It was not one I'd heard before, but so twisted by terror, I'm not sure I would have recognised it anyway. "For the love of *God*, let me in!"

"I'm not opening the door until you move away from it," I shouted back.

The hammering stopped, and I thought he was complying with my order, but the next thing I heard was a muffled cry of fear, then his running footsteps, retreating.

I yanked open the bolt and came out of the cottage in a fast crouch, with the gun extended in my right hand, supported by the flashlight in my left. I caught a glimpse of a bolting figure disappearing between two of the cottages. He ran wildly, arms flailing for balance on the rough ground.

And then, out of the corner of my eye, I saw an animal, big and muscular, streak after him in the light from a clear moon. All I gleaned from that fractional view was an impression of a dark outline moving with speed and aggression, its head and jaws flecked with something like the phosphorescence I'd once seen trailing behind a night ferry.

"What the—?"

I took an involuntary step back. The solid reality of the cottage wall grounded me. I remembered Sir Henry's talk of the family legend that stalked the moor—the hell hound that might very well have frightened his uncle to death.

Squaring my shoulders, I clicked off my flashlight and stepped away from the cottage into a bright patch of moonlight, telling myself firmly that I did not believe in ghosts, and ghouls, and things that went bump in the night.

However, I did believe in the exorcistic powers of twelve 9mm hollow point rounds, and in my ability to place every one of them into the centre of a moving target, even in half-light.

I'd hardly taken half a dozen paces when there was a shriek in the middle distance, mingled with the rumbling bellow of a chase hound in full pursuit of prey.

The door to the cottage Sherlock Holmes had been using swung open, and two men burst out, causing me to duck behind the corner of another of the buildings, out of sight.

"The hound!" cried Holmes. "Come, Watson! Great heavens, if we are too late!"

The pair ran past my position without pause and were soon swallowed up by the gloom. I considered my options.

Stapleton wished to get rid of Sir Henry Baskerville, that much I knew. If this weird apparition was all part of that plan, then it was not my business. Besides, I'd noted the old army Browning in Watson's hand as he passed. They were at least as well equipped to deal with whatever the strange animal might be.

And there were *two* of them . . .

I only had it confirmed who the stranger was a day or so later, when I called in to Grimpen again to pick up my email, and buy milk and bread. I happened to meet Dr. Mortimer just leaving his surgery, bag in hand.

"You will no doubt be pleased to hear you need not worry about the escaped prisoner, Selden, any longer, Miss Fox."

"Oh? Has he been captured?" I asked, although it hadn't taken much working out what was the likely fate of the man. Who else might have been loose on the moor?

"In a way," Mortimer replied. "The poor man was no doubt stumbling around in the dark when he seems to have fallen and broken his neck—the night before last, it would be."

"Poor man?" I queried. "If *half* of what he was supposed to have done to his victims was true, it's hard to feel much real sympathy for him."

Mortimer blinked a couple of times. Not the response he'd been expecting, clearly. But I'd never subscribed to the tradition of not speaking ill of the dead.

To cover his confusion, he asked, "And have you otherwise been enjoying your stay so far?"

"I think I'm starting to get to know the moors a little," I said, thinking of the GPS in my rucksack. "How is Sir Henry?"

If anything, Mortimer's frown deepened.

"I am on my way to see him now."

"He's not ill, I trust?"

"Oh no, but he is . . . concerned. Dr. Watson promised to stay with him until this business was over, and now I understand he has gone back to London on some urgent business, leaving Sir Henry to his own devices."

"Well, I'm sure he will appreciate your company."

"Indeed. Although he has been at Baskerville Hall only a short time, already he has made many friends in the area. The Stapletons have invited him to dine this evening."

I left the doctor climbing into his old BMW and hurried back across the moor path to the cottage. Sure enough, the one Sherlock Holmes had been using was empty, the door locked, and no sign of his occupation visible through the windows.

Had he really gone to London with Watson, and left Sir Henry so vulnerable? Something about that just didn't sit right. I could only hope that his actions were somehow for the sake of the game in which Sherlock Holmes—if Watson's blog was anything to go by—seemed to take such delight.

It was not only in the hope of finally convincing Beryl Stapleton to put her escape plan into action that I took up station watching Merripit House as afternoon slid into evening. If Holmes had indeed gone to London with Watson, I felt I owed it to him to keep an eye on his charge while I was here.

The lights in the house came on, shining like navigation lights across the moor. The Stapletons' housekeeper could be seen bustling in the kitchen, preparing food for their guest, and setting the table in the dining room.

But of Beryl Stapleton, I failed to catch even a glimpse.

Even when Sir Henry arrived, and the two men sat down to eat, she didn't put in an appearance. Stapleton had hospitalised her several times in the past, although he'd always managed to talk or threaten her out of pressing charges. For a few moments I wondered if he'd done so again, or even if Holmes had taken my words to heart and had somehow whisked her off to safety in London with him, but dismissed the idea as soon as it formed. To do so would mean abandoning his duty to Sir Henry, and I remained unconvinced that he would act that way, even to rescue an abused spouse.

So, where was she?

I circled the house, staying out of range of the lights. Still, I didn't see her, but I hesitated over going in to find out. Suppose Jack Stapleton had realised what she was planning, had locked her up somewhere, and was now waiting for me to reveal myself?

The soft scrape of boots behind me on the path had me scuttling into cover. Against the darkening sky I could just make out three figures approaching, and my pulse began to pound. So, Stapleton *did* suspect something was amiss, and he'd called in reinforcements.

Then I caught a quiet voice I had come to recognise ask, "Are you armed, Lestrade?"

And a new player, his outline small and wiry, answered, "As long as I have my trousers I have a hip-pocket, and as long as I have my hip-pocket I have something in it."

There were so many ways to take that I didn't know where to start. I smiled in the darkness. So, Holmes had not abandoned his post. It didn't take much guessing to work out the identity of the third member of the group. Where Holmes went, Watson was sure to be alongside him. And who better to have there in the rough stuff than an ex-army medic who'd seen action in Iraq and Afghanistan?

But not everything was going according to plan. It had started out as a clear night, but gradually a mist began to roll across the moor, swamping all before it in a thick impenetrable cloud. The three men moved back towards the higher ground, where their view of the house and the path leading away from it was clearer. I worried, though, that they would be too far away to act in case of trouble.

I used the mist as a shield to creep closer to the house. The kitchen was now in darkness, the door unlocked. I slipped through and up the rear stairs. Just as

I reached the landing I heard Stapleton and Sir Henry in the hallway below, and flattened against the panelling.

The two men sounded cordial enough. Stapleton was expressing doubts that the baronet should drive himself home after the wine and the brandy he'd consumed. Sir Henry said he was happy to leave his car and walk across the moor, although his voice betrayed a certain trepidation.

"In that case, I'll see you on your way," Stapleton said.

Knowing I had little time, I hurried along the upper corridor, trying doors quickly as I passed until I found one that was locked. With no time to consider an alternative, I kicked the panel just inboard of the lock, twice, and heard the screws tear out of the frame.

Inside was a study, the walls covered by blow-up photographs of butterflies and insects. In the centre, tied to one of the beams that supported the roof, was a wide-eyed figure, bound to the pillar with plastic zip-ties, and gagged with a towel.

I eased the gag away from her mouth. Beryl's face was swollen, one eye closed to a bloodshot slit. Her clothing was bloodied where she'd been beaten and had fought against her bindings.

I pulled out a knife, snicked the blade into place and sliced through the tough plastic ties. She all but collapsed onto me.

"Let's get you out of here," I said, biting back my anger. "Right now!"

"No!" Her voice was hoarse, her eyes bright with pain and humiliation. "He plans to kill him—tonight! You *must* save Sir Henry."

"Bollocks. It's you I have to worry about."

"*Please!*" Her eyes overflowed with tears. "Quickly, before it is too late!"

I let out an exasperated sigh. "Holmes and Watson are out there—they'll save Sir Henry."

She sagged with relief, then stiffened again almost at once. "But my husband will get away! There is an old tin mine on an island in the heart of the Mire. That's where he kept the hound, and he has a refuge there. Leave me and go after him, I beg you!"

With a muttered curse, I propped her gently against the base of the beam and whirled away. If that was what she wanted, that was what she was going to get. I ran down the staircase and out through the still open front door into the foggy night. By the time I hit the gravel driveway, the SIG Sauer was in my hand.

I'd spent the last few days carefully going over the moor, logging the paths with the GPS. Stapleton might like to think he knew the only safe ways through the Grimpen Mire, but his methods relied on landmarks and sightlines.

Mine relied on a series of thirty satellites orbiting the planet at a distance of 12,500 miles, and speeds of up to 7,000mph. The receiver I carried would work through glass, plastic, or cloud. Yes, it could be fooled by snow, but it wasn't snowing. The signal could also be delayed by tall buildings, or heavy foliage, but fortunately the moor boasted neither obstacle.

Standard civilian GPS units were accurate to around three metres, but for somewhere like the Grimpen Mire that distance could easily be the difference between life and death. That was why I'd come equipped with a military-grade receiver that was accurate to less than 300mm.

I used it now as I jogged into the territory of the Mire, trying to trust in the technology and to avoid listening to the sucking of the bog at the soles of my boots.

Suddenly, over to my right came a cry of outright fear, and the same roaring growl I'd heard the night that Selden had been run to his death.

I froze. There was a pause, then gunshots, their sharp report muffled by the fog, followed by a yelp of pain that I could hardly tell if it was human or animal in origin.

The GPS guided me on. I kept one eye on the screen and the other scanning the landscape ahead of me, as far as I could see into it for the fog. After another fifty metres or so I began to imagine it might be thinning. Then I knew for certain that it was, as the figure of a man sprawled on his back solidified ahead of me.

"Help!"

As I approached I saw it was Jack Stapleton. He'd stepped off the safe path and the Mire had grabbed him as far as his knees in a heartbeat. But he possessed a coolly logical brain and was not a man to panic easily. He'd taken the recommended action, lying down flat with his arms outstretched to spread his weight across the surface, which was not stopping him sinking farther, but was at least slowing his rate of descent. With his legs buried to the knees, he could not extricate himself unaided. He daren't even lift his head at my arrival, and only his eyes swivelled to meet mine.

"Ah . . . Miss Fox. Thank God," he began. "I don't have much time. I—"

And then he saw the 9mm in my right hand. His mouth worked soundlessly for a second, and I watched his mind considering whether to admit defeat or try to brazen it out.

"Well, well," he said at last. "I didn't think Sir Henry would call on the services of another—not when he had the great Sherlock Holmes at his disposal."

"I'm not working for Sir Henry," I said. "I'm actually working for Señora Maria Pablo de Silva Garcia."

"Who?"

"Oh, you really should recognise the name, Jack. She's your mother-in-law. A very formidable lady, who does not appreciate the way you've treated her daughter."

I squatted down as close as I was prepared to get to either Stapleton or the bog that had him in its grip.

He bared his teeth at me. "So what are you waiting for." His eyes flicked to the gun. "Just get it over with, why don't you?"

I shook my head. "Not my brief to kill you, Jack."

I watched the play of emotions cross his face then. Doubt, chased by logic into hope, and relief. "So, give me your hand then. Get me out of here."

I shook my head again, rising to my feet. "Sorry, Jack," I said without regret. "Not my brief to save you, either."

"I'll admit everything!" he cried. "About Sir Charles, about the hound. About—"

I smiled. "Do you really think 'the great Sherlock Holmes' hasn't worked it all out for himself?" I asked. "The only thing he needed was the proof. And I think you've provided him with plenty tonight. That, and Beryl's testimony."

"She can have the divorce uncontested! I won't fight her on anything."

"Too late, Jack." I looked at him, cold-eyed as the mud sucked at his clothing, plucked at his hair. "Ask yourself which is worse—the long, slow death of drowning? Or the even longer, even *slower*, death of life behind bars?"

He was still for a moment longer, then he began to thrash, grunting with effort. His actions agitated the Mire beneath him, so that it drew him under ever more quickly. After less than a minute he'd driven himself below the surface, which continued to bubble and heave for a while, then returned to malignant stasis.

I slid the 9mm back into its rig and glanced at the screen of the GPS, stepping carefully onto the patches of solid ground in the direction of the cottage.

The sky was beginning to lighten, and a breeze had sprung up to disperse the remaining fog. I reckoned I'd just time to pack my gear and walk to the station in time to catch the London train. Beryl would be safe in the hands of Dr. Watson and Dr. Mortimer.

And not even Sherlock Holmes would be able to say with any certainty what fate had befallen Jack Stapleton.

ABOUT THE CONTRIBUTORS

PETER S. BEAGLE is best known as the author of *The Last Unicorn*, and, more recently, *Summerlong*, the Nebula-nominated *In Calabria*, and the short-story collection *The Overneath*. He met Sherlock Holmes on a BART subway station, falling into conversation with him when they realized that they were both old friends of the late Avram Davidson, admirers of the Victorian ballads of poet John Davidson, and devotees of the scientific writings of Professor George Edward Challenger. They parted at the 24th Street and Mission station—Mr. Holmes being bound for the San Francisco Airport, on his way to meet with the legendary Irish revolutionist Erskine Childers—and never encountered one another again. Mr. Beagle says that he has no idea of what became of Holmes afterward, but that he does speculate about him fairly frequently, even now. www.facebook.com/TheRealPeterSBeagle

RHYS BOWEN is the *New York Times* bestselling author of two historical mystery series: the Molly Murphy Mysteries, set in early 1900s New York City, and the lighter Royal Spyness novels, featuring a penniless minor royal in 1930s England. She is also the author of the #1 bestselling Kindle historical thriller *In Farleigh Field*. Rhys's books have won fifteen awards, including Agatha, Anthony, and Macavity, and have been nominated for the Edgar best novel. Rhys has always enjoyed spending time in the foggy streets of London with Sherlock Holmes, ever since she discovered him when she was first allowed into the adult section of the library and his was the only name she recognized! www.rhysbowen.com

REED FARREL COLEMAN is the *New York Times* bestselling author of Robert B. Parker's Jesse Stone series and the author of four other series characters including Gus Murphy and Moe Prager. He is currently writing the prequel novel to the movie *Heat* for director Michael Mann. Reed is a four-time Edgar Award nominee and a four-time winner of the Shamus Award for Best PI Novel of the Year. He met Sherlock Holmes in black and white on a sick day home from elementary school. Elementary indeed! www.reedcoleman.com

JAMIE FREVELETTI is an internationally bestselling and International Thriller Writers- and Barry-award winning author of seven novels and four short stories. She writes her own Emma Caldridge thriller series and also writes for Robert Ludlum's Covert One series. Her short stories include "Risk," "Gone," and "Run," featuring her Emma Caldridge character, and "The Last Bad Morning," in the true crime anthology *Anatomy of Innocence: Testimonies of the Wrongfully Convicted*. She first met Sherlock Holmes in elementary school, when she would ride her bicycle to the local library in her rural area and pore through the mystery section, landing on a complete set of the stories and checking the book out over and over again. www.jamiefreveletti.com

ALAN GORDON is a Kleban Prize-winning librettist, lyricist, fiction writer, and storyteller. He first encountered Sherlock Holmes in third grade during the non-stop reading binge that was his childhood, and remembers *The Sign of the Four* as being like a fever dream. He is the author most recently of *Where Werewolves Fear to Tread*, as well as eight Fools' Guild Mysteries, starting with *Thirteenth Night*, from St. Martin's Minotaur Books. His short fiction, covering multiple genres, has appeared in numerous magazines and anthologies. He has written the book and lyrics for several musicals that have received productions and staged readings across the country. As a story-teller, he has appeared in three GrandSlams at the Moth in NYC, and on *The Moth Radio Hour* on NPR. He would like to thank violinist Andrea Segar of the Lydian String Quartet for her answers to violin-related questions, as well as Professor Lisa Berglund of Buffalo State College for the correct nineteenth century pronunciation of the word "Thames." www.alan-gordon.com.

GREGG HURWITZ is the *New York Times* and #1 international bestselling author of nineteen novels, most recently *Hellbent* (2018). His novels have been shortlisted for numerous literary awards, graced top ten lists, and have been published in thirty languages. He is also a *New York Times* bestselling comic book writer, having penned stories for Marvel (Wolverine, Punisher) and DC (Batman, Penguin).

Additionally, he's written screenplays for or sold spec scripts to many of the major studios (including *The Book of Henry*), and written, developed, and produced television for various networks. Gregg resides in Los Angeles. www.gregghurwitz.net

TONI L. P. KELNER was in junior high when she first read the Sherlockian Canon in her father's 1930s hardback edition, and it was her father who took her to a shooting tournament where the target was the letters VR (her father won second place.) So she can't wait to give him a copy of this book, with her own homage to the Great Detective. Kelner is the author of eleven mystery novels, has co-edited seven anthologies with *New York Times* bestseller Charlaine Harris, and has published more than thirty short stories. As Leigh Perry, she writes the Family Skeleton mysteries and has written even more short stories. She's been nominated for the Anthony, Macavity, and Derringer awards multiple times, and has won the Agatha Award and the *RT Book Reviews* Career Achievement award. No matter what you call her, she lives north of Boston with her husband, two daughters, a guinea pig, and an ever-increasing number of books. www.tonilpkelner.com

WILLIAM KOTZWINKLE is a novelist, children's writer, and screenwriter. He won the World Fantasy Award for Best Novel for *Doctor Rat* in 1977, and also won the National Magazine Award for fiction. Kotzwinkle wrote the novelization of the screenplay for *E.T. the Extra-Terrestrial*. Together with the artist Joe Servello, he created two books about the fascinating Inspector Mantis and his companion Doctor Hopper, *Trouble in Bugland,* published in 1983, and *Double Trouble in Bugland*, published in 2016.

HARLEY JANE KOZAK was born in Pennsylvania, grew up in Nebraska, graduated from NYU Tisch School of the Arts, and eventually migrated to Los Angeles. She worked as an actress for twenty-five years (*Parenthood, Arachnophobia, The Favor*, etc.) before turning her attention to crime fiction. Her first novel, *Dating Dead Men*, won the Agatha, Anthony, and Macavity awards, and was followed by four others, including the paranormal *Keeper of the Moon*. Her short prose has appeared in *Ms. Magazine, The Sun, The Santa Monica Review,* and the anthologies *Mystery Muses, This is Chick Lit, A Hell of a Woman, Butcher Knives and Body Counts, The Rich and the Dead*, and *Crimes by Moonlight*. After a fifteen-year maternity leave, Harley has returned to the big screen in such instant classics as *I Spit on Your Grave III*. Her affair with Mr. Holmes came in a roundabout fashion: her friend Bonnie MacBird's *Art in the Blood*, written in the style of Conan Doyle, so charmed Harley that she went to the source material, listening to *The Complete Works* while painting the entire upstairs of her house. The rest is history. www.harleyjanekozak.com

D. P. LYLE is the Macavity and Benjamin Franklin Silver Award-winning and Edgar, Agatha, Anthony, Shamus, Scribe, Silver Falchion, and USA Today Best Book Award-nominated author of seventeen books, both nonfiction and fiction, including the Samantha Cody, Dub Walker, and Jake Longly thriller series and the *Royal Pains* media tie-in novels. His essay on Jules Verne's *The Mysterious Island* appears in *Thrillers: 100 Must Reads,* and his short story "Even Steven" is in ITW's anthology *Thriller 3: Love Is Murder.* He served as editor for and contributed the short story "Splash" to SCWA's anthology, *It's All in the Story.* He is International Thriller Writer's VP for Education, and runs CraftFest, Master CraftFest, and ITW's Online Thriller School. Along with Jan Burke, he was co-host of Crime and Science Radio. He has worked with many novelists and with the writers of popular television shows such as *Law & Order, CSI: Miami, Diagnosis Murder, Monk, Judging Amy, Peacemakers, Cold Case, House, Medium, Women's Murder Club, 1-800-Missing, The Glades,* and *Pretty Little Liars.* He first met Sherlock during his early teens when he began reading crime fiction. Since then, revisiting the stories and using them as reference material has been an ongoing process. www.dplylemd.com Blog: http://writersforensicsblog.wordpress.com

WESTON OCHSE first met Holmes on the shelves of his grandfather's library amid the Time Life Photo Books and books on trout fishing. Weston went on to work in the military and engaged enemy combatants, terrorists, narco smugglers, and human traffickers. His personal war stories include performing humanitarian operations over Bangladesh, being deployed to Afghanistan, and a near miss being cannibalized in Papua New Guinea. His fiction and nonfiction has been praised by *USA Today, The Atlantic, The New York Post, The Financial Times of London*, and *Publishers Weekly.* The American Library Association labeled him one of the Major Horror Authors of the 21st Century. His work has also won the Bram Stoker Award, been nominated for the Pushcart Prize, and won multiple New Mexico-Arizona Book Awards. A writer of more than twenty-six books in multiple genres, his military supernatural series SEAL Team 666 has been optioned to be a movie starring Dwayne Johnson. And sometimes, when he's spent a day fishing and contented with the universe, he'll read a little Holmes and remember his grandfather. www.westonochse.com

JOE SERVELLO has worked as an actor, art and drama teacher, and art director for television. As a commercial artist, Servello is best known as an illustrator of children's books; his most prominent assignments were the covers and interior art for several books by William Kotzwinkle. He has also done covers for republished detective novels by Fredric Brown and books by A A Attanasio and Leigh Brackett. Joe has lived all his life in Altoona, Pennsylvania.

ZOË SHARP was brought up living aboard a catamaran on the northwest coast of England. She opted out of mainstream education at the age of twelve and, after an early diet of Leslie Charteris' "The Saint" and Conan Doyle's Sherlock Holmes stories, she wrote her first novel at fifteen. She created her ex-soldier turned bodyguard heroine, Charlotte "Charlie" Fox, after receiving death threats in the course of her work as a photojournalist. The latest in this series, book twelve, is *Fox Hunter*. She has also written more than twenty short stories and two standalone crime thrillers, plus a joint novella, *An Italian Job*, with acclaimed espionage author John Lawton. Her work has won or been nominated for numerous awards on both sides of the Atlantic, as well as being optioned for TV and film. Lee Child has said: "If Jack Reacher were a woman, he'd be Charlie Fox." http://www.ZoeSharp.com Blog: http://MurderIsEverywhere.blogspot.co.uk

DUANE SWIERCZYNSKI is the Anthony and Shamus-award winning author of *Revolver* and *Canary,* whose work has also been nominated for the Edgar, Hammett, Macavity and Barry awards. Duane first met Mr. Holmes in his clever Sesame Street guise ("Sherlock Hemlock"), but later made his formal acquaintance in *The Crimes of Dr. Watson*, an interactive mystery (with pull-out clues!) published in 2007. A Philly native, he now lives in Los Angeles. http://secretdead.blogspot.com

F. PAUL WILSON is the award-winning, bestselling author of fifty-plus books and nearly one hundred short stories spanning science fiction, horror, adventure, medical thrillers, and virtually everything between. He is perhaps best known as the creator of the urban mercenary, Repairman Jack. As a boy he discovered Holmes through the Basil Rathbone films but got into Holmes when his mother ordered Doubleday's *The Complete Sherlock Holmes* from the Book of the Month Club and he read both volumes cover to cover. Paul's most recent novels are *Panacea* and its sequel, *The God Gene*. He resides at the Jersey Shore and can be found on the web at www.repairmanjack.com.

ACKNOWLEDGMENTS

Any anthology is a team effort, from writer to publisher, and we've been thrilled to be working again with the dedicated people at Pegasus Books, including publisher Claiborne Hancock, and the staff at Pegasus, Bowen Dunnan, Maria Fernandez, and Sabrina Plomitallo-González. Many thanks as always to Don Maass, who shepherded the book through the contract stage, and to Jonathan Kirsch, whose legal savvy about books generally and Holmes writing in particular is unmatched.

We're happy that the little club of contributors to these books has grown, and once again, past contributors are stalwart cheerleaders for each volume. Our gratitude continues for the support of all those who joined us in playing The Game, especially with publicity—all their names are below. In fact, the books seem to have become "recruiting" tools for the Baker Street Irregulars, with Jan Burke, Dana Cameron, S. J. Rozan, and Nancy Holder becoming active members of the Baker Street Irregulars, and Sara Paretsky and Alan Bradley as "Distinguished Speakers" for the Irregulars weekend celebrations. (Jerry Margolin, Neil Gaiman, Michael Dirda, and Michael Sims had previously been involved in the BSI, so the road goes both ways.)

ACKNOWLEDGMENTS

To our friends in the Sherlockian world—too many to mention: thanks for supporting our little game. These books are for you, pals!

Finally, to *the* women, the two who always stand by us: Zöe Quinton and Sharon Klinger. Without their enthusiasm, patience, love, and proofreading skills, these books would never happen.

Laurie & Les

Volume 1: *A Study in Sherlock* **(Random House & Poisoned Pen Press, 2011)**
Alan Bradley, Tony Broadbent, Jan Burke, Lionel Chetwynd, Lee Child, Colin Cotterill, Neil Gaiman, Laura Lippman, Gayle Lynds & John Sheldon, Phillip & Jerry Margolin, Margaret Maron, Thomas Perry, S. J. Rozan, Dana Stabenow, Charles Todd, and Jacqueline Winspear

Volume 2: *In the Company of Sherlock Holmes* **(Pegasus Books, 2014)**
Laura Caldwell, Michael Connelly, Jeffery Deaver, Michael Dirda, Harlan Ellison, Cornelia Funke, Andrew Grant, Denise Hamilton, Nancy Holder, Leslie S. Klinger, John Lescroart, Sara Paretsky, John Reppion & Leah Moore, Michael Sims, and Gahan Wilson

Volume 3: *Echoes of Sherlock Holmes* **(Pegasus Books, 2016)**
Tasha Alexander, Dana Cameron, John Connolly, Deborah Crombie, Cory Doctorow, Hallie Ephron, Meg Gardiner, William Kent Krueger, Tony Lee, Jonathan Mayberry, Catriona McPherson, Denise Mina, and David Morrell